BOOK 1 OF THE DRIFTERS' SAGA

Graves FOR Drifters AND Thieves

SOPHIA MINETOS

Cover by Franziska Haase, www.coverdungeon.com.
Edited by Josiah Davis.

ISBN: 978-1-7355933-0-2 (paperback)
IBSN: 978-1-7355933-1-9 (hardback)
ISBN: 978-1-7355933-2-6 (epub ebook)
IBSN: 978-1-7355933-3-3 (mobi ebook)

www.sophiaminetos.com

For Mom and Dad

Prologue

S ummer was over. With the mountains behind them, the Oldridges began their ride to the Mesca territory. There, they'd sell the pelts Pa had snared over the summer, then wait out the northern winter in the desert haze. Jae rode behind her father, whose gaze flicked between his compass and the surrounding pines. Their horses trotted steadily, the dust clouding around their legs.

A chill crept across Jae's neck. She tugged her patched-up jacket around her shoulders. "How much farther?"

"Six miles or so, I reckon," Pa answered. The sun was below the treetops now. "We'll eat supper, then stop somewhere for the night. It ain't wise to ride in the dark."

The woods had grown foggy with the setting sun. Jae shuddered, squinting at the winding trail before them. It was as loopy as a diamondback's tracks. The trees' branches knit together in a knotted canopy and shrouded the road in shadow.

"It's a shame our usual route flooded," Jae said.

"Ain't that the truth," Pa said with a snort. "I've been on this trail before, though. It's a tad crooked, but it'll get us where we need to go."

Pa studied the road carefully, which made his face lengthen an inch or two. People always told Jae she looked like her father, but she wasn't so sure that was true. Pa wore buckskins and furs like a proper mountain man. He sported a shaggy goatee, and his brown hair was even shaggier. It was long enough to mostly hide the puckered scar on his neck—the remnant of a wound from a grizzly's claw. His brown eyes were steady, never straying from what lay ahead.

Jae's own blue eyes were prone to wandering. Often, she reckoned that she looked too small for the world around her, with her baggy clothes sagging from her thin limbs, her hat sitting crookedly on her head no matter how many times she pushed it back in place. Pa's years had hardened him, and she always felt awfully delicate by his side.

Soon, a clearing opened up on the east side of the trail. The patch of grass was small, about half the size of their cabin. Wildflowers decked the ground, surrendering their colors to the cooling air, wilted and tired. The trail cut through a steady incline, and the ground sloped steadily on either side.

Pa gestured for Jae to dismount. She hopped to the ground, then he passed her a flask of lukewarm tea. She sipped the strong, earthy liquid as Pa counted their bales of furs for the thousandth time. Beaver, marten, nutria.

"We should sell the furs in Kalstira one of these years," Jae said. "We could see the ocean. And those redwood trees you told me about."

Pa replied without looking up from his furs. "I don't think there's a market for furs in Kalstira. People don't need beaver hats down there. Too balmy."

Jae rubbed a bit of warmth back into her stiff fingers. "Must be nice."

Pa's laugh was soft. "I'll take you there, one day. But if you're anything like me, you'll always prefer the woods to the sea."

Maybe that was true, but the difference between the woods and the sea was that she'd never *seen* the latter. Jae leaned against a ponderosa tree, smiling into the darkening woods, at all she could not see. "I swear, when I'm a Ranger, I'm going to ride from coast to coast. I'll see every bit of the Outlands." Apart from Banderra, Mesca, and the road between them, there was little in this world that she'd actually seen.

Pa jostled the pelts back into place. "I hate to break it to you, Jae, but the Rangers don't have much of a say in where they go. Most of the time, your captain will assign you a case and you'll go from there."

She wrinkled her nose. "Is that why you left them? To go exploring by yourself?" She'd heard droves of stories from his days as a Ranger, but she never grew tired of them. One day, she hoped to have stories of her own.

Pa chuckled. "Nah. Well, maybe a little." He gazed off into the distance. "Ten years in the depths of the Outlands. I came back much crazier."

"Because of the things you saw?"

"That, and because I had a daughter."

"*Hey.*"

"Sorry, sweetheart." His dark eyes brightened. "Couldn't resist."

"Still," she said. "I want to see it all. The wilds. Sometimes I can almost feel them calling me. Like they're whispering my name."

Pa laughed again, then took a step away from his stallion. "You've got enough spark in you to light a wildfire. I wish I had that much spirit left in me."

"*I* think you do," she said. Grinning, she lifted her chin. "Do you miss it? Being a Ranger?"

"Sometimes. I was a wild one when I was younger. It's a painful thing to be too careful. But being reckless ain't any better." He smiled. "Besides, I've got everything I need right here, and fewer worries than I did when I was young. It's a simple life."

Jae did not want a simple life. She wanted to hurry down a long, winding trail and leave a string of tales behind her.

"You ready to go?" asked Pa.

"Just about." Jae straightened her hat, and began walking back to her mare.

Before Jae could saddle up, her horse trotted forward, then stopped at the eaves of the forest. She pawed at the ground, tapping her hoof as if she was trying to stamp out a fire.

"Whoa, girl." Jae stroked her mare's neck. "Easy. We'll rest soon."

"Yep." Pa adjusted his stallion's reins. "It's getting mighty chilly out here. Before long we'll have to…"

His voice trailed off.

Jae's lips parted. "Pa?"

He raised a hand to quiet her. His face turned blank as he stepped away from the horse. He ran toward a mound of brambles, then dove arms-first into the gnarled branches and pushed them apart to clear a window into the mist-veiled woods.

Jae stepped in Pa's direction, hoping to glance over his shoulder. A cold gust sliced through the air like a bullet. The sharp wind stung her eyes and gripped at her face and neck. Her fingers went numb.

Something rumbled across the earth, like rain splattering on rock. The air chilled her throat as she opened her mouth, but no sound came from her lips.

A voice drifted over the air. "*Oldridge.*"

At first, she thought she'd imagined it. Then, her father leaped away from the bushes and ran like he'd just glimpsed hellfire. His hands seized her waist and swept her off the ground.

She squirmed and began to protest, but he shut her up right away. "Jae. Quiet. Not a word."

Pa hurried into the trees, weaving around upright trunks and fallen logs. He brought Jae to a circle of pines and tucked her into the shadows. Her feet stumbled over the roots, trying not to fall. "What's happening?" she asked, biting back tears. There was a flame in Pa's eyes that she'd never seen before.

Pa swallowed, then placed his compass in her hand, the metal cold against her palm. There was a sad, kind look on his face. "Stay here. I'll be right back." It did not sound like a promise. He slipped away.

Jae dared to move a little and found a gap to peer through. Pine needles grazed her chin. The fog and branches obscured her line of sight, but she could make out Pa's figure at the clearing's edge. Somewhere deeper in the woods, a few horses snorted. Then came a faint, raspy laugh.

"*You've come back.*" The words hung in the fog.

Pa trembled but did not run. He waited. The silence was unbearable. Just as Jae was about to dash down the hill and join him, two-dozen faces emerged from the fog before him.

The riders surfaced from the trail's western border, passing through the trees as if they were made of steam. They wore buttoned uniforms as soldiers did, but their clothes were stained and glassy, like soiled hailstones. Fog circled the bluish bodies of the men and their horses. There was no warmth in their faces, and their eyes were too wide, like someone had ripped their lids clean off. Their mouths were cracked and smeared with what Jae could only guess was blood. They moved like feathers on the wind, their bodies wispy as smoke.

Ghosts.

Terror bolted Jae to the ground.

The spirits halted near the trail's edge, leaving only a short stretch of earth between Pa and themselves. The ghost heading the riders spoke. "*We've been looking for you, Ven. We smell your blood. Twice over.*" Jae could make out his brittle hair, his lined face, the sneer that he'd carried with him into death.

Pa reached for his gun. "Don't you *dare* touch my daughter."

Then came the thunder. The horde charged forth. Pa wavered, shouted, then disappeared in the army of ghosts. Jae swore she heard him crying her name, but the hoof beats smothered the sound.

A rush of icy fear tore through her.

Jae screamed as she tumbled to the ground, thrown over by a burst of wind. Her hands flailed against the earth, and the dirt stung her eyes, clouding her sight.

Over the pounding hooves, her father cried out again. Sputtering, she tried to get up, but something held her down. Whether it was the cold or fear, Jae did not know. Were they passing ahead of her, or fleeing west? The pounding hooves seemed to sound from all around her.

A final cry escaped the chaos, and it was not from Pa. It was faint, but Jae made out the word. "*Outlands.*"

Jae tried to push herself up. Everything, save for her trembling hands, had frozen still. Silently, she begged the Wandering God to let her move again, but she could only lie there helplessly.

At last, the hoof beats disappeared. Just as she began to wonder whether she was going to die on the forest floor, warmth found its way back into her bones. She pushed herself up, gasping and coughing, soil tumbling from her clothes. Her eyes burned.

Jae summoned the strength to whisper. "Pa?" Her knees knocked together as she stood, and the shout burned her throat. "*Pa!*"

There was no answer besides the echo off the pines.

Jae wanted to break, then—to sink to her knees and crumple to the ground. But those ghosts wouldn't wait for her.

Damn it. Which direction had they gone? She searched. She ran forward, and when she came to a wide, sunken gorge, she went backward. The mist weighed down on her like a slab of stone.

Jae wandered through the trees, climbing over boulders, exposed roots, and long-dead logs. Except for the twigs cracking under her boots, the woods were quiet as death. Pain scraped at her muscles, but she urged herself to keep moving, to search until she glimpsed those restless souls again.

Every now and again, she shouted for Pa. The forest mocked her with its silence.

Soon, she found her mare in a frenzy by the river, but Pa's poor stallion was nowhere in sight.

"Oh, sweet girl, I'm here," she cried, clinging to her horse's reins.

Her mare's hooves brought up the river's mud, and it splattered Jae's boots. Jae nuzzled her horse's neck, whispering, trying to keep her voice straight. "Come on, I need ya. We gotta find Pa."

When the horse quit crying and stomping, Jae swung herself onto the saddle and rode away from the trail.

There was no time to stand around and let pity put shackles on her ankles. If those ghosts were nearby, then they didn't deserve a moment of ease. She'd already let fear chain her to the ground once tonight, and she wouldn't disgrace Pa by waiting another second.

She went east. Then west. She roamed until the fog disappeared and the forest once again looked green and fresh. When she reckoned she'd go mad if she kept trudging through the pines, she headed back to the road.

Jae did not speak again until the next day when she reached Fort Sheridan. The sun was fading in the west. The log fort rested on a flat plain, its sharp posts stretching toward the rosy sky. The ruts from wagon wheels formed a straight path toward its entrance.

A tall, mustached fella spied her riding his way. She was still shaking like a madwoman, and her eyes itched with exhaustion.

The man hurried up to her, his boots leaving faint prints in the loose earth. "Miss, are you alright?"

"I need to speak to the captain."

Without another word, he took her to the fort. As the structure came closer, Jae could make out the smudges on its windows, the woodpile resting beneath its awning, a stack of barrels banded with steel.

She felt like she was sinking.

The mustached man led Jae's mare to the stalls, then helped Jae inside. Fort Sheridan's captain was a man called Berion Drake. Captain Drake had fine, straw-colored hair and sunburned cheeks. His blue eyes were kind, but he couldn't coax a word out of Jae while she washed up and sat down in his office.

Jae stroked the arms of the chair he'd offered her. Plush leather, cracked and worn. "Thank you." Her voice was small. She felt like grit covered everything—her clothes and tongue and heart.

"Pleasure," he said softly. "How old are you, miss?"

"Fifteen in November."

"Nearly fifteen. Alright. Your name?"

She watched the twilight streaming in through the window and the dust dancing in its path. "Jae Oldridge. I'm Ven Oldridge's daughter."

"*The* Ven Oldridge?"

"Mhmm." She swallowed. "They took him. He's gone."

"*Who* took him?"

And she told him. Every bit of it.

Captain Drake did not have much to say. "Ghost riders, you say?"

She nodded.

He drew in a long, deep breath. "I'm not sure what we can do, miss. Ghosts are something that we don't fully understand. If they've taken him, then—"

"You *have* to," she interrupted. "He's a Ranger. I mean, he used to be one, at least. There must be *someone* you can send after him."

Drake only stared.

Jae's lip quivered. She regretted snapping at him like that. "I'm sorry. Please. I don't know much about ghosts either. But... they sounded like they wanted *him*. If they wanted him dead, they would've just killed him on the trail. They took him instead. Pa can't be dead. He's got to be out there."

Berion Drake was a good man. She knew this because he didn't tell her what he must've been thinking. *It's not possible.*

"Please," she said. Her throat was getting tighter. "I heard them shouting. They said they were gonna take him to the Outlands."

Jae thought back to Pa's stories. Many times, he'd said that he'd pissed off a few bastards in his day, but he'd never mentioned their names. Who would hate him enough to come back from the grave?

"Miss," the captain said, "I'm sorry that this happened to you. We'll do what we can. I'll write to the Rangers in the Outlands. They're more familiar with this sort of thing, but I'm afraid I can't guarantee that there's anything they can do."

Jae counted the planks in the floor. She wondered how many folks had sat in this chair before, begging for an answer. Desperate pleas from desperate people like her. She couldn't bring herself to meet the captain's gaze. "I can help. I'll help them search for him. There might even be something in our cabin we can use. I'll—"

"Miss," he said again. "We'll do what we can."

Their conversation ended there. He offered her an empty room with a small cot, promising that he'd send word to the Rangers the next morning.

Jae wondered how long it would take the message to reach the Outlands. A few weeks, if they were lucky, but the snows would come before long.

Jae lay down with the setting sun. The calico sheets were soft against her bare legs. Outside, the wind sang, but panic stirred in her chest. When she closed her eyes, she saw Pa lying on his side, the ghosts circling around him.

What was she doing here?

She crept across the floor, then pressed her forehead to the window and stared at the night-kissed plain. Jae gazed at the silver crags of the Cannoc Mountains and the boundless sky. The peaks were high enough for the moon to hear their whispers, if they could speak. Starlight danced on the world below. Her legs ached, begging her to move toward those mountains.

And she would. Just not yet.

Beyond the mountains were the Outlands. Those ghosts were out there somewhere, and they had Pa. Where would they take him? Across the Outlands' sprawling taigas? North to its frozen tundra? The lakes? The sea?

She stood there for what felt like eons.

A tear slid down her cheek. She reached into her pocket and removed its contents with a fisted hand. Slowly, she unfurled her fingers and showed the object to the sky.

Pa's compass.

She flicked it open. Its needle swayed, then settled in the direction of the mountains. North. Toward the Outlands. Wordlessly, she asked the stars for help.

Etched on the back of the compass was the Rangers' sigil: an arrow laid across the crescent moon. The mark of Hemaera, the half-goddess who had roamed the Outlands herself, charted them, and presented the map to the first Rangers. Some of them, like Pa, still believed that. To others, Hemaera was a symbol. A myth.

But myth or not, Jae called upon Hemaera's spirit then, for

courage and guidance.

Jae put the compass back in her pocket, and there, she vowed; "I'm comin', Pa. I'll give this back when I see you again."

Chapter 1

The desert was not quite silent. A breeze drifted across the earth, rustling the dry, brittle grass. In the distance, the rust-red mesas touched the sky, bordered by miles of yuccas and scruffy shrubs. On the horizon lay a massive rock shaped like a fist, its knuckles brushing the full white clouds.

Murrieta's Rock. That meant Ameda was not far.

Jae Oldridge dismounted and draped her horse's reins over the branch of a mesquite tree. The gray mare blew a breath from her nostrils, then stretched out her neck and sniffed the air. Jae pressed her back to the mesquite's trunk, taking in the small patch of shade. March in Mesca often felt like winter at night and summer during the day, and the morning was already warm.

Jae reached into her knapsack. Her hand pinched a thick wad of folded paper. Her map. It was the second most valuable thing she owned, after Pa's compass. Touched by magic itself, it was. A strange gift from an even stranger person.

Jae's gaze flicked to the glimmering gold speck on her map.

Ameda's name, scrawled in brown ink, lingered a few whispers of space above the gold spot. As she traveled, the map moved with her. It showed her a radius of about twenty miles around wherever she was, but she could ask it to show her greater things—entire land-masses, or smaller places, like the streets of a city.

It couldn't show her anything tinier than a village, or anywhere without a name, of course. The map also only worked for places. She'd tried asking it to show her the whereabouts of men on the run before, to no avail.

Jae folded the map back up and put it away, then mounted her horse and headed north on the road.

Two days earlier, some cowboys in Carth had told her that a rustler called Thaddeus Glory had stolen their horses and fled north that morning. The cowboys had heard Glory gloating about his plan to swindle some horses from Ameda next. A man on the run would have few options in this part of the desert. Glory could take Murrieta's Road. Or follow the curves of the Pedora River. The men in Carth had sworn they'd seen him take the road.

Jae had snagged a copy of the warrant from Carth's sheriff. Glory's bounty was set at thirty crowns. That would buy her food for several weeks.

Jae frowned, squinting at the road for the hundredth time. Last night, winds had turned the sands, sweeping any tracks from the trail. Nerves prickled at her stomach. When she found Glory, would he threaten her, or shoot right away? With outlaws, it was often hard to say.

But scary as they could be, nothing scared her more than the thought of never seeing Pa again. Her folder of successful bounties grew fatter every few months. And she'd catch a thousand robbers, killers, and rogues if that was what it took.

It'd been more than two years since he'd gone. Somehow, it felt closer to ten. On long rides, when there was little to do but think to herself… Jae longed to feel like a child again, to laugh, to revel in stories, to sleep without fearing the ghosts that rode across her dreams. But such hopes were for folks without work to be done, and they were luxuries she no longer had.

She loved this land, but did not have a lick of respect for thieves. The west was beautiful, glorious… and to many, it was *new.* The folks on this side of the country were hearty people. They had to be. Many were honest. Others saw it as a climate where their wretched deeds could go unpunished. The land deserved protection from the rotten folk who flocked to it, believing they could prosper by shedding blood and feeding their greed. And if staving them off helped her get closer to Pa, all the better.

Her horse whinnied. Jae's fingers loosened on the reins. Murietta's Rock looked to be about four miles away. The Pedora flowed nearby as well. That was good. She needed more water.

The sun climbed toward the sky's center, and Jae rode until the road sloped down into a valley. Cottonwoods sprawled alongside the river, casting wide sweeps of shade. Folks often joked that the Pedora River was little more than a muddy ribbon cutting through the desert. Northerners had the real rivers, but in the desert, water was water.

Jae followed the river's curves, listening to the current pouring through the valley. The trail wound through the cottonwoods, then opened into a flat stretch of hard-packed land. Beyond the flat earth lay Ameda.

Like most desert towns, Ameda was small and boxy, its structures baked weak and pale by the sun. Wooden buildings with flat rooftops bordered a wide, arrow-straight road. The main street was unpaved, and save for the cacti growing by the storefronts, empty.

Jae stopped outside the town's church. The white, adobe walls were cracked, and the church's doors were carved from planks of oak. A bell glinted in the open window of the building's tower. A crow waited on its awning, flicking its head and croaking.

Jae dismounted. She hitched up her mare and triple knotted the reins for good measure. Jae glanced over her shoulder, then removed the pot from her saddlebag and unscrewed the lid.

Hackwort tar. Clearer than honey and ten times as sticky.

She heaped it onto the reins. Jae drew her knife, then used the edge to smear the liquid over the leather, careful to leave a bare spot near the bridle.

She was ready.

"Good girl," Jae whispered. She took the rope out of her saddlebag—two loops tied just wide enough for a pair of wrists and ankles—and tucked them under her shirt.

Jae peeked inside the church, scanning the area for parishioners. Empty. She slipped inside and shut the door behind her.

The church of the Wandering God always welcomed travelers. Jae had spent many nights in their storerooms and lofts. They rarely asked for anything in return, but Jae always left them a couple of deons, or food if there was no money to spare.

Jae's boots clicked on the floor. At the head of the altar was a carved walking stick: the symbol of the Wandering God. The holy books said that he had walked through the skies, and worlds sprouted from the seeds he sowed across the stars. Below, in frames of copper, were the sigils for the lesser gods of this world, whom the Wandering God had appointed at the dawn of the earth. A sun for Cressien, a mountain for Petreos, a river for Nerea. Jae eyed the pine tree representing Argun, the god of forests and travelers. Her father had always favored him, so she sent Argun a silent little prayer.

Her requests were simple: *Please help me catch Glory, and help me get away.*

Beside the altar was a narrow stairway. Jae hurried upstairs to the bell tower. The space was empty, except for the bell's rope hanging from the angled ceiling. A window cast a square of sunlight on the floor. There was no pane within its frame, letting the morning air stream into the room.

Jae hurried to the window. The ledge rose to meet her chest, giving her plenty of room to scout out the area.

Up here, she could see the whole town clearly, right down to the signs mounted over the shops' doors. She took the spyglass from her pocket. Pressing it softly to her brow, she gazed at the road, and waited.

Her fingers drummed on the ledge and grazed the rough bumps in the stucco. Somehow, the streets looked even emptier now.

In the past two years, Jae had learned a lot about thieves. They didn't carry themselves like common folk. They either acted like they had too much to do, or too little. Sometimes they'd go out of their way to blend in with the cowboys around them. Other times, they just stuck out like sore thumbs garbed in fine leathers and fringe.

The cowboys in Carth had said that Glory liked to steal horses in broad daylight, loudly threatening to shoot anyone who crossed him. Given that, along with a nickname like "Glory," Jae guessed he'd be the sore thumb kind of thief.

She waited. Her neck grew sore, and she was itching with sweat beneath her clothing. The breeze batted at her face, tossing stray hairs around her forehead.

She backed out of the wind, but just before she turned to head back inside, she spied a wiry figure riding into town, holding himself upright like a warlord, and her gut told her that her target was here.

Jae left her twin revolvers in a corner, keeping her knife and her smallest pistol hidden in her boots. She never approached a target without a weapon or two, but they didn't need to know that. It was better to let them think she was unarmed.

In a flash, she was downstairs.

Jae snuck out of the church's back door, careful not to let it slam behind her, then hurried to the street's edge. She wiped her palms on her pants, poked her head out just far enough to watch, and held still.

Two cowboys—one leading a strong brown workhorse—stood chatting on the roadside. Beside them, the rider came to a stop. His horse was a beauty with a glossy black coat. He reached for his gun, and lined the barrel up with the cowboys' eyes. As he cocked the pistol, his demand boomed across the hard-packed dirt.

"Give me the horse."

Glory indeed.

Jae couldn't make out what the cowboys said. One threw up his hands right away, but the other dared to talk back. Even from a hundred feet away, Jae knew a sharp tongue when she heard it.

Glory fired. Dust rose from the ground, but the man did not fall. Must've been a warning shot. Trembling, the sharp-tongued cowboy took a few steps back.

Glory took the brown steed's reins and bound them to his own horse.

"Don't talk to me like that again, boys," Glory called as he rode away. "Or I'll take more than the damn horse."

He was closer now. Jae cast a glance at her own horse, then crept out of the alley and sat on the steps of the church.

Slouching to make herself look small, she pretended to fiddle absentmindedly with the hem of her shirt. Her eyes wandered until the horse thief stopped in front of her. Glory's gaze met her own.

The rustler snickered. Gods. Why did they always laugh at her?

She held onto his gaze. His eyes were a dull, burnished brown, like a rusty old knife. Scratches covered his face, red and ripe beneath his whiskers. "This your horse?"

She let herself shiver before him. "Yes, sir," she croaked in a small, grating voice. She rolled one of her braids across her fingers. "Can I help you?"

"You sure can." He dismounted and brought out the gun. "I'd like your mare, if you don't mind."

Jae nodded, whimpering like wounded prey. "Y-yes. Go right ahead."

He looked the horse up and down. "Not a beauty, but she'll do."

Hmph. Thieves or not, she hated people who made a show out of being rude.

Thaddeus Glory holstered his gun, then braced himself to tether Jae's mare to the chestnut horse. He took up the mare's reins with both hands.

But he did not step away. Fingers tight around the leather, his eyes narrowed on the bridle. He jerked his arm, slowly at first, then frantically. The mare whinnied as the rustler flapped his elbows about. Glory did not see Jae retrieve the rock from the ground.

"Is this *tar?*" he shouted.

Despite the nerves twisting in her stomach, Jae couldn't resist a reply. "Yep." She brought the rock down on his head.

Glory's knees buckled. With a startled cry, he fell to the ground. Jae drove her heel between his shoulders, then whipped out her boot pistol and clicked it right by his ear. She kept her voice firm and level. "Not a word out of you. Don't move."

A low moan came out of Glory's mouth. He could hardly even move as she slipped his wrists and ankles through the loops of rope and pulled them tight. In her periphery, she could see the two cowboys from the street approaching them.

Glory finally squirmed a little as she yanked on the rope binding his ankles. She planted her heel on the small of his back again. "I told ya, don't move!"

He shuddered a moment, then settled. The cowboys eyed both of them, not moving much.

"Hey," Jae said. She pointed to the workhorse, who was still hitched to Glory's black steed. "Don't worry, I've got him. Your horse is fine."

One of the cowboys stepped toward her, his brown eyes brimming with confusion. "Ma'am? What did you do?"

"Hit him with a rock." She cleared her throat. "You folks got a sheriff?

Chapter 2

S heriff Arlington was asleep when they entered his office, resting his head on his forearms, his body slouching in his desk
chair. Jae and the cowboys carried Glory, still tied up like firewood,
between them. The daze of being whacked must've faded some-
what, because now, he was writhing like a beetle on its back, probably
chafing his wrists raw.

Sunlight leaked in through the window's dusty blinds. At the back
of the room was a set of two cells, barred with iron and barren, save
for two shoddy cots and stray bits of hay. The sheriff murmured as
the door slammed shut. He rubbed his eyes, fetched a beat-up hat
from the side of his desk, then got to his feet and trudged to the
doorway. "What's goin' on, folks?"

Jae grunted, struggling to haul Glory along the wooden floor.
"Caught ourselves a rustler. Thaddeus Glory."

The sheriff blinked. "That horse thief from down south?"

"Sure is," said one of the cowboys.

The sheriff grabbed a pair of cuffs from a hook the wall. "Set him down."

They did as they were told, and Glory started thrashing as soon as they released his limbs. The sheriff placed his boot on the thief's back, cuffed Glory's wrists, then slipped off the two loops of rope. As he brought Glory to his feet, the sheriff tried to pass the rope to the cowboys.

Jae took the rope and slung it loosely over her arm. The sheriff gave her a sour look, but said nothing.

Glory didn't so much as glance at the three men. Instead, he kept his glare aimed at Jae the whole time. When the sheriff yanked the cloth from Glory's mouth, the thief said, "Gotta say. I thought that if I ever wound up gettin' caught, a lawman would haul me off. Or did the Rangers get desperate enough to haul *you* outta the gutters?"

Jae said nothing. Coarseness from thieves scathed her about as well as lukewarm milk.

"Keep your mouth shut, Glory," said the sheriff. "Your trial will run a lot more smoothly if you do." The cell's iron door shut with a high-pitched creak. The sheriff locked it, then motioned to a log bench before his desk. "Have a seat, y'all."

Jae lowered herself onto the bench in front of the sheriff's desk. The seat's ledge dug into her thighs. Even if the blinds weren't down, Jae guessed the sheriff's office would still be dim. The smell of dust and stale paper filled the room. The walls and wooden floor were plain, save for the sea of handbills plastered to the wall. Faces of outlaws, sketched by careful hands above their promised bounties, stared right back at her.

The sheriff plucked a pen from the mess of papers on his desk. He cleared his throat. "Alright. What happened?"

The older of the two cowboys pointed to Jae. He straightened his hat, tucking a few strands of silver-black hair under the brim. "This young lady bound him up. We just helped her haul him off."

Sheriff Arlington coughed. "Either of you get hurt?"

"Nah," said the cowboy. "He just took a shot at the ground, then stole my horse. Got the horses back after this gal took care of Glory."

The sheriff scribbled down the report. "Can I get your names, gentlemen?"

"Juan Silva," said the graying cowboy.

"Breck Barlon," answered the other, scratching his neck.

The shape of Jae's name formed on her tongue, but the sheriff cut her off. "That'll be all from you, gentlemen." Arlington sipped his coffee, then pointed at Jae with his pen. "You stay."

The men tipped their hats. Juan gave Jae a polite smile, then left at his companion's side.

"Thanks for the help," she said as they headed outside. When they were gone, she turned back to the sheriff, leaning forward in her seat. She itched to collect the bounty, for the coins to fall into her hands.

"What's your name, miss?" asked Arlington.

"Jae Oldridge."

"How'd you happen to come by this rustler?"

"Tracked him for a few days."

Clicking his tongue, the sheriff set down his pen. "And who taught you how to do that?"

Jae took the knapsack off her shoulders, then pulled out the folder holding her records. "I'm sorry to be curt, sir, but I have other business to take care of. I need to leave soon. If I could get my bounty and a receipt for it, that'd be swell."

"Settle down. You ain't going anywhere until you tell me how you caught this fella."

Jae suppressed a sigh, wondering how long it would be until she could get her coins and hurry out the door. She explained the events of the morning to him.

The sheriff looked at her like she'd just asked him to teach her how to breathe. "Tar?"

"Tar," she said.

The sheriff clasped his hands and leaned on his forearms. "What business has a young lady got chasing horse thieves through the desert?"

"Why is my profession any concern of yours?" she asked. "If the job gets done, it gets done."

The sheriff snorted, a hefty wheeze coming out of his nostrils. "Profession?" Before Jae could shift back, his plump hand reached out to seize her folder. "Let me see this."

If it weren't for her pending payment, she would have yanked it back and hurried outside, but she let him open it. She watched the sheriff leaf through the receipts, warrants, and records with wide eyes.

"Hang on here. You passed yourself off as a landlord's daughter, then lured two bandits into a locked room at a boarding house?"

"Yes."

The sheriff thumbed the next page. "And you traveled with the Brenner gang for a few days before you drugged their water supply, bound their hands and... got the sheriff before they woke?"

She folded her hands. "Yes."

Sheriff Arlington flipped over the third report. "And you caught the... Clarence twins? Freed their horses and broke their wagon wheels?"

"Yes," she said, tapping her fingers on the bench. The wooden legs creaked as she adjusted her position. She wasn't keen on being here all afternoon.

The sheriff fingered the records again. "Are these real?"

"Of course." Why on earth would she have wasted time forging them? Besides, she had no money to throw away on *paper,* of all things.

"So. You're a bounty hunter?"

"I am." The phrase itself didn't bother her. What bothered her was the way most men said it, like they were forcing the words out of their stomachs.

"You know, miss, this ain't a game. Most bounty hunters don't last long. The only ones the job don't kill are the ones with enough sense to walk away."

Jae shrugged. "I'm still alive."

Solemnly, Arlington squinted. "For now. You know, vigilantism ain't legal out east."

Jae laughed. "That's because they don't *need* it there. Why do you think all the thieves come out west?"

The sheriff's gaze was tired and heavy.

"Same reason the settlers do," Jae finished. "Opportunity."

"Lawmen are coming with those settlers," the sheriff replied, his voice laced with scorn. "*Real* lawmen. Not rogue bounty hunters and children who want to play at being gunslingers. How old are you anyway?"

"Twenty," she said quickly. She was seventeen now, but her age wasn't his damn business and she didn't mind lying if it would cut this conversation short.

"You wanna know the truth about bounty hunters? Most of them don't give a damn about justice. They just like the thrill of it, and the pay that comes with it. I don't respect most of 'em."

She took no offense. "I don't care about the thrill. I make enough to get by. But for now, it's a necessary job."

The sheriff gave her a thoughtful stare. "Why?"

"I'm gonna be a Ranger."

The ghosts were in the Outlands. Common folk couldn't get to the Outlands. And there was only one safe way in. Hemaera's

Pass—wide and flat and swarming with the Rangers' watchmen. If you weren't a Ranger, then you didn't make it through.

The sheriff answered with another wheezy laugh. "In that case, best of luck."

Tempted as she was to snap, she answered him as delicately as she could. "Much obliged." Men turned to buzzards if they sensed a speck of desperation in her. They liked trying to pick her clean of her words like meat from a bone.

Jae felt that she'd sat through this conversation many times before, though she supposed she shouldn't have been surprised. There were nearly three hundred Rangers in Hespyria. Only twenty-one were women, and every single one of those women started as a bounty hunter. Jae had tried using her first bounty to pay three Rangers to search the Outlands on their own. When she told them that she didn't know where Pa was exactly, they'd all backed off. One had even laughed.

There was no shortage of danger in the Outlands—harsh weather, beasts and monsters, strange happenstances of every kind. Then there were the Nefilium—the hidden-folk, with magic pulsing through their veins. The Rangers guarding Hemaera's Pass were not lenient about letting common people through.

The breeze whistled through the crack of the doorway. The sheriff blew a puff of air from his lips. "Want some free advice?"

"Sure," said Jae, though the phrase in question struck her as odd. Who was out there charging money for advice?

"Settle down," the sheriff said. "There are plenty of suitable jobs for a woman your age. Jobs that have pride in them. Jobs where you won't end up with a bullet in your gut."

She tried to smother her agitation, but her reply still came out sounding flat. "Thank you for your suggestions. I'll certainly consider them." A suitable job wouldn't help her become a Ranger or get her to the Outlands.

The sheriff snorted. "Don't turn your nose up. I'm trying to help you out."

She didn't need his help. She brushed the old papers back into her folder, closed it, and stashed it in her bag. "If you don't mind, sir, I'd like to collect my bounty and be on my way. I'm sure you've got a busy day ahead of you."

"Yeah, I'm busy today." The sheriff scribbled down a few more notes, then opened a drawer full of bronze crowns, silver deons, and copper pennies. "I'm leaving for Calora on business this afternoon."

Jae shifted to the side. She looked down at her boots, trying to ignore the feeling of splinters prickling under her pants. The shadow of the desk was a graveyard for moths and flies. Finally, Sheriff Arlington slid her the coins. Jae counted them twice. Twenty crowns. "Sir."

"What?"

"You underpaid me." She pulled the warrant from her pocket. "Glory's bounty was set at thirty crowns."

The sheriff glanced at the scrap of paper. "Where'd you get that from?"

"Carth."

He sniffed. "Then ya should've caught Glory in Carth."

Jae traced the price with her fingertip. "Same county, so I should receive the same bounty. It's—"

The sheriff stood, thrusting his chair behind him. He shoved a finger an inch in front of Jae's face. "You watch your mouth and take what you've earned. Frankly, there are men in my position who wouldn't be half as generous."

Glory laughed from inside his cell.

Though she felt like it would kill her, Jae held her tongue. She figured Arlington was the sort of man who would yank the coins right back if she didn't take what he'd given her. But as she scraped them into her satchel, blood burning with frustration, she hoped she'd never have to return to Ameda.

She tipped her hat, pushed her chair back, and stood. "Have a good day, sir. I hope you don't run into any trouble on your way to Calora."

She didn't look back at the sheriff, or Glory for that matter.

Chapter 3

*L*ife on the road offered few comforts. Roadhouses were one of them.

Halston Harney and his gang came across the house an hour after sundown. All day, they had traveled on a twisting road bordered by cacti and heaps of red stone. The house looked small and charming against the wide desert sky. Blue letters stretched across the awning, reading "Dalton's Roadhouse." Firelight illuminated its windows, the shutters swaying gently on either side of the panes.

Halston rubbed his hands together, blowing hot air onto his fingers. His breath rose like smoke in the winter night. "Let's stop here. We have enough to spare."

"Thank goodness," Lorelin breathed. She patted down her trousers. "I'm sick of sleeping on dirt. I'm dusty enough to give someone a cough."

Halston's brother, Hodge, rode close beside him. Halston watched Hodge adjust his battered, pinched-front hat, a leftover from their days as cowhands. The boys were both tall, and they shared the same olive skin, black hair, and brown eyes, but Hodge always looked... looser. His tousled hair fell just below his jaw, while Halston kept his short and straight as a soldier's. Halston was slim, but sturdily built, while Hodge was lanky. And Hodge always seemed to be moving... tipping his hat and grinning, stooping and swaggering and in and out of doors, pushing up the cuffs of his sleeves and unrolling them again.

A shaft of moonlight lit up Hodge's eyes. "Do we have enough time to stop here? We have to reach the railroad by noon tomorrow."

Halston nodded. "We'll be fine. If we set out by sunrise, we'll reach it with time to spare."

They led their horses to the stable. The structure was small, about six stalls wide and framed by a short, slightly crooked fence. A stable boy in a wrinkled shirt waved to them, then set about getting their horses into stalls. "You folks came right on time. We're boarding up for the night in about half an hour. Where are y'all headed?"

"Calora," Halston lied. Long ago, lying had dismayed him. Now, it felt as natural as stretching his arms out in the morning, though he wished it wasn't so. Honest people didn't last long out here.

While the stable boy took the reins, Halston adjusted his brown gambler's hat, hoping the brim would hide his face. There were probably some thousand tall, dark-haired men his age in Mesca, but he often wondered if the warrants mentioned anything more distinct, like his scars. His shirt covered most of them, and he usually managed to hide the rest under his bandana. People rarely recognized him, but he never could be too careful.

Quietly, they made their way to the front of the inn and walked inside. Warmth sank into Halston's bones. There was a woven mat before the threshold, and ristras of brittle peppers dangled from the ceiling. Flames danced in the fireplace. Wood was stacked artfully on either side, and brass candlesticks decked the mantle. The smell of baking bread and roasting chilé wafted across the air.

The short innkeeper and his plump wife welcomed them as they eased into the foyer. "How many rooms?"

"Two, please," said Lorelin. She had a voice like a bell, and she turned heads whenever she spoke. She was nineteen, just a few months older than Halston, but she had a way of making herself sound as old or as young as a situation required.

"Names?"

"Lucinda," said Lorelin, brushing the blonde curls off her shoulders. She tugged at her black lace gloves, then gestured to Halston, then Hodge, then Gryff. "And this is my husband, Alphonse, his brother, Marion, and Andreas."

The innkeeper smiled at Gryff, though Halston spied a twinge of discomfort behind it. The expression was civil, but not welcoming. "We'll give you our biggest bed, sir."

"Much obliged," said Gryff. The firelight shone on his moss-green scales. He was an Azmarian over seven feet tall, muscled like an ox, with the build of a man and the head of a snake. His wide mouth stretched from one cheek to the other, the tips of two fangs visible beneath his upper lip. At the end of his snout were two wide nostrils, and while his eyes were gold with slit pupils, they were somehow the most human part of him. Despite their snakelike features, Azmarians didn't hiss. Gryff had the rugged voice of a rancher who'd spent his fifty years shouting, smoking, and drinking. He garnered his share of stares, but he seemed good enough at ignoring them.

The innkeeper's wife led them upstairs, then down a hallway illuminated by brass sconces. The wooden floor creaked under their feet. Lorelin chatted with her about the weather and the best shops in the nearest town.

They stopped between two rooms, and the innkeeper's wife passed Lorelin two brass keys. "We hope you'll be comfortable here.

If you need anything, don't hesitate to ask." She disappeared down the hall.

Hodge's eyes flicked to Lorelin. *"Marion?"*

Lorelin placed her hands on her hips. "I just thought you could do with some humility."

"It'll take more than a name to do that to me," Hodge jested, his mouth curving into a fiendish grin.

Gryff snorted. His long, clawed fingers pinched the brim of his hat, then hung it on the rack by the door. "Let her have her fun, kid," he told Hodge. He opened the left door, then peeked into the room. "This one has two big beds. Who's going with me?"

"I will," Hodge said, then pointed to Lorelin. "Next time, *I* get to pick the fake names."

"Fine, fine," she giggled. "Sleep well, Marion."

Halston raised a finger to his lips. "Everyone get some rest. We're riding at dawn."

The room's wallpaper was the same greenish-blue as Lorelin's eyes, the color of water-tarnished copper. They had two narrow beds with gingham comforters, a nightstand made from an old vegetable crate, and shelves overflowing with books of all thicknesses. Halston hurried up to it immediately and ran a hand across the bindings, murmuring the titles.

At last, he pulled himself away, dust coating the skin of his palm.

"I agree," said Lorelin, flopping onto her bed. "It would be lovely to read again."

Halston was tempted to grab his knapsack and stuff it with as many books as he could carry. But he wasn't *that* sort of thief. There was no sense in stealing just for the sake of it.

Lorelin began fixing her hair in the mirror, which was almost as tall as she was. Scuffs covered its frame, tarnished beyond hope of it ever gleaming again.

Silver.

"Do you think we could get that mirror out of here without dropping it?" Halston whispered.

"Maybe," Lorelin replied. "But it looks awfully heavy."

That was probably true… but it was tempting. Tempting enough for Halston to consider it. He'd take a pile of corroded silver over a sea of gold any day, and weep for joy at the sight of it.

They'd get all the silver they needed, someday soon, and then they'd never have to steal again. At least, that was what he told himself.

Lorelin took off her jade-studded boots, then sat down on her bed, patting the mattress. "Come join me, honey."

"*Honey?*"

She pointed one shoulder at him. "We're supposed to be married, aren't we?"

He sighed. "Yes, I guess we are."

Lorelin flounced out her shirt and batted her eyes at him. "Shall I bake a pie while you go out and rob a train? It's my only duty to serve you, you know."

"Stop," Halston said, but he was laughing now. "They might hear you downstairs."

She snorted. "It doesn't matter if they do. Most innkeepers I've met don't care who comes through their doors as long as they pay."

"Still. I don't want them to hear us. Not worth the risk."

"I know. Nothing is."

He would have argued, but they seemed to have this sort of conversation every night. It was futile to waste more breath on it.

Halston lay on his bed, sinking into the mattress. He settled beneath the comforter and welcomed the touch of cotton on his skin.

"It beats the sand, doesn't it?" Lorelin sighed.

"Without a doubt," Halston said with a yawn.

Lorelin stood and paced up to the window. Mist fogged the pane. "I like it out here. It's quiet."

"I thought you didn't like the quiet."

She shrugged. "I do every once in a while. It keeps things interesting."

Halston rolled onto his side. After a day of traveling, it was hard to find a comfortable position. The sensation of riding seemed to stay with him for a long time after dismounting. "Lorelin?"

"Yes?"

"Can you ever... feel yourself *still* riding at the end of the day?"

"All the time."

"My father said the same thing happens after a few days of sailing. You can still feel the ship pitching under you, even after you've stepped onto the ground. 'Sea legs,' he called it." After years of riding through miles of sand, it felt strange to speak of the sea again.

Lorelin threw herself back onto her bed, squealing as she buried her face in the pillows. "I'm exhausted."

"You didn't seem tired two minutes ago."

"Well, I am now. I'm going to sleep forever."

"I'm not paying you to sleep forever," Halston grumbled.

"Yeah, yeah." A yawn muddled her voice. That was the last he heard of her that night.

Halston only found himself tossing and turning. He tried to sleep like Lorelin, to keep his mind from racing a mile a minute. Tireless, he was. That's what everybody told him when they caught him sitting awake at night, scribbling his thoughts down. They said it like it was a good thing, but he didn't need to be tireless now. He needed sleep.

The usual thoughts danced across his memory, but most were about the train. It wouldn't be the first they'd robbed. Chances were it would all be fine.

That was what he told himself until he fell into a shallow slumber.

———

Hodge wasn't used to sleeping under a roof. He preferred the feeling of openness, of drawing fresh air into his lungs.

When he woke up, he reckoned he hadn't been asleep for long. He sat up and looked out the window to find that the moon had barely shifted in the sky. Gryff lay still as stone in the bed across the room.

Hodge tugged on his boots and slipped out of the room. The March night would be cold, but he figured he might as well take a walk outside and tire himself out.

He headed downstairs. He stepped into the foyer to find it glowing with candlelight. A slender girl in a blue nightdress stood beneath the bookshelves, slipping a title back in place. She was around his age, with copper curls and lips pink and full as cherry blossoms. She glanced over her shoulder and caught him looking, though he didn't mind.

"Don't mind me," said Hodge. "Just stepped out for a walk."

Grinning, she moved toward him. "I saw you riding in earlier tonight. I'm afraid I didn't get the chance to say hello. I'm Mira."

"Mira," Hodge said. "I'm... Marion." He bit down on his cheeks. *Damn it, Lorelin.*

She giggled. "Couldn't sleep?"

Hodge shook his head.

"Me either. If you want, I can show you around. My folks have run this roadhouse for twenty years. I don't mean to brag or nothin', but it's mighty pretty."

Hodge smiled. "Sure thing, ma'am."

Flashing him a foxlike grin, Mira led him back into the hallway. He followed her to a room at its end.

Quietly, Mira shut the door. Inside the room was a small desk, a trundle bed covered with a red-and-yellow quilt, and a wooden chair carved with patterns of daisies and vines. White curtains dangled from the window, and a round woolen rug lay on the pine floor.

"Your room?" asked Hodge.

Mira nodded and paced over to her bed, her skirt swaying around her ankles. "The best part of living in a roadhouse is all the people you get to meet."

"Meet a lot of interesting folks?" asked Hodge, moving toward the bed.

"Yes," Mira said, grinning. She sat down on her bed. "Plenty."

Hodge shoved his hands in his pockets. "Wish I could say the same."

Mira laughed. "I'm sorry to hear that."

Hodge sat down beside her, stretching out his arms. "Well, maybe that ain't the right way for me to put it. I meet plenty of interesting folks. But… we don't always seem to get on well."

"Why not?"

Hodge shrugged. "Don't know. They get jealous of me, maybe."

Mira laughed again, then brushed a few strands of hair off her face. She tilted her head, shining like a gem against the dull, faded wallpaper. "How old are you?"

"Eighteen." Well, not eighteen yet, but nearly so.

"So am I." She ran a hand over her skirts. "My friend Tillie is six months younger than me, and she got married this past Sunday. She's been rubbing it in my face ever since."

"Oh, I'm sorry to hear that."

Mira scoffed. "He ain't even good looking, really. All he does is talk about meat. Smoking it, chopping it, eating it."

"I mean… meat's nice. But there are better things to talk about."

"Like what?"

He leaned her way. "Like you."

It was nice, meeting someone friendly and new. There were times he reckoned that his gang got a little tired of listening to him talk.

Slowly, Mira lifted her brows. "Must you leave tomorrow? It seems like you could use a few days of rest."

"In a perfect world," Hodge replied. "But we have work to do. This job can't wait."

"What's the job?"

"Driving cattle," he said, almost too quickly. "We're taking them up to Monvallea. The market is good there right now." It wasn't true, of course, but he didn't feel too bad about saying it. That *had* been his job, and not too long ago. There were still days where he woke up thinking he was still in the ranch's bunker.

"Have you ever thought about settling down? It seems like cowboys never stop moving."

Ain't that the truth. "Maybe one day. But that's a far cry from now."

Mira shifted closer to him, the bed's springs squeaking. She pressed a hand to his chest, and Hodge's heart jumped.

"There's a sweet little bookstore in Calora. Pa took me there when I was little. He bought me a bunch of old novels for a deon apiece. The ladies in those books were always riding off with cowboys into the night. I used to wonder if that would happen to me."

Gently, Hodge wrapped his hand around her wrist. "There ain't nothing wrong with staying here."

"Maybe not," she sighed. "But I *would* like to get to know you better." Her finger traced his collarbone.

He smiled. "I'd like that, too. But my brother will be mighty angry if I'm not out the door by sunrise. He'll start shoutin' fancy words at me. Turns into a real smart-mouth when he's mad." They had a job tomorrow, too, which always made Halston even more uptight.

Mira's free hand found his back. "Don't listen to him, then. Won't he get over it?"

Hodge shrugged. "Eventually. He's a killjoy. But I'm used to it."

They were quiet for a while. Mira began playing with his hair, twisting it 'round her long, clever fingers. "We'll have to be quiet."

His hands traveled to her waist. "You sure?"

She kissed him.

Eyes closed, he told her, "I'll be gone tomorrow."

"Don't care."

Tomorrow, he would leave, and she would never know his real name. Then her smooth hands traveled down his neck, her skin warm as coffee in a porcelain cup, and he forgot all about tomorrow.

He kissed her rhythmically, listening to her rising breaths. Each second was more thrilling than the last. Gods, she was beautiful.

"Will I get to ride away with you?" she asked between kisses.

"Oh, definitely," Hodge answered before he'd even really thought about the question.

She lowered her voice. "Don't say 'yes' unless you mean it."

He almost let go of her waist. He wanted to say yes. Pretty girls had a way of milling his mind.

No, he'd have to stop this. He shouldn't let it go this far—

A slamming door shattered his thoughts. "Mira!"

The innkeeper stood in the doorway He had one hand propping the door open, and the other was already curling into a fist.

Mira scrambled away from Hodge, her red curls flying over her shoulders. She dug her fingers into the comforter. "Nothing happened!"

The innkeeper ignored her and pointed to Hodge. His eyes flared like hot iron. "You. Outta my inn. You've got one minute, boy, and you'd better not be in my sight by the time it's up."

Hodge stood, not daring to look back at Mira. The innkeeper stepped out of the doorway, his face coal-red. Hodge darted away before anything else could be said, thankful that he'd received a warning rather than a beating. He slipped into the corridor, then raced up the stairway. He pounded on Gryff's door, then Halston and Lorelin's. "We gotta get out of here!"

He ran back downstairs, through the foyer, and out into the cold night. He carried himself across the silent, windswept earth and stopped to catch his breath. He stood there, shuffling quietly in the sand. Even outside, he could hear Halston's confused exchange with the bellowing innkeeper. Then came the hurried footsteps. The rest of his gang hustled out the front door, looking dull-eyed and dazed.

"*Don't come back!*" The door slammed behind them.

Hodge winced.

Halston and Gryff were moving slowly, their eyelids still heavy. Lorelin stared Hodge down with what might have been the sharpest glare he'd ever seen her wearing. She bent over and scooped something off the ground, and before Hodge could even think of explaining himself, she started throwing rocks at him. "You miserable oaf!"

Hodge caught one rock in his hand and dodged two more. "Stop! I didn't mean anything by it!"

Lorelin must have calmed down a little, because then she started throwing pebbles instead. "You got that poor girl in trouble! What were you thinking?"

"She ain't in trouble!"

Lorelin glared. "Then what was all that yelling about?"

Hodge waved his arms. "Old men don't like me! Everybody knows that!"

Halston let out a staggered breath, then covered his eyes with one hand. "Hodge. You told me you were *done* with this sort of thing."

Hodge scratched his neck, looking to the darkened shapes of mesquite trees instead of his brother. "I am. But I ran into her and... she wanted to talk."

"If you were just *talking* to her, why'd he toss us out?"

muttered Gryff.

Hodge didn't have an answer for him. "Y'all think I went in there *planning* to rile him up? I didn't mean to get caught."

"Of course, you didn't," Halston said. "Nobody *means* to get caught."

Lorelin waved a hand. "Oh, just forget it. We'd better get the horses before he chases us off the land."

"She's right." Gryff snorted. "Next time, Hodge, do us all a favor and don't speak to anybody."

"Wasn't my fault," Hodge said under his breath. "Just some rotten luck is all."

They walked to the stable in silence and found it unlocked. They trudged inside, stepping over horseshoes and lumps of hay, then fetched the horses and saddled up. Guilt tingled down Hodge's spine, but he reckoned apologizing to his gang would just make them angrier. Silently, they headed for the railroad.

He hoped Mira's pa wouldn't be too angry with her. Maybe another cowboy would come sweep her off her feet soon.

"Maybe it's a blessing in disguise," Halston said when they were far enough away. "Gives us more time to brace ourselves for the job. Do you have the powder, Hodge?"

"Yeah."

"Good. By the way, I'm forbidding you to speak to a woman ever again."

Don't count on it, thought Hodge. But next time, he'd be smarter about it.

Chapter 4

Halston stood in the sand, facing the horizon. There, the buttes loomed like giants in the distance. He raised his fingertip and traced their outlines, trying to focus on breathing steadily.

After they'd left the inn, it hadn't taken long for them to reach the tunnel. Hours had passed since then. They'd tried to occupy themselves, but they could only go over the plan so many times without losing their minds. He'd considered talking to Hodge again, but decided against it. He wanted their heads clear as possible for the job, not clouded by frustration.

Halston stretched, then turned around to get another look at the tunnel. A lengthy ridge of knurled, rust-colored earth spread out at the end of a flat stretch of desert. It rose about as high as a barn, but there were plenty of boulders strewn around it for them to climb. The tracks plunged into the tunnel's entrance—a dark and perfect square in the center of the ridge, bolstered by thick wooden beams. Past the mouth of the tunnel, he could not see anything. The winds were heavy today, tossing up the dirt and howling like restless ghosts above the rock. Halston had stuffed his hat inside his satchel to keep it from blowing off his head.

Lorelin sat near him, polishing the sleek handles of her guns. Halston could never help but chuckle to himself at the sight of them. The handles were carved from mother-of-pearl, the likenesses of peacocks engraved in them. How out of place they looked in the calloused hands of a woman on the run. The gods only knew how much they'd cost.

"*Pretty guns,*" Hodge had once said. "*Looks like you could set a table with 'em.*"

Lorelin sighed, then slid one gun back into its holster. She tugged on her gloves, biting her lip. "Six hundred crowns. Think the train will have all of it?"

"Can't imagine why it wouldn't," said Gryff. "Sterling himself had the records for it."

Hodge folded his arms with a grin on his face. "We've got about seven guns between us and a horn full of black powder. We ain't got *nothin'* to worry about."

Gryff rolled his eyes. "Still ain't sure how I feel about trustin' you with explosives."

Hodge had won the powder in a shooting contest with a miner. The man said it would blow through a chunk of metal thick as a man's thumb.

A gust of wind drifted over their heads. Halston shuddered. He fiddled with the buttons on his coat, making sure they were snug enough, and stared at the straight, dark strip of the train tracks.

In the distance, a whistle sang a note. It was faint, far on the other side of the tunnel, but that meant it was time to brace themselves.

"Let's go over the plan one more time," Halston announced, itching to start moving.

"We've got it, we've got it," Lorelin replied. "You and Gryff will wait above the tunnel, then hop on the car before the caboose. Gryff looks out for men on the train while you take out the pin."

"Then the car rolls to a stop," Hodge continued. "We climb into the car, then pour the powder on top of the safe. I light it. It goes off."

"And as soon as it goes off, we collect the money and run," Halston finished. He squinted at the powder horn hanging from Hodge's belt. Its bone curve caught snippets of the morning light. "You tested the powder, right?"

"Yep. Works like a charm."

Halston glanced at the revolver in his own belt. It was a sturdy, practical thing, as fine a weapon as he could afford. He'd had it since his ranching days. Wooden grip. Aluminum frame. Light as the gun was, it felt like a weight as he moved. He hoped he wouldn't have to use it today.

Hodge nudged Halston as he stared at the mesas again. "Hey. You alright?"

"No," Halston replied. "If this goes wrong…"

"What?"

Halston wiped a slick mixture of sweat and sand away from his brow, leaving a muddy film on his fingertips. "Sterling…"

"I know," Hodge finished. "You don't gotta say it, alright? It won't happen. We'll make it out of this."

"Come on," Gryff broke in, motioning over his shoulder. "You two can talk later. It's comin'. We don't have much time."

Lorelin pressed her lips to her fingertips and blew each of the Harney boys a kiss. They all tugged their bandanas over their mouths and noses, pulling them taut. Lorelin and Hodge made their way north, following the tracks. Halston whistled three notes to Hodge, and Hodge whistled back. One high note, a low note, then another high. It'd been their signal ever since they'd turned to robbery—the first three notes of an old sailing song their father had taught them. Even when there was no pressing need for it, the brothers found themselves sounding it off whenever they began a job.

Without another word, Halston and Gryff began trekking toward the tunnel.

Grunting, Halston dug his heels into the sand and hoisted himself uphill. Gryff's boots left marks the size of griddles in the earth. Their steps brought up the dust, sending it off on the breeze. They took to the rocks, moving swiftly, but not without care. Halston climbed boulder after boulder, hands scraping the grains in the sun-warmed stone. The winds chafed his bare forehead, and he squinted against the particles of airborne dust.

When they finally reached the ridge, Halston breathed in the metallic scent of the engine's smoke. The train whistled again, its volume escalating. Gryff and Halston squatted, looked down, and waited. Halston ran his tongue across his teeth and tasted the grit of the desert. Shaking out his arms, he leaned forward.

The whistle sang out thrice more, echoing off the tunnel's walls. Halston braced himself to leap.

Finally, the black engine surged beneath them, and a hefty plume of smoke rose from the tunnel. Car after car followed it, rattling as the train barreled out of the darkness.

The caboose was coming. Gryff counted down. "One, two… three!"

They took to the sky.

Halston landed after Gryff. A jolt shot through his legs, and he wavered to the side, then lost footing. He broke his fall, palms slamming into the cold metal roof. Fighting back a shout, he bit into his cheeks and pushed himself up again.

Up ahead, someone within the train shouted.

"Come on," Gryff urged, hustling to the edge of the car. Halston rose and followed, his boots pounding on the flat roof. The train tee-tered and shook beneath their feet. Fear nipped at Halston's stom-ach, like the hollow feeling before a tumble, but he fought it back and raced for the edge.

A pair of ladders stretched down the caboose's front. Halston took the right-hand ladder, Gryff took the left, and they descended into the gap between the cars. The iron rungs chilled Halston's palms.

Gryff bent down. The link-and-pin coupler was as large as his fist. The tracks whirled by under the mechanism. They'd be goners if they slipped—splattered on the rails.

Gryff wrapped his fingers around the pin and yanked. The narrow bar rose reluctantly from the cavity, the metal creaking as it emerged. Halston clung to the ladder as the car shuddered, then parted from the link.

Someone up ahead shouted, "Stop the train!" At the same time, Gryff shouted, "Jump!"

Gryff leapt to the left, Halston to the right. He landed on his knees, sending a wave of impact up his body, then rolled, sprawling in the sand. The train sped away from them, and the shouts of the men inside were faint beneath the locomotive's clamor.

When he'd rolled off the shock, Halston leapt to his feet and ran. The caboose barreled up the tracks, following the line of cars.

Halston chased it, and Gryff followed the car on the other side of the tracks. A stitch formed in his side. He drew in a breath and ran faster as the wind pushed against his body. They couldn't let the car outrun them.

A minute later, the wheels began to slacken. The car slurred to a steady halt. The rest of the train had turned into a rapidly receding speck on the tracks ahead.

Hodge and Lorelin caught up to them, their horses stealing down the side of the rails. Hodge didn't bother with a careful dismount. He leapt from his horse's back and ran to the car.

Lorelin and Halston ran after him. Staring forth, steady as a soldier, Gryff remained outside and brandished his rifle.

They approached the back side of the caboose. Halston threw the car door open, gun at the ready. The trio took a step into the car.

Inside, the caboose was dim and shoddy, reeking of hot metal and coal. No passengers. Orderly stacks of crates lined the walls, and a few empty, splintering pallets lay on the floor. In the very back was what they'd come for—a small but bulky combination safe, just waiting to be blasted open.

Hodge removed the powder horn from his jacket. He twisted the cap, then began lining the top of the safe with the black powder.

A shot rang out from outside.

Halston darted back to the entrance. Gryff wore a cold stare, crouching behind the caboose with his rifle. "The hell are you guys waitin' for?"

"We're almost ready!"

"Hurry! I think they're sendin' folk after us now!" Gryff fired a second warning shot into the air.

Halston turned back. "We're out of time. Light it!"

Hodge struck a match, and a thin trail of smoke drifted from its head. The flame met the powder. "Run!"

They ran from the ensuing hiss. Lorelin vaulted herself over the railing. The boys followed her.

Silently, Halston counted to nine, then—

BAM.

The gang turned around, met with the dull scent of smoke. Gryff cocked the rifle, poised to shoot again.

The trio coughed as they entered the car. Halston tried to wave away the smoke, his eyes burning.

"No!" shouted Hodge. "Nonononono!"

Halston squinted through the haze. His heart sank. A hole brimmed in the center of the safe, its edges curling and freshly melted. Inside, a fire blazed.

Hodge touched the sides, then drew back with a wince. "Too hot."

Without another word, Lorelin splashed the contents of her canteen onto the safe. The flames died with a sharp squeak.

Three shots came from outside, all a higher pitch than the low blare of Gryff's rifle. The men were shooting back.

"They're ridin' our tails!" shouted Gryff. "Just take what you can! We've gotta get out of here!"

The safe held seven bars of silver and four gold. There were bills, too, but now they were nothing but ash. Halston took all of the gold bars and one of the silver. Still hot from the explosion, but not impossible to touch. He tucked them into his jacket, and they hurried out the back, then ran for the horses.

Halston swung himself on to his stallion, grasping for the reins with one unsteady hand. At last, he got a decent enough hold on them, then drove his heels into his horse's side. The gang charged along the rails, the caboose waiting behind them.

Halston looked over his shoulder as they approached the tunnel. A shadow emerged from behind the smoking car. A man. Before Halston could react, the man raised his pistol. It cracked.

The bullet exploded at the head of their path, sand flying about. Lorelin's horse screeched and bucked to the sky.

Lorelin tumbled from the saddle. She hit the ground, yelping as the earth met her chest. The metal bars fell from her arms.

"Lorelin!" Halston shouted.

Scrambling to pull the metal back into her shirt, she mounted her mare with one arm, but nearly ate the dust again. Another shot sailed through the air, then disappeared somewhere in the tunnel. When Lorelin climbed onto her horse again, Halston gave his stallion a firm kick. They kept riding.

They plunged into the tunnel, the horses' hooves drumming on the tracks. Shadow covered them. Wind moaned off the dark, arched walls. Minutes later, the gun thundered behind them again, but its echo was faint. "I think we lost them," Hodge said, breathless.

At last, they emerged from the tunnel. They rode on, abandoning the train tracks. Soon, they returned to the flat expanse of desert. Murrieta's Rock loomed in the distance. Halston glanced over his shoulder every few moments, searching the area for pursuers. Nothing but miles of sand and desert plants beneath an enormous blue sky.

At least they'd all made it out in one piece.

Hours passed. They spent them alternating between a trot and a gallop, bound north for Murrieta's Rock. When the sky began to turn rosy with dusk, Halston decided it was safe to stop.

He jerked his reins. The gang rounded themselves up in a circle. Halston dropped the metal bars into the sand. Hodge added the second set. Lorelin surrendered what she'd scraped up in the scuffle.

"I dropped one," she murmured without looking up.

"Damn powder," muttered Hodge.

"Hey," said Halston. "It's nobody's fault. We did what we could, and it could've been much worse. We all made it out of there." Though it certainly would've been better if Sterling had mentioned that some of the crowns would be bills, not coins.

"Sure, we're all in one piece now," Hodge pointed out, "but what about when we see Sterling?"

"We better think of somethin'," said Gryff. "We're half empty-handed, and we've got two days to get him what we promised."

Halston exhaled and looked to the sky, at the wisps of clouds turned gold by the setting sun. The fear began to surface inside him. He tried to breathe in, to draw his mind away before the panic caught onto him. For a moment, he felt like he was back in that cell in Arrowwood, wondering if they would make him watch his brother hang. But they'd made it out of there alive. They'd make it out of this, too. They still had time. They just needed a plan.

He raised his thumb to Murrieta's Rock, trying to gauge its distance. From far away, the formation looked even more like a knobby fist than it did up close, like a giant punching its way out of its own desert grave. "Murrieta's Rock is close. We can get to Ameda from here. It's probably an hour or so away. There's a bank there."

"Been there?" asked Gryff.

"Once," said Halston. "Small town. They've got a sheriff, but I doubt he's anyone special."

"Don't mean the bank is an easy target," said Gryff.

Halston shrugged. "We'll find out when we get there."

"Hal, this is nonsense," Lorelin said, shaking her head. "We can't improvise *now*. We've never leapt into a job without looking before."

"I know, but I'd rather show up with something to say for ourselves than admit what happened here." He wiped his hands on his pants and slid one foot into a stirrup, then grabbed the pommel of his saddle and hoisted himself up. "Sterling doesn't care where the money comes from, as long as he gets it."

Halston looked to Murrieta's Rock once more. "Let's set out. Keep a low profile when we reach Ameda. We've got a… brief ride ahead of us."

Chapter 5

S tars painted the sky as the gang rode into Ameda. It was built like most towns in Mesca, a couple miles long, but with a solitary street cutting through two rows of buildings. The buildings were black, identical silhouettes against the backdrop of night. Wind whistled through the structures, a lone, dull note. The air smelled of cigars.

The street was empty. Halston scanned the area, trying to catch a glimpse of the bank. Muffled laughter flowed from a tall building to the north. Halston squinted. "Elona's Saloon" read the crooked sign above the doorway.

Lorelin pointed. "Let's go there." There was a spark in both her eyes and her voice.

"I don't know. It doesn't seem wise to spend money on drinks when we're already short," said Halston.

Lorelin raised her canteen, flicking her head to the side. "Mine is bone dry. I've never been to a saloon that charged me for water. I'm persuasive, you know."

Hodge held up his own canteen in agreement. Halston's was a little less than half full.

"There's a perfectly good river running around this town," Halston said.

"Oh, come on, let's go." Lorelin bobbed as she spoke, as though her excitement would make her burst at the seams.

Lorelin adored saloons. She loved cheap wine, piano music, and laughing freely, when nobody could tell her to quiet down. She disliked the wooing from drunk, greasy men, but she loved the looks on their faces when she beat them at poker. Lorelin always left in a fit of giggles. Halston always left exhausted, trying not to look at the men who'd started throwing themselves at Lorelin, fawning over her shadow like lovelorn fools.

"We're meeting with Sterling the day after tomorrow," Halston reminded her. "We'll have to scout out the bank. *Tonight.*"

"And we will," Lorelin said. "C'mon. We've all had one hell of a day. Half an hour, tops. We can go jimmy bank locks and whatnot when we're done."

One day, Halston would learn how to say no to her, but he wasn't sure how much energy he had to keep protesting. He sighed. "Alright. Half an hour. I'm holding you to it."

Lorelin let out a delighted squeal, then hopped down from her horse.

"I'll be out back," decided Gryff.

Gryff had a way of sensing whether the residents of a town would take kindly to his presence. Usually, the further east they were, the less surprising it was to see an Azmarian. But Azmaria was thousands of miles across the sea, so it was a surprise to people regardless of where they were. That was one point on Gryff's list of reasons why he disliked talking to people, which the gang had heard many times.

"You sure?" asked Lorelin.

"Sure as can be," Gryff said flatly. He adjusted the pack on his broad shoulders before trudging away.

"We'll miss you!" Lorelin called after him.

"You'll live," Gryff replied, and veered off.

Halston said nothing as they tethered up the horses, then stepped into the haze of drinking and shouting. The saloon was large, overflowing with tables and lit by a chandelier with curled arms. The air stank of tobacco and stale beer, and peanut shells littered the floor. A mural of two skeletons locked in an embrace spanned across the back wall. One wore a flowing gown, the other a wide-brimmed hat and a collared shirt. Halston furrowed his brow, wondering what would prompt someone to paint such a thing.

There wasn't an unoccupied table in sight. Men sat clutching mugs of ale over tabletops blanketed with battered cards and poker chips. Lorelin's eyes grew wide as they glimpsed a crowd overlooking a dice game at a center table.

Halston nudged her. "Remember what we talked about?"

"I know," she sighed. "No betting what we have."

"Exactly."

"I wouldn't do that," she said. "But I think you should learn to live a little."

"Keep your voice down. Besides, we—"

He stopped when she threw back her shoulders—a sign that she was braced to mimic him.

Part of him wanted to be frustrated that she could make light after a botched heist, but he couldn't blame her. It was her way of playing the cards they'd been dealt.

Halston just shook it away. "Hmm. Looks like all the tables are full." He turned to look at the row of booths to his left, then pointed to one in the corner, where the windows met the mural. "Looks like there's space there."

One side of the booth was empty. On the other sat a girl, likely a bit younger than Halston's nineteen years, judging by what he could see. The brim of a hat shaded her face, painting everything but her nose and pink mouth in shadow. Two thick, mussy brown braids fell over her shoulders. Though she looked young, there was something ancient about the way she sat, holding still as a statue.

She lifted her head when she caught him looking, and her mouth stretched into a small, slightly crooked grin. With that, she went back to reading a large, wrinkled paper in her hands.

"Good idea," Hodge hooted, smacking Halston on the back. "Let's sit there."

Halston frowned.

Hodge hurried up to the booth as Halston and Lorelin trailed behind him. "Hey there," he drawled, flashing the girl a smile. "Mind if we sit here?"

"Go ahead," the girl said in a low, clear voice. She did not look up.

Stiffly, Halston followed Lorelin's lead and settled down in the booth. Hodge joined them. He was there for all of four seconds before his eyes widened at something nearby. He said, "I'll be right back," and left.

"What's your name?" Lorelin asked the girl. Lorelin was never one to pass up a conversation, whether or not the time for it was convenient.

"Jae," she said.

Halston wanted to tell Lorelin that they needed to get some water, thank the bartender, and leave. He nudged her on the leg, which Lorelin either did not notice or ignored.

"So. What brings you here?" asked Lorelin.

"Planning a journey."

Lorelin laughed. "I know the feeling."

Jae finally looked up. Her eyes were blue with gray flecks, like stones in a riverbed. "You do?"

"I certainly do." Lorelin gestured to the mural. "That's an interesting sight. I think it's supposed to be the drifter and the duchess."

"Drifter and the duchess?" asked Halston.

"You know," said Lorelin. "That old legend. It's about this Weserian duchess who sails across the sea to escape a war, and she meets a drifter from Mesca. And they fall in love and are killed by the men he stole from and haunt the desert forevermore."

That was one way to tell a story. Halston nudged Lorelin again. "Remember. We can't stay here long."

"Fine, fine." Lorelin surveyed the room. "Where's—" She stopped herself from saying his name. "Where's your brother?"

Halston spied him on the other side of the saloon. Hodge was talking to a pair of girls with sequined dresses and tightly coiffed hair. He spoke with his hands, probably telling a story dazzled with hyperbole. By the looks on the girls' powdered faces, they weren't as interested in the story as they were in whatever amount of money he had in his pockets.

Halston slapped his forehead. "This happens *every time.*" And after last night, too.

A snide smile tugged at Lorelin's lips. "Should I go warn those girls that he's a cad? I could pretend to be his former lover, or something. *That* would teach him a lesson."

"No. No need for a scene." Halston spoke quietly. "But I'm tired of him getting us into trouble."

"He's almost eighteen. He'll probably grow out of it." Lorelin paused thoughtfully. "Well, I guess some men *never* grow out of it."

"That's assuring," Halston grumbled.

Lorelin chuckled. "And then there are boys like you. You must have come out of the womb acting like you were fifty years old." She stretched out her arms. "But if *he* gets to make new friends, then I think I should, too. I'm going to go watch a game."

"We just got here," said Halston. "You said we were just going to get water."

Lorelin sighed, rolled her eyes, and rested her chin on her hand. "And we'll do that. Don't you think we should make the most of the night?"

"Yes." *By scoping out the bank for our job tomorrow.*

Her frown disappeared, stretching into a small, curt smile. She gave his ear a tug. "Come on. You know I'm not trying to ruffle your feathers. I just think you could stand to loosen up. You deserve it. We all do."

"Not when we're on a deadline."

"You're denying me life's simple pleasures."

"There are plenty of people who live long, fulfilling lives having never played poker."

"I'm sure there are, but I'm not one of them." Lorelin straightened her derby hat and tucked a few stray curls under the brim. "I get it. Jobs are jobs. I just think we ought to give ourselves half an hour to stop, y'know... worrying about failure." Playfully, she rested her head on his shoulder. "Besides, how can you say no to me?"

"You make it difficult, Lorelin. That's the problem."

She giggled. "I don't blame you. Everyone says I'm irresistible."

"Sometimes you're exhausting."

She jabbed him in the ribs. "You're cruel! Fine. I'll stay here."

Halston said nothing. He turned to Jae, surprised she hadn't looked up from her paper to comment on their argument.

The paper's edges were soft, worn with age, creased and browned. Something about the map uneased him. It called to him, like someone trying to wake him from a dream. It didn't look like something you could pick up at a dock or a bookshop. It didn't look *natural*.

The corner of the map bore the symbol of a crescent moon. Through the moon was the thin outline of an arrow.

The *Rangers' sigil.* The mark of Hemaera.

This girl had a Rangers' map!

In the center of the map, the word *Ameda* shone in gold. It didn't catch the light like paint did. The letters almost seemed to flicker, like candlelight. Wondering if he'd imagined it, Halston blinked. The gold lingered.

"Um—miss?"

"My name's Jae," she corrected him.

"Sorry. Jae. Could I take a look at your map, please?"

She raised an eyebrow, sinking back into the booth's cracked leather seat.

Rangers' maps were hard to come by. They'd spent years trying to find one, but they hadn't quite figured out how to get close enough to a Ranger to snag one.

Could this girl be one of them? Halston had never met a Ranger, but from what he knew, they were usually men with years of experience under the law.

Jae was still wearing a slightly sour look, so Halston went on. "It's—it's beautiful. I've never seen cartography like that before. I would love to take a look, if you don't mind."

He could hardly believe it. *Tonight,* they could leave this place with a map of the Outlands in hand.

She folded the map, then pushed back her shoulders. "Dontcha got your own map? Listen here. I mean no disrespect, but I didn't come here to show off my belongings."

Lorelin gave Halston a wide-eyed, knowing look. *Ranger?*

Halston nodded, then said, "I'm afraid our map got drenched in a thundershower a few weeks ago. We're short on money, and we're not too sure where we're headed next." He bit down on his cheeks.

A poor excuse.

Jae tilted her head. "Well, if you take the road north, Duraunt ain't too far."

"Duraunt," Halston repeated. "Thanks."

Jae narrowed her eyes. Halston hoped that she couldn't somehow sense the thoughts scrambling inside his mind. If they snatched the map from her, there was a chance she'd chase them, and they still needed to get a look at the bank. He doubted a sheriff would go out of his way to catch someone for stealing a map, but he'd once met a man who'd lost three fingers for taking a lump of soap from a general store.

Lorelin reached into her pocket and placed something on the table. A set of knucklebones and a die clattered on the wood. They weren't real knucklebones, hewn from rose-colored marble rather than marrow-flecked bone. A relic from Lorelin's past.

"You seem like you'd be good at games," Lorelin told Jae. "He could play you for a peep. Best two out of three?"

Jae shrugged. "Well, I don't see what's so interesting about my map, but alright. I enjoy a game every once in a while. Do I get to pick *my* prize if I win?"

"Of course," Halston said quickly.

"Good." Jae stroked a set of initials someone had hacked into the tabletop. "Cause I think there's something' you ain't telling me. If I win, you tell me why you're so interested in my map."

Halston tipped his head, breathing in. It was fair enough. If she won, then they'd hurry out of here immediately. Her suspicions didn't matter.

Halston rolled first. Three. He tossed the knucklebones to the level of his eyes, then caught two on the back of his hand.

Jae's turn. She rolled a six. Halston hoped the bones would tumble off her hand, but to his surprise, she caught them all without even twitching.

They rolled again. Halston caught four of four, Jae two of four. One more round. Halston: two of three. Jae: one of five.

"Thank you," said Halston, sweeping the die and bones into his palm. "Good game."

Jae said nothing, then unfurled her map without blinking. "Alright. Take a look. Be quick about it."

Part of Halston cried out to him. An urge to snatch the map and run. What would she do if he took it? Sit by and let him? Swat his arm? Start a fight? Maybe they should just leave. It wasn't worth uprooting trouble when they had a deadline hurtling their way.

As it turned out, it didn't matter one way or the other, because the moment Halston touched the map, the ink disappeared.

They all gasped. Halston, Lorelin, and Jae gazed down, unblinking, at the newly blank paper. Nobody moved a muscle.

Slowly, Jae touched the map again. The images reappeared. "Touch it again," she told Halston.

Twice more, Halston touched the map and the ink faded. Each time, Jae returned the dark lines with the tap of a finger.

Jae locked eyes with Halston. "Well," she sputtered, "if it helps, I didn't know it did that either."

Hodge came strutting back to the table, then. His smile sank into a bewildered frown when he saw the three of them staring down at the map, then back up to each other.

"Hey. What happened here? Everyone alright?"

"You," boomed a harsh, guttural voice, the word followed by the jangling of spurs.

Hodge swerved.

A husky, broad-shouldered man approached Hodge. Unkempt hair coated his chin and fell from the brim of his hat. His frayed shirt was covered in liquor stains the size of handprints, and his sallow face was knit into a scowl. Two more men walked at his sides. They were not nearly as burly, but their glares were just as sharp. One was stocky, with a red, tangled beard and fingers thick as sausages. The other was tall and lean, dressed all in black, with dark, greasy hair and features sharper than glass.

Halston barely had time to conjure up a thought before the man in the center hurled himself forward and shoved Hodge against the wall, his forearm wedged beneath Hodge's throat. The man towered over his brother.

Hodge wheezed, "Get off of me!"

Halston and Lorelin jumped to their feet. The man dug his fist into Hodge's pocket and pulled something out.

Coins rattled on the floor. Next to Hodge's boot lay a drawstring pouch, the money spilling from its mouth.

Damn it, Hodge.

"You thought you could steal from me?" the man snarled, spittle falling onto Hodge's face.

Hodge opened his mouth, but Halston broke in before his brother could say something else and make matters worse for them all. "Sir, please. Calm yourself. You have your money back. No harm done."

The man turned his head. "The hell are you?"

Halston kept a level tone. Over the years, he'd mastered the art of keeping a steady tongue. "Not important. Let him be. He's sorry."

People behind him laughed. So did the man, in spite of himself. "He's sorry, eh? If so, he oughta tell me himself. There's a price to be paid for stupidity."

"Stupidity?" Hodge blurted. "At least *I* know how to keep an eye on my money!"

The brutish grin slid from the man's face. Slowly, his hand moved toward the broad knife in his belt. "Bet you won't be so pretty if I slash that smirk off your face."

Halston and Lorelin scrambled out of the booth, and Lorelin jumped for the thug. "Stop!" she cried, grabbing for his big shoulders.

The man snorted, then pushed her back with one hand. Lorelin stumbled into the path of his buddies. The thin one snickered, scrunching up his nose. "Want a part of this, sweetheart?" he asked as he pinched Lorelin's hip.

Lorelin drove her heel between his legs, grabbed him by the arm, and flipped him across the table.

The man yowled as the patrons roared with laughter. The man pinning Hodge swerved, gasping. "Skeet!"

Hodge's fist rammed into his throat, and the man gagged and stumbled back. Halston tried to lunge toward his brother, but the redheaded knave slid into his path and lifted a grimy fist.

Halston raised his guard. Hard knuckles dug into his forearms. He took a breath, then kicked at the man's shins. He grunted as Halston dipped to the right, away from the table that Jae was now hiding under.

A storm of hollering roared around them. Some men scrambled away, while others hurried forth, eager to join in.

The stocky man threw a punch at Halston's gut. Halston jerked to the side, but the fist still slammed into his hip. He grunted. Gritting his teeth, he swung his fist at the man's face and nailed him in the cheek. The man cursed, and his hand flew up to cradle his jaw.

Halston snatched the moment he'd just won and hustled backward, then hurried toward his brother's figure. He watched Lorelin slip out from beneath a man's arm, circling around a nearby table.

They'd put a stone's throw of distance between themselves and the men. Hodge snatched two bottles from the nearest table and hurled them at the fighters. The glass shattered on the wooden floor, scattering green and amber shards around their feet.

Lorelin leapt over the glass and drew her gun. Halston joined her. Finally, Hodge got a grip on his pistol and raised it. Voice booming over the floor, he bellowed, "Left skeleton's eye, eight ball on the pool table, and that big blue liquor bottle on the bar!"

The patrons screamed as he shot, but the bullets hit only the targets that he'd promised.

The saloon fell silent. The brawlers all held still now, staring ahead with wide eyes and parted mouths. Nobody dared to twitch. Halston held his breath, still gripping his gun. He and Lorelin flanked Hodge as they worked their way toward the door. The scent of gun smoke filled his nostrils.

"Great," called Hodge. "Now you know that I can hit any target I damn please, including you." Smirking, Hodge lifted his chin up at the man who'd pinned him to the wall, who now stood holding the knife limply as if it were a frayed length of twine.

They walked backwards. Without blinking, Halston kept a steady grip on his gun until they reached the door. Lorelin kicked it open.

"I don't miss," Hodge called. "So think about that before you pick fights with the Harney gang again."

IDIOT.

They slid away from the door and dashed outside. As they sprinted, Halston could only think one thing.

He was going to kill his brother.

He was going to get them to safety, thank the gods that they'd escaped, and then *kill Hodge.*

Chapter 6

They bolted to the hitching posts. Confused shouts boomed from inside the saloon. Halston snatched up his horse's reins and unwound them. "Gryff!" he shouted.

Gryff came running from the side of the building. His golden eyes glowered as he stepped out of the shadows. "What happened?"

"Hodge made a scene." Halston swung himself onto the saddle. "And they might come after us. Hurry."

Gryff leading, they took off. The horses tore across the earth.

"Where are we going now, exactly?" shouted Gryff.

"Away!" Halston yelled. "Hodge just let a few dozen people know that the Harney gang is in Ameda."

"You did *what?*" yelped Gryff.

Hodge said nothing.

It didn't take long for Halston to hear the hoofbeats pursuing them. The end of the town was in sight, the wide road spilling out between the rows of run-down, wooden structures. If they fled down the main road, they were goners. Halston drove his heels into his horse's sides. They sped up. The hoofbeats behind them grew fainter, but Halston did not dare lower his guard.

He'd have to lead them into the open desert. Then they'd ride for Murrieta's Rock. If they reached the landmark, they'd come to the Pedora River. They could continue on the trail from there.

He tugged his reins, steering his horse to the left, and led his gang through a gap between two splintering buildings, deep into the shadows.

Hodge swore.

Gods damn them, they'd reached a dead end. A pile of barrels loomed at the end of the alley, stacked at least twelve feet high.

Precious seconds gone, just like that. Nothing to do but back out into the street.

Just then, someone hollered from along the road, audible above the sound of several horses running fast. Halston prayed they weren't outnumbered. He clutched the reins in one fist, and his free hand traveled to his gun.

"This way, gentlemen!" someone shouted, the voice low and clear.

Halston froze. It was Jae.

The gang stayed tucked away in the darkness, the barrels close enough for them to count the bolts on the bands. Halston faced the open end of the alley and waited. Panic closed around his chest, but he forced himself to hold steady.

Jae rode into his line of sight on a slim, gray mare. Halston waited for more shouting, for gunfire—but none of that came. Jae stretched her arm to the west… in the opposite direction of the alley.

Had she seen them flock to their hiding spot? She must have, if she'd followed them.

"You sure?" someone asked. Halston spied the scowling face of the man who'd held up Hodge, his eyes following Jae's extended arm. Only one of his pals was with him now. Halston guessed the man

Lorelin had kicked was out of commission.

Halston felt himself go stony, and he stalled his own breath.

Again, Jae jerked her arm to the west. "I'm sure. I saw them ride past the blacksmith's. They must be heading for the river."

With a hiyup, the horsemen rode in the direction she'd motioned. But before Jae could join them, her eyes fell on Halston's darkened figure.

She *could* see him.

And she smiled.

She rode off then, following the cowboys.

For a moment, Halston couldn't move. The moment had washed away his other thoughts. The stranger from the saloon had saved them, for no reason at all.

"Halston," snapped Gryff. "C'mon."

When the street was completely clear, they hurried out of the alley, then curved around the shops into the lonely, open desert. The horses galloped over stiff grass and heaps of moonlit sand. They were off-road, but as long as Murrieta's Rock was in sight, they could reach the trail again.

Before long, they came to a water hole. Starlight glinted on its murky surface. It wasn't much more than a puddle, but it would do. Plants with thin stalks and sharp leaves sprouted at the water's edge. A cluster of boulders wrapped around the water, huddled over the damp earth like men around a campfire.

"We stop for a few minutes. No more," said Halston.

They dismounted, their boots sinking into the mud. They crouched before the hole and lowered their canteens into the cool water. Halston leered at Hodge, bracing himself to speak, but Gryff beat him to it. "Tell me what happened."

Hodge kicked at a stone on the ground. It hit the water with a soft splash. "Stole something."

"Stole what?"

Hodge shrugged. "Pouch of coins. Guy wasn't even watching it."

Gryff let out a strangled sigh.

"What? It's not the first time I've done this. Just the first time I've been caught."

"Hodge," Halston started. "We made an agreement. We don't take from individuals. We don't steal from the innocent."

Hodge laughed. "Innocent? You're gonna tell me that guy was innocent?"

All of Halston's composure vanished. "You started a *brawl*. You could have landed us in jail, Hodge. You could have gotten us killed."

"Well, I *didn't* get us killed."

Lorelin waved her arms. Halston could practically see the steam puffing from her ears. "Both of you. Stop it. I'm tired of this. All this bickering. Can't we just have a *civil* discussion, for once?"

"The boy's gotta learn somehow," Gryff said solemnly.

But he never does.

"Look," Gryff went on, glaring down at Hodge. "Kid. This ain't a game. You start playin' around, then you'll wind up as buzzard food."

Hodge made no reply.

Gryff tapped a claw against the side of his head. "Use what's between your ears. You're lucky that fella didn't kill ya. I've met folks who'd set you on fire for snaggin' a single coin."

Halston stepped away from the water hole and sat down in the sand. A few silent moments slipped away.

"What?" asked Hodge.

"Tell me why."

"Why *what?*"

"Why do you think this is all a show? Why do you insist on making a spectacle of yourself?"

Halston wasn't sure why he'd bothered asking, because once again, Hodge didn't have an answer.

Halston said, "Maybe you don't care whether you live or die. But I do. We're not invincible. Elias was proof of that."

Hodge went tense at the name. They spoke of it rarely now, but not without reason. The memory that came with it still burned like a fresh wound. Hodge lowered his head, but it didn't hide the pain on his face. Halston bit his lip. *Gods. Maybe I shouldn't have said that.*

"Fine," Hodge said at last. "It was my fault. It was stupid. I'm a reckless son of a bitch. Is that what you want to hear, Hal? 'Cause if it'll get you to clear your head so we can figure the rest of this out, then I'll do it."

"Enough," Gryff said with a tired rasp. "It happened, and it don't matter now. What matters is gettin' out of here."

Halston wasn't sure how many lawmen a town like Ameda would have, but he wasn't taking his chances. There was no going back to rob the bank, and they had to meet Sterling in less than two days. Finally, he said, "The closest town is Bluefield. Nothing but ranchers there." He drew in a breath. "We'll have to face Sterling with what we have. We'll ask for more time."

"You're crazy," said Hodge.

"It's honest," Halston told him. "If we tell them the truth, they won't come after us. I don't want them to think that we're deserters."

"Honesty is nice," came a voice from above. "But it won't buy you time."

Halston jumped.

Lying on the boulders above, staring down with an impish grin, was Jae.

Chapter 7

There they had it. First, she'd led the townsfolk astray, and now she'd snuck up on them like a riptide.

"Don't fret," she said. She reclined like she was perched on a cushioned seat rather than a shelf of rock. "Y'all have already had a long night."

Hodge was reaching for his gun.

"*Don't*," Halston whispered.

"Yeah," Jae added, patting a revolver at her hip. "*Don't*. I ain't here to cause trouble. I must say, you boys seem to be living a life more... complicated than I'd expected. You owe *Sterling Byrd* money?"

Halston was tempted to shoo her away, but by the way things were looking, this girl had saved them from the mercy of a jail cell. He at least owed her... *something*. "Yes."

"Why?"

"Ain't your business," Hodge answered.

"Alright," Jae drawled. "Fine by me. I don't need all the details."

She jumped down from the rocks, landing with a catlike grace that Halston couldn't help but admire. She wore a men's jacket that was likely older than she was, its sleeves rolled up at her wrists and stitched in place, exposing a thick scar that marred one of her hands. Patches covered the legs of her pants, and she wore worn, supple boots—simple, practical things. Her hat still shaded her face, masking everything but her crooked smile.

"Who are you?" Gryff murmured.

Jae paced before the gang, perusing them as though they were a horse she was considering buying, and braced to haggle. "It's a good thing I led those men away from you back in town. Otherwise, we'd have to talk in the sheriff's office. Wouldn't want that."

Halston pressed his fingers to his temple. "And I appreciate it, really. But you'd best be getting home before they find you with us."

"Home? Don't have one."

Halston sighed. "What do you want?"

"Something in return," Jae answered. Her eyes danced around as she spoke, as though all of her surroundings fascinated her and she couldn't pick just one thing to focus on. "There's only so much I can steal on my own. Not without being gunned down, at least. I get by, but I'm sick of picking up scraps. I'm ready to thrive."

"*Jae,*" Halston said, stressing her name. "Again, many thanks. But you should go." Perhaps he did owe her more than his thanks, but sending her away was better than whatever trouble she'd find with them. He wasn't in the mood for bargaining, nor was he especially used to it.

She shook her head. "I led those brutes away from you back there. Point is, you owe me. I want in on a job with you. If you're working for Sterling Byrd, I can only imagine how much coin y'all can haul away."

Halston scratched the back of his neck. Fine. He'd hear her case, but he didn't have to take it. "This isn't a life you want a part in.

Besides, we're not a typical gang."

"You ain't dead or in jail yet. That speaks wonders about y'all," she said sweetly.

"We have more than a few heists ahead of us," said Halston.

"Even better."

Halston bit his lip. He wasn't sure if he should pity the girl or be wary. Besides, if it was money she was looking for, she'd best be served joining a different gang. His crew wasn't intent on spending most of what they stole. As long as they had enough money to get by, Halston had no interest in taking more than they needed.

It was silver they were after, and they'd never cared to become rich.

Lorelin stepped toward Halston, then whispered in his ear, "The map."

Halston nodded, then looked back to Jae. "Your map. Show me again."

"Gladly," Jae said, pulling it out of her pocket. She unfolded it before Halston's eyes.

He scanned the paper, disappointed at what he saw. Despite the Rangers' sigil, it wasn't a map of the Outlands, after all. It showed the surrounding desert, Ameda, Bluefield, the Pedora River… nothing he hadn't already seen.

Jae said, "It's magic."

"What?" Gryff blurted.

"A gift from an old Nefili man," Jae answered.

Hodge laughed. "Magic map? Interesting. And I have a golden seed that's gonna grow a golden tree when I plant it."

"Neat," said Jae.

"She's not lying," Halston told Hodge. "I saw it myself in the saloon."

"It only works when I touch it," said Jae.

Hodge teetered back. "What?"

"Go ahead," said Jae. "Touch it."

Raising an eyebrow, Hodge reached out and stroked the map. The ink disappeared, then reappeared when Jae touched the paper. Hodge and Gryff could only stare.

"There's more to it, too," she said. "The map moves with me. If I stay here, it shows me Ameda, the Pedora River, the lands around us. If I went to Kalstira, it would show me the whole territory, down to each curve of the coast. When I go down the road, the map's image moves south with me.

"I can also ask it to… show me places. Anywhere in the world with a name. As long as it's larger than a village."

Halston's heart pounded. The silver was only the first part of their journey. The rest of it would take them north, to the unforgiving Outlands. Without a navigator, they were as good as dead.

Hemaera's Pass was for Rangers alone, but there were also old Nefilium roads and tunnels scattered across the Cannoc chain. Somehow, he knew what Jae would say if he told her how they planned to get there: that it was lunacy. The elements killed most people who tried to navigate their own way through those mountains… if the creatures didn't kill them first.

Halston didn't mention the Outlands. "We could certainly use a navigator." He could bring up their plans later on.

"Gladly," Jae said. "I can guide you. I heard that you're short right now. I'll help get you what you owe Sterling, and I'll help you get silver to spare. Y'all could certainly use an extra gun. Just keep in mind that I need my cut."

Silver to spare. So, she was part of the rumor mill. Halston knew that his gang mystified everyone in Mesca. People loved trying to unravel their own questions. He had no doubt that they all had their own theories for why the gang horded the metal. What he doubted was that any of them were correct.

Halston locked eyes with Hodge, trying to silently toss the issue back and forth. They needed that map. Who knew if they'd ever come across another?

"Alright," Halston said. "I'm not here for games, and I'm not here to make friends."

"Neither am I," Jae replied.

"I'll make you a deal. We've got at least four or five more heists before our retirement. You can help us with the first job. I'll give you your cut, since you led those thugs away from us. Overall, if the job goes well, you can stay for the rest."

"No worries," Jae answered. "It'll go well, and I'm staying."

"Good." He held out his hand. "Do we have a deal?"

She shook his hand with a firmness that caught him off-guard. "Deal."

It was settled, then.

Chapter 8

A fter that, they saddled up. Jae had tethered up her mare
behind the boulders. She climbed onto her slate-colored
horse as Halston lifted himself onto his own saddle.

They set out and rode across the flat bed of desert. Lorelin traveled in front of Halston, and Jae rode behind him. Hodge rode at
the end of their line, with Gryff hustling at Halston's side. Murrieta's
Rock towered on the horizon, the moonlight bringing out the
grooves of its stone.

"So," Jae said at last. "You the leader?"

"No," said Halston without turning to face her. "There are no
leaders out here."

"Why not?"

"Leaders cause envy," he explained. "Disarray. If I were the
leader, they might decide to rise against me one day."

"Not if you were a good one," Jae pointed out.

"Well, that depends on what a good leader looks like to you." He
hoped her questions would end there.

They didn't. "So. Sterling Byrd?" Jae asked. "I take it you got mixed up with him somehow?"

Halston stiffened. "Yes."

"Hmm." She considered it mildly, as though he'd just described the fundamentals of driving cattle to her. "How did that happen?"

"An ill twist of fate," Halston answered as he looked to the stars.

Lorelin turned around and smirked at him. "Why do you always talk like that?"

Halston fingered his reins, stroking the rough stitches in the leather with his thumbnail. "I've known Sterling a long time. He got us out of a pinch. We've worked for him ever since."

In a different time, they might have been able to say no, but Sterling Byrd's career had been long and profitable. He'd never once been caught. So he gave them the weakest links in the chain. The most surefire jobs. Sterling knew Mesca like the back of his hand. He provided the gang with work, and in return, they gave him a cut of what they snagged.

Sterling paid them well and paid them quickly. The profits they could make from holding up an occasional bank were nothing compared to what Sterling could clue them onto—even minus his cut.

"Do you really *want* to work for them?" asked Jae.

"Of course we don't *want* to," said Gryff. "You ask a lot of questions."

"I think," Halston said slowly, turning at last to face her, "that this deal will work better if we try not to ask too many questions."

She answered quickly. "Alright."

"It's a hard truth," said Halston. "but sometimes, we don't get choices out here. I'm sure that's something you're familiar with."

Jae shrugged. "Not so much. Guess that's one good thing about working alone."

"I used to do that," said Lorelin. "Ride and fend for myself. I almost went mad." She brushed the grit off her embroidered sleeves. "I'd be a raving old spinster if I hadn't found these boys."

"A spinster?" Gryff said. "You're nineteen."

"Yes. Old enough to declare myself a spinster, should I choose to." Lorelin lifted her chin. "How old are you, Jae?"

"Seventeen."

"Well. I guess the boys and I are on our deathbeds, then. And you, Gryff?"

Gryff said, "No."

"Oh, that's right," said Lorelin. "The Azmarians use a different calendar, yes?"

Gryff nodded. "We don't measure in years. We measure in seasons. Equinox to equinox."

"How many seasons old are you?"

"No."

Lorelin chuckled. Halston wasn't sure how old Gryff was, but he guessed that the Azmarian was hardened by five decades, at least.

A few quiet hours ticked away, and Halston's eyes were itching with tiredness when they finally stopped. There wouldn't be a chance for them to rest much. They still had a day of riding to reach the Mouth—one of Sterling's many hideouts. Still, even a sliver of a night's sleep was better than nothing.

They tethered the horses to a circle of shrubs. Jae's gray mare stood several paces away from the others—Halston and Hodge's palominos, and Lorelin's lean brown mare. Lorelin took the first watch. Halston took out his bedroll and settled beneath it, rubbing a bit of warmth into his hands. The day had been mild enough, but now, the air was cold and sharp. Surely, his face would feel like ice in the morning.

He rolled over and looked at Jae, who was positioned about ten paces from the rest of them, sitting by the branches of a sagebrush.

She had her face raised to the sky with a distant, almost sad gaze, looking at the stars as though reading a long-forgotten tale.

Halston was a quiet sort. At least, he tried to be. Still, something urged him to talk to her.

Wherever that urge came from, he ignored it. Jae was an asset, not a companion. Hodge, Lorelin, and Gryff were the only people in this world he trusted fully. Just three… but some days, that still seemed like too many. And on nights like tonight, Halston hated to admit that his brother was looming closer to the edge of his trust.

He wished he were more like Hodge at night. Hodge could fall asleep in a matter of minutes, and waking him was like trying to raise the dead.

Halston was different. His thoughts and memories ran like wild horses when he tried to sleep. He'd never learned to shut them down.

Tonight, he took to imagining all the different things Sterling might say when they met again.

She'd seen the handbills before. *Five hundred crown reward for information leading to the capture of the Harney brothers.*

Jae knew exactly what Pa would say if he saw her here.

"*Jae.*" Then, he'd sigh and close his eyes. "*What on* Earth?"

He'd said that all the time when she was younger. She hadn't been easy to raise. It was a miracle she'd never broken a limb or set herself on fire. The world fascinated her—and she simply couldn't keep her hands to herself.

She felt a little dirty about it… leading those cowboys astray just so she could turn the gang in herself. Maybe it was selfish. Irresponsible. But if it got her back to Pa, she didn't mind being either of those things.

They were thieves, and thieves belonged in jail cells.

Out here, they were more a legend than anything else. About a year ago, Elias Harney had killed the sheriff in Arrowwood and fled with his brothers. After their arrest, they'd fought alongside jailed outlaws in what folks dubbed the Arrowwood War. The skirmish had left twelve men dead. The Harneys left unscathed.

Jae had been to Arrowwood twice. Some of the people there said that Elias Harney was a scoundrel, but others said that he was a charmer, a gentleman caught in the wrong place at the wrong time. They didn't have much to say about his brothers.

But Elias appeared to be gone now. Jae knew better than to ask why.

Jae wondered what Elias had looked like. Halston and Hodge both had dark features and wide-set brown eyes, but Halston's were larger and calmer than Hodge's. Less fiery. Halston was a man carved from stone, while Hodge was something plucked from the wind.

Jae wasn't sure how she'd get them to a sheriff, but it would have to be quick. She didn't have any of the tinctures she'd used to put the Brenner gang to sleep four months back, and those were hard to come by. They'd also cost her over five crowns.

But if she wanted to claim the gang's handsome bounty, she'd have to figure something out. Her heart felt a little warmer when she thought of hearing Pa's laugh again.

She flipped open her compass, watched the needle swivel north, then go still.

Bounty hunting required flexibility, but Jae had never been fond of it. She preferred certainty—knowing where she was heading and what she would do. Sure, she didn't have much of a plan now… but the gang had fallen for her ploy. For now, that would be enough.

Chapter 9

Usually, Halston was the first to wake up. Today, Lorelin had him beat. She sat at the edge of the camp, resting her chin on her hand.

Halston stretched, then made his way to her. "Were you up all night?"

"Nah. Gryff took the second watch. He went back down at dawn. I was tossing and turning anyway. Figured I'd take up the last of it."

Halston looked around, then spied Jae's empty bedroll beneath the sagebrush. "Where's Jae?"

"Went off to find nuts. Something like that."

Hodge lay sleeping with his blankets tangled around his legs. Halston walked over to his brother and shook his shoulder. "Come on. It's time to be alive again."

Hodge stayed still, splayed out like a ragdoll. Halston removed his canteen and splashed water on Hodge's face, and he bolted upright, flailing. Halston bit back a laugh, which became even harder to do when he saw the pinched-up look on his brother's face.

"Sorry to raise you from the dead, but we've got a big day ahead of us."

"I'm gettin' real tired of not being dead," Hodge murmured with a slight grin.

"Nope. No dying today. My rules." Halston nudged him. Frustrated as he'd been the night before, the worst of it was over. Lorelin was right. Bickering would do them no good now. "Come on. Nobody has found us yet, so… what do you say? Truce about last night?"

"Yeah, alright. Truce."

"Good. But if they find us, it's your responsibility."

Hodge brushed the sand off his hat, then put it on. "Yeah, yeah."

Halston pointed over his shoulder with his thumb. "I saw some prickly pears about a quarter mile back."

Hodge got to his feet. "We'll be right back, Lorelin."

"Don't miss me too much," she said with a wink.

The boys made their way across the desert. The sky was cloudless, and the spines of the cacti glinted in the sun. A horned toad scampered across their path, his clawed feet leaving few marks in the loose sand. Up ahead, the cacti stretched their paddle-shaped arms to the sun. Their purple fruits were bright and plump. They'd be firm, and not quite sweet yet, but they'd be easy enough to pluck.

Hodge settled on his knees and started harvesting the fruits, avoiding Halston's gaze. He was too quiet.

"Tell me what you're thinking," said Halston.

Hodge shrugged.

"Hodge, I told you. We're putting last night behind us. If you're angry with me, you can say so."

"I ain't angry with you," Hodge said. "And… look." He reached into his pocket, tossed the bag of coins from the bar into the air, and caught it.

Halston's eyes went wide. "You got it back?"

"Yeah. Decked that fella in the nose. Snatched these back up when he wasn't looking. It ain't much, but it'll help our case." Hodge breathed out. "Listen. If Sterling pulls the whip on us, then I'll—"

"No," Halston said. "Don't... don't say that, alright?"

"Why not?" Hodge snorted. "I'll take it. It's my fault we didn't rob the bank in Ameda. If he's in a bad mood and wants to remind us of it, then I'll take it."

"No, you won't," Halston said. "We'll explain it to him."

Hodge grunted, straightening his hat. "You say that like he's reasonable."

"Sometimes he is."

"I wish we could tell with him," Hodge muttered.

Halston would never forget the first time they'd come up short. It'd been one of the first robberies Sterling had assigned them, a stagecoach packed with copper. They'd scraped up about half of it before the driver, an old man with the brightest eyes Halston had ever seen, finally spoke.

"This might kill me, but to hell with it," he'd said. *"This copper is from Shada. Mining camp out west. You take it, and the miners won't get their pay for the next month. They have families. Those men have likely worked harder in their lives than the lot of you ever have."*

They'd dropped the copper and rode off.

When the boys showed up with empty hands, Sterling had asked for an explanation. Halston had still been young and stupid enough to tell Sterling the truth. He made it about halfway through his response before the hard ground plowed into the side of his face.

They yanked the shirt over his head. Sterling had him whipped once for each pound of copper they'd surrendered. Halston felt as if a fire was blazing on his back, his own blood fueling its flames. He wished to black out, at the very least, so he could stop listening to the others screaming for him. Sterling made sure the whip cut deep so Halston would have the scars to remember what would happen if they ever crossed him again.

They'd arrived shorthanded a few other times, but never with nothing to show for the job. Sometimes, Sterling wrote it off and considered it a meager addition to their debt. A few other times, he'd felt that punishment was in order, whether it was with the whip or a few pairs of fists. He kept them guessing.

Hodge said, "I have an idea."

"Let me hear it."

"Well, if we hit up some folks on the road, we could—"

"No," Halston said firmly. "We aren't robbing individuals. End of discussion."

Hodge frowned. "I never said we had to take from men who ain't done nothing wrong. I'm talking about the folks who got everything they have by lying and working good, honest folk to the bone. Can't imagine they'd be hard to find." His face went stiff. "I mean, really, Hal. Why do you like to pretend that we're noble or something? We ain't doing the right thing, but you seem to think that we're better than all the other crooks out here. We ain't. If the Rangers catch up to us, they'll haul us in. Good looks and pretty words won't stop 'em."

Halston considered it. "Maybe not. But we haven't been caught yet. Or killed."

"If I die, I hope they sing songs about me," said Hodge. "The tale of Hodge Harney. Shot well, fought bravely, died young."

Halston shook his head. "It scares me when you say things like that."

"Don't worry about it."

"I mean it." Halston's hand closed around a prickly pear. "Stop talking like that."

"I said don't worry about it. Like you said. You ain't our leader."

Halston ignored the remark. They began paring off the spines of the fruits. Pink juice stained their fingers.

"I need you to promise me something," Halston said after a long silence.

"I can't make any promises."

Halston touched Hodge's shoulder. "You can for me. Promise me you won't sneak off again. I don't want a repeat of last night. We stick together. We'll last longer than way."

Hodge paused. "What do you think of the girl?"

Halston frowned. "You're changing the subject."

"Yeah, 'course I am. What do you think of her?"

"Answer me."

Hodge sighed, then put down his knife. "You worry too much, alright? We haven't died yet, and we ain't gonna die anytime soon."

Hodge still hadn't offered Halston a promise, but he decided it was best to drop it now. Arguing wouldn't put the remaining crowns in their pockets. Still, part of him wished he could crack his brother's stubbornness with a hammer and chisel.

"So. Her. What do you think?" asked Hodge.

"Well, like her or not, she's got what we need. Even if Sterling helps us get our silver, it's all been for nothing if we can't get to the Outlands. She's got that map."

Hodge raised an eyebrow. "Are you sure you want some-body new?"

"I'm not sure what I want," Halston said. "But she's got what we need."

Soon, they were hurrying back with the fruit. Jae sat several paces away from the camp, staring out into the open desert and popping pine nuts into her mouth, one at a time. Hodge ventured off to go feed the horses.

Gryff nudged Halston. "I hope you talked to him this mornin'.

Did he tell you he was sorry?"

"No. But he said he would take the blow. If Sterling decided to pull the whip out."

Gryff frowned. "You're goin' too easy on him."

Yes, perhaps he was.

"Lord, Halston. You still must be angry with him."

"Maybe?" said Halston. "I don't know, Gryff. Sometimes I feel like we argue enough as is. I don't want to keep things on a sour note if I don't have to."

Gryff snorted. "Well then. Guess we'll all have to hope and pray that Sterling lets it slide. Hope you're okay with that."

Halston wasn't, but that didn't matter.

———

When they set out, Halston announced that they'd ride into the evening, then settle down for the night. They'd reach the Mouth the following morning. There, they'd give Sterling the money from their latest heist and collect their next few jobs.

Jae had thought about how she could snag Sterling's bounty, too, but she waved it off in a jiff. Sterling Byrd's gang was notorious for raiding entire towns, then slipping away without a trace. They didn't hesitate to gun down folks who stood in their way. Often, they left towns with burning buildings and shattered windows and blood pooling in the streets. Jae would be hopelessly outgunned, no matter what strategy she might come up with.

When Jae overheard Halston mention his involvement with Sterling Byrd, a knot of anger had twisted in her stomach. She wasn't typically concerned with the motives of thieves, but any man who associated with the likes of the Byrd gang was no one who deserved to be running free.

Still… if all went well, she would know the location of one of the Byrd gang's hideouts. She'd report that to the sheriff when she took the Harneys in. Maybe that bit of information would be the beginning of the end of Sterling Byrd's reign.

The sand, shrubs, and cacti went on for miles. Murrieta's Rock and the surrounding mesas stretched proudly to the sky, their red hues rich in the morning sun. In the distance was the outline of the Briarford Mountains. Some people called the chain "Sleeping Val," because the shape of the peaks looked like a sleeping woman. A sleeping woman with no feet and a mighty small head.

Until midmorning, they rode in silence. Jae couldn't help but take a moment to admire the others' horses. Halston and Hodge both rode palominos, while Lorelin had a thin, elegant mare with a coffee-colored coat.

Gryff didn't ride a horse, but he kept up with them all the same, his boots leaving hefty marks in the sand... gods, where did they even make boots that large? Slung across his back were a knapsack and rifle, and there was a small pistol at his hip. Jae squinted at a gold coil emerging from his pack. Some sort of fancy rope?

Curiosity got the best of her. "Is that a golden rope?"

Gryff twitched his head. "Sure is."

"What's it for?"

Jae had no doubt that Gryff had heard her question, but he decided not to answer her.

Jae's nerves twitched at the thought of Sterling Byrd. Tomorrow, she'd see him up close, and she wasn't sure how she felt about it. She figured she might as well learn what she could now. "So, Sterling promised you a share for the heist?"

"Yeah," Hodge replied, snorting. "We won't be getting it now. We lost some of it running from the train. I reckon Sterling will keep it all for himself, now."

Now was as good a time as any to ask. She looked at Halston.

"Why the silver?"

She reckoned Halston understood the question, but the boy played dumb anyways. "Silver?"

"C'mon, Hal," said Hodge. "She knows. Everybody knows."

"He's right. It's made y'all a legend," said Jae. Rumor had it that silver was the bulk of what the Harneys stole. Even if they took crowns of bronze or paper, copper pennies, or gold, folks said they'd swap it for silver whenever they had the chance.

Hodge beamed. "You hear that, Hal? We're legends. I didn't need to hear someone tell me that, but it's always nice to hear."

Lorelin rolled her eyes.

"Believe me, Hodge," murmured Gryff. "you don't *wanna* be a legend out here."

Hodge didn't respond to Gryff. "So. You wanna know why we steal silver?"

Jae nodded.

"'Cause we feel like it." Hodge turned around without another word.

Well… she hadn't expected that. Jae hoped the look on her face wasn't too stupid.

"Have you thought about swapping what you have for deons?" asked Jae. "They're silver."

"Deons are worthless," said Hodge.

"No, they ain't. You can buy a couple meals for a deon," said Jae. Money was money. She'd never even taken a penny for granted.

Halston shook his head. "There isn't much silver in them. They're mostly zinc and nickel, with a silver veneer. They wouldn't be much help to us."

"Why not go to a silver mine, then?" asked Jae. "There are lots of them in the territories."

"No. We don't take from miners," said Halston. "It would be

unprincipled."

"Who *do* you take from?" Jae was tempted to ask why they bothered to steal at all, if Halston was so damn concerned with being virtuous. Given that they worked in the service of Sterling Byrd, it made even less sense.

"The Fisks. The Bronsons. The Graydens," Halston said.

"All the scumbags running this damn county," Hodge muttered. "Rich bastards who let Arrowwood happen."

"The Winters," Lorelin added.

The realization crossed Jae's mind. She couldn't believe she hadn't considered it yet. A couple years ago, Lorelin Winter's name had spanned the newspapers' headlines. A Calora-born aristocrat, she'd tied her husband-to-be up to his bedpost, threatened to kill him, and fled without following through.

Jae didn't give Halston's claims credence. Arrowwood didn't happen because of rich old bastards. It happened because some men would rather spill blood than adhere to the law.

Before Jae could say anything else, she caught Halston looking at her, a finger pressed to his lips. The gesture bothered her more than anything he could have said at that moment, but she swallowed and held still, remembering his request last night.

Alright. She'd watch the questions. For now.

———

At dusk, they came to a clump of long-forgotten buildings on the roadside. Rocks dotted the ground. Not much grew here besides a few boughs of spindly, withered shrubs. Log structures surrounded old tent posts and steel beams, and there was a series of pits spread across the sand.

An old mining camp, dry as dust and empty as the hollow of a pipe. Men had come west for years to dig up gold from Mesca to

Kalstira. Their mining camps either flourished and turned to cities or dried up into ghost towns. This wasn't much of a town, though.

Three graves marked with sun-bleached planks lay on the road-side. There had once been names scratched into the wood, but time had muddled them. They reminded Jae of a song she'd learned long ago, about an old man left to die by bandits. He heaved himself up and tried to walk home, bleeding everywhere, just so he could be buried next to his wife. He died too soon. So cowboys found him and buried him, nameless, in the open desert.

Hodge stooped under the opening of a cabin and walked inside. "Looks good in here."

They followed him. Grit covered the floor, and two wooden chairs with crooked legs sat in what was left of a kitchen. A rusty cookpot hung in the fireplace, and a stairway in the back of the cabin led to a loft. There were still panes in the window frames, though the glass was smeared with dust. In the corner was a bureau, which still bore a hint of gloss on its wood.

Hodge walked over to the bureau and started leafing through it. "Hmm. Nothin' but papers in the top drawer."

"I wouldn't do that," warned Jae.

"Why not? I don't see any scorpions."

Jae answered with a half-shrug. "You won't find scorpions this far north. Black widows are more likely. Or rattlesnakes."

Hodge frowned. "That's worse."

"I didn't say they were better. Just more likely. Besides, that's not the only reason you shouldn't be sniffing around."

He was on the second drawer now. "Why not?"

"You shouldn't take from ghost towns. It's bad luck," said Jae. She hoped her tone made it clear to him that she was no longer kidding.

"I don't believe in luck."

By the self-assured flare in his eyes, Jae knew he meant what he said.

"If that's true, it's odd that you test yours so much," Gryff remarked.

"Really," Jae said. "I've talked to cowboys who took trinkets and tools from ghost towns. Woke up the next day with scratches on their skin, or went home and found their livestock dead. Ghosts don't like thieves."

"How could a ghost hurt you?" asked Hodge. "I don't see any here."

The question shouldn't have made her angry, but it did. A little. "Doesn't mean they ain't around. They can hide themselves."

Hodge was on the last drawer. He reached into it briefly, then drew back his hand and closed it. "Nothing good in there, anyway," he muttered, though Jae thought she saw him shiver for a split second.

They untied their bedrolls and sat down on the cabin's floor. The gang chewed on underripe prickly pears and old biscuits while Jae nibbled on the nuts she'd gathered that morning. The cabin held back enough cold air that there was no need for a fire. Wind bustled outside, the sound grating against the cabin's walls. Gryff lingered by the window, his clawed hand perched just above his knife.

"It's just wind, Gryff," said Hodge.

Gryff snorted and kept his stance by the pane. "Can't be too careful out here."

"Where did you learn so much about ghosts?" asked Hodge, breaking his biscuit into quarters.

"My Pa was a mountain man. They're superstitious folk," said Jae.

"Once I heard someone say 'superstitious' means the same thing as 'stupid,'" said Hodge.

"That ain't true," Jae replied. "Ghosts are real." She hadn't seen a ghost since Pa was taken, but after that, she figured she couldn't be too careful.

"There are some wild things out here, that's for sure," said Gryff. "But most of them don't make it this far south. They stick to the north, where it's cold and bleak and men are few and far between."

"Have *you* seen a ghost, Gryff?" Hodge asked, droning.

"No," said Gryff. "But I've seen things that are much worse."

When they settled for the night, Jae considered taking her blankets to the loft, but at a closer look, the old thing looked fragile as a moth's wings. She picked a corner by the fireplace instead.

She changed her position no less than eight times. She tried to lull her mind, thinking of rivers and what the sea would be like when she saw it someday. Nothing helped. She couldn't stop wondering if she would wake up to find that the Harneys had made off with her horse and the rest of her belongings.

No. There was nothing to fear. They wanted her map. They wanted *her.*

She propped herself up on her forearm and traced circles on the floor with her finger. Halston was on watch nearby, sitting on one of the old chairs with a battered paper in his hand.

Jae squinted. No, not just a paper. A portrait, though the details were so fine, she had reckoned it was a photograph at first.

Four children, three boys and a girl, stood in the middle. Jae recognized Halston and Hodge. A bearded, stony man stood upright on the left. He looked like a war hero, holding himself like a king. On the right was a woman with thick hair and delicate hands. She had a gentle, soft beauty about her, like a desert bloom, and her dark eyes smiled. Jae could almost hear her laughter through the picture.

She didn't recognize the little girl. In the picture, Halston looked no older than nine. He stood between a teenaged boy and Hodge, who wore a grin stretching from one ear to the other.

Before Jae could persuade herself to turn away, Halston

caught her.

"Sorry," she said. "Couldn't sleep."

Halston folded the picture, but did not meet her gaze. "You have nothing to apologize for."

She asked, "Your family?"

"Yes." Hardly more than a whisper. He stared at the ground, unmoving, his mouth a hardened line.

Jae dug her fingers into her blankets. What had taken that family in the picture? And what had led Halston to Mesca, whittling that child from the picture into the young man sitting here?

Now wasn't the time to dwell on it. Besides, she didn't want to ruffle him up with more of her questions. "Sleep well," she mumbled, pushing the thoughts away.

"You too," he said.

Sleep came quickly after that.

Chapter 10

Fifteen miles outside Bluefield, there were the foothills. In the foothills, there was a slope. And at the bottom of the slope, there was a cavern.

The stone on the cave's floor was smooth, while the top hung over in jagged spires. Sunlight glinted off the arches of the sandstone, and the rock swept over the land like the towers and barracks of a wide, crooked castle. A pair of sprawling buckhorn cacti rose on either side of a wide arch, perched like guards before a drawbridge. The Mouth.

Halston scanned the area, glimpsing little besides the curves of the sandstone. "I don't see anybody. Maybe we're early." He supposed it worked in their favor.

"I've heard plenty about these fellas," Jae said, hopping down from her saddle. "Though most of it is about how they always seem to get away in the nick of time. What're they like up close?"

"Sterling and Pierce are the ones you gotta watch out for," Hodge told her. "Their cronies got nothin' but rocks between their ears."

Halston's head whirled in his brother's direction. "Hodge!"

"What?" The unheeding look on Hodge's face sent a wave of frustration through Halston.

Halston pinched the bridge of his nose. "When they get here, show them some respect, *please*. We're relying on mercy today."

Hodge said nothing more. Halston did his best to fight off his irritation and prepare himself for the meeting.

They were early, but not by much. Before long, a cluster of men on horses emerged from the hills, led by a sturdy rider. He rode with a loose sort of slouch, looking as if he didn't have a care in the world. There was a rifle on his back, pistols at his sides, and a wide-brimmed hat on his head. His large eyes were dark brown, flecked with russet, like embers on blackened wood. Smooth beard, sun-tanned skin. A silver ring circled his right index finger, sleek and unadorned. He was very handsome, despite a few scars on his face.

Sterling Byrd.

Riding behind him were his brothers. First, there was Sterling's burly, big-jawed brother Pierce, who always seemed to be scowling, with or without reason. He had a knobby nose that hadn't quite healed from a breaking, and white scars peppered his knuckles. Pierce lifted his chin up at Halston in acknowledgement, which was his manner of a cordial greeting.

Then there was Argus, the youngest. He was at least several years older than Halston, but his face still had a boyish softness that the others had lost. His mustache was little more than a narrow strip of dark fuzz above his upper lip. His hair was thin and almost wiry, falling past his jaw in wispy waves.

Besides their last name, they didn't share much. Every one of their features differed, and they certainly didn't look like any set of brothers Halston had ever seen.

"Ah, the Harneys," Sterling announced, riding forth on his slick black stallion.

Halston gave him a curt nod. "Glad to see you, sir."

"Likewise." Sterling gestured to his gang to dismount.

Halston studied the faces of Sterling's men. The Byrd brothers were no portrait of finery, but the rest of the gang always looked shoddier, dressed in baggy clothes, their faces caked with soot and cuts. Evia, Sterling's fair-haired, beautiful lover was the exception. Then there were the pale, blue-eyed Calder boys: Maxim, Ned, and Lyle, who claimed they could shoot flies out of the sky. Behind Sterling was a man called Flynn, who was almost as tall and brawny as Gryff, without being an Azmarian. There was Thumbscrew, Sterling's demolition expert, and Gallows, who supplied the weapons. Wolf stood near the back, folding his arms. He was one of Sterling's quietest recruits—an immigrant from an isle far across the sea. On Sterling's right stood Stone Slade, an old man who likely only tagged along because at this point, he knew nothing else.

At the edge of the gang, looming near the rim of the sandstone, was a man Halston had never seen. A shabby hat rested atop his shorn hair, and a thin layer of stubble coated his jaw. His skin was ashen, as though he'd been gathering dust on a shelf for years. Pale eyes narrowed under his thin brows, which appeared to be locked in a permanent crease. It was hard to say how old he was. Halston decided he was probably in his twenties, but he had the looks of a man who'd seen enough hardship to strip decades off his life. The man looked to the east with an empty stare, evidently disinterested in whatever business was to take place here.

After tethering the horses, they entered the Mouth. The sandstone formed a wide cavity, the rock rising from its edges like warped sheets of copper. It stretched high enough to paint its floor in shade, with plenty of nicks and troughs along its foundation.

Sterling had an array of hideouts and rendezvous points scattered across Mesca. He'd only introduced Halston's gang to a fraction of them. For some reason, the Mouth eased a part of Halston's fear. He preferred the red sandstone to the shady, dank-smelling hideouts they'd met in before. He felt as if there was something old and powerful in these walls, something that whispered to him and helped him stand his ground.

They settled around a flat-topped lump in the cavern's foundation, a sheet of rock about the size of two tables pushed together. Sterling's men stood on one side, Halston's gang on the other.

Halston caught Thumbscrew eyeballing Jae. He was a muscular man, built like an ox or an anvil, with a toothy grin and snuff-colored eyes. "Didn't tell us you were bringin' someone new," he said, and clicked his tongue.

"She's an extra gun," Halston said. *What's it to you?*

"Which one of yer beds is she warmin'?" Lyle asked with a wheezy snort. He grinned at Jae, raising his eyebrows. "I think I saw a whore in a saloon that looked a lot like you, though she had a much prettier smile."

Lyle's voice grated on Halston. Jae just stared at the thin strip of sky above the tips of the rocks, as if Lyle's words weren't any louder than the drop of a pebble in her ears.

"Tell me something, Lyle," Hodge said. "Do you think it would *kill* you if you shut your mouth for once?"

"*Hodge*," Halston snapped at the same time Sterling said, "*Lyle.*"

Hodge bit his lip and took a step back. Jae said nothing, merely staring up with her arms folded.

Sterling shot Lyle an extra glare. "I told you to keep your comments to yourself. You're wasting everyone's time."

Lyle stuck out his lip. "Why'd they bring her?"

"No business of yours," Sterling said. "If she's helping them hold up their end of the deal, then I don't much care who she is."

Lyle snorted and backed into the crowd, and Sterling stepped up to the table of rock and set his palms down on it. "First things first. The train."

Halston and Hodge surrendered all they'd managed to gather in their escape. Halston was glad he'd mastered staying the shaking in his fingers, or his fear would've been plain as day.

Sterling began to count the spoils. Halston held his breath.

Sterling finished the count and raised his eyes painfully slowly. "You're a bit short, boys."

"We can explain," said Halston.

"Can you?" snarled Pierce.

"We can," came a clear voice.

Everyone looked at Jae.

"Mr. Byrd," she said, "which town did you get the totals from?"

Halston's stomach lurched, but he couldn't bring himself to try and quiet her. He wasn't sure what she had in mind.

Sterling blinked. "The records were from Alistair, where the train was loading up."

"It made a stop in Calora," said Jae. "All trains that cross through the capital have to stop for inspection. It's the law." She went on. "There's a fee if they don't pass. Not sure why this train had to pay up, but if time allowed, we would have hit it before it got to the capital. How much are we short by?"

"Ninety-seven crowns," Sterling replied matter-of-factly.

"We'll have that in no time," promised Jae.

A strange feeling hung in the air, like thunderclouds looming over a canyon. Finally, Sterling said, "Alright, then. I'll let it slide. I'm taking a bigger cut, though."

Halston's shoulders dropped. "Thank you, sir."

Gallows pointed to Jae. "Where'd you find this bitch?" he asked, yellow teeth flashing through his chapped lips.

Halston tried not to glare at him. He was used to Sterling's men, but that didn't make their manners any less atrocious.

"They didn't find me," Jae said, without a hint of irritation in her voice. "I found them."

Gallows gave her a tight-lipped smirk. "Didn't think the boys were that desperate."

"Enough," Gryff fired back. "She's givin' you an explanation. It ain't our fault the train wasn't up to bar."

The breeze sang outside the sandstone walls. Sterling waved a hand. "Calm down, Gallows. It ain't what we were hoping for, but it can't be helped if the train didn't pass inspection."

Sterling pocketed most of the money, but left the gang ten crowns. Halston pointed to it bemusedly, but Sterling just pushed it Halston's way. "Don't get too excited. It's a loan. You'll be on the road for a few more weeks, and I'm taking bigger cuts from these next couple jobs. You make them work by my deadline, deal?"

Halston nodded, sweeping the crowns into his palm. "Deal."

Sterling took a map out of his pocket and unfolded it. "I've got your route planned out." He traced a line on the map. "You'll start in Duraunt, head to the Taracoma Valley, and we'll meet in Mourelle when you're done."

"What have you got for us?" asked Halston.

"First up is the Fisk bank in Duraunt," Sterling said. "New bank, old building. Used to be a steel mill, but they split the place in two a couple years back. Now there's a bank on one side and a theater on the other. 'Bout a month ago, they tore down a chunk of the wall after some fella in the audience shot it. If you can slip in that way, you can get into the bank. You may have to jimmy a few more locks, but I snagged you the combination to the vaults. I'd like at least four hundred crowns from this job."

He passed Halston a photograph of the building. "Hank Sawyer

Theater" one-half read in dazzling letters. The other half bore the unmistakable emblem of the Fisk banks: a lion, mouth open mid-roar. On the back of the photograph was the combination: 13-27-01-29.

Sterling scratched the back of his neck. "Second… well, it ain't exactly a heist. It's more of a dig."

Halston wasn't sure what to think. "A dig."

Sterling's hand returned to the map and pointed to the area surrounding Duraunt. "I'm seeking a treasure near the Taracoma River. Statue of our Lady Cressien. Solid gold one."

Cressien, the goddess appointed by the Wandering God to watch over the skies. Halston had seen sculptures of her before, the stars abundant in her skirts, a crown of sunlight on her head.

"A treasure?" asked Halston. "I don't mean to derail, sir, but… what if it's not there anymore?"

Sterling answered with unmistakable certainty. "Oh, it's there. Friend of a friend told me that the gentleman who buried it had passed. Gave me these to prove it."

Sterling handed Halston a folded scrap of paper, its creases worn and soft. Halston quickly unfolded it and skimmed the directions. The handwriting was just shy of illegible, but fortunately, each step was accompanied by sketches of landmarks.

"From what he said, it's a bit… out of the way," Sterling went on. "Tucked off in a rocky area of the woods. Might take a bit of a climb to get there, but it won't be too much trouble."

Halston fought the urge to raise an eyebrow. This job wouldn't call for gunplay, nor was it exactly stealing. Why wasn't Sterling playing Halston's crew to their strengths?

Sterling must've read the look on Halston's face. The crime boss said, "The dig doesn't line up with the route I've got planned for my men. Clashes with a few of our own jobs. Figured we'd get it sooner if I gave the job to you. Consider it a gift." He lowered his voice and said, "Hope you don't refuse my generosity."

"Not at all, sir."

"Good." Sterling pointed to the map again and leered at Halston like a bull about to charge. "Listen well. Typically, if you bring me the sum I asked for, I ain't concerned how you get it. But in this case, you'd better bring me the artifact itself. No haggling. No debts. No making up for it. You return with what I asked for. We clear?"

Halston nodded.

"Gold is poison," said a wavering voice.

They turned to look at the haggard man in the back of the cave.

"You got something to say, Spec?" snorted Pierce.

"Adamite and gold," Spec drawled on.

Halston had heard of the metal before, but never seen it. Adamite was rarer than diamonds, strong enough to forge knives that cut through stone, and powerful enough to shoot a ghost into the netherworld.

"I've seen men go after it," Spec retorted. His eyes were so wide, he may as well have stitched them open. "And it drove them mad."

Argus spoke gently, casting a sidelong glance at the scraggly man. "Spec. Remember our deal?"

Spec was silent, then.

Sterling continued, prying Halston's attention from the withered man in the corner. "Now then. The dig." Sterling went still for a moment, simpering in a way that almost confused Halston. He leaned forward and raised his chin. "If you bring me the statue, I'll give you half its weight in silver, and the other half of the blade."

Hodge started coughing, like he'd just choked on air.

Halston blinked, not sure if he'd heard that right. "The... the other half?"

Sterling's mouth smiled, but his eyes stayed wide and steady. His hand disappeared inside his black coat, then emerged holding a leather sheath. The sheath was long and narrow, with curved, intricate runes spanning its surface.

Halston's heart cried out to him, begging him to snatch it. Artifact. Treasure. *Salvation.* It was just inches from his fingertips.

But it wasn't theirs yet.

"Thought you'd like to see it *again.*" Sterling passed Halston a cold, joyless smirk. Halston didn't look away from the sheath as Sterling stashed it back inside his coat. "And the deal's about to get better, too. You bring me the four-hundred crowns from the bank *and* the statue, then our partnership will come to a peaceful end. No questions asked."

As soon as they were out of here, Halston was going to climb the nearest hill and shout to the heavens.

Weeks, mere *weeks* from now, it would be over. They'd never have to hide beside the railroad or stage lines, guns loaded, waiting for their next set of bonds. They would ride out of Mesca and leave the rumors and crimes behind them.

No more Sterling.

It took every ounce of willpower for Halston not to gush like an overexcited child. "Thank you, sir. We won't disappoint you."

"I hope not. We don't like being disappointed," said Pierce. His tone always had a way of rattling Halston. His icy eyes flicked to Jae. "Ain't sure I like the new one."

Jae's face stayed vacant in the shadow of her hat.

"Well, it's a good thing you don't have to ride with her, then," said Halston.

"Maybe so," Pierce admitted, still fixated on Jae. "But nobody likes a smart mouth."

Jae didn't even blink. "I was just stating facts, sir."

Sterling's lip curled as he shot his brother a look. "Settle down, Pierce. The deed is done. Ain't like they lost the loot on purpose."

He pointed back to the map. "Duraunt is about a two days' ride from here. Taracoma Valley's another week or so from there. I'll give you a fourth week for margin. We'll meet on the last day of March. Mourelle Manor." Sterling extended his hand. "Deal?"

Halston shook it readily. "Deal." His hand felt limp in Sterling's firm grip.

Halston let Sterling's men move out of the cave first. Silently, they exited the formation and mounted their horses. Halston did not look back to Sterling's gang as they rode away.

He couldn't take his eyes off Jae.

She finally caught him looking—or had she known the whole time?

"Train inspection?" Halston coughed out.

Jae shrugged. "Yeah. It wasn't a lie. Not entirely. They do go through inspections in the capital. But I ain't sure what the fee is if you don't pass it."

"Whatever it is, they believed it. You got us out of a pinch back there."

She turned from him. "Don't mention it."

Halston doubted Sterling's men had bothered her, but he still felt a little sore from the way they'd treated her. "I'm sorry that you had to witness his men's behavior. And that Gallows called you... that. Gods."

Jae shook it away. "It's fine. It takes a bit more than 'bitch' to make me angry."

Hodge raised an eyebrow. "Like what?"

"Something cleverer. Think about it. 'Bitch.' It's one word. It's lazy. A good insult should at least take some effort." She spoke swiftly, as if she'd written out her words beforehand.

———

They wove around the hills beneath the afternoon sun, bound northeast for Duraunt. The horses' hooves sank into the dry earth. Halston's throat was parched and cold at the same time. The horses' breaths were relaxed, and there was little more to stifle the silence. It was almost peaceful. *Almost.* Nobody spoke, but Halston was sure that the others were still too stunned.

Our partnership will come to a peaceful end.

Shortly before dusk, they stopped to rest. They found themselves a lump of boulders and short, puffy junipers, which gave them a pocket of shade just large enough to freshen their eyes. Lorelin and Hodge started a card game, while Gryff set to polishing his rifle. Halston stretched out his arms, looking to the shape of the Briarford Mountains. Their bluish tint was soft against the cloudless sky.

That's where they were headed. Duraunt lay at the Briarfords' roots, the Taracoma valley in its depths. Whatever waited for them there, he hoped it involved a pocketful of coins and a bloodless trail behind them.

Jae rested several yards away, gazing at the mesas in the south— in the direction of Ameda, the train they'd robbed, and the saloon they'd escaped.

Halston ambled toward her, the sand crunching under his boots. He tapped her on the shoulder. Slowly, she peered over her shoulder, and he pointed to their ephemeral camp. "Do you want to come sit with us?"

"That's alright." She turned back to the horizon.

"Thank you," he said. "For helping us out."

She chuckled. "It's a part of the job, ain't it?"

"Still. Thank you."

Her smile was faint as she turned away. "You're welcome."

He ventured back to the circle of rocks and trees, thinking it best to let her be. He recalled her sitting in the corner of the saloon, and he wondered how long she'd been wandering on her own. Did she enjoy it—the solitude? Or was she lonely?

Halston had never been without Hodge. He did not know what loneliness was, really, but he could not imagine anyone preferring it.

Chapter 11

They spent the next two days on the road, and Jae spent every minute of it waiting.

She'd turn to her map every so often, wondering if an outpost or a village would spring up on the road, but there was nothing but tiny houses, ramshackle cabins, and the occasional ranch, hour after hour. Without a doubt, the nearest lawmen were in Duraunt. She'd have to find one before the gang made it out of the heist.

The closest she'd ever been to a gang was when she'd gone after the Brenners, and that case hadn't taken her long. There were four of them, and she'd only traveled with them for a day before slipping the tinctures into their water supply. After they'd fallen asleep, she'd disarmed them, bound them all to the trees circling their campsite, and led the sheriff back to the gang.

It was difficult not to speak to the Harney gang. Still, she pushed herself to watch her words. She reckoned that her lie about the train inspection had wrung a few more drops of trust from them, but she was still walking on a length of brittle rope.

Eventually, they came to the Taracoma River and began follow-ing its curves toward Duraunt. Winter had yielded the last of its snow to the river's silvery waters, and the current cut swiftly through the land. The cottonwoods cast their downy seeds into the air, danc-ing like snowflakes on the wind.

The towns looked less battered the further north they went, and soon, the Briarford Mountains were closer than ever. At the foot of the mountains lay the town of Duraunt.

After days of riding in the desert, with little to look at but rocks and plants covered in thorns, the trail sloped up. Soon, pines grew in line with the cacti, and with each hour of travel, the trees grew taller and the air became crisp. Jae inhaled it as if it were water. She had always liked the lands where the desert met the mountains. The air was cool, but the earth felt dry, and folks there still celebrated rain as they would a holiday.

They rode past barns and log cabins. Soon, they spied a train chugging across the silver cliffs, spilling smoke into the air. A flock of black birds swooped above the pines, and the tangy scent of the forest swirled with the smell of train smoke.

Before long, they came to a wide bridge, and beneath it flowed a stream thriving with runoff. They replenished their water supply, crossed the bridge and entered the cluster of buildings, far different from the sad little structures in Ameda. In this settlement, there were rows after rows of buildings. The planks were polished, the shut-ters painted, the shingles sleek and new. Many of the buildings had carved awnings with arches and balconies. Some even had window boxes, already blooming with flowers. Jae had always found those to be mighty silly. Why hang flowers from your window instead of walking through a meadow?

"This ain't no ghost town," she murmured.

Then came a commotion up ahead. Two boys, no older than

nine, stood roughhousing in the street, spewing foul names at each other. The bigger one took the other by the arms, guffawing, then stopped suddenly when he spied Gryff. They stared at the Azmarian like he'd just stepped out of a dream.

The big kid dared to approach Gryff. He had auburn hair sticking every which way, and his shirt buttons were off by one hole. "Are you a snake?"

"Yes. What were you doing to that poor kid?"

"He's my brother," said the boy. "He told me that I wasn't tough enough to take him down, and I wanted to show 'im."

"Hmm. You know, I haven't *always* been a snake," Gryff told him, completely straight-faced. "Do you wanna know why I look like this?"

"Why?"

"Because when I was younger, I wasn't a nice fella. Lied. Stole. Picked a bunch of fights."

The boy's eyes widened.

"And then *this*," he continued, pointing to his nostrils and flicking his forked tongue over his lips, "happened to me. So you go be nice to your brother there, alright?"

The boy shuffled away obediently and hurried back to his brother.

Hodge turned to Gryff. "What was that all about?"

"Helpin' a boy out. There. I've done one good thing this week. That's more than any of you can say for yourselves."

They traveled down the main street, then turned left onto a new road. Jae spied the sheriff's office on the corner and made a note of it in her mind.

At last, they found the building Sterling had mentioned. It didn't take them long. The theater was as ritzy-looking as the rest of the town, and it sat close to the forest's edge. Jae scanned the theater, paying close attention to the fancy oak doors, the windows with their

104 : Sophia Minetos

ivory frames… anywhere she could make an exit. How could she reach the sheriff in time?

"Should we go in?" asked Hodge.

"Not now," said Halston. "Lorelin?"

"Yes?"

"Care to be a patron of the arts today?"

She tossed back her hair. "Always."

"Good," said Halston. "In that case, I think you have a show to attend."

A small squeak came out of Lorelin's mouth. "Will you check the times for me?"

Halston dismounted, then headed up to the ticket booth. The sign above advertised "dirt cheap tickets," which seemed like a poor phrase for an advertisement, along with free shows for ladies on Tuesdays and Sundays. As he chatted with the spectacled man in the booth, Jae looked over the distance from the sheriff's office to the bank, wondering how she could get the gang there when the time was right.

Halston returned. "The show starts in an hour. Fortunately," he said, looking at Lorelin, then Jae, "we came on a Tuesday."

Heat rose into Jae's cheeks. This was the first time she'd seen anything close to mischief on Halston's face. "What are—"

Lorelin didn't let her finish. "Come on! Right this way. We've got this."

Lorelin led them back a few hundred yards from town, through the woods and into a clearing. After they both dismounted, Lorelin grabbed Jae by the wrist and pulled her into the shade. Jae leaned dumbly against a tree as Lorelin riffled through her saddlebags, then removed two lacey gowns.

Jae blinked twice. "Why do you have those?"

"What?" asked Lorelin. "You think I'd leave home without taking my favorites? Not a chance. Here, put this on. It matches your eyes."

Lorelin tossed Jae a dress as blue as northern cornflowers. Just holding the fabric made her skin crawl. She'd handled ropes that were softer than this.

Lorelin lifted her chin up at the others and waved her finger in a circle. "Turn around, boys. Nothing to see here."

"Wouldn't want to," called Hodge.

Lorelin gasped, raising her hand up to her mouth. "Hey!"

Jae waited until Lorelin made the others walk several stones' throws away. The gentlemen ducked behind a pile of logs. Lorelin slipped into her dress, a sleek pink thing with cloth-covered buttons down the back. Lorelin was a hand taller than Jae, with long legs and plenty of curves. Jae wondered how one of Lorelin's frocks would take to her own slim, boyish figure.

With a sigh, Jae lifted the dress in defeat. *C'mon. It's for Pa.*

She shed her jacket, shirt, and pants, then slipped into the gown. The fabric hung in bloated bags around her chest and hips, and she'd have to hoist the skirt up above her ankles to keep from falling on her face. Her skin begged her to strip it off.

This had better be worth it.

"Marvelous!" Lorelin gushed, though Jae couldn't tell if she was serious or just trying to be polite. "I'll fix your hair."

Jae let Lorelin unravel and arrange her twin braids into something more... suitable. Her scalp was screaming by the time Lorelin was done, but she didn't say a word about it.

Lorelin sighed. "Those braids leave such lovely waves in your hair. Oh, you look wonderful. I think this will be our grandest scouting trip yet. Let's pick out our fake names."

"Fake names?"

"Yes. That's the best part of this all. A few nights ago, we stopped by a roadhouse. I was Lucinda. Halston was my husband, Alphonse.

And Hodge was Marion."

Jae couldn't help but laugh. "I don't mind Marion. I'll be Marion this time."

"Oh, good. I wanted to be Lucinda again." She tapped her fingers on her chin. "Now, let's see. We need a feasible story. I'm your older sister, and I've helped you get back on your feet after the death of your husband, Peter. I'm a rich widow myself, so now I'm taking you to do all of the things Peter never allowed you the pleasures of."

Jae raised an eyebrow. "Is this… for the job?"

"No. But it's fun to come up with, is it not?"

"Lorelin," Halston called. "Are you ready yet?"

"Indeed, but I'm Lucinda right now." She twisted her curls into a snug knot, then passed Jae a damp cloth to wipe down her face. "Marion and I will head for the theater. I hope to return with a thorough review for you."

Jae did her best to put on an agreeable expression, but it was difficult with this lacey dress bagging over her body. They strode back to the town streets, and Jae tried to mimic Lorelin's graceful saunter. None of this felt real.

The ticket seller beamed at the girls when they came to the window. "Two tonight?" His cheeks went pink as he spoke.

"Yes please," Lorelin answered with a smile.

The man passed them two flimsy tickets, then watched them enter the theater without batting an eye.

They passed through a small foyer laid with a red-and-blue carpet. Framed portraits lined the walls, and two doors waited ahead of them. Jae looked back and forth to the narrow hallways extending on either side of the vestibule. "Do we pass through there?" she asked, pointing to the one on the right.

Lorelin shook her head. "The tickets are for the floor seats.

Those hallways lead to the boxes." She lowered her voice to a whisper. "We *will* use them. Just not tonight."

Lorelin led them through the doors and into the theater. Plush chairs crossed the floor in neat rows, and ivory paint coated the walls. Above the stage, a thick red curtain hung from an awning of gold. There were no more than fifteen people there, mostly women, and all of them had nestled themselves in the first few rows. The space smelled of shoe polish and dusty fabric. Lorelin chose a string of seats two rows from the back.

Surrounding the stage were boxes adorned with carved wooden railings and short velvet curtains. There was one box on the top level and one on the bottom on each side of the stage, four in all.

Lorelin pointed to the boxes on the right side. "There it is." In the ground-level box was the construction area Sterling had mentioned. While the room was dim, Jae made out a boarded-up hole about the size of a small doorway.

Jae frowned. "Wonder how many bullets someone had to put in that wall to get them to tear it down."

"The theater can be a bit of a madhouse, believe it or not," said Lorelin. "This one looks an awful lot like one I used to go to. I'd sneak out on Friday nights to watch the shows. There were parties sometimes, too. And poker nights in the basement. It was chaos... beautiful, musical chaos." She giggled. "That all ended when I got engaged. Gods, I miss it."

Jae wasn't sure she understood the appeal. "Why... why'd you go there?"

"I needed something different," Lorelin said. "I was born rich. Figured that if I wanted anything other than mundanity, I'd have to find it myself. I was tired of days filled with powdering my face and listening to my mother raving about suitors."

The curtain went up, then, and the audience clapped as two

actresses stepped onto the stage. They both had long, curly hair that shone like polished copper, and their printed dresses were covered in ruffles.

"What now?" Jae whispered.

"You'll see," Lorelin said without looking away from the stage. "We have to watch the show first."

The girls on stage began with a shrill, fluttery song, which seemed to put the audience into a trance. A vested man pounded on a piano beside the stage, the notes mingling with the girls' birdlike voices. Lorelin's eyes glimmered with awe, and an absentminded grin formed on her lips.

Jae had hoped that the show would at least entertain her, but so far, it had only succeeded in confusing her. The actors' voices boomed over the theater, chanting and bellowing and sighing and wailing as though the audience could not hear them otherwise.

The look on Jae's face must have been quite dumb, because Lorelin nudged her and explained, "It's *melodrama*. It's not supposed to seem real."

"Why not?"

"It's more fun that way."

Alright. Why not?

From what Jae gathered, the play followed a man named Branigan and a scoundrel named Veron. Veron and Branigan both loved a woman named Ilia, so Veron framed Branigan for murder and had him jailed. Now Ilia and her sister, dressed as male soldiers, were working to free Branigan and defeat Veron.

The audience had to shout and wail, too. Jae caught on to the rules with ease, though she didn't feel like participating. They were supposed to yell "boo" for Veron and cheer for Branigan and Ilia. Lorelin was taking full advantage of it all.

The show ended with Veron tumbling off a cliff. Branigan held

Ilia, still in his prison uniform, until the curtain went down. The crowd cheered and clapped for minutes.

Lorelin put a hand over her heart. "Oh, that was wonderful. What did you think, Jae?"

"I enjoyed it." Maybe if she didn't have business to take care of, she would've enjoyed it more.

Lorelin grinned. "Come now. The actors will be out any minute."

"Actors?"

Lorelin nodded. "We're going to convince one of them to give us a tour," she said with a dramatic wave of her hand.

The actors walked into the rows of seats, shaking hands and chatting with the patrons, who seemed more than eager to greet them. Lorelin motioned to the actor who'd played Veron, a tall fellow with chestnut hair and a mustache so glossy he must have combed it for hours. His eyes lit up at the sight of Lorelin. Jae figured the girl had that effect on people.

"Good evening, miss." He spoke like he was talking with his nose pinched. The tips of his mustache were sharp as fire pokers.

"Good evening yourself," Lorelin bid him. "I haven't been to the theater in ages. What a delight it was to come on the night of *your* performance."

Reddening, he bowed. "Thank you. I'm glad to hear it."

"I was in a show, once," Lorelin said with a mischievous glint in her eye. "But that was long before I married. I did love to go backstage. My friends and I would lurk in the darkness and try to frighten each other. Such wonderful memories, they are."

The actor laughed. "There isn't much backstage, but would you like to see it?"

Jae reckoned that Lorelin could probably sell a man a dead snail, and he'd smile while handing her the coin.

Lorelin gasped. "I'd be honored. Would Marion be allowed to

join us? She's never been to a theater."

"Gladly."

Jae gave him a polite tip of her chin. "Thank you."

The actor led them around the side of the stage. They passed a short stairway leading to a door painted with pink roses. "That leads to the dressing rooms. Off limits, of course." He led them down the narrow corridor, past a ladder reaching for a walkway above the stage. The scuffs of shoeprints covered the wooden floor. Ropes and sandbags stretched across the walls, suspended by a complicated web of hooks and knots.

The actor broke into a speech about costume changes, but Jae's eyes had settled on a door at the corner of the backstage area. An exit.

"Like I said, there's not much to look at," said the actor. "But a pleasure to show you, nonetheless. Are you coming to the show again tomorrow?"

Lorelin beamed up at him like a sunrise. "We certainly are."

Chapter 12

The world cooled rapidly as night fell. They set up camp in a patch of grass, which had started growing green and soft with the first breaths of spring. Jae kicked a mound of twigs to the side, then settled on the ground and waited for the gang to begin discussing their plan. She forced herself to hold still.

"How was the play?" asked Hodge.

"Oh, it was lovely," sighed Lorelin. "I laughed and cried the whole way through."

"Let me guess." Hodge tilted his head. "It's about a rich woman named... Eustanzia Nobiliana. And there are three men who all want to marry her."

"Yeah, I like that," said Jae. "And her suitors are all trying to impress her while sabotaging the others."

"Which is stupid of 'em, because she's really in love with a farmer," Hodge went on.

"And the farmer sings about how much he loves her, but how could a woman so rich and beautiful ever love someone as poor as—"

"We are planning a *heist*," Halston reminded them.

Jae grinned at Hodge. "You and I should write plays."

"Ours is *nothin*'," Hodge told her. He pointed to his brother with his thumb, grinning fiendishly. "Halston loved all those plays by... what's his name? Isaac Clearwalder?"

"Clearwater," Halston murmured.

"Yeah, that's it! Our pa had this big ol' tome full of his plays. Halston loved 'em almost as much as the Suryan epics. Hell, he even wrote his own, one time. Wanted us all to act in it. Drew up costumes and everything. What was it called, Hal? Something about pirates?"

"*Hodge*," Halston said, furrowing his brow.

Hodge sighed and leaned back against a fallen log. "Yeah, I know. The plan."

Halston prodded the fire. The flames danced with each other, climbing across the wood, and the air grew heavy with the smell of ash. "What did you find?"

"The breach is in one of the boxes," Lorelin explained. "Ground level. There's a hallway that leads to it from the foyer. There were several planks over it, but I think we should be able to take them down."

Halston nodded. "That should take us into the bank. There may be a few locks we'll have to pick, but we should be able to make our way to the vaults."

"There's also a back door in the theater," Lorelin said. "Behind the stage. One of us ought to guard it. Make sure the escape route is clear and that nobody else comes in."

"When's the last show?" asked Hodge.

"I checked the times," Halston replied. "Eight o'clock."

"Jae and I will buy tickets again tomorrow night," Lorelin said. "But we'll linger until the theater is empty. Hide somewhere. You guys wait outside, and I'll open the back door and signal when we're ready for you."

"Who's goin' into the bank?" asked Gryff.

"Me, for sure," said Hodge. "I'm the best at picking locks."

Gryff snorted. "We knew that, swank. I'm askin' who'll hang back and keep an eye on the theater."

"I'll do it," said Jae. "I'll take the back door. Someone else will have to keep an eye on the front. Make sure nobody comes in through the foyer."

"I will," Lorelin said.

Hodge chuckled. "Don't want in on the action?"

"The theater is beautiful," Lorelin sighed, tipping her head to the side. "I want to take it in while I still can."

"Got it," said Halston. "You and Jae keep an eye on the theater, we'll slip into the bank, then come back through the gap in the wall and exit through the back door. We can tether all the horses there beforehand. As for the sheriff... we'll have to do this quiet-like, right under his nose. If we keep things soft, he won't even know what happened until morning."

As they discussed their plan, Jae was developing her own. Once Gryff and the boys entered the bank through the gap, Jae would prop open the back door and hurry to the sheriff's office. From there, she'd lead him back to the theater before the gang could come out.

"How long is the show?" asked Halston.

Lorelin shrugged. "Hour and a half, I'd wager. But it felt like five minutes. Swept me away."

"Alright," said Halston. "If it ends at nine-thirty, then we should be able to start a little after ten o'clock. We saw that the bank closes at six, so the building should be empty."

Jae flicked a speck of ash off her shoulder. "Seems like you boys have gotten pretty good at this."

Hodge shrugged. "Been at it a couple of years. Tried to come by our fortune the honest way, but then we figured there's no one watchin' out for you in these parts. Don't matter if you're honest."

"Hodge," Halston warned.

Hodge continued anyway. "I miss being a cowboy. A few years back, we drove cattle from Mesca to the edge of Apalona, and I saw the Beltaire River for the first time in my life. So wide you couldn't even see the other side from the west banks. Made the rivers we've got out here look like puddles."

The Beltaire River split Hespyria in two. In the east lay the provinces, with their factories and velvet suits and whatnot. In the west were the territories: Mesca, Monvallea, Kalstira, Orliada, and Banderra, of course. Out here, there were few people and a whole lot of land, and settlers came to till it, or rip it up in search of gold.

Sometimes, Jae wondered if those folks knew what they were getting into. Yes, there was land out west. There were also burning deserts and men who would shoot you if you looked at them the wrong way.

Jae whistled. "Beltaire. Sounds nice."

"It was," said Hodge. "Some days were awful boring. And I did get a lot of blisters. But you got to see everything. Meet a lot of new people."

There was a longing in his voice, and Jae wondered if he yearned for his old life as much as she yearned for hers. Hodge longed to see the Beltaire River. She longed to wander the north of Banderra without a care in the world. Two drifters who could not roam where they pleased.

Jae scolded herself for such thoughts. She wasn't here to listen to Hodge's stories. Tomorrow, she would honor her duty to the law and the land, then forget the Harney gang.

Later, Lorelin took the first watch. Jae set up her bedroll next to Lorelin's log and brushed away the pine needles from her space. The ground was soft, here. She smoothed out her blankets, then sat down and hiked her knees up to her chest.

Her blood warmed her veins, feeling hotter with each beat of her heart. Somehow, she couldn't bring herself to close her eyes. Not even the smell of wood smoke and pine could calm her. Restless, she stared at the sea of ponderosas, their wide trunks tinted with moonlight.

At last, she settled back into her blankets and waited for the weight of tiredness to close her eyes. She rolled over, hoping that none of them had seen her twitching like a dead leaf clinging to a twig. Fear was a dangerous thing on its own, but showing it was even worse. She reckoned some outlaws had a knack for smelling it. It made their jobs a whole lot easier.

She drew in a breath, letting the mountain air steady her heartbeat. They'd granted her the lookout's job. She knew where the sheriff's office was. The theater would be free of people, and soon, the bounty would be hers.

Closer to home, to the northern skies, to putting this damn job behind her.

Closer to Pa.

Chapter 13

*J*ae couldn't see a thing down here.

With all her layers—Lorelin's blue dress over Jae's own clothes—she felt like a chilé roasting beneath its husk. Toward the end of the play, during what Lorelin called a "scene transition," the theater had dimmed. Jae snuck down the side of the room, then wedged herself between the corner of the stage and the dark stairs leading up to it. A few boxes and barrels also sat in the gap, hiding her head from view.

Sweltering, she listened to the sounds roll by. Actors' shoes pattering on the stage. Patrons chatting amongst themselves. The front doors opening and slamming shut about a hundred times. The voices softened, and the footfalls on the carpeted floor grew scarce. The theater went from quiet to silent, then turned dark.

A good while later, Lorelin's voice floated across the stage. "Jae?"

Jae stood, shoving herself out from between the wall and the stairway. Lorelin peeked out from the curtains, draped in the velvet like a newborn foal swaddled in blankets.

Jae followed Lorelin down into the back area, sneaking through the darkness. Jae urged herself to breathe, to focus on the plan she'd laid out. Soon, things would be alright.

Lorelin opened the door slowly, the hinges scarcely even squeaking. Gryff and the boys were waiting across the street, the horses tethered to a nearby railing. The road was quiet, and most of the town's windows had gone dark for the night.

The others shuffled in one at a time, scanning the area before sliding in through the door. Jae kept her mouth shut and ignored the wave of nerves creeping down her spine. For however long she had to, she'd remain quiet and calm and do whatever Halston told her to do.

Brushing off his jacket, he looked to her and said, "Good work. You stay here and guard the back. Leave it shut. Whistle at Lorelin if you hear anyone coming."

"Will do." Jae settled by the door, standing with one hand wrapped around her belt. She waited while the others made their way through the backstage passage and turned around the corner.

Before Lorelin disappeared, she waved and said, "Best of luck."

Jae smiled, then faced the door. She could do this. The bounty would fall into her hands, the sun would rise, and she'd turn her back on Duraunt and the Harney gang for good.

Still, there was a new feeling rising in her. Like nothing that had come with any other case before. It was heavier, somehow, like a stone chained to her ankle.

Could she do this?

Of course, she could. She'd done it many times before. Thieves were thieves.

She warned herself not to trust the feeling. As soon as she was certain that she could slip out unnoticed, she was running for the sheriff. She had a duty to Pa, and she'd learned better than to let second guesses slow her down.

———

They entered the box through the front by climbing over the short, gilded railing. Halston studied the construction area, surprised to find how few boards covered the hole. Five planks sealed the gap, some level, some crooked. The hole was about the size of a doorway, the edges splintered and rugged. A fine white powder sprinkled the floor beneath the hole, bright against the dark red carpet. There were two rows of seats before the gap, and a short path between the final row and the wall. An opening at the edge of the seats revealed the end of a narrow hallway and a stairwell leading to the upper level.

Halston, Lorelin, and Hodge squeezed between the back row and the wall. Hammers in hand, they wedged the claws under the nails and got to work.

One out. Two, three.

"Why can't we just break 'em down?" asked Hodge, shaking out his hand.

"Too loud," said Halston. He freed the final nail from a plank, grabbed the wood, and set it gently on the floor.

Hodge laughed softly. "Think of what the papers will say. 'Thieves break into bank, but leave theater construction nice and clean.' Common courtesy, eh?"

Lorelin lowered another board and said, "Almost done. I'm gonna head to my spot. See you boys when this is done."

Hodge jammed his hammer under the last nail, then grabbed the fifth and final plank and set it down. Lorelin shifted out of the box, then hurried down the corridor toward the lobby.

Behind the boards was a large, metal cabinet blocking the breach. There was just enough space for Halston and Hodge to reach in and grasp one of its corners. Heaving, they pushed the cabinet right to open the gap. The metal lurched, groaning as it slid across the floor.

At last, they'd pushed it far enough that they could climb through.

One by one, they stepped into the space, though Gryff had to stoop a good deal. The hole led to a storage room, about three times the size of a large closet. Stacks of paper and cramped bookshelves lined the walls, and a thick layer of dust covered everything. A door with a square window at the top waited across from them.

Hodge walked to it and jiggled the knob. The door opened up, and Hodge held it in place as Gryff and Halston filed through.

They entered the tellers' area, a section split from the front of the bank by a counter and a long window. Five adding machines sat on the counter. Through the glass, Halston peered at the front of the bank. The sight of a Fisk bank never failed to make Halston laugh to himself. Burgundy wallpaper embellished with gold swirls, curled, glossy lamps that looked like they cost more than a house, even the statue of a lion's head mounted to the wall. What would it be like to be so rich that your banks had to look like mansions?

At the end of the counter was an iron-barred door. Before they could move toward it, Hodge said, "Let's check the cash drawers."

"Not now," Halston whispered. "We're here for the vaults. We'll check the drawers if we have time."

Hodge shrugged and reached for the door. He removed the lockpick from his pocket, but before he set to work, he twisted the doorknob...

And pushed the door wide open.

Halston gasped.

The door hadn't brought them to the vaults at all.

They'd come to a lamp-lit office. Two desks sat in line before another barred door, and two pale men in crisp black suits sat at the desks, clutching pens in shaky hands and staring at the thieves who had just broken into their bank. One was short and slender, with blue doe eyes and round spectacles, and the other was middle-aged, full-lipped and round-bellied.

Slowly, Halston raised a finger to his lips. "Shh."

The bankers both screamed. Loudly.

Gryff lunged forward. The small banker leapt from his seat, and the glasses flew off his face. Halston jumped his way, and the man jammed a hand behind a bookshelf. He brought it down between them, books clattering on the hardwood floor.

Halston's hand fumbled for his revolver. He drew his gun and pointed it toward the thin banker, who was shouting, "Help! Somebody help!"

Halston bit his lip, wondering if these men had ever even *heard* of a robbery if they didn't have the good sense to keep quiet. He tried to ignore the fear in the man's eyes. They'd never caused an innocent harm, but at times, inspiring fear was an unfortunate necessity.

"Quiet!" Hodge snapped, pistol pointed the portly man's way. "Shut your traps, will ya?"

Halston looked at Gryff. "Do you have any rope?"

Gryff shook his head. "Guess we'll have to make our own." He turned and faced the bankers. "Arms out. Both of y'all."

Trembling, the men complied.

"Take off your jackets."

They did. Gryff started with the chubby man. He tore the sleeves off the jacket and set to binding his wrists behind his back. Gryff said, "I hope you fellas manage to keep your voices off until we're gone. I'd say you're stirrin' up more trouble than we were hopin' for."

Halston waited with the other man, whose long nose and cheeks were turning whiter with each passing second. Hodge said, "We gotta get into the vaults. Will that door take us there?"

The men nodded.

"Got a key?"

"The sheriff won't let you get away with this!" snapped the

portly man.

Gryff loomed over him. "The sheriff ain't here. No funny business. Now tell me where the key is or I'll toss you into the afterworld."

He gulped. "My—my suit pocket."

Gryff rummaged through the pockets, then tossed the key to Hodge, who caught it with one hand. Hodge grinned. "Much obliged, bud."

Gryff finished binding the last man's wrists. Behind them, the doorknob rattled.

Halston jumped, pivoting toward the door. He brought up his revolver, braced for whoever waited for them on the other side.

The door opened. The first thing Halston saw was a derby hat crowning a head of golden hair.

Lorelin sauntered in, gun raised and strutting like they'd all been expecting her. "Good lord," she said, looking down at the bankers. "What kind of miserly bastard has employees working this late?"

"Come on," Halston urged, taking her arm. He pointed back to the bankers. "Gentlemen, we'll need you to stay completely silent until we're out of here. Deal?"

Eyes wide, they bobbed their heads in agreement.

Halston turned to Lorelin. "Why'd you leave?"

"Heard the commotion," said Lorelin. "Came to check on you. Jae's still at the back door."

"Good."

Hodge unlocked the door, then pushed it open. They stepped into a cramped, narrow room, just wide enough for the four of them to walk side by side. Dozens of locked, gleaming deposit boxes lined the walls, and in the middle of the boxes was an enormous, circular door. The combination lock was in its center.

Halston sped up to it, pulled out the paper from Sterling, then rolled his thumb across the number wheels. He worked quickly, the metal cool beneath his skin. With a soft click, the final number slid into place, and he pushed down the handle and yanked. The hinges screeched, and the door opened, revealing rows upon rows of bills.

Their arms flocked greedily into the space, seizing as many bills as they could. The paper felt crisp and firm in Halston's grasp.

Halston counted three-hundred-fifty crowns. With Gryff and Hodge's loads, they'd meet Sterling with more than enough money to spare. When they'd all loaded their bags, they shut the vault and ran back through the office. The bankers said nothing as they bolted into the teller area. As they raced in the direction of the theater, Halston couldn't help but feel that he was racing toward a new day—one that would bring their freedom with it.

———

Jae ran.

She'd waited at the back door for a while, listening as best she could while they took the boards down. At last, they'd slipped into the bank. She'd overheard Lorelin announce that she'd wait in the foyer. A couple minutes passed. Just before Jae finally reached for the door, faint shouts and a crash boomed from the other side of the building.

Jae wasn't sure why, but she ran backstage toward the curtain. Lorelin shouted, "Jae!"

"Yeah?"

"Sounds like they're in trouble! I'm going in after them! You stay here!"

Jae heard the sound of Lorelin's hurried footsteps in the corridor leading to the boxes. For a moment, Jae wondered who those shouts had come from, but there was no time for much wondering. She had to find the sheriff.

She didn't see Lorelin run through the hole. Jae turned her back and sped away to the back door. It was time.

She placed a thick, knotted rope between the door and the wall to prop it open, then slipped outside. Night air cooled her face. The streets were empty, the moon high and bright in the sky. Her feet carried her down the road, flying over the dusty wagon ruts and bits of gravel. She veered right around the corner and raced toward the sheriff's office at the end of the lane. The windows glowed with candlelight.

The building had a pointed, shingled roof and a wooden stairway leading to a narrow porch. Jae leapt up the stairs, nearly tripping on the last step. She pounded on the door until the impact began stinging her knuckles.

The man who answered was short, dark-eyed and barely older than Jae herself. Good-looking boy, with a shiny copper badge and even shinier hair. He wore the cleanest clothes Jae had ever seen on a deputy, and maybe anyone in a Mesca town.

"There's a robbery happening," she said between short breaths. "Fisk Bank and theater. Harney boys."

The young deputy parted his lips, but said nothing.

"Harney boys?" boomed an older voice.

A fella with broad shoulders and a big, glimmering badge hurried to the front. Pistols with fine ivory grips rested in his holsters, and his shirt was a similar color. A silky bandana was tied neatly around his strong neck. He was tall, but the way he held himself made him look even taller.

"Yes," said Jae. "We gotta hurry."

"Dalton, Rhodes, this way," the sheriff ordered. The kid and another deputy with long, reedy features followed him outside.

They broke into a swift jog. "Where did you see 'em, exactly?" asked the sheriff.

"They got in through a hole in the theater's wall," said Jae. "I reckon they'll leave the same way. I got out through the back door. This way."

When they reached the back door, the sheriff entered first, his two deputies at his heels. Jae followed them and kicked the rope away, letting the door fall shut behind them.

"This way," Jae whispered through the darkness. She moved past the deputies, allowing the sheriff to walk beside her.

"Don't hear nothin'," the young deputy murmured.

They reached the end of the backstage corridor and walked around the curtain. When they stepped onto the stage, Jae pointed to the box. "They'll come out through that gap, there. Should be any—"

"*She's with them!*" someone yelped. "Sheriff!"

Jae whirled in the direction of the voice. A man stepped out from the other side of the stage, emerging from the shadows of the curtain—the mustached actor who'd shown them around the night before. "Don't move! She's a thief!"

The actor eased toward her, a pistol in his hand. Jae wondered if he knew how red his face was.

"Thief?" asked the sheriff.

Jae shook her head. "You're out of your mind. I got the sheriff to stop them!"

"She's a liar!" wailed the actor. "I was cleaning the dressing rooms when I heard the voices! She let the bandits in through the back while I hid! She's bluffing!"

"If I were with them, wouldn't I be *in* the bank?" She motioned behind her. "I got the sheriff to—"

"Put your hands up," the sheriff said.

Jae turned around. "What?"

"I said, *put your hands up.*"

Guns drawn, the deputies spread out around her, holding back like they'd just learned that she had some sort of disease. The sheriff pointed his revolver as well. The gun had the longest barrel she'd ever seen on a weapon. She stood there, too stunned to say anything, caught in the sights of three different guns.

Her heart was pounding fast as a horse running through hell. She lifted her hands limply, but said, "I ain't with them."

"If that's true, then it shouldn't matter that I'm asking you to put your hands up," the sheriff said, lowering his eyebrows. "Now take a step forward."

This guy was really gonna make her push her luck, wasn't he? "Listen to me! You have to—"

"Drop your guns!" someone shouted.

Hodge.

What happened next seemed to last both a blink and an hour.

Fear flashed on the young deputy's face. He jumped like a startled grasshopper.

As he jumped, his gun went off.

Jae had always expected it to hurt, if it ever happened. It didn't, at first. It felt like a smack from a low-hanging branch. A single hit. An instant. Then came the burn, rising in her upper arm and spreading to swallow her elbow, her shoulder, her wrist.

Her eyes fell to the red cloud staining her sleeve. Her balance wavered, then disappeared, and the floor struck her head.

Lorelin shouted Jae's name. The gang's four figures stood in the box, all of them looking so still Jae briefly wondered if time had stopped.

Three more shots thundered in a row, and three screams followed them. Jae lifted her head, wondering if the sheriff's men would join her down on the floor with fresh wounds.

They didn't. Their guns slammed against the stage, though. The men all raised their hands, bleeding from their fingers. The actor sank to his knees, hands in the air, his face scrunched and his eyes shut tight. "Stop shooting! Please!"

Hodge shouted, "If you reach for those guns again, I *will* shoot! Y'all better stay where you are!"

A hot, spinning haze clouded her mind. It was like being drunk, but fueled by fury instead of a light and careless joy. Boots pounded on the floor. She rolled her head over and faced the ceiling, watching the curved wooden panels blur above her.

They were going to leave her.

She'd lost the bounty. If she didn't bleed out, someone would come and haul her to a jail cell. They'd wring out any information they could about the Harney gang, and there she would stay. Gods above, she'd failed. Whether she wound up in some dumpy cell or in her own grave, she would never see Pa again.

"Stay put!" Hodge shouted. "I mean it! I'll shoot again if one of y'all makes a false move!"

A shadow fell over her. A light groan escaped her lips as she turned her head, then saw a hand outstretched before her, arm clad in a brown sleeve.

Halston leaned above her body. His face was faint in the darkness. "Jae. Take my hand."

She reached for him. It wasn't like there was anything left for her to do here. She raised her good arm, trying to ignore the pain flushing down the other. Her hand shook violently, and a tingling warmth spread through it, rendering her fingers useless. Halston pulled her upright, but her trembling legs kept her from standing.

A strong hand supported her back. She felt someone tucking her into the crook of a scaly arm. Gryff. He raised her up like she weighed no more than a feed sack.

Then, they were moving.

Jae stared at the floor. Each of Gryff's steps sent a new jolt of shock and numbness through her. She watched the smooth stage turn to planks, then dirt and gravel when they reached the street. They were all shouting at each other, four voices stirring together like grit and soot and leaves in the wind. They might as well have been speaking in some dead foreign tongue, because Jae didn't catch a word of what they were saying.

At last, Gryff lifted her onto a saddle. She sat up best she could, one leg on either side, settling against whoever sat behind her.

She was in no position to run, to bluff, to do anything but sit there and wait.

Behind her, Lorelin said, "Hal. Put pressure on her wound."

A firm, light brown hand settled on her arm and pushed. Jae gritted her teeth. Halston's other arm wrapped around her side. He took the reins and whispered, "Hold on."

They rode through the streets, weaving around the town's sprawling structures. The town's limits turned into forest, and they rode until they found a dark, misty glade in the woods.

Until they dismounted, Halston's hand did not leave her arm.

Lorelin spoke. "Halston, help me lay her down."

That was the last thing Jae heard—the last thing that made sense to her, at least. Her vision seemed to flicker on and off, like a candle's flame being blown out, lit, and blown out again. She could feel her heartbeat and hear it at the same time. Every inch of her skin was damp with sweat or blood. Something soft and thin covered her legs—a blanket, probably. She was cold. Colder than she had been while wandering through the Banderra winter after Pa disappeared, or when she lay helpless on the forest floor when the ghosts took him away.

They took him. They took him and she did nothing. She was useless then and useless now.

Something cool and wet poured over her wound. It stung, but not in a way that she resisted—it was clean feeling, like a sin being purged away. Voices hummed around her. She opened her eyes and glimpsed firelight, then a vast, black sky. For a moment, she forgot the earth beneath her legs, and the sensation of sinking flooded her body. The world was slipping—from her grasp, from her sight.

A groan surfaced from her lips. Something soft lodged inside her mouth.

Fire seared her arm. She screamed, but the bough of cloth smothered the sound. The pain wrapped around her like a hand, and she could not slip from its grasp before she blacked out.

Chapter 14

There was pain.

Jae opened her eyes.

Light, blurry trees, and more pain.

Jae tilted her head. Lorelin sat on a nearby log, stitching up a hole in one black lace glove. "Oh, good! You're awake. How do you feel?"

Groaning, Jae touched the back of her head. There she found a large and tender lump, but the skin seemed to be intact. She was sweating beneath her clothes, but her nose was mighty chilly. Her eyes darted to her arm. She unbuttoned her shirt and freed her shoulder. A thick, clean bandage circled her bicep, marked with a dry red stain.

The memories came flooding back to her, and she cursed herself. She'd failed.

They'd gotten away with it.

Damn that deputy for not having a proper grip on his gun. Who even taught him to hold it?

"Don't worry. The bullet didn't lodge in your arm," Lorelin said, making her way toward Jae. "It just skimmed you. You lost quite a bit of blood, though. I cleaned the wound and seared it shut last night, but you passed out cold after that. Still, it was a lucky stroke. You should be good as new in a few weeks."

Jae swallowed. "Thank you. Where… where'd you learn how to fix a wound like that?"

"Oh, an old friend of mine. She taught me the basics, but she was far better at it than me. If she were here, you would've been up and about twenty minutes after the bullet hit you. She… she's got a magic touch."

Jae looked at the ground, biting her lip. "Gods, I was… I should've been more careful."

Lorelin lifted her shirt, then gestured to a round, white scar above her navel. "See? Nothin' to be ashamed of. Happens to the best of us. You lived through it."

Jae tried to stand, legs wavering like a drunken fool stumbling out of a bar. Nausea latched onto her, and bile climbed up her throat. She leaned over a rock and emptied out her stomach.

"Whoa, whoah!" Lorelin hurried over and pressed a hand to the small of Jae's back. "Careful. Drink some water."

Jae spat, then took a swig from her canteen. She stayed bent over, hands glued to the rock, until the sickly pangs stopped clawing at her stomach. The world spun around her head. Lorelin kept her hand on Jae's back until she stood straight again.

Jae breathed in, trying to recall the night before. She remembered the bullet hitting her arm, falling, Gryff hustling her out of the theater. Then there was the race to the forest, Lorelin cleaning her wound and sealing it. It all felt like fevered glimpses of a long-lost dream.

She was grateful to be up again, to be moving, to be *alive*. Her head was still a little bleary, though. "I'm glad I didn't die." Silly as it sounded, she didn't care.

Lorelin laughed. "Yes, we're all glad we didn't die."

Jae scratched her neck. Lorelin had patched her up. The gang could've left her bleeding on the theater's floor, at the mercy of that wounded sheriff. Instead, they'd brought her here.

She'd never been in anyone's debt before, let alone a band of wanted outlaws.

Jae tried not to think of it. She'd sort things out once she felt functional again. She rubbed the sleep from her eyes, and the morning light stung them. They stood on a small hill, nicely shaded by the trees. Black logs smoked in a crackling fire. The horses grazed happily in a patch of newly green grass, and she could hear the deep rush of a river somewhere downhill. "Where are we?"

"A good many miles outside of Duraunt. We've got time to rest before we start riding toward our next job." Lorelin pointed over her shoulder. "The boys are hunting with Gryff. If you're up for it, I thought we could make gravel biscuits."

"Gravel biscuits?" Hunger scraped at Jae's stomach. She didn't have any food on her besides a handful of pine nuts and a strip or two of dried pork.

Jae helped Lorelin remove a pan from her saddlebag, along with a sack of flour, salt, a bowl, and a tin of lard. Lorelin greased up the pan. "You take your batter," she began, blending the flour with the lard, salt, and water, "then you throw in everything else you've got."

"Like what?" asked Jae.

Lorelin jogged back to the horses and fished through the boys' saddlebags. She came back with raisins and seeds, then tossed them into the dough. "Got anything that might be good in here? Try not to use your right arm."

Jae fetched her knapsack, then tossed a handful of pine nuts into the dough.

After adding a pinch of salt, they worked the dough into a

smooth, stretchy mass. They shaped it into balls, then placed them in the heated pan. The biscuits sizzled over the flame.

Jae stretched out her neck while they cooked, watching the clouds trail across the sky. Birds sang in the treetops. The biscuits let off a warm, hearty smell, and she thought of sitting with Pa by the campfire, cooking their supper.

When the biscuits turned golden brown, Lorelin removed them from the fire. Jae asked, "Should we wait for the others?"

"Gods, no," Lorelin said, shoving half a biscuit into her mouth. "I'm starving."

Jae chuckled, then picked up a biscuit. She spent a few minutes picking it apart and nibbling on the crumbs. "Lorelin?" she said.

"Mhmm?"

"How long have you been part of the gang?"

"Hmm," Lorelin said. "A little over a year. Why?"

"Just wondering." Jae tilted her head. "I was just a little curious. About why you joined 'em. I hope I ain't being too bold."

Lorelin perked up and lifted her chin. "Not at all." She tossed a stray curl behind her shoulder, then started on another biscuit. "Lord, don't let me eat all of these, even if I try. Anyway, I was the youngest of three. My father died when I was two years old. I don't remember him, but everyone said he was kind. I think his passing changed my mother for the worse. When she wasn't fussing over me, she was holed up in her room.

"My sister, Magdalena, wasn't much different. I don't recall her ever saying anything kind to me. Then she married a city slicker and left home. The most I ever got from her was a letter each summer. My brother, Killian, inherited our fortune and married a quiet girl from the east.

"My mother wanted me to join them—find a husband and spend my years staying pretty for him. I did my best to scare all the suitors away, but Adwell… he stayed interested. Not that I blame him. I'm a very interesting person."

Jae laughed.

"Things were fine, at first. Better than fine, really. Every time he visited, he'd have something new for me. Some pomade, gown, or pocketbook. I never loved him, but I enjoyed him. He seemed to be the only person who ever cared what I had to say, and I wanted to leave home. So when he proposed, I accepted.

"He took me into the city one day. We walked down a plaza where artisans were selling their goods. I saw a merchant being robbed. The bandits left him stranded. Adwell told me to leave him be, but I ran.

"He was hurt. I… I couldn't just leave him there. When Adwell wasn't looking, I took off my comb and slipped it into the merchant's hand. This dainty little gold thing, trimmed in pearls. I hoped it would help him pay for what he'd lost.

"But that comb was a gift from Adwell. When he saw it was missing and learned what I'd done, he struck me in the stagecoach. My mother didn't believe me when I told her."

Jae's mouth parted. "That's awful. What did you do?"

"I asked her if I could break the engagement. When asking didn't work, I begged. The first time I tried to run, she sealed our windows shut and hired servants to guard the doors at night. I stopped paying visits to Adwell myself, so she arranged for him to visit me.

"He called me ungrateful. He said I should feel lucky, that he was the only man who'd ever find any worth in me after I'd failed to do anything but embarrass my family all my life. The worst part was that I believed him.

"I asked him what he wanted. He told me he wanted obedience, if not the kindness I showed him at the start. So I promised him that I would obey.

"But one night, I couldn't take it anymore. I collected everything

I couldn't bear to part with, then I gathered all the money I had and bribed a servant to let me outside. And I saddled up and rode to Adwell's manor.

"I ran up to the front door, crying, with a length of lace tied to my wrist. His housekeeper answered, and I sobbed and told her that bandits had robbed me on the road.

"When I reached him, Adwell just kept shouting at me to stop blubbering. He told me that it was past midnight. If I was found in his home, still unwed, it would tarnish both our reputations. He asked me if I wanted a scandal. So I looked him in the eye and said, 'Yes.'

"The rest was a blur. He put up a fight. I won't say I didn't walk away with bruises. But the next thing I knew, I'd lodged a kerchief in his mouth and strung him up to the bedpost with my lace. I found his gun, then, in his bureau.

"I could've killed him, but I didn't. I *wanted* them to find him there. I wanted them to know that I looked him in the eye and *won*. He wanted an obedient wife, and I wanted them to know that I took that away from him.

"So I fled. And that's the last I ever saw him."

Jae spent a moment searching for the right words. "I never knew. That... he treated you that way."

"Most people don't." Lorelin fingered the bark of the log. "I robbed three of his family's banks before I met the Harneys. I kept some for myself, but I gave the rest away. Tipped merchants when I bought brooches from them. Gave it to cowboys in the woods when they let me warm myself by their fires. Figured they needed it more than the Fisks did."

Lorelin paused to draw in a breath. She closed her eyes. "I try not to let anger get a hold on me. Like poison, it is. I've let him go.

I was strong enough to set myself free. I don't have to forgive him, though, and I'll never have to see him again, provided I do my share to keep Sterling happy."

Jae frowned, setting her biscuit aside. "What's Sterling have to do with it?"

"He says that he has a way to tell Adwell where I am… if one of these days I don't comply. I have my doubts, but Sterling has moles and cronies all over Mesca. I can't be too careful."

Jae swallowed, wondering what she could say. Pa always said it was wrong to pray for the misfortune of others… but Jae wondered *how* wrong it would be to ask the gods to strike down Adwell.

"Thank you," Jae said. "For… for being so nice to me." She winced, realizing that wasn't the proper thing to say.

Still, Lorelin smiled. "I don't know where you're running from. Or to. I love my gang, but… sometimes I don't think they understand what it's like to be a woman on her own. I do. You don't run into many girls like us, sleeping on roadsides, guns in our belts. It's hard to take things into our own hands with men turning up their noses at everything we do."

There was a warm understanding in Lorelin's eyes, the kind Jae reckoned mothers had, and it made her wish that her own hadn't died so young.

"You know how to look after yourself," said Lorelin. "It's admirable."

Finally, Jae found something to say. "You're not what I expected."

Lorelin had a thunderous laugh. "I hope not. Adwell made sure the papers turned me into a monster. But I found the boys and Gryff, and… that's all that matters, really. I don't much care what anyone else thinks of me."

For a while, they talked and tended to the next batch of biscuits, watching the steam rise from the pan and disappear into the air. Until the others came back, Jae didn't think of Sterling, or the bank, or even the twinges of pain flaring from her wound.

Chapter 15

S everal days passed, and Jae was surprised at how fast they flew by. She didn't say much, and she searched for her own food whenever she could, keeping her distance from the gang. They discussed their next plan, of course, and of those to come, but Jae spoke as little as she could.

She tried to listen, though. There was some talk of Sterling, but simple tasks filled most of the days on the trail. When they made camp for the night, Gryff set up snares, and Halston checked them in the morning. Hodge chopped wood. Lorelin fetched water. Jae gathered roots and greens and nuts. They rode and rode, mile after mile, bound for the Taracoma Valley.

Each night, Lorelin helped Jae slip down the bandages and clean the wound with alcohol. It stung less as the days went by, but her skin was still tender, the wound slick with a clammy sheen. They talked as they worked together, and Lorelin always seemed to be wearing a smile. Jae wanted to stay quiet around her. Carry her own weight. But in this regard, she was powerless to do so, and for some reason she didn't mind.

Though Jae didn't dare say so out loud, she thought she might miss Lorelin when she left.

Several mornings after the bank job, Jae sat with Lorelin by the fire, plucking a turkey Gryff had trapped. "Is turkey even *worth* all the feathers?" Lorelin asked, shaking out her hands.

Jae licked her lips. "*I* think so." She loved wild turkey. Pa preferred the white meat, and she liked the dark. He used to give her the legs, and she'd bite into them like a hungry bear.

Jae pushed the pile of feathers to the side with her heel. When they finished plucking the turkey, Lorelin lined a circle with stones and began snapping her flint over the firewood. Sparks jumped from the rocks and glowed hot against the tinder. "Would you mind getting us some more water, dear?"

Dear. In spite of herself, Jae liked the sound of that. "Sure thing." She took up the bucket, then headed for the river.

The Taracoma River was shallow but wide in these parts, its waters a bright, inviting blue. Jae walked downhill toward its rush, welcoming the soft touch of the earth under her boots and bouncing the wooden pail off her knees.

She came across a crook in the river, half-hidden by aspens with pale, pearly bark. They sprouted close together, like rungs on a ladder. Two boulders and a slab of rock formed a small bridge overhead. Jae watched the waters pass beneath it. A line of trout darted through the current, the sun glinting off their slim, silvery backs.

After Jae filled the waterskins, she decided she could use a quick wash and fetched a dollop of soap from her knapsack. She undid her braids, then removed everything but her underclothes and waded into the water. She did not wade out far enough to let the water rise above her waist, careful to keep her wounded arm above the river. Slick stones poked her soles. The runoff was like ice, but she welcomed the numbness it brought her aching bones. She dipped her head into the water, then came back up to wash her hair. She rinsed it out before stepping back to the bank.

Jae patted herself mostly dry with a rag, then put her clothes back on. Beads of water clung to her legs, and the mist kissed her face. She breathed in the sweet, cool smell of the river and sat back.

It was one of those mornings where the trees seemed particularly alive. There was no sweeter music than the swish of their arms dancing in the breeze. Jae traced the rigid bumps of an aspen's bark. For a moment, she felt a bit like her old self, in those quiet days before Pa slipped away. Like she could run on her yearning to see this world's beauty alone, instead of her anger at those ghosts for taking her father.

Maybe she could feel that way again, one day. What mattered now was her work.

When she finished dressing again, she gently prodded her right arm. The bandages were still tight, the wound dry. Jae had heeded Lorelin's warnings about keeping it clean. If it started to bleed again, Jae would have no clue how to treat it.

She swallowed. What if she left and the wound became infected? Would she be able to slow it herself? Would she have the time to make it to a doctor, let alone afford one? She'd heard stories of folks who'd sustained bullet wounds and lost their limbs from blood poisoning and other foul things, if the infection didn't take their lives first.

But as soon as her arm healed, she'd pack her things and leave in the night. She wouldn't leave them an explanation. They'd all do just fine without one. Another week or so of traveling with the gang was preferable to losing her arm.

Besides... when she thought about the statue, it tempted her. It was all a bit exciting, the thought of treasure beneath the earth, like one of Pa's old stories. It wouldn't be stealing, if she stayed with them while they looked for it. Not really.

Jae finished dressing, filled the bucket, and started back for the camp. As she moved, she heard someone whistling up ahead. Then the whistling ended, and a voice began to sing.

"Come down to the valley
And I'll show you hordes of old
From plundering and pirating
Rubies, emeralds, gold
Show you the glint and gleaming
Of treasures vast and true
But dear, I do not love them
Half as much as I love you."

She craned her neck over the bushes and looked downhill. Halston sat on the banks of the river, scribbling something in a journal.

"You have a lovely singing voice, Halston," she called.

Halston yelped in surprise and flung his pencil to the side. He jerked his head forward, looking at Jae with wide eyes.

Jae clapped a hand over her mouth, biting back a laugh. "Oh, gods. I'm sorry. You alright?"

Halston straightened himself up, then fetched his pencil from the arms of a bush. "I didn't expect to see you here."

Maybe she'd been cruel, scaring him like that. "Sorry about that," she said as she made her way through the bushes, then stepped onto the bank to join him.

Halston bent down a few yards away from Jae. He placed his open canteen into the water and let the river feed it. He looked different this morning. With his hair still mussy and the sleep still in his eyes, he looked less like a rugged, commanding outlaw and more like… well, just a boy. In the sunlight, his eyes were gold.

His shirt rode up above his hips, revealing a portion of his back. Long, jagged marks covered his lower back and disappeared under the fabric of his shirt. Jae's stomach twisted, and she wondered what had put those scars there.

Halston stood straight again, slinging his canteen over his neck. "How's your arm?"

"Fine, as long as I don't touch it."

"That's good. After our business with Sterling, I'll get you your share for the heist."

Oh, right. Her share. "You sure? I don't think I added much."

"A deal's a deal."

The thought of her share hadn't trailed across her mind in days. Maybe after she left, she'd give the money to a church, or somewhere else that needed it. She didn't want stolen money in her pocket for long, and besides, she hadn't helped the gang, really. In fact, she'd done nothing but lead some lawmen inside, and taken a bullet to the arm for it.

Halston asked, "Those deputies who came in. Where did they enter?"

"The front door," Jae said quickly. "That actor in the theater must've snuck out to get them while Lorelin was with you. Sorry I didn't hear him leaving."

"Don't worry about it. I'm just glad we all made it out of there."

Her gaze fell to the journal in his hand. Halston noticed her looking and said, "I was just doing some business in here. Calculating our shares and whatnot. Making sure we have what we need. Boring stuff, I know."

"Ah." She straightened her shirt, then stretched out her neck.

"I'm hoping we'll reach our destination in a few days," Halston said. "The directions Sterling gave us say the statue is buried close to Marcelena."

"Marcelena?" asked Jae. "Hell, we'll reach that in a day and a half. And that's if we take our time."

Halston nodded. "Good." He paused. "If you don't mind my asking… you said that you got your map from a Nefili man."

"Sure did."

"How… how did *that* happen?"

She swallowed, her eyes darting to the thick scar on her hand.

———

Jae had left Fort Sheridan the day the Rangers stopped looking for Pa, and it was probably the stupidest thing she'd ever done.

Snowflakes fell onto her face, and she could hardly feel her fingers anymore. The cold dug down to her bones. When she first saw the campfire glowing through the white-capped pines, she thought it was a blessing.

She dismounted and hurried toward the fire, but she heard shouting when she approached the site. When she looked through the bushes, she spied a man crouching in the snow. Dirt covered his clothes, which hung like floppy sacks on his thin frame. Locks of dark, inky hair hid his eyes.

What she remembered best of all was the thin coating of moss on his hands and neck.

Two surly, big-shouldered men stood before him, hurling every obscenity Jae had ever heard at the thin man. *"Please,"* he coughed. *"All I asked for was a bite."*

What happened next was a mangled blur, but Jae knew that the thin man would die if she didn't step forth. So she did. "Stop!" she cried, lunging through the bushes.

They did stop, then. They looked at her, and their laughter was the most wretched sound she'd ever heard. Before she could move, one man knocked her into the snow and jammed a forearm beneath her throat. Jae flailed to fend him off. She screamed when his blade slashed her hand. She wheezed, gasping for breath as his fingers dug into her pockets, taking what little money she had.

Though her hands were numb and stiff, she reached for her boot pistol while his weight kept her rooted to the earth. She finally gripped the handle, and each action that followed came as easy as blinking.

The shot tore through her assailant's neck. The next two brought the other to his knees, then his death. The snow turned crimson.

She struggled to free herself from the man's weight. The thin fellow helped her, pushing the corpse to the side. The outlaw's blue eyes stared back at her, wide and angry even in death.

Too stunned to cry, she faced the thin man. He gazed at her with a simple, almost childlike curiosity.

"*Who were they?*" she whispered.

"*Thieves*," he said. "*Scoundrels.*"

Jae glanced at his narrow face, and the clothes flapping on his limbs. *He's still hungry.*

Jae removed her knapsack with trembling fingers, her hands slick with hot blood. She took out the rations she'd gathered—a loaf of bread and two apples. She split the provisions in half and passed what she could to the thin man before dragging herself up to the fire, wrapping her hand in her handkerchief.

She lost consciousness, then, huddled in her jacket, and when she woke at dawn, the bodies were gone, the snow clean and white. Though it was small and wispy, the fire still blazed. At first, she figured it had all been some kind of hallucination brought on by the cold.

Then she saw the scar on her hand, pink and plump but fully healed, and found the map in her knapsack.

When she opened it, the words appeared in gold ink.

Many thanks, young drifter. May you never lose your way again. Speak "hence" to know where you are. Ask, and let the map guide you.
-Grove

She rose and looked around, hoping for the Nefili man to emerge from the woods. Then, a gnarled piñon tree snatched her attention. About as tall as a man, with two branches pointing toward the sky, their middles bent like the crooks of arms. She could almost feel that tree grinning at her.

But then she cried. For her sin—the blood she'd just spilled—for her dead mother, and for her missing father.

Grove had given her the map to help her find her way, but never before had she felt so lost.

————

Jae looked at Halston. "I got the scar in a bar. Card game went wrong, and the fella accused me of cheating. Slashed my hand before I got away."

Halston shuddered. "Does anything good ever happen in bars?"

Jae laughed softly. "I reckon not."

Chapter 16

*H*odge, Gryff, and Lorelin sat on a pair of mossy logs, feasting on the turkey. It was good, fatty meat, salted and roasted. Weeks on the road gave Hodge an appetite like no other. He turned the drumstick in his hand, savoring each bite.

Soon, they'd reach the site of their next job. Aside from Jae getting shot, their last robbery had gone off without a hitch. Now, this dig was all that was standing in their way. Hodge reckoned he should be more excited about it, but he knew better than to be so hopeful. Part of him wondered if they'd meet up with Sterling only for him to dangle the dagger over them and give them three more jobs. Hodge certainly wouldn't put it past him.

Heist after heist, rushing away down winding roads, and the smell of gun smoke. It was all he'd known for years now. What would it feel like when it ended?

It didn't take long for Lorelin to pick a topic of conversation for the morning. "What do you think of Jae?"

Hodge turned to Lorelin, swallowing a mouthful of meat. "Why?"

Lorelin shrugged, then dug back into her food. "Just making conversation."

Hodge thought about it. "You know, it's pretty strange how you always have to like someone, or hate them, or love them. Why can't you just *know* somebody?"

"So, you have no opinion, then?" Lorelin asked, tilting her head.

"She's pretty. I guess," said Hodge, but not in the way he preferred. Something about Jae told him that she wasn't afraid to slug him in the ribs if he crossed her.

Lorelin pinched her fingers together. "Hodge, let me give you some advice. Girls are more than just 'pretty' and 'not pretty.' You can't talk about them that way and then wonder why none of them like you."

"Plenty of girls like me," Hodge said with a grin.

"That's because you run away before they have a chance to talk to you for very long."

"A charmer indeed," Gryff said flatly.

Hodge frowned. They'd jabbed at him like this before. He wondered if they truly thought they were going to better him, or if they just liked trying to rile him up. "Does it matter? I ain't taking a wife or anything."

"You say that now." Lorelin's eyes were bright. She peered back in the direction of the river. "Halston and Jae have been gone a long time. I wonder what they're up to."

She looked back at Hodge, a curious glint in her eye. "Alright, let's say you don't ever fall in love. I don't believe it, but I'll humor you for now. What if Halston did?"

Hodge and Gryff exchanged a glance, then both of them burst out laughing.

Lorelin scoffed. "Stop it. Both of you. You're being cruel."

"Yeah, I guess we are," replied Gryff, rubbing one eye with his knuckles. "Maybe it's our fault. The boy has nobody to teach him. I could tell him about Azmarian matin' bonds, but I reckon that would be no use to him. And it ain't like Hodge is a good influence."

"I'm younger than him. It ain't my job to be his influence."

"Exactly. It's your job to drive him up the wall," Lorelin agreed.

"I don't know. Halston hardly ever laughs nowadays."

"You're thinkin' too much," said Gryff.

She sighed dreamily. "I suppose I am. But I want Halston to be happy."

Lorelin was always swooning and sighing over something or other. Hodge reckoned she could look at a musty spider web and find something pretty about it. She could gush over the idea of Halston falling in love all she wanted, but that wouldn't make it any more likely. Hodge knew his brother, and he knew that Halston was a frigid bastard. Halston was dear to him and all... but he was still a frigid bastard.

Jae and Halston came marching back to camp. Jae's hair was wet, and she was carrying the water bucket in her hand.

"Good morning," Halston greeted them, then took a seat on one of the logs. "Let's take a look at our next job." Halston riffled through his knapsack for the instructions Sterling had given him, fetched them, and unfolded them.

"Take the road four miles north of Marcelena." Halston nudged Jae. "May we see the map?"

Jae pulled out her map and unrolled it. "Like I said, it ain't far."

Halston continued. "You will pass a sign pointing east to the town of Glyson. Head directly west of the sign for one mile.

"When you reach the banks of the Taracoma River, you should come to a bear tree." He raised an eyebrow. "*Does* that say 'bear tree'?" he asked, showing it to Jae.

Jae nodded. "Sometimes black bears will claw and bite a tree to talk to each other. It could be easy to miss, so look carefully."

"Alright. Let's see... head north at the bear tree. Follow the river for five-hundred paces, then you will come to a boulder." He lifted the directions to show them. The boulder resembled a knobby chess piece.

"Twenty paces north of the boulder, you will come to an upward slope. The statue is buried beneath a spruce tree with this symbol etched into the bark." He pointed to the final sketch on the directions—a simple drawing of a songbird.

"Straightforward enough," said Lorelin.

Hodge shook his head. "That statue is of Cressien, right?" He wasn't sure if he believed in the gods, but digging up a statue of one didn't feel quite right to him.

Lorelin beamed up at the clouds. "Our Lady of the Skies. Wonder what he wants with it."

"Call it a hunch, but it might have something to do with it bein' made of pure gold," said Gryff.

Lorelin waved a hand. "You know what I mean."

Hodge furrowed his brow. "What if it's cursed or something?"

"Why would Sterling want *cursed gold?*" Gryff asked.

"Cursed gold is more expensive than plain gold, Gryff," said Hodge, voice rising. "Everybody knows that."

"Let's be serious," said Halston.

"Really, though," Hodge went on. "What does he want a solid gold statue for? Why can't we just rob another bank or two?" It didn't make much sense to him. Sterling had never given them a job like this before. They fled most of their jobs with bruises, and often to an accompaniment of gunfire in the background. "Something about this feels odd."

Halston sighed, lowering the paper directions. "You're right. Sterling told us to consider it a gift, but—"

"—he ain't exactly the generous type," Hodge finished.

"I reckon Sterling didn't get them directions from a friend," Gryff added. "Knowin' him, someone doesn't want him goin' after that statue."

"That has to be it," said Halston. "It must be on somebody's property. Something like that." He nudged Jae. "Think your map would show us that?"

Jae nodded. "It might not be labeled, but buildings usually pop up on it, depending how big they are."

Hodge snorted. He'd met plenty of strange folk in Mesca, so the thought of someone burying a golden statue on their property was no surprise to him. "I don't feel too right about this."

"We don't have a choice," said Halston. "If this were a chest of bills and coins, we could probably find it elsewhere. But Sterling demanded *this* statue. If we show up without it—"

"I *know*," said Hodge.

Everyone was silent for a few moments, then Halston said, "I've got an idea. We still have a few days to spare before we rendezvous at Mourelle. When we get to the site of the dig, we'll scout it out first. When we have a solid understanding of the area, we'll make a plan before we jump in."

The others nodded in agreement. Hodge wished he had something more to add, but if the gang was content to ignore his concerns, then all he was left with was his eagerness to pack up and get the job done.

They smothered the fire, rounded up the horses, and set out on the mountain path. If a problem waited for them at their next job, he'd face it same way he faced most of his problems: with a grin and a pistol.

Chapter 17

Light dappled the ground in netlike splotches, shining in through scattered gaps in the branches. Few pines grew this close to the river, and leafy trees sprouted in their place. Leaf litter covered the loam, browned and brittle, and the gentle rush of the river was the only sound for miles, save for the hoofbeats of the horses.

As they moved across the forest floor, Jae felt heightened, alive. She had not felt free—*truly* free—in years, but the woods helped her feel close to it. The desert was harsh and unyielding, and the forest was a savage, untamed thing. But it was kind to those who knew it. There were few things dearer to her heart.

They passed the road sign, pointing crooked on its broken pole, then started downhill for the bear tree. Jae kept half her focus on her compass to make sure they hadn't strayed off course.

She didn't sense any suspicion from them, but for good measure, she helped out whenever she could and spoke as little as possible. While the thought of the treasure enticed her like an apple tart cooling on a stovetop, she couldn't shake the notion that she'd be wasting her time entirely if it weren't for her wound.

She should be on the road again, on her own, not aiding criminals on a job.

But while she wasn't sure where they'd find the statue, she doubted whoever buried it was the original owner. It didn't deserve to be forgotten, shrouded by heaps of earth for years to come.

When they reached the river, they dismounted and tethered the horses to a cluster of willows. Their long branches cast wide, soft shadows on the rock-strewn banks. Halston said, "Someone should watch over the horses."

Jae almost offered, then remembered that Halston needed her map. Nobody else volunteered at first.

Finally, Lorelin gave in. "I'll do it, but if you find any jewels to go with the gold, I get the first pick."

"Wouldn't dream of giving first pick to anybody else," Hodge said with a wink.

Jae took out her map, and the search for the bear tree began. "Look closely at the trunks," Jae called to the others as they paced nearby, scouring the tree trunks. "Check for scratches. Chunks of missing bark."

She found it about ten yards from the horses—a thick, sturdy fir tree, its shredded bark beaded with golden sap. "Over here!"

The others hurried uphill, Gryff at the lead. They bid Lorelin goodbye, then started their five-hundred-pace trek. Onward.

Jae counted the paces under her breath. At one hundred, the river curved away from them, and soon, its rush softened into a faint whisper. At two hundred, Lorelin and the horses were out of sight.

They moved ahead. Jae looked forward, side-to-side, then back. The woods were quiet, and the shadows thickened. The trees grew close together here, like headstones in a cramped graveyard. They shoved past low-hanging branches and crowded mounds of green-ery. Jae listened for a songbird or chattering squirrels, but nothing came of it. All was still.

She ran a finger along her map. The gold spot moved east with them, but there wasn't a structure in sight, as Halston had suspected. If they kept going in this direction, they'd only wind up marching through more forest.

A sudden pang of unease hit her. Her boots felt like weights, urging her to bolt herself to the earth. She sank her teeth into her cheeks as chills poured over her skin. Jae swore she heard some-thing humming, a soft drone beneath the earth. Breathing out, she crinkled her hair next to her ears to have something else to listen to. Maybe it was just a product of her discomfort.

When she was younger, she'd wondered if the forest could speak. Not in the way humans did, with voices and language and written let-ters, but in songs of its own. The sighs of its wind, the calls of its creatures, the way the earth and growing things seemed to answer to a person's touch.

Jae felt the forest whispering to her.

And it told her that they weren't supposed to be here.

Jae stopped. "Hold on." The others halted in their tracks.

This area was more open than what they'd just hiked through, but still dense with shadows. A small hill rose before them, and there were large, gray rocks and fat logs scattered around the trees. On all the other sides of them, the forest continued like a vast ocean.

Pointing to the gold spot on her map, Jae said, "Look. We ain't near anybody's property like we thought. Just empty woods."

"Ain't that a good thing?" asked Hodge.

Jae's muscles went tense. She looked around at the trees, which seemed to glare down at her like she had blood on her hands. "We— Sterling really told you that this was a *gift?*"

Halston said, "I try not question him."

Why the hell not? "That doesn't sound like an ideal way to make your way in the world."

"We take what he gives us, alright?" said Halston. She must've shot him a slight glare, because he raised his voice. "He has something valuable of ours. We need him, but the moment he decides he's done with us, he can toss us to the rails for all he cares."

"Calm down, kid," Gryff said with a frown.

There was something Halston wasn't telling her, and Jae wished that it didn't bother her... but it did.

Before she could say anything else, a new voice beat her to it. She jumped as it drifted over the earth, speaking words she didn't quite catch.

She'd cocked her revolver before she was even aware of the action. Hodge followed her lead. Had someone followed them here?

Up ahead, a ghostly bluish light hovered beneath the trees. There stood the blurry figure of a man, raising a hand at them. Jae could stare straight through him and still make out the outlines of the pines behind him.

Hodge pointed his gun at the man.

"Stop!" Jae shouted, waving her hands. "Stop!"

Jae hurried toward the figure. His form was so hazy, she could barely make out his face.

This was no ghost. Ghosts moved stiffly, like their limbs were partly frozen. Despite his faint glow, this man's motions were as life-like as anyone who still had skin and bones.

"A memory," Jae whispered. "A Wyrdrian memory," she said, her tongue almost tripping over the word.

"Wyrdrian?" asked Hodge.

"The Rangers," Gryff broke in. "I... I didn't think it was true. The early ones had... some sort of language. They spoke memories into the land."

Jae had seen memories before, winking like trails of steam in Banderra's woods, but she'd never seen one this far south. Glimpses of the past, they were, that men of old planted for all to see, to live in the world long after they'd died.

A tear welled up in the corner of Jae's eye. She'd never known this man, but the apprehension on his ghostly face summoned a breath of resolve in her. She stifled her fear and braced herself to listen to him closely. Jae stood before the flickering memory like she was bound up to it. The man's figure quivered, disappeared for a minute, then rose again like smoke from a candle. A muffled sound came from him. He raised his hand, and vanished once more.

"Did he..." Hodge stammered, "did the *memory* say anything?"

For a moment, Jae held still. She waited, hoping the memory would reappear. At last, she choked out her answer. "He said... 'Turn back.'"

The Rangers used memories to talk to each other. They could tell future travelers where to find food, point out caves where they could stay the night, or warn them about nearby dangers.

"I'm going back," said Jae.

Gryff looked to Hodge. Hodge looked to Halston. Halston said, "We're on a mission."

Jae's mouth fell open. "This fella here is *warning* us! Does that mean nothing to you?"

"It's from the past, isn't it?" Halston said. "How do we know that whatever he saw is still here?" He didn't sound sure of himself, as he so often did. He sounded more like a lost soul trying to breathe truth into his words, even if he knew better.

"Are you *crazy?*" Jae blurted. "You're really gonna take that chance, Halston?"

Halston stood a few yards away from her, and his answer was

soft, but she could still make it out. "Whatever it is, it won't be worse than what Sterling has in store for us if we fail."

The memory appeared again and announced his warning. *"Turn back, turn back."*

Jae spun on her heels and walked back the way they came.

"Where are you going?" asked Halston.

"I told you, I'm *leaving*," said Jae. *"Goodbye."*

"Remember our deal," Halston told her.

Damn the deal! "Are y'all comin' with me? Or are you gonna walk into danger's wake to please your scumbag boss?"

No answer.

She turned around and kept walking.

———

Jae wasn't out of sight yet. Hodge and the others stood there, watching her move back toward the river.

Hodge turned to his brother. Halston had a blank, icy look on his face, one that Hodge saw most often when they met with Sterling.

Hodge didn't want to admit it, but he said, "She's right."

Halston breathed out. "Sterling won't bargain if we come back without the statue. Damned if we do, damned if we don't." He paused. "Tell you what. We'll scout the area. Any immediate signs of danger and we'll leave."

Save for the Wyrdrian memory, nothing looked out of place. "Gryff, you know about memories, right?" asked Hodge.

"Sure. Heard a bit about 'em, at least. Like I said, I didn't know they were real."

"How long do you think this one's been here?"

"Don't know," said Gryff. "But I heard that there ain't anyone left who speaks the language. I'm guessin' this one's been here for years."

"Damn, Gryff, why didn't you say so?" asked Hodge. "Should I go get Jae?"

"No," Halston murmured, taking a few steps forward. "She won't change her mind."

They'd lost count of the paces, so they just kept trekking in the same direction. No more than two minutes passed before they spied the boulder, jutting out on the crest of a large hill that rose like a tide on the forest floor. Hodge thrust his pointer finger in its direction. "There it is!"

A jolt in the ground sent them stumbling in their path.

Before any of them could move again, the ground began to stir. Their feet stumbled across the earth, trying to catch their balance. The smell of rot and singed flesh wafted from the surface.

Three figures emerged from the loam, soil rolling off their bodies, thin as starving deer. They shuddered and twitched for a moment before standing. Tattered capes dangled like shrouds from their shoulders. Beneath their cloaks, bones and teeth and feathers and hair covered their chests. Their heads weren't much more than skulls wrapped in graying flesh—one resembled an owl, one a bull, and the last one, a ram. Each of them carried a long-bladed spear in a clawed, skeletal hand. The jagged blades didn't *look* very sharp, but Hodge didn't dare get his hopes up.

Son of a bitch, they should've turned back.

The owl hissed.

"*Trespassers,*" the creatures shrieked. Their voices were wailing, brittle, snapping like twigs in a fire and grating down Hodge's spine.

They took off. Halston whipped out his gun and fired back at them. The bullet slammed into the ram's shoulder, its bone splintering. It lurched back for a second, then jerked itself forward.

Hodge's hands fumbled over his hips and waist, desperate to draw his guns. His chest flamed. Finally, he took hold of one pistol as Halston shouted, "*Get to high ground!*"

Gryff flipped his rifle from over his shoulder, jumped forward, and swung. The butt of the gun crashed into the ram's neck, which then let out a sharp crack. The ram tumbled to the ground, limbs flailing. Before it could move again, Gryff lifted his rifle and brought it down on the creature's head. Its horned skull split down the middle. Gryff hiked his rifle back up in both hands, then hurried to station himself behind a boulder.

Hodge raced halfway up the hill and grabbed a tree branch. He began to scale the pine, trying to find a solid limb where he could perch. Halston hurried around the tree and braced himself behind the trunk, firing at the last two monsters.

"*Trespassers, trespassers!*" they squawked.

Hodge raised his pistol. The hammer clicked, then he aimed and fired twice. One bullet found the owl's shoulder, and the other plowed through its gut. Black blood seeped from the wounds. Halston put a bullet in its thigh, then another by its neck. Still, the creature shrieked and writhed.

"Damn it!" Hodge fired once more. The bullet plowed through the owl's head. Sinking to its knees, it rattled its arms for a second... then went still.

The bull's head perked up. Its black eyes flicked from Halston's spot to Gryff's head poking out from behind the boulder. It raised its spear, screamed, then charged toward Gryff.

Hodge shot. The bullet skimmed the creature's chest, scattering a few feathers into the air, but it kept running. Gryff's rifle boomed twice. Each shot plowed through the monster's stomach. It stumbled for a moment both times, then snarled and pushed forward again.

Gryff shot a third time, but the monster had reached him. The bull clubbed its spearhead against Gryff's rifle, and the gun fell from his hands.

Hodge aimed and shot again... but the pistol did not jolt.

He cursed.

Empty.

Gryff reached out and grabbed the bull by the horns. Its clawed hands reached to pry Gryff's fingers away. The creature slashed at him. Gryff cried out, then fell. Hodge glimpsed Gryff's blood pooling on his scaly forearms before he started rolling down the hill. The monster picked up its spear and followed him.

Hodge leapt from the tree.

The ground struck his knees, the impact hot as fire. He let out a pained yelp as the force tore through him, but he got to his feet all the same. Nothing felt broken.

"Hodge!" Halston swerved past him with an outstretched hand. Hodge took it, Halston helped him to his feet, and they raced in Gryff's direction. Hodge drew his knife and held it ready.

The Azmarian lay at the foot of two more rocks, groaning, trying to push himself forward. The bull stood a yard away from Gryff, pumping its spear in its arms. Halston raised his gun, braced to fire.

Three shots sounded from the east. Two black spots exploded in the monster's chest, one in its neck. The bull wailed. Before it could take another step, a fourth bullet struck its spear, and the weapon fell to the ground.

Halston shot at its knees, and the noise was like knives in Hodge's ears. The beast lurched, then fell. It shuddered on the ground, long fingers grasping at the sky, its legs a broken mess.

They were close enough to see its eyes now. Tar-black, but pricked by small beads of light, glowing like coals in a dying fire.

The final shot came from the east. This one ripped through the bull's temple, blood pouring into its inky eyes. The monster stretched out its arms and screeched like steel grinding on stone, then collapsed.

Hodge and Halston stood above it, their breathing heavy. The creature lay still, nothing more than a bloody heap.

Gryff moaned and got to his feet. "Damn things oughta learn to mind their own business…"

Hodge looked east. Jae stood several yards away, brandishing a smoking revolver, her face white as sun-blanched bark.

Hodge shook, trying to slow his breathing. Black blood soaked the earth. He could almost feel the monster's bony hands on his shoulders.

Jae paced over to the corpse of the bull and craned her neck, her braids swinging over the beast's broken limbs. "I've never seen one of these before."

"What *are* they?" asked Halston.

"Lorthans. My Pa told me about them. Told me that… warlocks and witches could create these. No brains to speak of. They'll do whatever their warlock demands." She prodded the body with the toe of her boot.

"I guess, in this case…" Halston said slowly, "it was to fight off trespassers."

"So, poor saps like us," murmured Hodge. "Wonderful. A warning from Sterling would've been real swell."

Perhaps in Sterling's eyes, this was no different than sending them on any other heist. It wasn't as if they were ever safe, really. Hodge just wished Sterling had enough gods-damn dignity to tell the truth.

He walked in Jae's direction, still clutching his knife, then stopped beside the bull. Hodge's stomach sank at the sight of the teeth and bones covering its chest. It looked helpless in death, silly even, like a heap of waste thrown out by a butcher. "Who in their right mind would make one of these?"

"Madmen," said Jae. "This here is wicked magic. My Pa told me about a warlock in Monvallea who tried to make a lorthan out of cow bones and pig flesh. When his neighbors found out, they stuck him with a pitchfork and burned his corpse, his house, and his barn for good measure."

Hodge snorted. "Lovely."

Gryff looked around. "Stand your ground. Let's look for the statue and get out of here."

The statue was the last of Hodge's worries, now, but he doubted any of them wanted to walk away from this with empty hands.

In the corner of his eye, Hodge glimpsed a large, dark shape looming in the treetops, the thin outline of a spear resting in its hand. He saw it a second too late.

"Hodge!" cried Jae.

Her weight slammed into him, bringing them both down to the earth. Hodge's hands fumbled with his knife, then closed around the blade. The steel slashed through his skin, and the wet warmth of blood spread across his palms.

Hodge ate the dust. Face down, he could see nothing, but the sound of screeching and gunfire thundered above him. At last, another heap of weight thudded on the ground. Jae gasped, her breath hot on the back of Hodge's neck.

Hodge groaned. "Damn it, Sterling…"

Jae rose. Hodge sat up, wiping the dirt off his face with the back of his hand.

"Hodge!" Jae touched his wrists, holding them gently. "Oh, gods, I didn't—"

Hodge winced, drawing his hands back. He raised them to his eye-level, biting his lip. Two thin gashes ran along his left palm, one on his right. Further up the slope, another lorthan lay dead. It had a narrow snout and long, twisted horns, like an antelope.

Halston ran for Hodge. "Hodge!"

"I'm fine," Hodge said, gritting his teeth. "I was holding my knife when she knocked me out of the way. Cut my hands. I'll be alright. Gods. What happened?"

Jae motioned to the fresh corpse. "Jumped out of a tree back there. I shot it in midair." She took a waterskin out of her coat, then poured cool water over Hodge's hands. Halston helped Hodge tie a pair of spare bandanas around each wound, knotting them securely.

"Thanks," Hodge said to Jae. "For... y'know."

Jae smiled, though her eyes still looked weary. "Uh... don't mention it. You okay?"

"Yeah, I'm fine." Hodge stood. "Well, we may as well finish those last dozen paces. I'll dig the hole myself if it means we can be done with this damn job sooner. Everyone keep your guns ready."

They moved uphill toward the boulder. It was every bit as knobby as it was in the picture. It resembled a plump man with a small head, tucking his arms into his chest. Weeds grew in its shade, their stems motionless, without a breeze to rustle them.

They strode downhill for about twenty paces and reached a wall of bushes and short, scruffy trees. Hodge was the first to burst through the shrubbery and into a clearing. Sure enough, there grew a spruce tree with a songbird etched into the trunk.

Before the tree lay a mound of bare earth. Here they were.

Gryff took the shovel out of his pack. "Let's get this over with."

Gryff took care of most of it, but the others did what they could, sweeping the dirt away or occasionally taking a turn. Hodge kept his eye out for more lorthans, but the forest was still and calm as ever each time he checked.

It wasn't long before the shovel slammed into a chunk of wood, no more than three feet beneath the surface. Digging, tossing, dusting, they brushed the earth away from the box. It was made out of branches of all colors. White aspen, golden oak, and dark walnut, bound together with shabby twine.

Halston's palm grazed the lid. "This looks like a coffin."

Jae grunted. "If it's a life-sized statue, I guess a coffin *would* make sense."

For a moment, there was silence, then Halston asked, "What if Sterling sent us to rob a grave?"

"Wouldn't be the first thing he failed to mention," muttered Hodge. He lowered one bandana, peeking at his scratches. They were sticky, which meant they were already scabbing over. A good sign. Hopefully they wouldn't scar. "I've got an idea. Let's just peek inside. If it's a body, we leave. If it's gold, we take it."

They all waited for someone to volunteer to open it.

Hodge sighed and reached into the hole. "Y'all owe me." Oh, well. This wouldn't be the first time he saw a dead person, if this really was a grave.

He looked around for a latch, hinges... something to open the box. Then, he found the two lengths of twine that held the lid down. He drew his knife and cut them. The string was so brittle it snapped at the slightest touch of the blade. When he'd severed all of it, he took a breath and lifted the lid.

There was no statue. There wasn't any gold, cursed or not cursed, or magic jewels.

There weren't any bones, either.

Inside was a girl.

Long hair, oval face, a small nose... young, too. Her skin was brown and firm, with a youthful, healthy glow.

His heart jumped when he looked down from her face.

Because her chest... *rose and fell.*

He pressed his fingers to her wrist. It was warm, and he could feel her blood pulsing in her veins. He held his palm over her nose. Her breath was soft on his skin. When he took his hand away, her inky eyes stared back at him.

They both screamed.

Chapter 18

odge fell back.

The girl shot up straight, dust flying from her skin. She shouted something in a language he did not understand, then leapt from the coffin.

The others jumped back as she sprinted north, bound for the river. Hodge got to his feet, pulled himself up, then ran after her. He couldn't stop himself from calling out. "Wait!"

They followed her all the way to the river. Light on her feet, she raced to the water's edge, then skittered back, spilling onto the shore. Her palms broke her fall, and she scooted away from the water. Black hair flying, she whirled in their direction, then raised her hands and sobbed. "Please don't hurt me."

Halston shook his head. "It's alright. We aren't going to hurt you."

Swallowing, she stared at them with up-tilted eyes. She was short and slight, with small hands and narrow shoulders, and she looked to be about sixteen years old. A blue and white pattern decorated her buckskin shirt, the colors bright as a summer sky. The girl cupped her elbows in her hands, shuddering. "Who are you?"

Halston spoke softly. "We didn't mean to alarm you. I'm Halston, and this is my brother Hodge. That's Gryff and Jae."

"What's your name?" asked Gryff.

The girl thought about it for a long moment, then replied, "Tsashin." *Saw-sheen.* "Shining Water."

"Do you remember how you got into that hole?" asked Hodge. He wished he could tell her there was nothing to be afraid of, but after leaping from a coffin guarded by monsters... he wasn't sure how much truth there'd be to that statement.

She shut her eyes tightly, like the sun had burned them. "Men laughing around me. Wicked. Running. Shouting. Something covered me." With each word, she shivered more. She cradled her head in her hands. "Darkness. And nothing else."

Tsashin opened her eyes stared across the treetops, moving her head as if she were reading them. "How did you wake me?"

"We don't know. Opened the box, I guess," Hodge explained. He thought about asking her if she'd heard of Sterling, but the poor girl seemed scared to death. They had to get out of here. To somewhere safe.

"Come on," Hodge urged. "We need to get out of these woods. There were monsters guarding where you were."

Tsashin's face fell. "*Monsters?*"

Hodge bit his lip. He had to be more careful when he spoke to her. "No. I mean, they're gone now. But let's get out of here and set up camp."

Tsashin's lips parted. She straightened her back, her hands trembling. "Are... they... still there?"

"No," said Jae. "We took care of them. It's safe now."

"What kind of monsters?"

"Lorthans," said Jae.

Tsashin frowned. "I don't know what those are."

"So you didn't know they were surroundin' you?" asked Gryff.

"No."

"Come on," Hodge said. "We've got some food and firewood. We'll help you figure this out."

Hugging her forearms to her stomach, she took a step toward Hodge. They made their way back to the horses. Tsashin trailed beside Hodge as they made their way east, following the river. Nobody wanted to see those monsters again, dead or alive.

Jae asked, "Can you tell us where you're from?"

"No," said Tsashin. "All I can think of is… fog."

Jae's face softened, her eyes heavy with worry. "There's quilling on your shirt. Are you from the Lapahi tribe? I've seen designs like that on their clothes before."

"Lapahi?" Tsashin said slowly, with a hint of tiredness in her voice. "No."

Hodge swallowed. "What *do* you remember?"

"No names," Tsashin said without looking at him. "No names, no faces, no places. Only fear."

At last, they reached the clearing where Lorelin waited with the horses. Lorelin gasped, then put a hand to her lips when her gaze fell on the small, shivering girl. "What *happened?*"

Hodge muttered, "Oh, y'know. Got attacked by monsters with spears. Turns out there was no statue. Gonna have a word with Sterling when we see him."

Halston gave Lorelin a more sophisticated explanation.

Tsashin's fingers twitched across her stomach. "Where are we going?" she asked, her voice not much stronger than a whisper.

"Well," Halston started. "We have to meet with our boss tomorrow night. But after that, we can try to find a way to get you home." To the others, he probably looked as sure as anyone could be in a situation like this, but Hodge knew better. He saw the whirlwind spinning behind his brother's eyes.

Tsashin said, "I don't know where home is." She pressed her fingertips to her scalp. "I think someone's screaming. Do you hear it?"

Hodge frowned. "I—no."

She shut her eyes. "Something swallowed me. You set me free."

Hodge wished there was something he could say. Something to comfort her. An answer. But that was far from their reach.

They set up camp in sight of the river, where the grass grew thick and soft. Tsashin wandered in circles as Gryff snapped his flint over the woodpile. Sometimes, Tsashin would stop for a moment and press her hands to her stomach, or whisper something in her language. The glassy, faraway look never left her eyes. Finally, she settled a few yards away from the fire, hugged her knees up to her chest, and began to cry softly.

Lorelin hurried up to her, Jae close behind. Hodge followed them. Lorelin passed Tsashin a mound of blankets and said, "It's going to be alright, Tsashin. You're safe here."

Jae added, "We'll figure this out."

Tsashin took the blankets readily and hugged them to her body. The night was warm enough, but she swaddled herself like she'd just crawled out of a snowbank, and shivered.

"You alright?" Hodge whispered.

Tsashin said nothing.

Hodge fetched two plates of food—squirrel meat and mallow greens—then sat with her again. Tsashin finished her plate like she hadn't eaten in years. When Hodge thought about it, he wondered if she really *hadn't* eaten in years.

Hodge told her something Elias said all the time. "Tomorrow's comin'. It'll be alright, if we all stick together." He didn't always believe it, but it had often helped him feel a little less afraid.

Tsashin pursed her lips. "Thank you."

Carefully, Hodge studied her face. Her brown eyes were still foggy, and damp streaks trailed down her cheeks.

"We've got business to take care of," he said. "But we'll do what we can to get you home. I promise." He almost bit his tongue. *Promise.* What was he thinking? He couldn't promise anything.

"Thank you." She touched her cheek. With that, she lay on her side, huddled in the blankets, and went to sleep.

Anger flared in Hodge's stomach. Did Sterling have something to do with this? Did he know who'd buried Tsashin here and taken her memory? Who would do this to an innocent girl? There had to be answers.

Hodge, Lorelin, and Jae paced back to the fire. "Well, she's scared to death."

"Don't blame her," murmured Jae.

Halston glanced Tsashin's way. "She said she isn't from the Lapahi tribe."

Jae rubbed her chin. "Maybe she's from the Ayahe tribe. Or the Yunah. The Tanaa nation ain't far, either."

Gryff sighed. "So we'll be hard-pressed to find her family, won't we?"

Grimly, Jae nodded. "Big tribes. All of 'em."

"Maybe she'll remember her family if we give her time," said Lorelin. "Poor thing. She's terrified. Maybe she just needs a few days to rest. Then it'll come back to her."

"What if it doesn't?" asked Hodge.

Nobody had anything to say about that. They sat quietly for a few moments, watching embers escape into the night and listening to the wood crackling under the flames. Hodge watched a little black bug climb up a blade of grass, then settle at the tip and stop, as if waiting for someone else to talk.

Hodge spoke up again. "If no one else is gonna say it, I will: Sterling lied to us."

"He might not have known," Halston replied.

Hodge shook his head. Sterling was no fool, and Halston knew it. "Sterling's never given us false information before. He knew. He threw us to those monsters like scraps to the wolves, Hal. I mean, *shit,* doesn't that at least *bother* you?"

Halston skirted around the question, as he often did. "Of course it does. What matters is that we made it out alive. We got Tsashin out of there. Even if Sterling *did* know about the lorthans, then—"

"Damn it, Hal, don't be a bootlicker."

Halston sputtered. "I ain't—I'm *not...*" He sighed and hid his face in one hand. "It's not for much longer, Hodge. We're close to finishing our time with him."

"There *was* no statue," Hodge said. "And we've gotta face him tomorrow without it. I ain't in the mood for a beating, or to have a hot iron shoved in my face or whatever else Sterling's got up his sleeve. Yeah, we made it out safe today, but that ain't gonna matter when Sterling finds out we failed!"

Halston drew back. Hodge bit his lip, wishing he could reel in what he'd just yelled, like that would blot it all away.

Of course, Halston feared what was going to happen. He just kept that fear buried deep.

"Stop it," said Lorelin. "Hodge, calm down. Halston, listen to me. Shouting about tomorrow won't solve this mess."

Jae sat up, pushing her brown braids behind her shoulders. "Sterling said he got that map from someone who *knew* whoever buried the statue. Not saying it's ideal, but... maybe he'll have an idea about the fella who put Tsashin there. Where she came from."

"He's got his sights set on the statue," Halston added. "If whoever put Tsashin there replaced the statue with her, I'm sure he'll be *eager* to find the man."

"We ain't leaving her with Sterling," Hodge said.

"I'm not suggesting that," said Halston. "But maybe he'll have an answer."

Hodge tried not to look at Halston again. Sometimes, when he looked at his brother, it was too much for him. There were days where Halston just looked... *different*. They used to be able to read each other with ease. Hodge feared that one day, Halston would look like a stranger to him.

"Yeah, yeah," Hodge murmured. "But if you don't tell Sterling we ain't putting up with this again, I will."

To his surprise, Halston said nothing. As a matter of fact, no one did.

Hodge took the first watch. He wasn't much in the mood for sleeping. As everyone else drifted off, he caught himself watching the stars as they rose and sank across the sky, his mind flying every which way. The darkness watched him sitting and thinking, and he stared right back. There was something welcoming about it—a moment's peace after a day of surprises.

He wondered what Elias would say right now. He'd probably know exactly what to do.

Whether he'd known it or not, Sterling hadn't sent them to a buried treasure. He'd sent them to a tomb.

When they buried Elias, they'd dug a grave near the river where he'd drowned. No coffin. No headstone—just a boulder in the woods.

Hodge would probably never see that grave again.

"I wish you were here," he whispered, hoping no one was listening.

During the day, Hodge kept Elias off his mind. It did no good to think about him on the road. He didn't want the others to think him weak, getting all bleary-eyed on a ride. But Hodge did think about him at night, whenever he took the watch. He had to. If he didn't, he feared that he'd forget the sound of Elias's voice.

Once, Lorelin had told him that eventually the grief would go away and the memories of Elias would only bring him fondness. The grief hadn't faded, nor had the fondness come.

He snorted. *Look at me. Thinking like a fool and wishing things were different.* Maybe part of him believed things *could* be different. And every time, he remembered how stupid it was to consider it.

Regardless, tomorrow would come, whether or not he wished for it. That was all that mattered. Nothing to do but get through it.

Chapter 19

Jae woke early the next morning. She took a few moments to listen to the river's strain and the forest's creatures chirping to each other. She sat up, smoothed the flyaway hairs back against her braids, and donned her hat. Halston sat before the fire pit, piling tinder on top of last night's ashes. A layer of dew speckled the ground, and the sky was bright and blue.

Halston glanced at her, then turned back to the firewood. "I want to speak with you."

Jae pushed her blankets down and stood. She raised an eyebrow. "Do you?"

"Yesterday," said Halston. "Thank you for coming back. For helping take out the last lorthan. But you turned your back on us."

"I didn't..." She drummed her fingers against her thigh, thinking of the right thing to say. "Yeah, I walked away. The Rangers used Wyrdrian to *warn* each other. I've seen those memories before, Halston. They don't just put them there for no reason." *Sorry you had to learn that the hard way.*

"When we met, you told me you were used to working alone." Halston snapped the flint over the wood. The sparks jumped to the twigs and winked into a small flame. "That won't cut it here. You don't walk away from the others. And *Hodge*. He got hurt because of you."

"Excuse me?"

"You jumped on him while he was holding his knife."

"I did what I could!" Jae blurted out, throwing up her hands. "I didn't see the knife in his hands! I saw the lorthan jumping his way, and I did what I had to do!"

"We're lucky that knife didn't slip between his ribs!"

"Well, it didn't! And we're *all* damn lucky those lorthans didn't crack our skulls!" Jae's arms fell to her sides. Halston stared back at her with that stupid, stony look of his. Jae murmured, "This ain't workin'."

"What?" said Halston.

"Nothing." She touched her bandages. They'd gone a little loose overnight. Lorelin had cleaned them before they went to bed and said the wound was healing nicely. "Why do you work for Sterling if you're so scared of him, anyway? Why put us all in danger because you want to please him?"

Halston blinked. "I beg your pardon?"

He's a wicked, rotten man. He's burned towns and shot down folks who stood in his way, and he disappears every time. And you put money in his pocket.

Jae cursed herself, knowing that she'd had a hand in it, too. She'd faced Sterling and let him be. She wasn't blameless.

"You could leave, y'know," she said. "Get away from him."

"He'd find us."

"How do you know?" she asked. "You don't. But you choose to stay with him, and—"

"You think I have a *choice?*"

She breathed out, trying to stop the heat rising to her head. Halston did not have a fierce glare. It was a mild one, like the one Pa gave her when she used to get herself in trouble.

She was wasting time here. The day before, she'd wanted to be angry. Angry at Halston for taking this job, angry at Sterling for giving it to him, angry at herself for diving headfirst into this mess. But as she'd stared at the lorthans' broken bodies on the forest floor, she could only bask in her own relief.

Now she was angry. Pa was waiting for her, and here she was on a trail helping a gang collaborate with another crew of outlaws. She was no closer to becoming a Ranger. Served her right for spending this much time in the company of robbers.

Halston stood and brushed off his pants. "Gryff set up a few snare traps last night. I'm going to go check them. Consider what I said, alright? Think about whether you really want to be here." He walked away from the camp and stepped into the trees.

When he was far enough away, Jae swallowed the deepest breath she possibly could, then sat down.

Even after fighting monsters and tackling Hodge yesterday, her wound hadn't popped open. Maybe Lorelin would lend her some alcohol to keep it clean.

She had to leave.

She wouldn't turn them in. They'd saved her during the bank heist, and she wouldn't forget that kindness as long as she lived. She didn't have the heart to turn them in now, but she didn't belong here. It was time to find a new bounty to go after.

Besides, if she told the Rangers the location of one of Sterling Byrd's hideouts, maybe they'd finally catch him. Perhaps some good would come out of this after all.

Their camp was just two stones' throws from the river. Jae made her way down to the banks, hoping its sweet song and cool water would help clear her head.

Jae stepped over a cluster of damp greenery, then planted her feet on the short, muddy bank. A few yards away, a small figure stood beneath a ponderosa tree, hands resting on the trunk. Tsashin.

The dark-haired girl raised her head to the open sky. Water droplets beaded on her face. Whether they were tears or river mist, Jae couldn't tell.

"Tsashin?"

Without turning toward Jae, Tsashin said, "I'd hoped my dreams would give me answers. Last night, I had one where the walls sealed me in, shrinking until they crushed my chest. I felt confined." She breathed out, shoulders trembling.

Jae wasn't sure what to say. "We'll help you. However we can."

Tsashin swallowed. "Thank you. For the kindness you've shown me." Her fingers skimmed the ponderosa's bark. "I told myself that I mustn't be afraid. But time has been stolen from me. Years of it, perhaps."

She breathed in, pushing on her chest as though forcing the air in. She said something Jae didn't quite catch, but it might have been "lost."

And just like that, Jae felt Tsashin's fear, and the anger that came with it. Who had put Tsashin there? Why? Jae couldn't think of anything much worse than being crammed—still breathing—into a box and buried. What reason would anyone, even a warlock, have for this?

Jae asked, "Is there anything you remember about your home? Anything at all?

Tsashin said, "I remember what I wanted to be when I left."

"What's that?"

"A storyteller."

"Go on."

"I remember a few legends," Tsashin began. "Though I don't

remember who told them to me. When I woke last night, I repeated them until I grew tired." She paused. "I remember what it felt like. To wake up in that hole, with no memory of how I got there. It fills my head with fear." She shuddered, then closed her eyes.

And before she could stop herself, Jae said, "I'm leaving today. You could come with me."

There. She'd spoken it and made it true. She'd leave before the mess thickened.

Tsashin turned, looking bewildered. "Leaving?"

"Yeah." Jae cleared her throat. "The Harney boys and I made a deal, but... I'm starting to think it's not for me. It'll be best for everyone if I go."

"*I* don't think it would be best," said Tsashin. "I think they would miss you."

Jae forced herself to laugh. "Nah. I... I don't think they would."

"Of course they would." Something close to a smile lifted Tsashin's mouth. "Hodge told me it's better if we all stick together."

Jae was tempted to tell her that Hodge was not the most knowledgeable sort, but she couldn't argue with what he'd said. Strength did come in numbers, but Jae had always been strong enough on her own. "Maybe," said Jae. "But... it's something I gotta do."

Tsashin tugged at her sleeve. "You don't sound certain."

Jae said nothing.

"You're angry," said Tsashin.

"Huh?"

"The way you're holding yourself. Your muscles are stiff." Gently, she went on. "You shouldn't make great decisions when your head is fogged with frustration."

Jae wanted to argue. But it was sound advice.

Tsashin's eyes wandered back to the river. "You should wait a while. Let your anger fade away before you leave. *If* you leave. I can't tell if you really want to go."

"I *do* want to go," said Jae. "Don't you?"

"No," said Tsashin. "I'm going to stay. Your band saved my life. I want to talk to… Sterling is his name, yes?"

"Yeah." Jae exhaled, then took in a long, deep breath. "Tsashin…"

"I know what you're going to say," Tsashin said. "But I spoke to Halston this morning. I don't fear Sterling. What I fear is spending more time not knowing… who I am, where I came from, why I was left to sleep in that hole. If he has even part of an answer for me, then I want to speak to him."

Jae had nothing else to say. If Tsashin had her mind made up, then Jae had no right to try and sway it. Besides, in good faith, Jae couldn't tell Tsashin that staying with this gang was a mess waiting to happen, or that it was lunacy, because she was doing the same thing.

Jae rubbed her neck and realized that Tsashin was right—she *was* clenching her muscles. "Bye," she murmured, and headed back to the camp.

Halston would be back any second, and she didn't want an interrogation if she left this morning. Tonight, they'd meet Sterling. Jae would offer to watch the horses, and then she'd be on her way. It would be easier to leave with no goodbyes.

Jae rolled up her bedroll and tied it off with twine. She wanted to speak to Lorelin again, and to find a way to properly thank the gang for saving her life. And to see Tsashin's memory return somehow.

But Pa was waiting for her.

This past month had brought her nothing but trouble. She didn't mind flirting with danger if it got her closer to the Outlands, but the trouble she'd found with the Harneys was different. Once, Pa had told her that when he was her age, trouble was sweeter to him than honey. Was this what he'd meant? Or was she just getting stupid?

Halston came back, then, carrying a few ropes. Jae guessed they'd had no luck with the snares. If he tried to rekindle the argument, she wouldn't even spare him a glance. She turned her back to him, but he just rustled in his saddlebags before starting to rouse the others.

Maybe Tsashin was right about anger fogging her mind.

No matter, though. The roads she and Halston traveled were just too different. Letting them run alongside each other this long would just brew more trouble for the both of them.

They'd saved her life, and she couldn't forget that. Pa had always told her that if someone did you a kindness, you should return it. If Jae left, she wouldn't have a chance to do that... but perhaps leaving was a kindness in itself.

Chapter 20

Nobody spoke much that day. Halston tried to hold himself steady, to keep from losing his composure.

Sterling was not *incapable* of mercy. When Jae had covered for them at their last muster, Sterling had shaken the matter away. Would that happen again?

In the end, it probably wouldn't matter. Until Sterling released them from their debt, things would not change.

As evening came, Halston glimpsed a crumbling stone tower above the treetops. Moss and vines covered the broken walls, joining the ruins to the forest itself, sweeps and arches of silver and green.

He wondered what Mourelle had looked like, long ago. It had been a large, sprawling manor before, but now it had a new life. The wind-stripped walls were home to moldering foundations, rampant vines, and criminal negotiations.

When he was a boy, he and his brothers had roamed in halls of stone not unlike these. Halston never spoke of them. Those memories belonged to another life, another time.

The past slowed you down if you fed it too much, but often, he caught himself fanning its flames.

They dismounted several dozen yards outside the walls and tethered the horses in a thicket of spruce trees. They looked like small, blue children beside the towering ponderosas.

Jae loosely slung her reins around a branch. "I'm watching the horses."

"What?" said Halston.

"I'm staying here," Jae went on. "You said it yourself—this could take a while. Someone ought to stay with them."

Fine. After bickering with her earlier, he was in no mood to argue again. "Suit yourself," he muttered, draping his reins over a branch and knotting them tightly.

They approached Mourelle's entrance, which was little more than a crooked arch. Something lurched in Halston's stomach. He always felt this way before meeting with Sterling, but it was far worse this time. Heavier.

He wished that Sterling was predictable. Then, at the very least, Halston could better prepare himself for what was to come.

"Hey," said Gryff. "I know what you're thinkin'."

"You do?" asked Halston.

"Yeah. This didn't go as planned. Things almost never do." Gryff cleared his throat. "You're good with words, kid. This was outta your control. Tell him that."

"I will," said Halston. "But even if he accepts it, it's a hollow victory."

Gryff's chuckle was joyless. "There ain't no victories out here. Not really."

They paused outside the entrance, exchanging brief nods with one another. Ready as they'd ever be. Lorelin kept her hand on Tsashin's shoulder. Tsashin did not look fearful so much as lost, as though she'd been wandering in the forest for days.

Halston inhaled the mountain air and stepped inside.

The gang moved across the wide room, standing shoulder to shoulder in a close-packed line. Halston stood in the center, with Tsashin at the farthest end. The pointed ceiling rose high above their heads, and moonlight streamed in through the misshapen windows. Thin shadows of pine needles on branches danced on the stone floor.

For once, Sterling and his party were the first ones there. Shadows cloaked their bodies. Sterling's expression was vacant, perfectly unreadable. A prickle of fear ran up Halston's spine.

He pushed it away and started with the pleasantries. "Good evening, gentlemen."

Sterling's dark eyes smiled at them, then his gaze leapt to Tsashin. His grin widened, teeth brimming under his lips like a snarling wolf. "Good evening. I take it the jobs went well?"

"The first one did." Halston passed him the sack of money from the bank.

Sterling took the sack without even glancing at it, as if he hardly cared for its contents at all. Wasn't he going to count the bills?

Halston breathed in, then forced himself to deliver the news. "The dig was unsuccessful. There was no statue in the hole."

"I know that," said Sterling with disturbing serenity. "Everything I need is already here."

Halston blinked, trying to make sense of Sterling's words. Halston thought he'd been clear. Was there something Sterling didn't understand?

Tsashin stayed close to Lorelin, but she spoke more loudly than usual. "Sterling Byrd," she said. "My name is Tsashin. They found me in a tomb, where you sent them to find your treasure. I do not know why I was there. I came hoping you would know."

Sterling smiled again, and the expression caused a pang of nausea to flare in Halston's stomach. Slowly, Sterling said, "You were *there* for them to find you. You were there so they could bring you to me, little one." There was nothing genuine about his syrupy tone. It was sickening, like rotten fruit.

Disgust swarmed up Halston's throat.

Sterling *knew.*

Hodge pressed a hand to his temple. "You're *kidding me.*"

Pierce glared. "You got something to say, boy?"

"Yeah. You lied to us. You sent us to dig up a *statue.* Not a *person.*" Hodge's hands curled into fists. "And those *monsters* around the tomb almost killed us! Did you know about those?"

"Lorthans are complex creatures," Sterling said. "They can only be put to sleep by the warlock who created them, and he happens to be dead now."

"We were your *pawns,*" Hodge snapped. "Makes sense. We're replaceable, ain't we? Gotta do what you can to protect your own band of dunces."

Sterling's men each shot Hodge a sharp glare, but Halston couldn't bring himself to tell his brother to stop.

Gryff could. "Kid. Calm yourself. You—"

Hodge spoke over him. "Say it, Sterling. You used us. Tell us why you lied."

"If we'd given you all the details, you would have run," said Pierce. "And any man who chooses this life and expects others to play by the rules is a damn fool."

"*Shit,* no kidding!" said Hodge. "Why didn't you just shoot us the last time we met if you wanted us dead? Would've saved you a lot of time."

"Watch your mouth," Sterling warned.

Tsashin sank back toward Lorelin, and Lorelin wrapped an arm around her. Tsashin reached out to grasp Lorelin's forearms.

Tsashin's voice was small. "Did *you* bury me, Sterling?"

"Of course not, honey," Sterling replied. "Come. You'll be safe with me. As for the boys, I'll give them what they want." He grinned at Halston. "I have the dagger half with me. The blade is all yours, if you do as I say. Just think. You can ride home happy, and we're out of each other's business forever."

When Halston didn't answer, Sterling said, "Look, boys. I don't like to lie. But it's a necessary evil in business. You're reliable employees, but not loyal ones. Had I given you every detail, you'd have pushed the job away." He looked back to Tsashin, and she drew back at his gaze. "She is… very valuable to me."

Jae's voice echoed in Halston's memory. *Why do you work for Sterling if you're so scared of him, anyway?*

Halston fought the urge to fire back and held his tongue.

Hodge did not. His angry laughter echoed off the broken walls. "*Valuable*, you say? Why don't you stab one of your own men in the back and take him to the Rangers, then? The bounty on just *one* of you would be enough to retire on."

Sterling ignored the remark. "Come here, Tsashin. Surely you miss your family. I can get you back to them in a few weeks. I promise you, I'm nothing to be afraid of."

Tsashin stepped away from Lorelin. "Will you hurt them?"

"Not if you come with me."

"He's lying!" Hodge looked to Tsashin, who was now shaking. "Tsashin, don't listen to him."

Sterling sighed. "I'll give you one more chance, Hodge. Every one of the Calder boys is twice as good a shot as you. I'll have 'em take care of *you* first if you can't keep your damn mouth shut while we're trying to negotiate."

No.

It couldn't end like this.

Halston's arm itched, begging him to draw his gun. He'd spent years dodging bloodshed whenever he could, but damn it—Sterling would not take their freedom away.

But thinking of it now... he hadn't really *ever* been free, here.

He would not fight Sterling, yet. Surely, he could still use his words, but he found none.

Hodge raised his gun.

Hodge, no!

Then, Hodge began to shake. He lowered his gun and hung his head. "There's something else we found. In the tomb. I'll tell you about it. Just... just don't hurt them."

Halston's heart splintered.

Sterling lifted an eyebrow, looking perplexed, but said nothing. His other men were quiet as the dawn.

Pierce grunted. "Something else?" He walked up to Hodge, so close that there was no room for Hodge to move forward. "What was it?"

Hodge mumbled something.

Pierce leaned forward. "What?"

Hodge mumbled it again.

Pierce snapped, "Speak up, boy."

Hodge lifted his head and his gun. "*Run, Tsashin!*" he shouted, and shot Pierce in the shoulder.

Sounds exploded all around them. Halston swerved just in time to see Tsashin's slight form dart out of the room. Shots cracked on the walls, smoke pluming up from hot guns, stinging their eyes. Sterling bellowed at his men to stop shooting and find where the girl went.

Hodge ran out the doorway, followed by Gryff. Before Gryff made it, Gallows cut him off. With no time to draw his gun, Gryff seized Gallows's shoulders. Gryff yanked him off the ground and threw him against the wall. Gallows cried out, then hit the ground with a grunt.

Pierce lay on the floor, clutching his shoulder. Slick blood coated his fingers. Sterling crouched over him, desperately trying to stanch the blood from his brother's wound.

"Block the entrance!" Pierce demanded, wheezing weakly.

Two of the men dashed toward the arch, and Halston took Lorelin's hand. They ran down one of the hallways, leaping over crumbled heaps of brick, and tore through the hall. They made it to a moss-covered stairwell at the corridor's end. They had to get out of here. Find Hodge and Gryff and Tsashin and Jae and run like hell.

Lorelin hurried up the stairs. Halston took a breath, then poured all his hope into the short climb after her. Halston spared a glance over his shoulder to find the hall barren. They still had a few breaths' worth of time.

They reached the top of the stairway, then wove in and out of upper hallways until they came to a small room. The window had no pane. They rushed for it.

Leaning over the ledge, they braced themselves to leap. A thin patch of overgrown grass stretched out at the bottom of the window, then dipped into the thick, piney woods. The drop would be unpleasant, certainly, but no bones would break. Halston nudged Lorelin. "Go."

She looked at him, eyes wide with uncertainty.

"Go!"

She climbed onto the windowsill, inhaled, and jumped to the ground. Lorelin landed gracefully on the earth, then shot up running and disappeared into the trees.

Halston began to climb, then heard a raspy voice behind him say, "Move any closer to that window, and I'll shoot."

Halston faced his opponent. Thumbscrew had a gaze sharp

enough to cut steel. There wasn't a speck of mercy in his eyes.

"No, you won't," Halston told him. "You need me alive."

"Try me, boy."

So Halston tried him and shot.

He missed, but the bullet grazed the man's arm. Thumbscrew hollered and recoiled in pain, sending his long-barreled revolver sliding across the floor.

Halston tried to mount the windowsill, then felt the outlaw's iron grasp around his ankle. He cried out as Thumbscrew yanked him to the floor.

Halston threw a punch at his attacker's throat, and his knuckles dug into Thumbscrew's windpipe. He gagged, then Halston dodged a blow to his side and jumped up, nearly losing his grip on the gun. He sprinted out of the room and headed for the stairs.

He barely made it one step down before a fist slammed into his back. Halston lost his breath, then watched his gun escape his clutch and clatter down the stairway.

Thumbscrew's weight pressed against Halston's back, grimy hands squeezing Halston's arms. With a burst of strength, Halston jerked himself to the side. Thumbscrew let go of Halston's arms, and Halston pivoted, ready to throw another blow.

He brought a fist into Thumbscrew's jaw, then cheek, then nose. Blood spurted from his nostrils. Halston dodged a blow to his own face, then braced himself to run downstairs to his gun.

Halston choked as knuckles slammed into the base of his throat. Before Thumbscrew could throw another punch, Halston grabbed his biceps, then yanked them both to the side. Their bodies slammed into the steps. As they tumbled down the stairs together, the room became a blur.

Halston flailed as he reached for the faint gleam of his gun, trying to ignore the pounding in his skull.

"Stay there, Thumbscrew."

Through a watery blur, Halston peered to the side. Maxim and Evia approached him, and before Halston could react, they pinned down his wrists. The cold barrel of a gun pressed against his forehead.

They yanked him to his feet. The trio led him back through the corridor, where Sterling still knelt over Pierce, bandaging his brother's wounds. The rest of Sterling's gang stood with their guns aimed, and Halston had no doubt they would shoot if he so much as breathed the wrong way.

"If you find Hodge Harney, kill him," Pierce spat.

Short-lived relief passed through Halston. Hodge had made it out. He was alive. But if Pierce found him...

"We don't know where he is," said Maxim flatly. "No promises."

"I'll kill him myself!" Pierce snarled.

Had it not been for the gun against his head, Halston would have promised Pierce: *I'll kill you myself if you do.*

Sterling raised his head to face his gang. "I want the others alive. Don't kill them, if you find them. Nobody dies until we have the girl."

Anger burned inside Halston like an oil fire, and it terrified him. He hadn't felt like this since Elias died. Only then, there'd been no one to blame for it. Here, it was different.

They dragged him outside to their band of surly horses tethered in the pines. Thumbscrew jabbed at him with the gun again, forcing Halston onto a saddle. Most of Sterling's men were gone, hustling to chase down Halston's gang before they covered too much ground.

Run, he thought, wishing he could send the word out on the wind. *Get out of here.*

He'd smother all his fear if he had to. It was fear that had led them here.

Perhaps they would whip him, or brand him with hot iron, or shatter his bones. But it didn't matter if he had to drag himself out of Sterling's stronghold bloody and broken, because one way or another... he'd do it.

He was going to find his gang.

———

Jae didn't know what was keeping her here.

She had a horse, saddlebags full of rations, and a mostly healed arm.

Scratching the back of her neck, she stood in the spruce grove and stared at the ruinous house through the branches. She thought of the way Halston seemed to tense up at the mention of Sterling's name, of the sketches in his journal, of the odd knife sheath that Sterling had practically dangled over Halston's head back in the desert. It was like finding a book with the first half cut out of it.

Jae decided there that she could waste her time trying to solve this mystery, or she could ride out of here for Pa's sake.

She started unhitching her horse when a gunshot stopped her.

Jae whirled in the direction of the manor and spied a small form running from the entrance like a startled deer. "Jae!"

"Tsashin!" Jae raced away from the horses and in Tsashin's direction.

Tsashin bit her lip, brown eyes watering with fear. She ducked into the shadows of the trees and pointed through the low-hanging arms. "Hodge told me to run. They... they wanted me to go with them. Sterling, I mean. He... he tried..." There was a catch her throat, then, and she swallowed. "We have to save them."

Jae leaned forward, peering through the slash of space between twigs and pine needles. "Stay quiet. We can't let Sterling know we're here." Two more shapes fled the entrance and moved east into the woods, including a towering figure that couldn't have been anyone but Gryff.

Another man emerged from the manor, too thick and brawny to be Halston. Jae's hand closed around Tsashin's wrist to keep her from moving.

When the man disappeared into the trees, Tsashin pointed west, her breathing ragged. "Look."

The fire in Jae's veins went cool for a moment, and she looked to where Tsashin was pointing. Lorelin's tall figure leapt from a window, landed on the soft earth, then disappeared into the trees.

Another gunshot boomed from inside the manor. After that, muffled shouts stirred together, but Jae couldn't tell who they belonged to.

Jae felt frozen, then, as if someone had hammered her into the ground like a tent stake. Something had gone wrong. Was Sterling Byrd lying dead in those ruined halls? Were Halston and Hodge with him? A hollow feeling opened in her chest.

Tsashin's voice broke. "What do we do?"

Jae looked in the direction Lorelin had fled. West. "Let's get a horse and *go*."

"The others—"

"They'll be alright. They can handle themselves," Jae said, though a whip of guilt lashed her as she spoke.

"There!" someone shouted from the manor.

A bullet whizzed through the air and exploded by their feet. Without thinking, Jae grabbed Tsashin's wrist. They broke into a run, Jae at the lead.

Twigs whipped at their faces, and bent roots jabbed at the soles of their feet. The trees whirled by in Jae's periphery, crowding them in like wooden spikes around a fort. A stitch formed in her side, its sharp fingers plowing deep into her muscles. She cursed herself for not running back to the horses.

If there was one thing she had to do now, it was to at least get

Tsashin somewhere safe. She'd no clue what those bastards wanted the poor girl for, but she didn't belong in this bloody mess.

Behind them, someone shouted. They ran faster, though Jae's legs burned like red-hot iron.

The sound of the river came to greet them. The trees began to clear, forming a pathway they could easily run through. To the left, the ground steepened sharply and sloped down to the riverbanks. Jae looked to its waters, watching the current pour over lumps of stone.

The night wasn't too cold. They could jump in the river, let the current carry them elsewhere. Or they could find a cave along the banks and—

Jae didn't have a chance to look back before the shot came.

The ground exploded beside her heel. She felt no pain, but her foot did not find the earth again. The shock sent her veering to the side, then the ground plowed into her body.

"Jae!" cried Tsashin.

She was falling.

She rolled down the slope, grunting as her body slammed into the earth over and over again. Each hit squeezed the breath out of her chest. The night whirled by in circles overhead, not much clearer than a muddled blur.

At last, a pair of thick tree trunks brought Jae's tumble to a halt. One smacked against her shoulder, and the other slammed into her calf. She sank her teeth into her newly bloodied lip, holding back a groan. Her limbs and torso were throbbing, and her mouth was slick with blood from her lips and nose. She lay like a fallen pheasant in a patch of weeds, trying to summon enough strength to roll over and crawl.

Jae pushed herself up with her forearms, sat straight, and ran a hand across her foot. The boot was intact. No bullet hole in sight. The shot must've just missed her heel.

Jae spied her hat lying a few yards ahead. She dragged herself toward it and placed it back on her head, waiting for another sound. No more shots. She prayed that Tsashin had escaped.

Jae winced as she tried to push herself up again. The pain seemed to spread through her muscles with each heartbeat.

Damn this! Damn this mess, damn these woods, damn me for ever going through with this cursed idea!

At last, she managed to stand. Her limbs burned, especially her ankle, which felt about as useful as a wheel severed from its axle.

The river was mere yards away. She could hobble up to it, then let its waters sweep her away... but she couldn't leave Tsashin. Where was she?

Jae limped behind one of the crooked pines that had stopped her tumble, then scanned the crest of the slope. Tsashin was nowhere in sight. Had their pursuers disappeared? Jae stepped away from the tree for a better look and considered calling out to her.

Then, three silhouettes appeared at the top of the slope and pointed straight at her. "There she is!"

Jae turned and started to run, but the first step sent a new bite of pain through her leg. Gritting her teeth, she tried to ignore it and lunge away, but the weight on her ankle brought her spilling to her knees.

She was not going with them. She'd crawl and claw her way out of this if she had to.

"Freeze." Heavy footsteps pounded downhill. They belonged to armed men, no doubt bigger and broader than her.

There was no time to run. Only to fight.

Huffing, she propped herself up on her forearm. The men hustled down the slope, guns drawn.

She couldn't waste her shots. Not from this distance. As soon as they were close enough, she'd fire.

She was not going down.

She didn't know their names, but the three men all looked the damn same to her... big hands and crooked mouths and battered, soot-caked clothes. "You've got five seconds to put up your hands!" They were close now, near enough that she could count the buttons on their dirty shirts.

She stretched her fingers to the sky. Her heart twisted in her chest, and her breaths turned shallow.

She could see their scowls beneath their hats, now. They hurried toward her, boots snapping the twigs on the ground. Their shadows fell on her.

Her hand flew to her boot pistol, but when she grasped the handle, a rough, gritty hand seized her wrist. The assailant twisted her arm, pinning it behind her back as a scream burned her throat.

Another hand grabbed her shoulders. The fear and pain turned the world to fog around her, but she felt the men jostling her belt, freeing her remaining guns from their holsters.

Grainy rope tugged at her wrists. When the knot tightened, the strong hand let go of her arm. She lifted her head, a speck of clarity regained, then a boot toe to her head sent her falling again. Blobs of color knit together behind her closed eyes. Darkness. Waves of deadened noise.

"Get up. On your feet."

She groaned.

"Oh, for gods' sake, let's just carry her."

They peeled her from the earth, hoisting her up like a casket. She forced her eyes open and caught a glimpse of the stars between the branches before shutting them again.

She had to run. She should be throwing punches, fighting for her freedom. But her sore ankle and throbbing head had stripped away what was left of her good sense.

"Circle up!" boomed a deep, strangely musical voice. Sterling.

Anger flared in her belly. Her captors lowered her to the ground. A gun clicked next to her head. She almost snorted. Did they really think she was in any position to run away?

Her eyes fluttered open. Sterling's gang stood in a wavering circle, the horses pawing at the earth with frenzied wails. Off to the side, another man held a cloth to Pierce's shoulder, the fabric stained with blood.

Good. At least one of these bastards was coming out of this with a scratch.

Sterling loomed ahead of Jae, standing out like a gem in a flat face of stone. He stepped up to her, leering down with a hard gaze. "Where's the girl?"

Tsashin, you son of a bitch. Her name is Tsashin. "I don't know."

One of Jae's captors drove his heel into her side. She yelped, cringing.

"Stop!" Sterling shouted. "Damn it, Ned! You'll kick all the breath right out of her. I need her awake right now."

Jae gathered all the willpower she could, though she wanted nothing more than to use it to tell them all to go to hell. "I said I don't know! We…" She swallowed. The coppery taste of blood filled her throat. "We were running when you shot at us."

Sterling's face sank into a deeper scowl. "*Who* shot at you?" he asked, raising his head to study the three men who'd hauled her in.

Shuddering, she looked over her shoulder. For the first time that night, she got a decent view of them. A young, blue-eyed man with a pair of expensive looking guns. A man with silver hair and broad shoulders, much older than the others, but still sturdy. Then there was the fella who'd compared her to a whore he knew in that first hideout. She recalled that his name was Lyle.

He blurted, "Stone. It was Stone. And he shot at them *twice*."

Stone turned to him. "Bastard."

"So, it's true?" Sterling asked.

Stone stammered, "I-I wasn't aiming for the girl! I swear! I meant to hit this one in the legs!"

"They were running, dunce!" Ned bellowed. "Could've killed both! Sterling told you not to shoot."

"I—"

"Thumbscrew," Sterling said with sickening calmness. "Grab his hand. You know the rest."

Stone barely had time to yelp before Thumbscrew lunged his way and yanked him back by the collar of his shirt. Thumbscrew forced Stone's head down on a large, slanted rock, shouting at the old man to keep still.

"Which is your best shooting hand?" asked Thumbscrew.

Stone wheezed, trying to lift his head under Thumbscrew's grasp. "I shoot fine with either!"

"Liar!" Thumbscrew gripped Stone's left wrist and forced it down on the rock. "Thumb or forefinger?"

"Neither! Please! Stop!"

"Alright, I'll start with both." Thumbscrew reached for the hatchet in his belt, the handle bound in cloth. He lifted it readily, unmoved by Stone's pleas.

Thumbscrew brought up the hatchet, braced to strike it down. Before he could, Sterling sighed. "Stop."

Thumbscrew's brows knit together as he faced Sterling. "Why?"

"I can't afford to lose another gun," Sterling said. "Not when our prize is gone."

"He ignored your orders," Thumbscrew argued. He clutched the hatchet so tightly his knuckles were white as bone.

Sterling made a sweeping motion with his hand. "Put the axe away. Stone, remember this. If you choose to defy me again, remember the fear you just felt. Remember the pain that comes with disobedience."

Thumbscrew grunted, shoving the hatchet back into his belt. Stone stood up, shaking, and trudged back to Jae.

She turned, trying to get a better look at each of them, though her pounding head made it tough to focus on anything. Two men stepped to the side, revealing someone she hadn't noticed yet. A heavy, blunt feeling hammered into her chest.

Kneeling down, guarded and bound, was Halston. His lips were still, but his eyes met hers and stayed rooted there. The look on his face reminded her of a forest ravaged by a flood, barren and lost.

She pulled her gaze from him, searching for any other kneeling figures. No one. Sterling's words buzzed in her head. *The girl.*

They wanted Tsashin alive. So much that Thumbscrew had nearly struck off a man's fingers for endangering her.

Jae wanted to run, to find that sweet girl and take her away. If Tsashin fell into these demons' hands…

While her thoughts sprang up and ran like rampant beasts, another figure stooped in front of her. A thin-faced woman with watery blue eyes and hair the color of wheat. This was Sterling's girl, Jae recalled, though she couldn't remember her name.

The woman raised a vial to Jae's mouth, and a faint, bitter smell wafted from its open neck. "Drink."

Jae mashed her lips together.

The woman snorted. "It will put you to sleep. It may even ease any pain you have."

You must think I'm real stupid.

The woman pinched Jae's nose. Jae tried to fight the rising pain in her chest, but it was no use. As soon as her mouth opened to swallow some air, the woman forced the vial between Jae's lips.

Jae tried to plug the vial with her tongue, but the liquid poured beneath it. The woman forced her hand over Jae's mouth to keep her from coughing it up. The trail of sharp-tasting fluid streamed down her throat.

Already, her limbs were going weak. At least some of the pain was fading from her head and ankle.

Trapped. Defeated. Bound, like so many of the men she'd hauled to sheriffs for their bounties. She wondered if they'd felt as scared as she did now.

The last thing she remembered was Halston gazing at her with a look that cried, '*Help.*'

She reckoned her face looked much the same before she blacked out.

Chapter 21

Hodge waited.

He couldn't remember the last time it'd been this hard to breathe. He clutched his gun, itching to run, to fight, to move.

It was hard to say how much time had passed, but judging by the moon's place in the sky, he guessed an hour, at least. That meant Sterling's men were either waiting in Mourelle, on the road, or scattered throughout the woods like hunting dogs.

He could hardly recall what had happened after his bullet found Pierce's shoulder, though he *did* recall the anger that had poured through him like a restless current. They'd fled the gun smoke filling Mourelle's halls, leaping over roots and brambles until they found a hiding spot. They stood wedged under an earthy bluff. Pines with bent trunks and exposed, twisting roots hung from its ridge. A grove of newborn aspens, thin as lampposts, sprouted before them, and the ground sloped delicately down into the forest.

Fear surfaced inside him, but he pushed it back and kept his grip steady on his pistol. The others weren't lost. They couldn't be.

Hodge and Gryff would find them.

Gryff stood firm while Hodge paced and turned, looking in every direction. Gryff hadn't said a word since they'd escaped.

Hodge wasn't sure if he should apologize. Maybe he should've lowered his gun instead of shooting Pierce, but he'd be damned if they let Sterling and his brothers get away with this. The lying bastard.

At last, Hodge spoke. "We should move. We gotta find the others."

"No," said Gryff. "We're stayin' put. I don't want us runnin' into Sterling."

"We lost the girls. And Hal."

"We'll find 'em. When the mornin' comes."

"I ain't waiting that long." By the time the morning came, it might be too late.

"Keep your damn voice down and do what I say."

Hodge's shoulders went tense. "Why, Gryff? So we can lose them for good? Is *that* what you want?"

Gryff exhaled. "You ain't thinkin' straight. If you were, you'd've thought twice before you shot Pierce. You wanna go down in history, Hodge? As some gunslingin' kid who died too young because he couldn't keep his head screwed on tight? You ain't a hero. Don't try to act like one."

"What was I supposed to do?" Hodge spat. "Do you have any idea what they would've done to Tsashin if they took her? I would've been happy to bring Sterling all the gold he wanted. But never a person with blood in her veins. Thought this sorta thing was beneath even Sterling. She ain't his property."

"I ain't sayin' she is. I'm sayin' that we could *all* be in danger 'cause you couldn't keep your finger off your trigger!"

"They're liars! And I wish we'd killed Sterling long ago!"

"You don't think I've tried?"

198 : Sophia Minetos

A few seconds ticked away. Hodge could only stare. Had he heard that right? "...What?"

"Sterling. I tried to kill him."

"Wh—" Hodge stammered, trying to make sense of it. "When?"

"That day we came back from the copper coach."

The first time Sterling had beaten Halston.

When Sterling took out the whip, Halston had jumped forward, throwing his arms out before Hodge and Gryff. Sterling had warned Halston that if he didn't back down, he'd have to take the lashes for Gryff and Hodge as well as himself. Halston had stood his ground and said he'd gladly take them all.

It'd been just the three of them, then. At the first crack of the whip Hodge had screamed and tried to reach his brother. Gallows had flung him to the ground and put a boot on his head to keep him there.

He'd heard Gryff struggling, shouting, but it'd all gone by in a crazed blur. When it was all over, Hodge had run to Halston's side and cleaned the blood from his wounds. They stayed on that red, empty stretch of earth for what felt like days.

They hadn't spoken until Gryff returned and told them it was time to go. Hodge hadn't realized that Gryff had disappeared until he came back, looking even more sullen than usual.

But Hodge had never asked Gryff what had happened. He figured that Sterling had simply made Gryff promise never to return empty-handed.

Gryff said, "When they pinned Halston down, I leapt for Sterling. I was gonna yank the whip out of his hands and choke him with it. It was like someone else had reins on me. I couldn't think of nothin' else.

"Pierce and Flynn and Argus got a hold on me. Beat me down and dragged me away. They... they didn't think I wanted to kill him.

They just thought I was gonna try and stop him from beatin' Halston.

"They dragged me off. Pierce pointed a gun at me and said that if I ever tried to stop Sterling again… they'd kill both of you. Then they'd tie me up and leave me there to watch you rot in the sun."

Hodge swallowed, searching for the right words. "Gods, Gryff."

By the look on Gryff's face, Hodge wondered if he had ever meant to tell that story. Gryff had lived decades on this earth before Halston and Hodge stumbled across his path, and every time they asked him about his 'better days,' Gryff either said nothing or pushed the subject away.

Gryff said, "If we had a dozen extra guns, we might stand a chance against Sterling, but I don't trust that 'might' enough." He paused, taking a moment to survey their surroundings again. "We'll sort Sterling out later. Right now, we gotta figure out where the others ran."

Hodge fought against the panic rising inside him. Where *were* the others? Had they even made it out? His gaze dropped to the ground while his thoughts raced around his mind. "At Mourelle. Did you see them take anyone?"

"No."

Hodge breathed in, trying to steady the fear bouncing around in his head. "Shit! I *shot* Pierce!" It was like he'd realized it for the first time, just now.

"Yeah, you did."

"You ain't helping! If Sterling took the others, then…"

"Hodge," said Gryff. "Lower your voice. Here's what I'm sayin'. They want Tsashin. If'n she got out with Jae, they'll want some idea of where she went. They won't kill no one till they get an answer. I think we got time."

Hodge often doubted he'd live long, but if he couldn't keep his own gang safe, then damn it, what good was he?

He put his fingers in his mouth and whistled the signal. It escaped into the night without so much as an echo returning it.

Hodge paced over to an aspen and slid down the trunk. He sat on the ground, fingering his holsters. He whistled again. Nothing.

He glanced down at his hands and stroked the red stains on his bandages. For a moment, all he could think about was how much he wanted to put a bullet through Sterling's throat. Even if Sterling sent one Hodge's way at the same time.

Then, Hodge called on things he could not see or hear. His father's gods and his mother's gods. Whatever was left of Elias's spirit, and his father's, too. The kindness in the world, wherever it was hiding.

"Gryff."

"Hmm?"

"We're gonna make it."

Hodge whistled.

A few minutes passed. A couple more.

Again.

Just the wind drifting over their heads.

He sent the song across the breeze…

And this time, he got an answer.

Hodge jumped to his feet, heart pounding. He whistled the three notes once more, and the reply came from the west, past the aspen grove.

"C'mon!" He nudged Gryff, and they hurried away.

They hustled over dark, rich earth and gnarled roots, careful not to stir the branches too much. Hodge tried to move without faltering, to focus on the direction of the sound. The whistle came again. He answered.

If anything was watching over them, he'd thank it without knowing its name.

The ground rose into a gentle slope. Gryff and Hodge darted up the hillside and spotted the shine of golden hair at its foot, waiting behind the tree line.

Hodge bit his tongue. It was all he could do to keep from shouting her name.

Lorelin turned, a relieved smile crossing her mouth. A small, dark shape peeked out from behind her. Tsashin.

Hodge picked up speed as he raced downhill, leaping over stones and logs of fallen pine. They reached each other. Hodge threw an arm around each of them and pulled them in close. "Thank goodness. Where's Hal?"

Lorelin's voice cracked. "They got him."

Hodge drew back. "What?"

Tsashin spoke up. "I saw him. I… I tried. Jae fell down a slope, and I lost track of her. I tried to find her, but they were behind us. Close. I scaled a tree." She swallowed, looking down. "I heard them say that they'd already tied Halston up. Then I watched them hauling Jae uphill. I wanted to help. But I didn't know what I could do."

Gryff asked, "Did you hear them say anythin'?"

"No," said Tsashin.

"We scouted the area," added Lorelin. "They've left. But we couldn't figure out where they went. We lost the path after a couple hundred yards."

"Hey." Hodge touched her shoulder. "You did what you could."

None of them had ever been any good at tracking. Damn it. If only Jae was with them.

She was alive. So was Hal. But where would Sterling take them?

"Think," said Gryff. "All the hideouts we've done business in. Which one's the closest?"

"Mourelle," said Hodge without thinking. He bit his lip and winced, wishing he hadn't said that.

If things weren't so serious, Gryff might've called him an idiot. "*Other* than that," Gryff said.

Lorelin shook her head, her blue-green eyes watering. "Nothing's this far north. Mourelle is the only place in the Briarfords we've ever met."

Hodge breathed out. "They'll head for the Mouth, I reckon. Or that hideout near Calora. Both of those are more than a week away. We'll have to try one after the other."

Lorelin's face fell. "We can't take that long."

"Why not?" asked Hodge.

"Think," said Lorelin. "We can try going to Calora first, or the Mouth. And if they aren't at the first one we try, we can go to the other. But Halston and Jae... he'll beat them. Whip them. If we take weeks to find them... who knows what state they'll be in by the time we get there?"

An image barreled its way into Hodge's mind. One of Halston lying on a dirty floor, cold with a sheen of sweat, fresh wounds on his back.

Stop. That won't happen. They would find Halston and Jae, and as soon as they did, they were getting out of Mesca and never coming back.

He rummaged through his mind for all the nearby towns. Marcelena, Dolorosa, Sienna, Bruhn...

Bruhn.

"Gryff!" he blurted. "How long will it take to get to Bruhn from here? Probably a day or two, right?"

"Yeah, I'd wager two days without horses."

"Remember Coy?"

Gryff snorted. "I try not to."

"Who's that?" asked Tsashin.

"One of Sterling's old employees," Hodge explained. "He runs a shooting pit in Bruhn now."

Coy was young, good-looking, and a mighty fine shot. That being said, he'd always been a few apples short of a bushel. About a year back, he hadn't shown up to a meeting, and Hodge had asked why. Sterling kept his answer vague, but Hodge had no doubt that Coy had done something to rattle Sterling just enough that he'd fired the bastard instead of killing him outright. Not the most common retirement plan for one of Sterling's men.

They'd visited his club in Bruhn once before—a raucous pit full of laughter and gun smoke. Coy held nightly challenges for anyone who had the coin to enter. Hodge reckoned he'd made a life for himself more prosperous than banditry.

Tsashin's eyes grew wide. "A shooting pit?"

Gryff scratched his neck. "He likes havin' them fight, like roosters in a pen. That sort of thing only draws fools."

"So," said Lorelin. "You think we should pay him a visit?"

Hodge nodded. "He was part of Sterling's gang for years. I'm sure he knows more hideouts than we do."

"Sterling probably paid him off to keep quiet about them," said Lorelin.

"Yeah, probably," said Hodge. "But I doubt Coy will turn down a bribe. Or an offer of one."

"We don't have much money," Lorelin said. "And I say this with love in my heart, Hodge, but even Coy isn't dumb enough to trust you with a debt."

Hodge breathed in. "Yeah, maybe not. But I don't think we have anything to lose by asking. Sterling's got Halston and Jae, not us. Like you said, he'll take his time if he thinks he can get a word out of them. I think we gotta see Coy."

Why not? They'd done crazier things before.

They spent a moment looking at each other, at the sky and the ground and the trees. At last, Lorelin said, "Well, if we're going to see Coy, then we'd better start walking. I think I can get us to the trail again. Everyone keep your guns ready. C'mon."

Chapter 22

The smell of rot and dust filled her nostrils.

Jae didn't dare open her eyes. She listened, waiting for the rough voices of Sterling's men. Nothing came.

Her mouth was dry as dust. She opened her eyes and sat up to find her wrists unbound. Her weapons and knapsack were gone, but they'd at least left all the clothes on her body. She pressed a hand to her head and found a lump, then reached down and rolled her thumbs over her ankle. Tender, sore, but no sign of a broken bone. She snorted. At least there was one bright side to this.

She studied the room. Hard-packed dirt formed the floor, and faint light streamed in through cracks between the planks forming the walls. A single window was set high on the wall furthest from her, small and circular, revealing a dim, overcast sky. There was a bit of light streaming from it, but whether it was dawn or dusk, Jae couldn't tell. To her right, a narrow, wooden stairway rose to meet a door coated with chipped white paint, and a narrow loft with a beat-up railing met the top of the stairs.

This certainly wasn't the sort of place she'd expected to wake. It looked like the cellar of a poor rancher, not a place where an esteemed gang would store their adversaries.

Halston lay in the corner to her left, knees up to his chest. His shoulder rose and fell as he breathed. Jae crawled toward him, careful to keep her motions steady. She reached out and jostled his shoulder. "Halston, wake up."

He didn't budge. She shook him twice more, then gave up. If they'd given him the same wretched fluid they'd drugged her with, he'd wake up in good time. She had to scout out this room.

She stood up and tiptoed around the floor, running her hands along the walls. Splintering wood prodded her bare skin. Could there be a vent somewhere? Maybe there'd be a rusty nail protruding from the wall, or a loose, sharp chunk of wood she could chip off a board.

No such luck. She raised her head to the loft. Perhaps there was something up there.

She shifted as close to the wall as possible, clutching the rail to keep most of her weight off the stairs. She took one step. Another. Despite her efforts, the old, thin wood creaked.

Almost immediately, the door slammed open. The man who'd compared her to a whore stood in the doorway, one of those blue-eyed brothers, aiming a hefty pistol her way. He was a loose-looking fella, his shirt half unbuttoned, chestnut curls falling from his hat. A thin layer of stubble coated his chin.

"Nice to see you up and about, little lady." He had a terribly grisly grin, like a donkey with a split lip. "You're comin' with me. Boss wants a word with you." He ran a pointer finger along his pistol's ivory grip.

Jae grunted. Sterling couldn't have had a word with her before his lady shoved sleep medicine down her throat?

Still, she said nothing. If Sterling wanted her dead, he could've shot her while she was out, and if he wanted a chat, she'd give him one.

Holding her by the shoulder, the man guided her up the stairs, locked the door behind them, then led her down the saddest hallway she'd ever seen. It was narrow but long, with three doors on either side. Another stairway stretched up at the end of the hall. Beside the stairs, Jae caught a glimpse of a kitchen with a stove and a cracked, barren countertop. Stains and sawdust covered the wooden floor, and cracks and pockmarks ran thick as swarming gnats across the walls. They stopped before the second door on the right, and the guard knocked thrice.

"Lyle?" Sterling called from inside.

"Yep. Girl's awake. Got her here."

"Send her in."

Lyle opened the door and shoved her inside. Jae stumbled into the room and caught herself from falling, then the door banged shut.

Sterling sat in a bulky wooden chair at a long oak table. A thick layer of dust coated its surface. The room was small and stuffy, smelling of burnt wood and spilled whiskey, and save for the table and chair, it was completely barren, the wooden walls free of paint or wallpaper. Jae glimpsed the rosy sky through a lone, grimy window and guessed that it was dawn after all.

Jae stood just before the door. Sterling motioned for her to move closer. She took a few steps toward the table, and though this floor wasn't nearly as squeaky as the stairs, her footsteps seemed as loud as gunshots.

When she stopped, the silence lingered for a few more moments. Then, Sterling said, "You've no idea where the Yunah girl is, do you?"

So she *was* Yunah. Jae shook her head.

"I believe you." He steepled his fingers, elbows resting on the table.

The way he looked at her made her ill. Like she was a pig he was about to chop up and skin instead of a person. She stood there staring, thinking of how she could a better look at his chair. Maybe she could snap off one of the legs and beat him with it.

"Why'd you bring us here?" asked Jae. "If you wanted her so bad, you could've just waited by Mourelle."

"I had business to attend here," Sterling replied. "Y'all ain't my only employees. Had an arrangement I couldn't afford to miss. If it weren't for that, we'd still be scouting the woods around Mourelle. But it's alright. I could hunt your crew down, or I could bait them out. Either of them will get me the Yunah girl in time."

"She's innocent," said Jae. "I don't understand what you want with her."

"I ain't doubting her *innocence*," said Sterling. "But she can offer me something. Something more valuable than a sculpture of gold."

Jae tried not to glare.

"Are you concerned for her safety?" asked Sterling.

"'Course I am." His gaze made Jae feel hot, like the autumn when she'd caught herself a fever and spent the long nights sweltering under her blankets, too scared to sleep due to the fear she wouldn't wake again.

"I didn't think a common thief would be so… righteous," he said. "And I was right. We found some… interesting papers in your knapsack. And I daresay you ain't a common thief at all."

She bit her cheeks to keep the shock from showing on her face. He knew.

Sterling just laughed. "Gotta say, I've never met a bounty hunter who'd cling to a gang for so long without turning them over. Then again, bounty hunters tend not to last long around me."

Jae tried to think of a bluff. There had to be a lie she could throw his way. But each moment she spent fishing for one, the stupider she must've looked.

"I thought you could be useful." He reached behind the chair and pulled out her pack, then fished out the folder and spread her records across the table. "At first, I decided you might make decent bait for the rest of Halston's gang. But since you're a woman of the law, I can't think of a reason to keep you alive. I'm sure Halston will be just fine by himself."

She was not going to beg for her life. Surely, that was what he wanted, to see her grovel on the floor and plead for mercy. Once, Pa had told her that a few seconds of hard thinking could buy you many years of life. And damn it, that was what she was going to do. If she could stay alive long enough to find a way out of here, then she'd bluff until she lost her voice.

Jae said, "I've got something I think you'll want."

Sterling smiled. Still, he drew his gun slowly, letting it sit ready in his hand. "What is it?"

"Magic map."

His smile sank into a stern frown. "Go on."

She pointed to her knapsack, trying not to shake. "There should be a big piece of paper in there. Pull it out."

He did so, and then passed it to her. She unrolled it, tapping the gold brimming over their location. "Lights up wherever I am. I use it to find my way. I ain't never gotten lost, even once."

"Where'd you get this?" Sterling asked without looking up.

"A Nefili man."

Sterling rasied an eyebrow. "It marks your location?"

"That," said Jae. "and other things."

"Like what?"

"It can show me places in detail," said Jae. "When I say 'hence,' it shows me where I am, exactly. But if I want it to 'show me Calora,'" she said, pointing to the map as it changed, "then I get Calora in all its glory."

The map changed under their eyes. The brown ink spun and fused into Calora's twisted streets, its squares and villas and acres of land, right down to the city's perimeter.

"The ink disappears when someone else touches it," added Jae. "Only works for me. It's made my profession a lot easier, and I'm sure it would do the same for yours. It's no good if I'm a corpse, though."

Sterling touched it and watched the ink vanish. He reacted with an expression Jae would associate more with a man who'd just noticed a coffee stain on the paper rather than magic itself.

Jae tipped her chin at him. "I've lost a few enemies due to that map," she said. "Certainly made it harder for them to run from me. I reckon *you've* got an enemy or two."

The quiet was worse than a week of scorching desert heat, and it felt at least as long.

At last, Sterling spoke. "Here's how it's gonna go, Miss Oldridge. You'll wait in that cellar with Halston Harney. If you try to run, then I'll have my men dig a nice grave for you out back after I shoot you down myself. Is that clear?"

"Yes, sir. If I do what you say, you'll keep me alive?"

Sterling said, "For now."

He called for Lyle, then. The young man came back into the room and yanked Jae away by her wrist. As they walked back to the cellar, Jae could only think one thing.

Thank you, Sterling.

He'd given her time, and that was all she needed.

Chapter 23

The waves crashed outside the walls, veiling the sound of chirping gulls. A slender hand settled on his shoulder, then shook him. Lia shouted in his ear, "Father's back! Get up, Hal!"

Halston sat up, pushing the covers down. He tugged his boots on, then reached to smooth out the blankets, but his sister groaned and seized him by the wrist. "You can make your bed later. Quick. His ship is almost here. Elias and Hodge are already outside."

They ran out to the shore, under a sky pink and muted with the dawn. A crest of sunlight peeked above the sea, but late stars still beamed over the water. Elias and Hodge waited on the shore, skipping stones on the waves. Laughing, Halston and Lia raced for them. Their mother came to join them, then, her smile warm as summer's touch. They stood and watched the sails drift closer, moving past the crags of silver rock.

The ship docked.

Something was wrong.

His father had been gone for four months. He should have been smiling, approaching them with open arms. There was an urgency to his movement, but it *was not a joyful one. As he came closer, Halston saw the grim look on his father's face, bleak and motionless. Still, he knew his father well. Halston could recognize the fear behind his gray eyes.*

That world slipped away.

Halston reached out, though the floor was cold and hard beneath his back. In his mind, he grasped at that image of his father walking toward him, even though he knew how the dream would end.

He gave up at last, then opened his eyes to find himself in a dim cellar with a loft and a stairway. Jae sat a couple yards away, legs crossed, tracing circles on the floor with her finger.

She didn't look like someone who belonged here, locked in the darkness of a cellar. Up close, she looked lost and small.

Jae looked up from the floor. "You're awake."

"Where are we?"

Jae shrugged. "Not sure. Sterling spoke to me earlier. He wants to know where Tsashin is."

"Do you know?"

"No. I lost her before they took me," said Jae. "But he'll keep us alive. If he knows the others will want us back, there's no point in killing us, especially if he thinks they have Tsashin."

Halston nodded, then whispered, "We should scope out the room."

"Tried that," said Jae. "The walls are almost as bare as the floor. Nothing I could find."

Silence passed over them for a long while. Halston watched the clouds' shadows ripple over the floor. Hunger grated on his stomach. "The stairs. They look pretty brittle. Think we could rip out a chunk?"

Jae shrugged. "Maybe, but they're noisy as all hell. The guard opened the door when I tried walking up." She paused. "Do you think the others will come for us?"

"They'll try, definitely," said Halston. "But I don't know where we are, and I doubt they do, either. The only hideout in the Briarfords... at least, the only one we've been to, is Mourelle. If Sterling's taken us to another, we could be anywhere."

The thoughts bounced around like stray bullets in his head. Where were the others? Gods above, were they even safe?

Halston lowered his shoulders and released a breath. Wherever they were, he'd find them. Sterling could put all the mountains and deserts he wanted between them. Halston would find a way over them.

A moment passed, then Jae said, "I'm sorry."

"Hmm?"

Jae hung her head. "For walking away from you, back when the lorthans came out. And for the way I acted the day we went to Mourelle. I think I let my temper get the best of me."

Halston said, "I think we both did."

Jae shook her head. "My Pa always said my mouth was like a paper boat. Sometimes, I let it go without thinking of where it'll end up."

Halston chuckled. "My father had a few similar phrases for Hodge, when we were younger. He was always pretty even-tempered, but Hodge tested him. From time to time."

Jae tilted her head, a curious glint in her eye. "Maybe we can make the most of all this," she said, gesturing to the walls and ceiling. "We'll be spending a lot of time together, surely. Maybe we can learn how to have a civil conversation while we look for a way out of here."

In spite of himself, Halston grinned.

They were silent for a moment. Then Halston cleared his throat. "Listen. I know how confusing it must be. I..." He looked to the cellar door, then shifted closer to Jae and lowered his voice to a whisper. "I've wanted to get away from him for years. We all have. But without him, Hodge and I will never get home. We'll never see our family again."

"Your family?" Jae asked.

Halston nodded.

"I don't mean to pry, but... I keep thinking about that picture of yours. The one you pulled out in the mining camp."

He wanted to tell her. Saying those names would be easy. He repeated them to himself every night. "Listen," he said at last. "I... I could tell you. But I feel like—"

"You feel like you'll jinx your chances of seeing them again if you talk about it too much. That if you let fate know what you're after, it'll rip it right out of your hands, just to laugh in your face."

Halston hesitated. She'd worded it more earnestly than he could have himself. "How did you know?"

"Because when I lost my Pa, I felt the same way," said Jae. "Then I realized that I'm gonna find him one way or the other. Nothin' will stop me. So if fate wants to keep me from going after him, it's gonna have to put up a damn good fight."

Halston considered asking her about her father, but Jae spoke again before he could. "You don't have to tell me their names or anything, but... what were your folks like?"

He thought about what she'd said. She was right. Silence wouldn't get him home any sooner.

"I think you would have liked my mother. She was smart. And kind. She had a sharp tongue, though. Which was a good thing, looking back at it. Hodge has... well, I'll just say he's always been this way."

Jae chuckled.

"My father..." He thought of how to finish the statement. "He was different."

"How?"

"He was a sea captain. Sometimes, he made me wonder if it was possible to be born without a sense of humor. He loved us. He just didn't say so very much. He had other ways of showing it.

"Then there's our sister. She's honest. Principled. But she isn't *nice*." He laughed to himself. "If she disagrees with you, she'll let you know right away. Provided you can understand sarcasm."

"I like her already."

"Then there is… *was*, Elias." He swallowed. "Though I'm sure you've heard enough about him. Rumors and all."

Solemnly, Jae nodded. "Some are easier to believe than others. I've heard about the men who died on the day of your jailbreak. I've heard that half the women in the town were in love with him. Someone said he broke ten broncs on the first day of working at the ranch. There was another I heard where he made a pact with some ancient spirit to help him kill the sheriff."

Halston couldn't fight the laugh that came. "No spirits, I'm afraid. The truth isn't *quite* as exciting." He raised his head to the window. The sky was dim, covered by thick gray clouds. "What do they say about us? People in Mesca, I mean."

Jae put her hands in her lap. "Well, most of 'em don't hate you."

Halston laughed mirthlessly. "That's a rather low bar right there."

"Elias is the most famous out of y'all. People argue about him. They can't agree if he was an innocent hero or a scoundrel."

Hero. Scoundrel. "Interesting. Because to me, he was just my brother."

In his mind, a gun exploded. He saw his brothers rounding up their belongings, desperate to flee before the lawmen came for them. He saw the ranch fading in the distance, growing farther and farther away. Gone.

He almost forgot Jae was there. "I'm sure most of them think the Arrowwood War was about nothing but my brother's bloodlust."

He drew in a breath and shut his eyes. The words came tumbling out, fueled by only his frustration. "I heard someone talking about it once. The sheriff in Arrowwood, Jackson Poole. They think he was an innocent man. That Elias killed him for no reason, and the Arrowwood War was just a slaughter.

"I'm sure they won't tell you that same sheriff stole property from the people he'd promised to protect. That the sheriff pointed his gun at husbands and demanded to have his way with their wives. And he called himself a man of the law. That's how I learned 'man of the law' doesn't mean a thing out here."

To his surprise, Jae placed a hand on his shoulder.

He opened his eyes, feeling like he'd just jumped from a rooftop and hit the ground. Hard. "Oh. I'm... sorry about that. I just—"

"Shh. I understand."

He wasn't sure if she meant it, but he continued anyway. "We used to work for a rancher. Gus Emberhill. He was a good man. Better than most I've met. He loved Elias, especially. He always said he didn't have a favorite employee, but we all knew better. Elias was a good sport about it, though.

"Jackson Poole was good friends with a rival landowner. Landry Finn was his name. He and his thugs came for Gus one night. Gus went outside with a lantern while the rest of us watched from a window. Gus thought they were only there to stir up a bit of trouble. I don't think he thought they'd kill him. But they did."

Jae blinked. "And... Elias found Jackson Poole and shot him for it, didn't he?"

Halston nodded. "Sheriff Poole hated Gus, too. Elias and some of the other cowhands figured he was in on the murder. They knew Gus would receive no justice from the law. So they delivered it themselves." He shut his eyes. "They left early in the morning. None of us were awake to try and stop them.

"The next thing I knew, we were running." He rested his hands on his knees. "We just ran and ran and we've never stopped."

He thought she would say something else, but she didn't. She didn't even look at him. She sat with her neck bent, facing the floor. It was like she'd stopped listening to him, but he knew she hadn't.

The door creaked, and Halston almost jumped. A shaft of light streamed in through the doorway, and Sterling stepped onto the stairway, a lantern in hand. He tipped his hat at Halston, as though nothing had happened. Like they were two acquaintances passing each other on the street. He reached the bottom step and tossed a sack onto the floor. It landed by Halston's boots.

"Your breakfast is in there, and some water," Sterling said. "Eat. We'll talk again in a few hours. I have business to take care of." He turned to leave.

Halston didn't eat. He kicked the sack aside and stood. "*Tell me* what you want!"

Sterling stopped, hesitating before he turned back. "I want the girl, Halston. Don't be so daft."

"Her name is Tsashin."

"Her *name* ain't important." Sterling's fingers twitched on the lantern's handle. "Feeling a bit bolder than usual, Halston? Alright, then. Should I double up on your guards?"

Halston raised his head, looking Sterling in his coppery brown eyes. There were so many names he had for Sterling. Some were in languages his tongue couldn't form. He wanted to shoot them all Sterling's way.

"It won't make a difference," said Halston. "I'm not going to play games with you. It won't work anymore."

Sterling's face was vacant for a moment. Then, he began to laugh, the sound harsh and breathy from his mouth. "Alright, then. I can make this difficult, if that's what you want. You know, I wasn't going to take the blade off the table, Halston. As far as I'm concerned, if it takes you far away from me, it's best for both of us. You go home. I get my prize. Neither of us has to see the other ever again."

He paused for a moment, and his fierce gaze softened into an expression Halston could only describe as gracious. "Like it or not, Halston... I need you. For now, at least."

Halston wouldn't believe it for a second. Heat passed through his trigger finger, and Halston swallowed the guilt that came with the sensation. "You're lying."

Sterling grinned. "Yeah. Perhaps I am." He set the lantern down and waved a hand.

Jae screamed.

The ground jolted, sending a wave of shock up their legs. A circle rippled in the air next to Sterling, rimmed by a soft, hazy border. The shape grew, like a bloodstain spreading across a piece of cloth. At first, the surface glimmered like a pool of clear water, but through it, Halston could see a landscape. A pale, silver sky above an endless stretch of rock. Pebbles, cobbles, boulders, mountains, all the same flat, dull gray. They stretched for miles. For ages.

He felt his jaw drop, his eyes freeze open in fear.

He'd been here before.

He'd run through it, bound for the cold Mescan ground.

"Want to go back?" asked Sterling, motioning to the world through the portal. "I'm giving you a way out. Go and seek your freedom."

Halston sank back, pushing himself against the wall.

"Want me to give you a shove?"

"No!" cried Jae.

Sterling glowered at her. "Remember what I told you."

Jae winced, sagging back into the corner.

Sterling turned back to Halston. "Make your choice, Halston.

Walk back into the Median, or stay here and do what I tell you to."

"I'll do what you say!" Halston shouted. He lost the will to keep his eyes open. He shut them tight and prayed that the portal would be gone when he opened them.

"Good," said Sterling.

Halston waited a few more moments, wondering if he'd open his eyes and find himself trapped in that rocky expanse. He forced himself to lift his head and look around. He was still in the dank, clammy cellar, Jae at his side and Sterling at his front.

Sterling said, "Eat. Drink. I'll be back for you later." He retrieved the lantern and disappeared up the stairs.

When he slipped through the door, Halston fell to his knees.

"Halston!" Jae leapt to his side and knelt down.

He couldn't stop it. Pain flared in his chest, and his breaths escaped from his mouth in short, shallow gusts. Numbness crawled up his arms, his blood roaring through him like hot smoke.

He was sinking.

Jae's placed her hand onto his upper back. Her touch was soft, light as the summer sun streaming through a pane of glass. She whispered, "Halston. Stay with me."

She said it again, and again.

They stayed there, kneeling in that cellar until the night faded and the soft dawn turned to clouded daylight. When he could once more funnel air through his mouth, and the pounding in his chest settled, she was still whispering to him.

"Stay with me."

Chapter 24

"Hodge, wake up."

Hodge rolled over and rubbed his eyes. Tsashin stood leaning over him, the tips of her hair brushing his forehead.

"Look what I found." She held out her arms. A bounty of wild onions rested in her hands.

He grinned. "Where'd you find those?"

She motioned downhill through the ring of pines. "There's a clearing over there. I found a whole patch of them. I thought you could help me pick some before we set out."

He fetched his hat from its resting place and put it on. "Sounds good to me."

Tall grass tickled their legs as they moved, and moths fluttered above the ground. The air smelled of dew and sap, and already, the day was warm. Hodge had always liked spring mornings. They reminded him of his mother, warm and sweet like her.

Lorelin had insisted they all get a few hours of sleep, but Hodge hadn't fallen into anything but a restless stupor. Every time he closed his eyes, he saw Sterling perched over Halston, slashing his scars open again.

They'd come close to death before. Shaken hands with it and snatched coins out of its pockets. Hodge didn't care how many times he'd danced around his own grave, but damn it… he wasn't going to bury his other brother.

He tried to shake the dread away. Sterling wouldn't kill him. Not until he had what he wanted, at least, and it was Hodge's job to keep him from getting it.

The clearing was grassy and steep, and there were rocks all over the place. The area receded into a ledge—a jagged shelf looming over a drop of about four yards. Tsashin led him to a row of holes with earth scattered about them. "Here they are. I'm sure we can pick enough to feed everyone. They're not quite ripe yet, but they'll do."

Hodge pushed his sleeves up to his elbows, and they got to work, digging and scraping the vegetables until their hands were caked with dirt. Tsashin began sawing through the stalks with her fingernails.

Hodge drew the knife from his belt. "Here," he said, passing it to her. "Use this. It'll go by a lot faster."

She thanked him and took the knife. He watched her work. The sunlight cast a crown on her thick black hair.

"How're your memories?" asked Hodge.

Tsashin scratched her brow. "It's strange. I remember pieces. Running through the woods, laughter, and songs. The taste of fresh fruit. The touch of the river against my legs. The shade of a wickiup. I feel that I had a family. I can still feel the love for them stirring inside me. But I don't remember their names."

Hodge tapped the ground beside him. The grass was warm under his palms. "They'll come back to you. I'm sure of it."

She smiled. "Thank you. And we'll find Halston and Jae. They're nearby. I can feel it." She trailed a few yards from him, picked up the onions, and gathered them in her shirt. "Come. Lorelin said we'll have to move fast if we want to reach Bruhn by tomorrow."

Hodge took a step after her, but his thoughts were scattered by a *crack*. Tsashin screamed, swooping to the ground, hands locked to her head. Hodge whirled around to the tree rising behind him. The bark splintered. Someone had shot at him.

"Tsashin! Run!" Hodge hurried forward.

Tsashin flattened herself against the ground when their assailant shot again. The bullet thundered from a cluster of bushes near the drop-off.

Hodge glimpsed a shape through the bushes and shot, his bullets sending a few flowers to their deaths. Petals flew about as the gunman jolted in his spot and leapt to the side.

Although Hodge didn't get a good look at him, he recognized him by his wiry frame and the fine blonde hair sticking out in every direction. It was Wolf—Sterling's gunman from across the sea.

Hodge raced up the slope toward the ledge, weaving a hard-to-follow path. A bullet slammed into the rock. Instead of shooting again, Wolf ran Hodge's way. Hodge fired twice, but both were near misses.

Hodge shot a third time. The bullet landed near Wolf's left foot, and he flinched for a moment. Hodge snatched up the advantage, aimed for the gunslinger's stomach, and shot again. Wolf yowled like a starved coyote.

Hodge sprinted toward his opponent. One hand pressed to his stomach, the gunslinger raised his pistol with a shaking hand.

Hodge's foot lashed out, hitting Wolf in the calf and sweeping him off his balance. He shuffled, his boots stirring up the pebbles. Suddenly, his fist plowed into Hodge's stomach.

Hodge's gaze clouded over, his breath all but gone. When he recovered, Wolf had his gun raised again. Without a second thought,

Hodge hurled himself forward, bringing both of them to their knees, then their sides.

They spun across the earth, stones digging into their backs. The ground gave way to the feeling of nothingness beneath Hodge's head.

They'd rolled to the ledge.

Hodge found himself lying down with the man on top of him, a prisoner beneath the bow of Wolf's legs. Expecting to see anger in Wolf's eyes, Hodge looked there, but there was nothing fierce about his gaze. Just determination, like he was trying to scale a mountain rather than take another's life.

Hodge shouted, and with all his strength, he threw Wolf to the side. The gunman screamed as he went flying off the ledge, then yelped as he thudded at the bottom.

Shivering like a leaf, Hodge lifted himself up. Blood covered his hands, coating the scabs he'd received fighting the lorthans. He huffed down a heaping breath of air, then peered over the ledge. The man lay sprawled out at the bottom. Red bloomed under his back.

"Tsashin!" cried Hodge.

She poked out from behind a cluster of shrubs, then came running uphill, her hair flying behind her. "Hodge! Are you hurt?"

Hodge shook his head. "I'm alright. Stay away from him." He picked up his guns, then ran down the slope beside the ledge. The ground leveled slightly, and he made his way to Wolf without a second thought.

He wasn't leaving without an answer.

He cocked his gun as he approached the dying man. Wolf was now wheezing like an aging mule. He swallowed. Now that he had a closer look, he saw that this man couldn't have been much older than him. Twenty at the very most. He had a thin face, boots full of holes, and his clothes were so baggy they looked like they might slip from his limbs.

His shirt was soaked, the blood gushing from his gut.

Still, Hodge didn't lower the gun. "Where's Sterling?"

Wolf winced. "Oh, gods. I'm bleeding."

Hodge gritted his teeth. "Don't play games with me, Wolf. Sterling sent you. Is there anyone else?"

Wolf coughed twice, pressing his hands to his stomach. "I don't know."

"Where did Sterling go? Where did he take my brother and Jae?"

"I won't say." His breathing sounded more like gulping now. "I never thought it would feel like this. Dyin'."

"I can stop your pain. But you gotta tell me where they went," said Hodge.

"Why?" Wolf spat, a thin trail of blood streaming from the corner of his mouth. "I joined Sterling so I could pay a doctor. My wife wouldn't have lived to see her last summer if I hadn't. But she died that September anyway, and Sterling wouldn't let me leave him. If Sterling wants your brother dead, nothin' *you do* is gonna stop him."

"Stop!" Hodge snapped. "Is Halston alive?"

"Yeah. For now." Wolf raised a trembling arm, pointing at Tsashin. "I had orders to kill everyone but her."

Hodge opened his mouth to offer a merciful bullet in exchange for Halston's whereabouts, but a loud choking sound escaped Wolf's lips. A moment later, his chest went still, his blue eyes fixed on the cloudless sky.

Hodge shook his head, then slid his gun back into its holster. "I'm sorry." It didn't come out as much more than a whisper.

Tsashin sat on the ledge, covering her eyes to shield herself from the sight. "Hodge. We have to go back. We have to tell the others."

Hodge nudged the body with his boot. Gods, this man had had a wife. He'd joined Sterling to save her. Not for greed or glory or to taste the thrill of riding from a heist, guns blazing. He'd just wanted to protect somebody he loved.

"Hodge," Tsashin said again. "It's going to be alright."

Hodge finally forced himself to back away, but not before pulling Wolf's eyelids shut.

He started walking with Tsashin back to camp, thinking of a long row of faces he wanted to forget, but never would. Wolf's ghost entered his mind and took a seat.

They didn't have to walk far outside the clearing before they met Lorelin and Gryff. "We heard gunshots!" Lorelin cried. "Gods, Hodge! Are you bleeding?"

"It ain't mine," Hodge said. "It's Wolf's."

"Wolf's?" blurted Gryff. "The hell?"

"Sterling sent him after us," Hodge explained. "But… I got him to spill, a little. Before he bled out. We'll have to be careful 'bout covering our tracks, though. If Sterling finds out that Wolf is dead, I reckon he'll send someone else after us."

Lorelin looked to Gryff. Her eyes were worried, flickering, but Gryff's were hard, like he'd expected this. Hodge doubted there was much that could surprise the old fella anymore.

"Keep your eyes wide open, then," Gryff said, his tone even lower than usual. "We'll move fast. The sooner we reach Bruhn, the better."

Tsashin said, softly, "We should take the main road. Think of it. If our own prints merge with the other tracks, they will have a harder time following us."

It felt like a recipe for trouble, but she had a point. They were following the river, now that the only map they had was a plain, non-magic one. Hodge just hoped that any other trackers were far enough behind them that a day of covering their tracks and walking down a well-used road would throw them off for a while. Maybe they were still poking around in the woods outside Mourelle, if they were coming at all.

Gryff and Lorelin helped Hodge hide Wolf. They carried him into the bushes, brushed a bit of earth over his face, and left him there. Soon, the wind would sweep dirt and leaves over him, and his bones would sink into the ground. Hodge wondered if they should say a prayer or something, but he'd just killed this man. He doubted the gods would care much for any prayers of his.

He should've been angry. If he had a lick of self-respect, he would've spat on Wolf's makeshift grave. But he couldn't.

He didn't hate Wolf.

He hated Sterling.

They found the road and walked for a while. There wasn't any noise to follow them besides the wind shaking the treetops. Hodge almost liked the look of the road spanning ahead of them. It gave him a sense of knowing.

Before long, they stopped to rest. They settled on the side of the trail, nestling themselves in a cool patch of shade. Sipped water. Wiped the dirt from their faces. Hodge changed his shirt, then sat next to Tsashin, who was still. Hodge didn't blame her. He'd fared similarly the first time he'd seen a man die.

"I'm… I'm sorry you had to see that," said Hodge.

She shook her head. "Thank you. You saved me."

The man wouldn't have killed her. If he'd had his way, he would've gunned down Hodge and carried Tsashin off. The thought of that spiked another wave of anger in him. "There's something you ought to know. You don't have to stay with us. If it's too much. We'll understand."

"Where else would I *go?*" she asked. "There is nothing I remember. I doubt anyone else could help me. You've protected me. You saved me from the darkness. I would have stayed beneath the earth if you hadn't brought me out. I trust you."

Hodge swallowed. "I know. I just had to say so."

She said, "I don't want Sterling to find us."

Hodge said, "He ain't gonna. We're gonna get away from him. Right after we get Hal and Jae out."

Gods, he hated this. Tsashin deserved a better guide, to ride alongside solid company. He knew what it was like to be lost and afraid and trying to make sense of a world you didn't know.

He just wished he could tell her how to handle it, because he knew damn well that he hadn't yet learned to do it himself.

Chapter 25

H ours passed. Halston sat a yard or so away from Jae, not asleep, but as still as if he were, his brown eyes glazed over.

She'd tried talking to him, but Halston hadn't even acknowledged she was there beyond the occasional glance. Still shaken up from earlier, she reckoned. Jae hadn't wrapped her head around the circle that Sterling had opened in the air.

He was a *warlock*.

What was that place that lay beyond the outline? And why did Halston fear it?

At last, evening came. Jae sighed, rubbing her temples and trying to soothe the aching in her head. What would Pa do if he were here?

She'd grown up thinking there was nothing impossible for him. She never thought she'd lose him, let alone in the way she had. Snatched. Stolen.

Jae closed her eyes. She might as well try and get some sleep. She'd spent part of the day pacing around the room again, checking for any imperfections she might have missed in the walls. She slid down the wall and lay on her side, shifting until she was as comfortable as she could be on this dirt floor.

When she shoved her hands beneath her head, Halston's voice cut the air like an arrow. "It was a portal."

Jae lifted her head and rolled onto her other side to face Halston. "What?"

"Sterling," said Halston. "He opened a portal. To the Median."

Jae wasn't sure why, but the word struck her like the fall of an axe. "Median." She shivered as she spoke it. It felt like being a child and learning your first swear word. "What is it?"

"A whole lot of nothing," said Halston. "Grim streaks of left-over worlds where nothing moves or grows. And if he tosses me there... I'm done for."

Jae shook her head. "Worlds? More than one?"

"Yes," said Halston. "Far more than one. Too many to count."

Jae didn't speak. She waited for him to continue, wondering if he would elaborate. But even if he did, would it make a lick of sense?

Jae thought back to all the reports she'd read about Sterling Byrd and his gang. They were notorious for their quick and brutal raids, riding out of town and leaving without a trace. Some lawmen even said that their tracks disappeared in the middle of the trail, as if the gang had risen into the air.

Of course.

To most folks, it would have sounded like nonsense... but Jae knew there were stranger things in this world.

———

A few more days passed. They slept, ate what little food was brought to them, and drank muddy river water from a waterskin that Lyle brought to them each evening. From time to time, they'd walk along the walls, though they both knew it was futile. There was no escaping through the cellar itself. If they ran, they'd have to get past their guard.

Halston was less of a stranger than he'd been several weeks ago, but a stranger all the same. They'd buried the words they'd hurled each other's way after gunning the lorthans down. It did not matter if Halston was a stranger or a thief, because if she could not take him as an ally, then they were both good as dead.

On the night of what Jae guessed was their third day in the cellar, the doorknob clicked and rattled. Jae jumped a little, cringing. She sat up straight, then watched the door swing open. Lyle stood in the arch and motioned her way. One of his brothers stood with him, but Jae would be damned if she ever bothered learning to tell them apart. "Sterling wants a word with you both, now."

Jae took a breath and approached the stairs. Halston followed her. Part of her wanted to reach out and take his hand, just so neither of them would feel alone. But for a reason she couldn't name, she didn't.

Unceremoniously, Lyle and his brother led them back to the same room, shoved the pair inside, and shut the door.

Jae's map lay on the table, unrolled and ready to be touched. There were two more chairs sitting across from Sterling, now, frail-looking things with thin legs and arched backs. He motioned to Jae and Halston to sit down.

Jae snorted. How courteous of him to provide them with chairs. She took a seat and looked out the window, a pale moon staring back at her. Halston settled down beside her. He looked calm. Bored, even.

Sterling said, "Touch the map."

Jae placed her hands on the paper.

"Ask it to show you the Harney gang."

"It doesn't work for people. Just places."

"Try."

Gently, Jae said, "Show me the Harney gang."

The map remained the same. Sterling grunted. "Figured it couldn't hurt to check. Wolf still ain't back. Ain't sure I can rely on him, especially since the lot of us trampled the earth outside Mourelle, after your brother decided he'd make things difficult for us all. I'll get the girl eventually, but time is precious. I ain't too fond of using up more of it than I need."

Jae tilted her head, not sure what Sterling had in mind.

Halston's mouth stayed shut. His eyes were dull at first glance, but there was iron behind them.

"It's been several days since we left Mourelle. We had to come here on business, and there's no chance of your gang finding this place," said Sterling. "I'll keep a few men here to wait for my tracker. See if he returns without the Yunah girl or any leads. The rest of us will set out for a different hideout. I reckon they'll seek out all the places we've met before to find y'all."

Halston frowned.

Sterling simpered back at him. "Got somethin' to say?"

"It sounds like you have your plan worked out," Halston replied. "So I'm curious about why you called us here."

"Wanted to see if the map would work. Besides, I thought I'd be polite. Let you know we're leaving soon," said Sterling.

"No," said Halston. "There's something else you want from us. What is it?"

Silence passed over them, the air so thick, no one could even hack through it with a blade. It was only April, but heat swallowed them whole. Sweat baked under Jae's clothing, and she itched to rip off her jacket.

"I thought I might wait a night or two," Sterling said at last. "But I figured now's as good a time as any for you to make your choice, Halston."

"What choice?"

"I reckon your brother will come for you soon," said Sterling. "Now, Pierce is comin' through. Should be back to himself shortly. But Hodge has a score to settle with us." His grin widened. "Unless *you'd* like to take it from him."

Halston held firm, but Jae glimpsed a flash of fear on his face. "What are you saying?" he asked.

"I'll keep you around until your gang shows up," said Sterling. "But one of you must pay for the attempt on Pierce's life. I'm granting you the courtesy of taking it from Hodge. The first time you had to pay for your gang's blunder with a job, you seemed eager to take your brother's place. Thought I'd extend the offer again."

Halston leapt from his chair. "You—"

He never got a chance to finish his sentence. Sterling's hand flew to his belt and drew what Jae first thought was a gun. She screamed, but no shot came. Instead, Sterling swiped the object across Halston's face, and he hit the floor.

Sterling planted his boot on Halston's back. Halston struggled under Sterling's weight, blood pooling from the scratch on his face. Sterling lifted the knife—a fat, sharp blade curved near the tip. "Y'know, maybe I don't really *need* you alive. Your friends just gotta *think* you're alive."

Jae's hands shot out ahead of her and snatched the map off the table. "Stop!" she yelled. "Get away from him!" She hoisted the map into the air, then Sterling sheathed his knife. He drew his gun and aimed it her way.

Gritting her teeth, Jae held the map up with both hands. "I'll shred it. I'll rip it to bits if you kill him. And then it won't be any good to you."

Sterling's fingers twitched on the grip.

He wouldn't shoot. Sterling wanted her map. She was like a

nugget of gold, and shooting her would be like tossing the metal back into a river. He stared at her, watching her stand her ground. Halston remained on the floor, trapped under Sterling's hold. None of them blinked or twitched.

At last, Sterling snorted and slid the revolver back into his holster. "Lyle! Ned!"

A few moments passed. The door opened, and the blue-eyed gunslingers hurried in. "Sterling?"

Sterling took his foot off Halston's back. "Take Halston back to the cellar. I'll have a few more words with this one."

Halston stood, keeping his gaze off the two guards. The cut ran from his right cheek down to his mouth. Jae tried to focus on it, wondering how deep it was, but then the guards seized Halston by the arms and walked him away. The door slammed shut, clashing like metal on stone.

Sterling holstered his gun. "Put the map *down,* Jae."

Swiftly, she did.

Sterling shook his head. "You'd be wise to bargain for yourself alone. Leaping to defend a man who's done nothing for you? A fool's game."

Jae tried not to tremble. Gods above… she'd just bartered with him for Halston's safety. This man had threatened to gun her down if she ran off, and she'd still grabbed that map without thinking. "They saved me."

"When?"

"During the bank heist. A deputy shot me in the arm. I thought they would leave me there, but they carried me out. So… he *has* done something for me, believe it or not."

Sterling snorted. "You're the strangest bounty hunter I've ever met."

"Thanks."

She wanted him to call for Lyle so the gunslinger could drag her back to the cellar and shove her inside. Maybe she and Halston could discuss ways they could escape. She wanted to go back to him, to make sure he wasn't bleeding all over the place, to sit with him and speak.

Halston. Her ally.

Sterling fingered the handle of his knife. Jae frowned. "Why did you cut him?"

"Hmm?"

"Even if you wanted to give him a chance to take Hodge's place, why'd you do it *now?*" asked Jae.

Sterling folded his arms and chuckled. "Halston tends to fancy himself a leader. I like to remind him of his place."

"Seems unnecessary."

"Why do you care?" Sterling asked. "Thought you joined him so you could collect his bounty."

Silence stirred between them for a few minutes. Sterling asked, "The Nefili man who gave you that map. What was his name?"

"Grove."

"Hmm." Sterling settled back against his chair, drumming his scarred fingers on the table. His fingertips were white and calloused, and there was dirt caked around his nails. "Last night, I began to wonder if you'd met my father. He was... well known for meeting with women in the woods. My mother was a favorite of his. But he also enjoyed wasting his time drinking Nefilium wine and playing tricks on travelers."

Jae tilted her head, unable to contain her urge to hear more. Warlocks got their power from Nefili heritage. Folks said that the power was sometimes unpredictable, but generally, the more closely related they were to one of the Nefilium, the stronger their magic was. And Nefilium tended to stay away from humans, so warlocks were about as rare as veins of gold in the earth.

Sterling went on. "If there's one thing I can be grateful for in this world, it's knowing that I'll die one day. Endless life turns you into an aimless dunce. Fools, the Nefilium are. Every last one of 'em.'"

Jae couldn't stop herself from asking, "What do you mean?"

"They've got all the time in the world. So they waste it, free of ambition. My father would wander in the wilds, warm my mother's bed when he tired of it, then disappear again.

"I never cared for him. Pierce didn't either, but Pierce wasn't his son. Our ma claimed she didn't even know who Pierce's father was." Sterling glanced out the window at the cloudy night sky. "I envied Pierce, sometimes. Without magic, he had something to prove. It made him deft. Made him strong.

"Argus was the only one who loved our father. When he visited, he told us stories. Old legends from the Outlands. His favorite was the story of the Veyres."

"Veyres?"

Sterling grinned. "A warlock family. Big one. They grew unhappy with their own power.

"See... the Nefilium don't belong here. Never have. They crossed into this world from their own. I reckon they'd deny it if you asked one about it. It's been thousands of years, at least. They left the realm behind, and with it... magic. Magic thrumming like diamonds in the earth. Magic they could harvest and grow into their own power.

"So the Veyres tore a gash in the sky and vanished."

"Like you did in the cellar?"

Sterling nodded. "I've no interest in crossing to another world. Not when I can reap all this one has to offer. Besides, tearing a hole in the fabric of the earth is just one step of the way. The Veyres had no guarantee of finding what they sought. Probably spent their days searching for magic ore that they never found."

Jae said, "Seems a decent goal to me."

Sterling chuckled. "You'd think that, I'm sure. But think of this. There's a stack of bills in front of you. But you've overheard a rumor about a cave of gold, one that could be thousands of miles away. Would you take the bills, or go after the cave?"

"Bills," said Jae, though she didn't mean it. An adventure in the pursuit of a fabled cave sounded far more exciting. What a journey that would be.

Sterling nodded. "The Harney boys got a code for themselves. I've met plenty of men like them. Men who would steal but wouldn't kill, who'd lie but wouldn't fight. Out here, there's a difference between men who live and men who die: the living hold fewer things sacred.

"Men can wander forever in search of peace, or riches they'll never come by. Others can live fast and take what's right in front of them. I decided that was how I'd spend my time on this earth."

"Took a long time for you to say all that," said Jae. "The word you're searching for is 'greedy.'"

"Are you any different?" Sterling asked with a grin. "I line my pockets with the money I reap from these budding towns. You fill yours with the money you acquire from killing men like me. We both finish jobs with blood on our hands. Mine makes me a scoundrel. Yours makes you a hero, but I reckon it ain't any easier to wash off."

"I only kill when I have to."

"No," said Sterling. "You kill them every time. If they don't wind up in a noose, you confine them to a cell for what remains of their lives. Their freedom. Gone. Tell me how that's any more remarkable than death."

Trying to kill Sterling would be lunacy, but her trigger finger started twitching like a bird with a broken wing.

I'm different from you, thought Jae. *Men like you are the reason bounty hunters stalk across these lands. Men like you deserve to bleed. To rot.*

But she couldn't bring herself to say it.

Sterling reached for the map and rolled it into a tube. "I'm finished with you. Lyle will take you back to the cellar. Sleep."

Jae barely remembered the walk back to the cellar. The shabby hallway stretched ahead of her, but all she could see was Sterling's wolf-like grin.

She found Halston sitting in the corner, pressing his sleeve to his cheek. "Just a scratch," he said. "I'll be alright. Jae... thank you."

"What for?"

"For saving my life."

She wanted to say it was nothing. Sterling just wanted to remind Halston of who was in charge. Would he have killed him, though? The sorry truth was Jae couldn't say for sure.

"No... uh, problem," she said, then winced. It was a stupid thing to say, but it mattered not. While her mind told her that they needed to start scraping a plan together, her body didn't long for anything but sleep. "You should rest. If your cut starts bleeding again, let me know."

Halston didn't speak again, but the look he gave her was soft and gracious. She felt something small and warm budding in her chest, and she wasn't sure what it was. She hadn't felt anything like it before.

Jae wasn't in the mood to try and figure it out. She lay down and let the silence carry her away.

Chapter 26

The day passed without too much excitement, then another. When evening came, they passed a road sign on a bent post—a wooden arrow pointing in Bruhn's direction.

Most of the time, Hodge's memories didn't latch onto towns. If someone asked him to describe Carth, Ameda, and Sienna, he doubted his descriptions would be much different from each other.

Bruhn was different. He'd only been here one other time, but every yard of it had been etched into his mind after he'd first stepped onto its streets.

The forest thinned as they moved down the road, and the wind nipped at their faces. The view spanned ahead of them—the town of Bruhn resting in between a few small, knobby hills.

Even from up here, it was easy to see why Coy had picked this town to open a shooting pit. The whole thing looked like a bunch of clueless folks had built it. It was small, but the buildings dotted the ground in a messy, aimless pattern. The structures came in all thicknesses and many heights, like a lump of mushrooms growing in a damp, muggy patch of earth. Behind the town, a ridge of red cliffs stretched above the woods, their faces blocky and streaked with long grooves.

The sun was going down, a yellow arc dipping behind the horizon. They finally reached Bruhn's streets, if you could call them that. The paths were about as tangled as a heap of old rope. Trash sat on the storefronts: cigarette butts, broken glass, chunks of old wood.

Lorelin wrinkled her nose. "Let's be quick here."

Coy's pit was hard to miss. The building was closer to the size of an enormous barn than any other club Hodge had been to, its name scrawled above the double front doors in blocky white letters: "Rattler's Way." The gang was still a good walk away from it, but the sounds of drunken laughter and clanging metal still smothered out the sighing wind.

One of the front doors was propped open by a barrel. One by one, they stepped inside, Hodge at the lead.

He'd seen the crowds here before, but it was even more packed than the last time he'd stood within these walls. To the right, wood rose from the floor like the dock in a harbor, but instead of water, it sat above a wide pit of dirt. There were two levels on the deck, each one packed with tables and chairs. Men sat and smoked and drank at them, and the smell of liquor and gunpowder was sharp and heavy. A few girls with curled hair and dresses laced at the chest sauntered through the stands, carrying mugs on trays and giggling. A wall of bricks circled the pit, stacked about three feet high on all sides but the one parallel to the risers.

Hodge narrowed his eyes. The pit was massive, taking up most of the building's space. Upright logs spread across the dirt, targets painted on them, though they were all so full of holes Hodge could barely make out the lines. On the back wall, a stuffed moose head looked out over the pit. Hodge wondered how many bullet holes filled its skull.

A short fella with tan skin and a stiff hat stood in the pit, wearing a vest so red it almost hurt to look at. Hodge watched him fire two shots, then turned his attention to a long table before the sitting platform. A gentleman sat there, shifting coins across the wood and scribbling something down on a pad of paper. Coy.

Coy was young, thirty at the very most, and he was one of the handsomer fellas Hodge had met in Mesca. He was sturdier than Hodge remembered, fair-skinned and square-jawed, with a plump mouth and thick, reddish-brown hair combed back over his head. He wore a black shirt with big, shiny buttons and ropey ties by the collar. It didn't look like anything Hodge had ever seen an outlaw wearing. Too expensive. Coy must've built a good life for himself here.

"Coy!" Hodge called, running up to the table.

Coy looked up, and a slight scream came out of his mouth at the sight of Gryff. Gryff snorted, and Coy began to laugh. "Ya startled me there, big guy."

"Yeah, sorry 'bout that. My presence tends to be a little much for some folk."

Coy lifted his chin at Hodge, grinning. "Never thought I'd see you again, Hodge."

"It's good to see you, too," said Hodge. "We were hoping you could help us."

The bottom of Coy's jaw quirked to the side. "I've become a respectable gent 'round here, Hodge. The sheriff himself pays me to come and watch tournaments on Saturday nights. I don't do favors."

Lorelin placed a hand on the table, leaning Coy's way. "Come on, Coy. You won't leave us in the cold, will you?"

Coy looked away from her, though Hodge swore he saw the man's cheeks going pink. Coy grumbled, "What do y'all want?"

"Sterling took my brother," Hodge said quickly. "And… another friend. They left from Mourelle, and we don't know where they went. You were part of Sterling's gang longer than us. Where's their nearest hideout?"

A smug grin tugged at Coy's lips, the kind that made Hodge want to smack it off. Coy said, "How much money you got on you?"

"Ten crowns," Hodge said without thinking. If he remembered correctly, he only had five deons left in his knapsack, but he hoped Coy wouldn't bother to check. "Come on, Coy. Don't be so uptight. We're gonna give Sterling hell when we see him again. Thought you'd be mad at him for giving you the boot."

That certainly made Coy drop his stupid grin. "Yeah, 'course I am."

Tsashin spoke up, her voice laced with more gall than Hodge thought she had in her. "He only wants to save his brother! You act as if this is some market trade. Please. Can't you show us a kindness?"

A wheezing laugh came out of Coy. He slapped the table, then covered his mouth with one hand. "Where'd you find this one?" He cast his dumb simper Tsashin's way. "Look here, sweetheart. I don't know how things are where you come from, but here, you don't expect people to give you what you want just because you asked for it. Even if you're nice about it. I like these fellas well enough, but nobody walks into my club without paying their way. I'll make an exception for y'all. You can pay to play, or you can pay to watch. What'll it be?"

"Fine." Hodge reached into his knapsack and gathered up the coins sitting at the bottom. "How much is it to shoot?"

"Just a deon."

Hodge slapped the coin on the table. "What do I get if I win?"

Coy shrugged. "Depends on the challenge, and what the betters put down."

"How about this," Hodge said. "If I lose, you can keep my ten crowns. If I win, you tell me where the hideout is. No more bullshit."

Without looking away from Hodge, Coy smiled and slid the deon into his hand. "It's a deal. Looks like Antonio down there is about finished." He put his fingers in his mouth, turned, and whistled. "Luther! I've got our next contestant."

Hodge barely had time to close his sack before a man stomped over to the table. He was about Hodge's height, but seemed taller, like a straight beanstalk sprouting beside a wilted one. Hodge couldn't tell if he was scowling, or if his thick brows were so close to his eyes that it just seemed that way. Although they were close to the same height, they were nowhere close to the same width—Luther's torso was shaped like an arrowhead, and his arms were almost as thick as aspen trunks.

Luther pointed to Hodge's guns. "Six shooters?"

"Yeah."

"Bring one. You'll have six targets."

"Hold on," Coy said. "I used to work with this kid. I've seen what kind of a shot he is. Don't give him the regular targets. Give him the rattler's round."

Hodge hadn't the slightest idea what a "rattler's round" meant, but after the self-satisfied look the men shared with each other, he didn't want to guess. *Damn it, Coy.*

They followed Luther and Coy across the stands, approaching the other side of the floor. The crowd had quieted down. As the company made their way before them, the crowd whispered, and Hodge figured they were probably eyeing Gryff and sneering. Gryff muttered something about how they "couldn't teach chickens how to cluck."

Hodge didn't get a chance to speak to the others before Luther did. "Follow me. Leave one of your guns with them."

Hodge took one pistol out of his belt and passed it to Gryff. "Take this by the horns, boy," Gryff told him. "We didn't come here for nothin'.""

"Come on, Gryff, you say that like I might fail. I won't."

He gave Tsashin and Lorelin a smile. Something went cold inside him when he saw their worried faces, but he did his best to harden it. He wasn't about to walk away from this. Not from the challenge, not from Sterling, and certainly not from Halston.

Luther led him to the right, down a short wooden stairway leading to the dirt pit. A narrow gate divided it from the stands, like the door of a pigpen. Before opening it, Luther explained, "Usually I announce the targets, but Coy likes to have the rattler's round to himself. He'll let you know what to do."

"What'll I be shooting?"

Luther snorted. "Eager, eh? The first four will be card shots. Then there'll be a target over your shoulder. Last one... you'll have to shoot the knife."

"*What* knife?"

"You'll know it when you see it."

Hodge tried asking him to clarify, but Luther waved a hand. "No more questions. You're wasting everyone's time. They paid for a show, not to sit while you dawdle with me. Step into the pit."

Hodge clamped his mouth shut and turned away. On any other day, he'd have tried to snatch up the last word, but not right now. Luther was right. They were wasting time.

Hodge stepped in through the gate, one hand on his pistol's grip. He stepped across the dirt, and behind him, Coy's voice flooded the room. "Turn your heads this way, gentlemen! Our competitor has chosen the rattler's round. Perhaps he'll be the first ever to win."

Chapter 27

Hodge stood near the center of the pit, then faced the crowd. Gryff, Tsashin, and Lorelin sat at a table near the stairway, all of them holding so still it made him twitch. The rest of the crowd hadn't finished roaring with excitement.

Hodge certainly hadn't anticipated this. He'd thought that they would walk into this club, have a discussion with Coy, and leave straight for Sterling's hideout. Hodge supposed that he was old enough to know better than to assume just about anything. It was too hard for some folks to just keep things simple. Then again, Hodge supposed he shouldn't have been expecting any favors.

Coy stood in the middle of the stands, positioned on a length of the deck that jutted out a little further from the rest, like the prow of a ship. He raised a hand to shush the crowd, then leered down at Hodge. "Step back. Stand by target number one."

Hodge glanced to his left, at the log target resting a few paces away. The number twelve covered its base, the white paint scuffed and chipped. Hodge walked backwards… and walked. And walked.

Target number one was at the farthest end of the pit, no more than three feet away from the wall parallel to the front doors. Hodge snorted, wondering if they'd ever used target number one. He pitied the poor soul who could miss a shot that close.

He was at least thirty yards from the other side of the pit. He widened his stance. Then, he fingered his pistol and waited. The crowd went from talking, to whispering, to falling dead silent.

Coy said, "Your first four targets will be cards. When I toss 'em, you shoot. You miss one, you step outta the pit. Ready?"

Hodge looked to Coy, who was holding the playing cards like a small fan. Hodge didn't bother speaking. He simply nodded, then held his pistol ready.

The first card flew through the air like a dragonfly. Hodge shot, the sound cracking off the pit's walls. The next two came even more quickly, spiraling down toward the ground, but he fired twice, his arm whipping side to side. The cards came too fast for him to worry about whether he'd hit them or not.

He drew in a breath, and Coy sent the fourth card flying. Hodge squeezed the trigger, and the shot bolted from his gun.

Hodge waited in place and squinted at the ground by Coy, trying to count the scraps of cardstock on the pit's dirt floor. He watched Luther hustle up to them, then snatch them off the ground. Luther traipsed up to Coy and passed the cards to him.

Coy flipped through the cards, taking his sweet time. A minute passed. Hodge glared, trying not to think of all the choice words he'd have for Coy as soon as they knew where the hideout was.

At last, Coy said, "Got 'em all."

The crowd erupted.

Luther approached Hodge, then, wearing a stone-cold expression. Hodge raised an eyebrow, wondering what he wanted. Luther simply held out his arm. There was something round and shiny in

246 : Sophia Minetos

his hand.

A mirror.

Luther placed it in Hodge's hand, then turned and headed back for the gate. Hodge was tempted to ask what the mirror was for, even though he knew that was probably a stupid thing to ask right now.

Luther walked back to the other side of the pit and dragged one of the log targets to the center of the floor.

So, I'll have to shoot it over my shoulder. He'd done something like this before, once. He'd been a boy of thirteen, new to a cowhand's life, and had just gotten his first pistol. On his soonest day off, he made targets out of old discarded boards and set them up on a bare patch of the ranch. His friend Vince taught him to shoot, and they practiced when they both had time to spare until Hodge could shoot a target over his shoulder. Of course, they'd placed those targets much closer than this one.

Luther didn't stop there, though. He balanced something small on top of the log, the color of fresh clay. He stepped away, and Hodge got a better look at it. Some sort of jug, it was.

"Turn," said Coy. "Use the mirror. Shoot when you're ready."

Hodge turned, his back facing the jug. He planted his feet firmly on the ground, then took a look at the front doors. One was still propped open, the wind piping through it.

He ran his thumb down his pistol's wooden grip. Judging by his stance and the jug's location, he had two choices here. Hodge was good with both hands—he was born working with his right, but he'd trained himself to use his left. If he shot with his right hand, he'd have to pull the trigger with his thumb. If he shot with his left hand, he could aim over his right shoulder and shoot normally, but then he'd have to rotate the barrel.

Vince had taught him to shoot with his thumb, but that was years ago.

Still, his instinct whispered to him and said to choose his right hand, so that was what he did.

Hodge held the mirror at eye level, then moved it forward until he could see the jug in the reflection. The mirror was a near-perfect circle, rimmed with brass and tarnished at the edges. No matter how much he tried to steady his hand, the mirror seemed to keep wavering in it. Nerves clamped down on his stomach. He urged himself to push them away.

He aligned the barrel with the jug, still trying to keep the mirror still.

This must be what it feels like to shoot drunk.

But he fired it anyway.

And in the mirror, he watched the jug explode.

The crowd whooped and whistled once more, but Hodge didn't pay them any heed. He wasn't here for their entertainment.

One bullet left in his gun.

Hodge turned his head left and right, looking to the log targets, Luther, the walls of the pit, and the crowd. Luther said that his last target would be a knife, and that he'd know it when he saw it.

Luther slipped out of the pit, and Hodge raised an eyebrow. Where was he going?

The crowd was quiet again. Hodge cast his gaze their way. He expected them to look excited, all wearing dirty grins. They still looked eager, wide-eyed, but… confused, like they were waiting for an end that wouldn't come.

Hodge shook his head. No more wasting time. He started pacing down the side of the pit, scanning the walls. Was there a knife hanging up somewhere? On a rope, perhaps?

Coy still stood tall on his perch, his fingers drumming on the railing. He wasn't smiling, but his face had that smug, knowing look written all over it. The only man in the room who knew what was coming.

Hodge waited for his instructions, but Coy kept his bow-shaped mouth shut.

Someone screamed.

Hodge jumped, then froze in place. He aimed his gun in the direction of the scream, toward the side gate leading to the stands.

Luther marched back into the pit, and this time, he wasn't alone.

The world seemed to lurch under Hodge's feet.

Held fast in Luther's arm was a young woman, no older than Hodge himself. Younger, maybe. Her dress was wine-red, matching her plump lips, its skirt frilly and falling just above her knees. Brown curls bounced around her shoulders, and while she struggled under Luther's grasp, she didn't kick, didn't put up as much of a fight as she should've.

Hodge heard Tsashin's voice cry out, "Let her go!"

Coy raised a hand. "Calm yourself. Our gunslinger has proved himself a worthy marksman. None of y'all should have anything to worry about." He leered down at the girl. "'Specially not you, Carlotta."

Luther let her go. "Stand up straight."

She stood, placing her willowy arms at her sides. Luther unsheathed a long-bladed knife from his belt, then passed it to the girl. She clutched the handle with a shaking hand, then raised it an inch or two above her head.

"Shoot the knife," said Coy.

Hodge didn't shoot.

He didn't even move.

"Shoot the knife out of her hand, and you win," Coy drawled on. "Unless you'd like to forfeit. 'Course, if you do that, all your money's mine."

The girl—Carlotta—didn't flinch. She stared at Hodge with wide eyes, but she didn't shiver, didn't try to crouch or run.

Perhaps it was because she'd been here before, and none of the men standing before her had ever dared to shoot.

But Hodge wasn't gonna be the first.

Without blinking, without prying his gaze from Luther, he shoved the pistol back into his holster. He started back for the gate, but Luther and Carlotta didn't move. Very well. He'd shove past them if he had to.

"I knew it," Coy spat from his above, the start of a laugh mingling with his words. "I knew you'd walk away. Nobody's ever finished the rattler's round. No one's had the guts."

Rattler's round.

What a stupid name.

Hodge didn't even grant him a glance. Coy didn't deserve one.

At last, Hodge reached the other end of the pit, then stopped a few feet away from Luther and Carlotta. Finally, Luther snorted, and took the knife from the sullen girl. "Go."

Carlotta picked up her skirts and ran to the gate. She lifted the latch, then hurried up the steps without bothering to close it behind her. Hodge kicked it shut, locking eyes with Luther.

Luther snorted. "What're you lookin' at, kid?"

Hodge drew his knife and plunged toward the man.

Luther yelped, raising his own knife in defense. Hodge's blade smacked against Luther's, the metal screeching. Luther's bewildered expression sank into a deep, haggard scowl. Luther shouted, then drew his knife back.

The blade swiped at Hodge's stomach. Hodge shifted back, taking two steps away from Luther. As they realized what was happening, the audience began to murmur. Gryff shouted, "Hodge, you crazy son of a—What the hell are you *doin'?!*"

Luther's arm swung to the side. Hodge ducked, the knife swooping above his head. Hodge shot back up straight. While Luther's arm was still tucked off to the side, Hodge smacked a hand onto his forearm and clamped down. Snarling, Luther drove the knife toward Hodge's waist. Hodge jumped out of the way.

His heart was racing like a speeding train.

Luther brought the knife swinging down again, the motion like a woodcutter, this blow bound for Hodge's head. Hodge raised his own knife to block it. He did, but the impact sent a shockwave plunging down his body. Hodge fell to one knee, managing to keep his knife beneath Luther's as the strong man pushed and pushed.

Half-kneeling, Hodge kept his arm raised and fought against Luther's shove. As they grappled, Hodge gritted his teeth, then formed a fist with his free hand and rammed it into Luther's gut.

Luther grunted and recoiled from the blow, falling to his rump. Lightly, Hodge slashed a line atop Luther's forearm. Luther shouted, and the knife fell from his hands.

In two swift motions, Hodge snatched up Luther's knife and sheathed his own. While Luther was still on the ground, Hodge drew his pistol, then stepped Luther's way.

"Don't!" Luther shouted.

"*I ain't gonna*," snapped Hodge, and rapped him on the head with his pistol's grip.

Luther groaned, slumping to the side. His heads reached for his head, prodding the area Hodge had hit.

But Hodge wasn't done yet.

Luther's knife in one hand, pistol in the other, Hodge trekked back across the pit. The crowd did not cheer. They did not hoot or talk or even whisper.

Coy's beady eyes lingered on Hodge as he stopped before the man's stoop. Hodge maintained their two-way stare for a few moments, letting the uneasiness simmer in the air.

Without looking away from Coy, Hodge tossed the knife upward. He aimed his pistol at the weapon and shot the blade.

————

"You said I had to shoot the blade," Hodge argued, trying not to raise his voice too much. "And that's just what I did."

"You were supposed t'shoot it over her head!"

"Yeah, well, maybe you should've been more specific."

Hodge and his company stood before Coy, stationed between Coy's prow and the stands. Nobody in the crowd was speaking, and Coy stood with his back pressed to the railing above the pit.

Coy squinted. "My business, my rules."

"We made a deal." Hodge pointed to his knapsack. "Hell, I've got more money if you want it."

"I don't respect a smart mouth," Coy spat.

Gryff nudged Hodge. Hodge got out of Gryff's way. Gryff stomped forward, and Coy's eyes began to dance with worry.

"Think you can frighten me, big fella?" Coy sneered, though the sniveling fright in his voice was plain as day.

Gryff's glare did not disappear. "No more. Tell us where it is."

Coy's nostrils flared. "Fine. Here's what I know. Take the main road south of Sienna for six miles. There's a boulder marked with a green cross, and to its left is a pathway. It's hard to miss. Follow that to the river, then you'll see two aspens with their trunks wrapped 'round each other. Then go straight ahead and over the hill. It's at the bottom."

"Thanks," said Gryff. Then, without the slightest hesitation, his claws seized Coy's collar and heaved him down. Coy cried out as he slammed into the liquor-stained wooden floor. Hard.

"I'll let the gods punish you as they see fit," Gryff spat, looming over Coy as the man scrambled away from him, still on all fours.

"When you make a game out of threatenin' to spill blood, it's just a matter of time before you start drownin' in your own."

Coy's breathing was heavy. Gryff stepped over him. Hodge followed, then the girls. They walked past the stands, past the men gaping at them with half-open mouths, past the stink of stale beer and cigarettes.

"Have a lovely evenin', folks," Gryff muttered before they all slipped out the door.

Chapter 28

The hideout was a two-day walk from Bruhn, but Hodge figured it was less than a day's journey from Mourelle.

They spoke little on the road. Hodge kept Coy's directions alive in his mind, repeating them like a prayer. Twilight came, turning the sky from blue to gold. Hodge led the gang across the riverbanks. Mud sucked at their boots, and cattails and reeds grew on the water's edge in scattered clumps.

Every few minutes, someone pointed out an aspen. They'd hurry to it, and find a tree with a single trunk.

"Aspens," Tsashin said, her hand skimming the bark of one. "Watchers."

"Hmm?" said Hodge.

She motioned to the bark's dark, round knots. "The patterns on the bark remind me of eyes. I like to think they're watching out for us," she said.

Anything to watch over them sounded like a blessing, and Hodge didn't much care what it was.

At last, they came to the interlocking aspens. Their trunks looped around each other once, like a pair of crossed fingers. They grew crookedly, their roots exposed.

They made their ascent. The muddy banks gave way to a dry, rocky slope. By no means was it an impossible climb, but it certainly was nowhere close to a pleasant one. Hodge's muscles started to ache before he could see what lay at the top of the slope. Few trees grew here, and those that did were short and straggly.

Hodge stayed alert, not daring to let his mind stray from their path. Without the cover of the thick forest, he felt like prey in a vulture's eye.

But he wouldn't be prey. He didn't care how far he had to walk into Sterling's camp to prove it.

They climbed a while longer. At last, the slope came to an end, and with it, the tree line. When they reached the peak, they all stooped down, flattening themselves against the ground. Hodge narrowed his eyes and tried to make out everything he could in the dimming evening light. The hill stretched downward into a large basin, its land cleared, loose earth and brittle grass spread across it. A few trees grew around a cluster of three buildings. The largest was a run-down house, two stories high. It had a pointed roof brimming with gaps, and if its wooden walls had ever been painted, the elements had stripped all their color. There was also a shack, similarly shoddy, and a stable. The shack and stable stood close together, just several yards apart, while the house was at least a hundred feet from both.

Hodge pointed to a lean, long-maned stallion standing outside the stable, flicking his tail. "That's Pierce's horse."

"Where do you think they're keeping Hal and Jae?" asked Lorelin.

"I don't see a guard outside the shack, but it still can't hurt to check. If not, I'll bet they're in the house," said Hodge. He scanned the area once more. "The stable faces east. The slope ain't too steep, on any side. We should be able to scale it."

"That our escape route, then?" asked Gryff.

Hodge nodded.

Lorelin said, "Tsashin and I will wait for you there. I'll lay cover fire if they start chasing you."

"How will we reach them?" asked Gryff.

Hodge rubbed his chin. They'd need some sort of distraction. He could fire a couple shots into the night, but he didn't want to waste bullets on a diversion. Hodge looked at the pistols in his belt, his knife sheath, and patted his pocket. In it, he had one coin and some flint.

"The stable," he whispered.

"What about it?" asked Lorelin.

Hodge took out the flint. "I'll let the horses out, then light it. I've still got blasting powder. I can make a big fire fast. They'll have to run out to douse it. Not all of 'em will come. Still, it gives Gryff and me a chance to work our way into the house."

It would make Sterling's blood boil. Then again, it wasn't like they hadn't done that already.

It wasn't surefire. But it was something.

Lorelin pointed in the direction of the stable. "Tsashin and I will wait on the peak over there. Whistle when you head our way."

Lorelin squeezed Hodge's hand. "Best of luck."

Tsashin nodded at him, then at Gryff. "Please, be safe. Both of you."

Lorelin whisked her west, moving to the other side of the basin across the tree-specked ridge. There, they'd find a perch and wait.

Hodge looked back and forth again. "I don't see anyone. Let's go."

He got to his feet and started downhill with Gryff behind him. The slope feeding the basin was less steep than the one they'd just climbed, but with even fewer rocks. Less cover. Hodge prayed nobody was looking out of the house's murky windows.

They reached the bottom of the basin. Hodge stopped for a second to listen for a shout or a warning shot. Nothing.

They hurried off, and Hodge set his focus on the stables. Occasionally, he glanced at the house, checking for figures standing by the doors or spying through the windows.

When they reached the shack, Hodge drew one pistol and held it close. The last threads of dusk were fading fast, and soon, night would cover the earth. He wanted to make the most of the last bit of light while they still could.

Gryff trailed behind Hodge as they paced around the shack. When they came to the front, disappointment flared inside him. He guessed he shouldn't have been surprised that Halston and Jae weren't there, though. The shack appeared to be about as close to collapsing as a building could get. Planks were missing from the walls, darkened by years of wear and weather. The front door was gone. Inside, tall weeds and parched grass covered the floor.

After scouting the area, Hodge and Gryff crept to the stable. The doors wailed like wounded birds when Hodge opened them. He cast another glance at the house. All was quiet, still.

They stepped into the stable. Shadows and hay blanketed the floor. Hodge didn't bother taking longer than a moment to scan the area. He hurried along the stable's left side, and Gryff took the right. They opened door after door of the stalls and led the horses out. Some of them trotted readily outside, and a few of the others needed coaxing.

Hodge couldn't help but smile when he reached the final stall, where his palomino waited and gazed at him with round, welcoming eyes. *Good to see you.* He unfastened the latch and pulled the door open, and the horse trotted out of his stall.

Gryff took the stallion's reins and started for the door. "Be quick, Hodge."

When Gryff and the palomino made their exit, Hodge reached into his pocket and took out the flint. Indiscriminately, he snapped the rocks at the stable's threshold. The sparks leapt from the flint and settled on the dry, dank-smelling hay. A minute went by, but it felt far longer than that. The embers glowed on the floor for a breath or two before the light left them.

C'mon, dammit!

He snapped the flint faster. He imagined the sparks growing, turning to flames that would rise and turn the wood to brittle cinders.

At last, a few sparks held their heat for longer than a moment, and small flames began to dance on the hay. Hodge snapped a few more embers out of the stone and let them catch. The fire spread like a rose opening its petals. He jumped back when he felt the heat on his ankles and blew a little more life into the flames.

That was as much time as he dared to spend here. His brother was waiting for him. Hodge turned his back on the fire, then dashed outside to the other side of the stable—which was as close to the house as he dared go. He placed his fingers in his mouth and whistled.

———

"Jae!"

Jae whipped her head around. She waited at the foot of the stairs while Halston stood at the other end of the room, pressing an ear to the wall.

"What?"

"Did you hear it?"

Jae stood and jogged to the wall. "Hear what?"

"The whistle. Listen."

A few moments passed. Halston held himself stiffly, like a coyote braced to jump. Then, the whistle streamed in through the thin walls, its three notes sharp and pronounced. A short, relieved smile crossed Halston's face for a hint of a second. He whispered, "They found us. They're here."

Jae touched his wrist. "Then we're leaving. Now."

"Quick," said Halston. "We need to get out of the cellar. If Sterling's men find Hodge and the others, they'll start shooting."

Jae's gaze trailed up the stairs. "We gotta take out Lyle. He's the only thing in our way, really."

Halston's face darkened, but he nodded. "Lyle's a good shot."

Jae rubbed her chin, then ran a hand down one of her braids, her torso, her hips. Silly as it was, she probed her own body as if Sterling might have missed one of her weapons. But there had to be *something* they could use. She scratched her forehead, pushing her hat off her skin.

Her eyes went wide. "My hat."

"Huh?"

Jae took off her hat, then ran a hand around the inside. She pinched it, crinkling the band between her thumb and forefinger. Sure enough, she felt a firm, flexible line beneath the fabric. She raised it to her mouth, then bit down on it and yanked with her teeth.

Halston was looking at her like she'd lost her mind. "What are you…"

Jae took her mouth off it, then started ripping at the fibers with her fingernails. "Getting something out," she said, trying not to gag on the dry bits of lint covering her tongue. She bit back into the hat like a hungry wolf and tugged again. She chewed and gnawed until the fabric finally parted under her teeth. She'd opened a tiny slash on the inside band. Jae dug into it with her pinky, picking at the fabric to widen the hole. She reached inside and pushed until the smooth, thin wire touched her fingers.

A popping noise echoed outside, but Jae didn't stop to wonder what it was. She clenched the wire between her fingers, then said, "Halston. Hold the top while I pull."

Halston grabbed the hat's crown. Jae tightened her clutch on the wire and yanked.

The wire loop emerged from the hole. It was stiff, and it fought against Jae's pull, but she kept tugging as the loop grew bigger and the hole got wider. She yanked until the wire's ends popped out from the slash and sprung back up into shape.

Jae held the wire in front of her eyes, trying not to smile at it like a fool.

She whispered, "I'm gonna get to the top. You call for Lyle when I give you a thumbs up."

Halston added, "I'll disarm him when you loop the wire around him. We'll run into the next room and break a window."

Jae nodded, then hurried to the stairs. She pushed herself up and climbed onto the banister, dangling one leg on either side like a saddle. Clutching the metal with both hands, she shimmied up, trying to keep her breathing soft.

The gang was here. Somehow, they'd found them. They'd come for Halston and Jae.

She didn't care that she was getting away with outlaws. All she cared about was getting away.

When Jae reached the top, the door handle was close enough to touch. Both outside and inside, she could hear faint shouting, but it wasn't coming their way. If Sterling's men had already spotted the gang outside, then they had to be quick. She looked at Halston, nodded once, and raised her thumb. Lowering her shoulders, she held the wire with both hands. She pressed her shoulder to the wall and flattened herself against it as much as possible. When Lyle entered, she hoped he wouldn't think to look to his right.

Halston took off, stealing up the steps, moving quick as a whip.

The weak wood screeched under his weight. "Lyle!"

The door swung open as soon as Halston reached the top. Lyle stepped inside, frowning. "What are—"

Jae sprung forward, arms outstretched, and looped the wire around his neck. She yanked with all her might. Lyle gagged, heels slipping on the floor. He lost footing and toppled backwards. His hands shot to his throat, trying to pry the wire away, but Jae didn't dare let it go.

Halston dipped down and reached for Lyle's long-barreled gun. Lyle swatted at Halston's hand a second too late. Halston lifted the gun and aimed it between Lyle's brows. "Don't speak."

Lyle's nostrils flared, and he pinned his angry blue eyes on Halston.

Jae peeked out the door into the empty hall. Tugging the wire, she said, "Take us to our weapons. Keep your hands in the air. One false move and we shoot."

Legs trembling, Lyle stood, hands in the air as ordered. He pressed his lips together and motioned over his shoulder. He wasn't much taller than Jae, but she kept the wire in place with her arms raised up at an awkward angle.

They passed through the hall, then stopped at the door across from Sterling's room. Lyle pointed inside.

Jae said, "My map is in that room right there. You're going to walk across and get it for me and bring it back."

She released the wire, then watched Lyle make his way to the room across the hall. Halston kept the gun pointed at Lyle's back. Jae reached for the doorknob, turned, and lifted it, trying to keep some weight off the hinges.

The room was smaller than Sterling's. In it was a chair, a wood-pile, a few folded tarps, and a stack of rakes and hoes. Beneath the chair lay two packs, three revolvers, two knives, and Jae's boot pistol.

Jae hurried forth and slung both packs on. She fetched the knives, shoved her pistol into her boot and her other guns into her belt. Before she could pick up Halston's revolver, he cried out. She turned around just in time to watch Lyle shove him out of the way. Before Halston fell, a bullet blasted from the stolen gun, sailing through the ceiling and sending splinters flying. The stolen revolver fell from Halston's hand and slid across the wooden floor. Lyle stormed into the room, tossing a crumpled ball of paper at Jae's face. "Here's your damn map!" he shouted before charging her way.

She didn't move fast enough. Lyle's strong hands seized her shoulders and pushed. The force shot through her like lighting, and her body slammed into the floor.

Lyle stood over her, his hands clenched into fists. She rolled out of his path and leapt to her feet, then darted towards the corner where the farm tools were propped.

Lyle's feet pounded behind her. Jae gripped the handle of a hoe and swung. The head plowed into Lyle's side. A startled cry escaped his lips, and his boots skidded on the floor. The hoe veered down, and Jae heaved, hoisting it back up over Lyle's head. She clubbed it against his crown.

A groan left his lips. He swayed for a moment, then collapsed.

Feet clattered on the stairs, and shouts filled the hallway.

Halston finally dragged himself up and slammed the door shut. Jae heard shouts that sounded like "Fire!" and "Outside!"

"Toss it to me!" Halston shouted.

Jae tossed the hoe as gently as she could. Halston clumsily caught it in one hand, then shoved the tool's metal rim beneath the doorknob and wedged the handle against the floor

Footsteps creaked out in the hall. Jae fetched her map and shoved it into her pocket. Halston grabbed the chair and lifted it, grunting as he lunged forward and brought it against the window. The thick pane shuddered but did not break.

Outside, a husky voice shouted, "You've got five seconds to come out before we shoot!"

Halston hurled the chair at the window, then dropped to the floor. Jae did the same.

The chair smashed through the window. Glass rained down like jagged hailstones. Bullets flew through the door, slicing the air and leaving splintered holes in the wood. Jae drew one revolver, aimed for the door and tried to shoot.

Her gun was empty as a dust-dry skull. She guessed she shouldn't have expected anything else.

Another bullet flew over their heads. Lying on her stomach, Jae dragged herself to Lyle's gun. Bits of glass poked at her skin. Her hand closed around the grip, and she sent three of its five remaining shots through the lower half of the door. One man cried out.

She doubted she'd struck anything higher than a knee, but at least they knew she was armed.

In the lull of gunfire, Halston jumped to his feet. "Take my hand!"

Jae stood, Halston grabbed her hand, and they each put a leg over the window sill, glass pricking at their pants. Jae didn't have time to feel relieved that they were on the ground level, because the shots started again. One clanged off the pile of tools. Another slammed into the chair. One more split the wall, inches from Jae's shoulder.

Halston leaned forward and brought them down.

They spilled over the edge, falling face-first. The ground slammed into Jae's nose, dirt filling her mouth. She pushed herself up and spat out some of the grit.

They were in a wide basin, hills expanding in a circle around the plain. Jae breathed in, and a sharp, heavy smell burned her nostrils. She coughed.

Smoke.

Halston helped Jae to her feet. A burst of earth exploded beside them. Jae turned to see a rifle's barrel sticking out of a second-story window, pointing straight at them.

They took off, bullets cracking behind them. The land was firm under their boots. In the west, another structure was swallowed in flames, the yellow tongues flapping wildly, smoke billowing from their bright blue hearts. Horses cried and galloped across the plain, fleeing from the fire. The shadows of men crowded the burning structure and slapped at the fire with sacks. It was hard to say how many there were, but four at least.

She held onto Halston's hand. He led them west, racing past the burning stable. One man stopped fighting the flames long enough to reach for his gun and shoot, but they were running fast, and the bullet didn't find them.

About fifteen yards ahead, a figure rode crossed their path on a broad horse. Jae's heart leapt into her throat. Behind them, shouts thundered. Men were coming—to kill Halston and Jae if this fella didn't get them first.

The rider yelled. "Halston!"

"Hodge!"

Jae couldn't have hurried for him faster if the ground was falling away behind her.

Halston sped up a few yards ahead of her, then stopped before a handsome mare prancing across the ground. Jae recognized it as Lorelin's horse. Halston held up two hands, then stepped to the side and seized the horse's reins in one swift, graceful movement. Jae guessed that his several years as a cowhand had paid off. Halston swung himself onto the saddle, yanked his reins and rode toward Jae.

A bullet split the earth between Jae and the horse. The mare screamed, then took off in the opposite direction of Jae. Halston shouted, trying to get the poor creature back under control.

Damn it! Jae paused, then looked around. If she'd had the mercy of a moment to spare, she would have tried to find her own horse, but there was no time for that. Jae fixed her gaze on the closest horse—a tan, speckled mare about ten yards to her right. Jae sprinted toward her.

The slender mare still wore a simple, padded saddle. "Easy, girl." The mare was not prancing, but Jae could hear the poor animal's swift, staggered breathing even from where she stood.

At last, Jae reached the horse. Halston had regained control of the brown mare and was galloping west, racing to the slope leading back into the forest. "Jae! This way!"

Jae shoved her foot into the stirrup and swung herself onto the mare.

In spite of herself, a thought crossed her mind, one where she wondered if it was wrong to steal an outlaw's horse. But there was no time to consider the complications of theft. Jae kicked the horse's sides, and the mare charged west.

The earth whirled past them, the path lit by the flames roaring in the distance. Jae followed the Harney brothers' shapes, flying across the plain and straight to the rising earth. To the forest's edge. To a million shadows to wrap them up and keep them safe.

They rode uphill. The horse shuddered with unease, her thin legs quaking as her hooves plowed into the rough terrain. Rocks dotted the hillside. "Come on, sweet girl," Jae urged her. "Almost there."

Jae didn't look back. If bullets and men were flying their way, all she could do was ride faster.

When they reached the basin's rim, two shapes jumped out from a lump of shrubs and rock. Jae's stomach shrank, but when Lorelin's voice cried out, Jae yanked her reins and brought her mare to a halt. The boys stopped, too, and Gryff brought his own run into a jog, then steadied himself beside them.

Jae put out her arm and said, "Hop on!" without caring who took up the offer.

Lorelin rushed Jae's way. Her hand grasped Jae's, and Jae helped her onto the saddle. She sat behind Jae, shifting to get a solid position on the mare. Tsashin climbed onto the palomino with Hodge.

As they snaked through the trees, chests heaving, hearts racing... a hot, wild feeling carried Jae forward. It swept through her like strong wind and burned hot as coal.

Freedom.

They rode, leaving Sterling's hideout in a cloud of dust and smoke and fire.

Chapter 29

*M*aybe they rode fifteen miles that night, or maybe they rode thirty. Jae hadn't checked her map, trying to keep her mind only on the ride. They alternated between galloping and trotting, speeding through row after row of towering pines. The trees grew thickly in this mountain forest, some close as soldiers marching side by side. It was difficult to wind through them without a trail, but they had the map, and they hoped the droves of pines would discourage their chasers.

The sky shifted from black night to pale dawn, its final stars clinging to the blue like the last leaves before a frost. The sun rose behind them, and they kept trotting west.

They came to a ridge overlooking a small canyon. Uneven faces of stone rose up on either side, reddish tan in color, and flecked with moss and shrubs. Pines cut through the bottom of the valley like a narrow green carpet. The faint sounds of morning flocked from the canyon—singing birds and humming insects.

"Well," said Hodge. "Where to?"

"We should stop," said Lorelin. "At least for a while."

"They're probably chasing us," Hodge argued.

"The horses are exhausted," Lorelin said. "We won't get much further, even if we try. I think we lost them. Besides, they've lost their tracker. And we need a plan."

"Their tracker?" asked Jae.

"Wolf," said Hodge. "He snuck up on us the other day. We took care of him, but he tried to kill us. If they find us again, we're all dead but Tsashin."

It would be tougher, certainly, without a tracker, but Jae doubted that was enough to stop Sterling. Jae's heart twisted as she wondered how his portals worked. Could he use his powers to find them?

They settled a few yards from the ridge. Halston and Hodge tethered their stallion to a juniper branch. A gooseberry bush grew near the junipers, its delicate fruits ripening into a bright yellow-gold. Jae dismounted, trying to ignore her aching muscles, and dared to ask. "Halston?"

"Yes?"

"Could Sterling... use his powers to come after us?"

Halston shook his head. "He'd have to cross over a lot of the Median if he did. It wouldn't be very useful. His powers are good for hiding, not so much for traveling."

Tsashin spoke up. "Powers?"

Halston nodded. "Sterling can open portals. Doorways in the sky."

"I think I know about those," said Tsashin. "From the story of a wanderer, who opened a gateway to the land of giants. But what does Sterling use his power for?"

"To run away after jobs," said Hodge. "There ain't much else to it."

They let the horses graze, then formed a wide circle, most of them leaning against the trees with folded arms. Jae cupped her elbows in her hands, staring at the ground and wishing Pa was here. For a moment, she could almost feel his presence. Pa was there, his warmth pressed to her side, sharpening his knife and whistling a song he'd learned when he'd traveled with the Konohe warriors.

What would he say to her, if he knew what she'd done these past few weeks? The scary thing was that Jae wasn't even sure, and she knew Pa better than anyone.

I ain't a thief, she thought. She'd done the right thing. She wasn't going to leave Halston trapped in that decrepit house with that monster. That didn't make her a criminal… but did it make her a part of this gang?

Jae wrote the thought off. Hell, they were still on the run from Sterling's men. If they got Tsashin, then the rest of them would go down. She doubted Sterling would even bury them. He'd probably just leave them in the woods and let time turn them to moss and dust.

That ain't my fate. And it can't be the Harneys', either.

Lorelin stood with one shoulder against a ponderosa tree, one leg crossed over the other. "What now?"

The others exchanged glances for a moment, then Hodge spoke. "Easy. We get the hell away from Sterling. As far away as we can."

A soft gasp came out of Halston, then. He closed his eyes. "The knife. Jae, could I have my pack, please?"

Jae tossed it to him. Halston threw open the flap and dumped the contents onto the forest floor. Ammo, twine, a tin cup and a fork and plate. Then there was half a knife with an old-fashioned handle, looking more like something from a thousand years ago than anything you could buy from a blacksmith in town.

"Thank the gods," Halston whispered, stashing it back in the sack. His shoulders sagged. "Sterling still has the other half."

"Hal," Hodge said slowly, then walked up to his brother. "Sterling will *kill* us if he finds us again. We didn't come for you so we could head right back to him."

"If we don't see Sterling again, then we don't see the knife again. If that happens, then this has all been for nothing. The silver, and Arrowwood, and Elias."

"Don't you say that! Elias didn't die for nothing!"

"Hodge. If we lose our conduit, then we'll never see our mother again. Or Lia. They'll spend their days looking for us, and we'll die out here. We have to at least try."

The picture. That smiling woman and the little girl. They were alive. At least, Halston thought so.

But why on earth would the boys need a knife to see them again?

The realization hit Jae, then. When Halston was clamoring about Sterling having something he needed, this was what he'd meant. The knife. He'd looked at it so longingly back in the Mouth, like a drowning man reaching for the surface, his saving breath just inches over his head.

Hodge furrowed his brow. "So you're saying we should go back to Sterling, then? Waltz into his hideout and hold him up for the bottom half? That ain't gonna happen."

"I'm not suggesting that."

"Then what *are* you suggesting?"

"I. Don't. Know."

"Listen," Gryff broke in. "The knife can wait, Halston. Hodge is right. If Sterling wants to take Tsashin, then he'll knock the rest of us down if we get in his way. I think we've lost him for now. Still. We've got to put some distance between us before we worry about the damn knife."

Halston opened his mouth, but Gryff spoke before Halston could get a word in. "I know what you're gonna say, kid. But you won't be any good to your ma and sister if Sterling kills us all."

Halston turned his head, fixing his gaze upon the canyon beyond.

Gryff continued. "Here's the plan. If'n y'all want to argue with me, go ahead, but the way I see it, we have no choice. Hodge is right. We all want to live, and that means gettin' far away from Sterling. We should leave Mesca."

Lorelin's jaw dropped. Hodge's shoulders sagged, but he wore a mild expression, as though he'd been expecting this suggestion. And Halston... there was fear in his golden-brown eyes. Jae could see it, but she recognized the weathered hardness his gaze, too. It was that same grim look Pa had just before the ghosts took him.

Hodge said, "If we leave, then we have to get our silver. Take it with us."

Gryff nodded. "Tomorrow, we'll set out for our stash. As soon as we get the silver, we head out. Can we take a look at your map, Jae?"

Jae slid the map out of her pocket. They circled around it, leaning over the paper. The river looked to be about fifteen miles away, and Jae skimmed the towns dotting its edges.

"Do you see Sienna?" asked Gryff.

Jae tapped a finger on Piera, the northernmost town on the map. "Sienna is several miles north of Piera. Should take about three full days of riding to get there. Why?"

Halston said, "It's the setout point for our silver stash. Jade Valley and the Stonespine are several miles northeast of the town."

"Alright," said Lorelin. "So we pick up the silver first, but where will we go after that?"

"Monvallea," Gryff said. The others looked to him. "Think about it. It's another territory. It's even more mountainous than Mesca, so it'll be easy enough to hide. And... if we cross the Dentada Mountains, then that puts a whole chain behind us for Sterling to cross. Maybe he'll give up. Realize it ain't worth it."

"And the Yunah nation is there," Jae added, then faced Tsashin. "When we ride north to get away from Sterling, I reckon we can take you home."

Tsashin perked up. "I'm Yunah?"

Jae bit her lip. "Oh… sorry. Forgot to tell you."

"Yunah." Tsashin blinked and whispered the name again, as if testing its familiarity.

"Does it ring a bell?" asked Hodge.

"It does," Tsashin said, and the ghost of a smile touched her mouth. She swallowed. "But the tribe is large. I don't remember my family. I don't know how we would find them if we made it to the nation."

"Maybe some travel time will help," Lorelin said. "But… once we get to Monvallea, what's the plan?"

"We'll keep goin'," Gryff said drily. "It… it won't be like startin' over."

"We've lost our income," said Halston.

"Not really," said Gryff. "We'll just have to be creative, I guess. Take our own jobs instead of gettin' them from Sterling. It'll be slower. But we can still get the rest of the silver we need."

Halston said, "The silver doesn't mean anything if we don't have both halves of the dagger."

"Halston," Gryff boomed. "I will tie your mouth shut if you mention the knife again! Your pa told you there was more than one of 'em, right? We'll find one."

Halston just blinked, then cupped his elbows in his hands. "I don't like our odds."

"Odds, eh?" Gryff snorted. "How about the odds of us livin' if Sterling finds us again? How do you feel about those odds?"

"Stop!" Lorelin waved her hands. "This is exactly what Sterling would want. He'd love to see us divided, like this, lowering our guard so we can jump for each other. It's not going to do us a bit of good."

Tsashin sat with her knees up to her chest, though the early morning air was hardly even cool. Her finger traced the circle of her kneecap, and her lips moved ever so slightly. "I want to know who you are," she said to them.

All eyes fell upon her.

"I remember nothing. I have no one else right now. But I still find myself wondering about you, Halston. And Hodge. I'm confused."

Hodge sighed. "About?"

"I still don't know if Sterling had a hand in burying me," she said, resting her chin on her knuckles. "I can't imagine what he wants with me. There is nothing I can offer him. But I don't understand, Halston. You fear this man, and yet you are hesitant to escape him. Why?"

Halston released a breath. Without looking at Tsashin, he said, "He has the dagger. And we need it to get home."

"Home? Where is it?" asked Tsashin. Warmth glinted in her eyes. "Can I help you find it?"

Hodge said, "I… I don't know if we can explain it. You wouldn't understand."

"How do you know?" she asked, the question soft as a dusting of snow. "You're helping me find my home. Why can't I help you find yours?"

The boys looked at one another, as if trying to speak without words. A frown crossed Tsashin's face. "Surely, there's a way for you to get home without facing Sterling again. He's a wicked man."

"Maybe there's a way," murmured Halston. "Just not one that I know of."

Tsashin stood, flicking a few pine needles off her deerskin pants. "I owe you," she said. "For saving my life. I'll help you wherever I can, but you cannot let Sterling treat you as livestock, to be slaughtered when he has no need for you any longer. Don't put your lives in his hands."

They all stared at her in stunned silence.

Jae's muscles went tense. She longed to hear Halston speak again, to know what these boys were truly about.

If the Rangers found them roving about in the wilderness, she'd go right to jail with the rest of them. There was danger in staying, and each day that passed kept her from her Pa.

But could she leave them now? Knowing that Sterling cried out for their blood, and that he'd stop at nothing to take Tsashin away?

———

They spent the day riding, resting, and riding again. Jae did her best to cover their tracks, but with little time to spare, there was only so much she could do. Each time they stopped, she'd check her map. Then she'd scatter their markings with a branch before they set out on a new path, though she tried to keep them bound northeast for Sienna.

They used Jae's map to find the river, though no one wanted to stay close to it, in case Sterling's men were following its curves. About half a mile from the banks, they decided to set up camp for at least a chunk of the night, since no one had really slept in a day. They hitched the horses up, then settled in a small glade between the ponderosas and a grove of blue spruce. They dined on nuts and gooseberries Tsashin had picked earlier.

The spring night was quiet, the air just the right amount of warm. The sunset blazed orange. Birds sang their last songs before they settled into the night. Jae wanted to think it was beautiful. She wanted to find a morsel of peace in their view. But for the first time in months, she felt completely, entirely lost.

When they finished eating, Tsashin said, "I'm going to give the rest of the berries to the horses. They deserve a treat, I think."

When Tsashin had gone, Lorelin said, "She asked you boys for the truth, earlier today. Why can't you tell her?"

"The truth ain't pretty," said Hodge.

"The truth is never pretty," Gryff pointed out. "And I think you owe it to her. She's scared. Hell. You told me where you were from as soon as I met you."

"Yeah, 'cause we were desperate," said Hodge.

Gryff snorted. "Ain't you desperate now? And why'd you bring it up if you weren't gonna tell her the rest of the story?"

Hodge shut his eyes and took a breath. "Look. I ain't in the mood for this. I'm gonna... I don't know. Sharpen a stick on a rock or some shit. Holler if you need me." And he strolled about twenty paces outside the circle, found a dead branch and a stone, sat down, and did what he had promised.

Jae watched the point on his stick grow sharper. She looked to Halston, who was now sitting and rubbing his eyes, and Lorelin, who was staring at Halston with a look that could have sliced through a rope. She'd been to some awkward meetings before, but this was something else.

Tsashin returned, then, and nestled quietly back into her spot. "The horses are doing better. We'll have to look for water soon. They should be ready to walk again in a few minutes."

"That's good," Jae smiled. "Tsashin?"

Tsashin turned her head.

"Would you mind... telling us one of those stories of yours?" Jae felt that they could all use one.

Tsashin's eyes lit up. For the first time, there wasn't a trace of sadness in her smile. Her fingers moved across her knees, as though she were spinning the story in her fingertips. Then, she began.

"There was once a band who lived happily in the mountains. Season in and season out, they rode, and the land was good to them. But one summer, after the rains came, a sickness fell upon them. Their skin became hot, but they still shivered with chills. Their hands and feet grew numb until they could not walk. At last, their tongues went stiff, and they could not speak.

"One of their warriors, who was still well, left to seek help. He rode through the valley, following the curves of the river, hoping to reach the nearest band.

"He stopped by the river to drink, then heard soft weeping from nearby. He followed the sound until he reached a clearing, where a young woman lay. It was summer, but she wore furs, as though winter had not left. A bow was strung across her back. She was thin and gaunt and told the warrior that she was starving.

"The warrior stayed by her side, bandaged her wound, and built a fire. He offered her what food he had to spare and stayed until she could speak. Soon, she was well again. He asked her for her name, but she only said that she was called Hegi. Shadow.

"She asked him where he came from. He explained that his people were sick, and that he was riding to the nearest band for help, as he was the only one in his own band who could speak or walk. The woman asked how far his band was, and to take her there.

"When they reached the band, she promised him she would heal them. He asked how, but she only told him to trust her.

"When she walked away, she began to sing in a language the warrior had never heard. As she slipped into the wickiups and sang to the sick, they joined her, as though they knew her song by heart.

"Their tongues were healed, but their limbs were still numb. It was then she took each man and woman and child by the hand and danced across the fields with them, spinning under the sky. As they danced, warmth crept back into their bones. Their fevers vanished, and their hope returned.

"She stayed with the band for a time and brought joy to them all. The warrior wanted to marry her, and she told him that there were others she wished to heal, but promised to return to him one day.

And quietly, she wandered out of the valley, a shadow beneath the setting sun."

Lorelin clapped her hands together. "Beautiful, Tsashin."

"Thank you."

"I like the ending," Gryff said. "A hopeful one." He said that like it was some sort of rarity.

"A story should have a hopeful ending," said Tsashin. "If it doesn't, then it is not over."

Jae hoped that soon, Tsashin would remember where her home was, so she could be with her people again. She deserved to share her stories with them.

———

After supper, Halston and Jae led the horses to the water so they could drink, and so they could refill their own water supply. Here, the river was thin and shallow, its cool water lapping at the roots of the lush green plants along the banks. The horses gulped it down as Halston and Jae refilled the canteens. Halston lowered his canteen into the current, welcoming the tingle of cold on his skin, the push of the current on his tired hands.

When they finished with the water supply, they led the horses back to their glade. Jae dragged a dead branch behind her, scraping its blunt twigs over their tracks. She had a steady look in her eye, and she moved pointedly, like she'd just turned her mind away from everything else at hand. Halston envied her.

When they reached the camp, they found Gryff, Lorelin, and Tsashin asleep. Hodge sat with his back against a tree, sharpening another stick on a rock.

"You should sleep," said Halston. "You look tired."

"We should have two people on watch tonight," said Hodge. "Just in case one nods off."

"I'll do it," said Jae. "I agree with Halston. You could use some rest."

"Alright," said Hodge, trekking back to his bedroll. "When one of you gets tired, wake me up right away. Don't try to stick it out."

Halston sat down at the edge of the glade and stared into the dark woods. Jae settled down a few paces away. An owl hooted nearby, filling the night with its call. The river was close enough to hear, but far enough that its voice was only a constant whisper in the air. Gray clouds filled the sky, crawling over the moon and covering the land in darkness. Halston squinted, trying to see further into the forest.

Jae said, "Your gun. Where is it?"

Halston turned to her. "I lost it in the scuffle."

"Here." Jae shifted closer to him, then passed him one of her own revolvers.

Halston tried to give it back, but she said, "Keep it. I'd rather have one than you have none."

"Are you sure? They're precious to you."

"Yeah, well, so are... I mean... you gotta protect yourself somehow, right?"

"Thank you." Halston holstered it. "That means a lot to me."

Jae said, "So. How are you feeling?"

"Gryff is right," Halston said. "If Sterling finds us again, we're good as dead. But after we get the silver and set out..." He closed his eyes.

"The knife."

Halston nodded.

"Y'know, you didn't tell us what it does."

"It's not..." he almost said 'important', but that was nowhere near true. "I don't think you'd understand."

"Why not?"

"It's not any of your concern."

"We just got out of jail together. Well… more or less. I've got a right to know what your business is with the man who wants us dead," said Jae. "Do you think I can't handle the truth?"

"No." Halston kept his eyes off of her. "But Sterling is stronger than us. And I'm just trying to figure out how we can move forward. Right now, I almost feel like we're starting over. We've lost our income. We've lost—"

"The knife. I get it. You still won't tell me what it's for." Jae breathed out. "Also, he ain't stronger than you."

"What?"

"Sterling. He ain't stronger than you. He's got some gold, some magic, and a bunch of thugs. But he's got a rotten spirit. You're a fool if you think he's stronger than you. I don't know how you fell so far in with him. You're right. Maybe it isn't any of my business. But if we're lucky, we won't have to face him ever again. I still can't tell if that's what you want."

He didn't know what he wanted.

She stood and turned on her heels. "Listen. I'm gonna go watch on the other side of the clearing. I've got some things to think about. I'll talk to you tomorrow."

Without peering away from the woods, he listened to her walk away.

When he closed his eyes again, all he could see was Sterling, sitting at a table across from him. Halston had been a boy of fifteen, a couple years into his new life.

"*Name your price,*" Halston said.

Sterling had already given him the first half of the knife, but he'd warned him that it was a loan, not a gift. He'd have to pay it off, and the second half was collateral. He'd also told Halston that if they disclosed the location of his hideout, he would torch the ranch where he worked and gun down everyone inside.

"*Ain't sure,*" Sterling answered. "*That knife is magic. I'm doing you a kindness by even letting you pay it off in increments. I could fetch a great price for it if I sold it.*"

"*You won't,*" Halston said. "*We'll work for it. I don't care how long it takes.*"

"*You told me you were on a deadline,*" said Sterling.

"*We have time,*" said Halston. "*Our deadline is there, yes, but it's years away. Our jobs at the ranch pay well enough.*" Not as well as robbery, of course.

"*That'll mean interest.*"

"*I don't care,*" Halston said. "*I'm not going to steal for you.*"

What a sad lie that turned out to be.

They spent years roping, breaking broncos and driving cattle, sleeping in a bunker in the winter and under the stars during the summer. It was an honest life. So different from the one Halston grew up with. He remembered Elias laughing by the fire. They sat with the other cowhands, the night filled with laughter and music and the smell of burning wood. In spite of all they'd lost, they were happy.

Then Elias killed Poole, and they couldn't think of a reason not to steal. They were wanted men anyway. Why not pay off Sterling faster?

You're a fool if you think he's stronger than you.

He was a fool for other reasons, too.

If he'd never met Sterling, never gotten involved with him... they wouldn't have the dagger, part or whole. But they also wouldn't be fighting for their lives.

Halston wished he could believe Jae. But even if Halston had less blood on his hands than Sterling Byrd, that wouldn't stop a bullet, and it wouldn't get him home any sooner.

Chapter 30

A day passed. They stopped earlier than usual that evening, because as soon as the sun disappeared, the clouds and fog made it damn near impossible to see.

They set up camp in a rocky clearing, where the boulders were as abundant as the trees. It took Jae a long while to dig enough rocks out of the ground to make a comfortable sleeping area. The air was thick with moisture, and Jae prayed to Cressien to hold off on the rain.

Jae remembered sitting in the cabin with Pa, back in Banderra. She was small, then, full of laughter and dreams. Their fire had gone out that night. Outside, a storm raged, and she cried beneath her blankets, wondering if the thunder would split their roof in two.

"Jae," Pa said. *"Thunder can't hurt you. There ain't nothin' in this world that can hurt you. It'd have to get by me first."* And Pa had survived grizzlies and worse, so she'd believed him wholeheartedly.

He'd kept those ghosts from her. Protected her. She had to do the same for him.

She swallowed, thinking that even if she became a Ranger, she wouldn't be half the person Pa was. Once, she'd gone on another rave about seeing the world, and Pa had answered with a gentle reminder. *"It's a glorious world, Jae. But remember… Rangers have a job to do. They keep our lands safe. They look out for those who need it."*

Jae settled back against the earth, lying on her blankets and watching the clouds roll by. What would Pa think of the Harney gang? He'd always liked just about everyone he met… but this was a band of criminals.

For days, she'd fought the terror fogging up her mind. Was she slipping away? Just months ago, she'd been trailing rustlers and bank robbers. Now, she was riding with a band of thieves. That scared her, but it didn't scare her enough to walk away.

Folks seemed to have a solid grasp on right and wrong, law and chaos, peace and violence. She'd thought she understood the line between them perfectly well. Now, she wasn't sure anymore.

There were lawmen like Pa. There were lawmen like Jackson Poole. There were thieves like Sterling, and… dare she say it, thieves like the Harney gang.

That night, she and Halston took the first watch again. They found a spot on a long, flat rock and sat down. Up here, Jae couldn't see much besides the outlines of the plateaus against the cloudy sky. She wished the stars would come out. Miles away, thunder rolled off the earth, and nearby, a coyote cried.

They sat quietly for a long while, but Halston broke the silence first. "I've been thinking a lot. About what you said. I know you must be feeling frustrated with everything. I thanked the others, but I haven't thanked you yet. You helped us escape with our lives. I'm grateful for that. It was… uncouth of me not to thank you sooner."

She couldn't help but snicker a little at 'uncouth.' She said, "Well… you're welcome. And thank you. I don't think either of us could've done it alone."

Though she was tempted, she didn't bother asking about the knife. It'd probably send him spiraling into a grim mood again.

Halston said, "I wanted to ask you something. Wyrdrian. The language that gave memories to the earth. What else do you know about it?"

Jae thought back to the memory in the Taracoma Valley, the man who tried to warn them about the lorthans. Who was he? "I've seen a few memories up north, but nothing this far down. It ain't an easy language to learn. Wyrdrian is... half a language, half magic."

Halston leaned toward her.

Jae smiled. She liked having someone who listened. "It was a gift from the gods." Hemaera was the daughter of a mortal woman and Argun. He taught his daughter to speak it, as a gift to her followers.

"Hemaera explored the Outlands and charted them. She taught the language to the first rangers, when they were established. And they would learn how to give a memory to the land, and the land would keep it. They could watch it unfold, right there. Forever." The ghosts of the past, planted in the earth to grow until the planet stopped turning.

Halston said, "Sounds almost too good to be true. I'm not sure I'd believe it if I hadn't seen it for myself."

"My Pa used to warn me about that. Said that closing your mind can be a dangerous thing," said Jae. "It ain't healthy to believe everything you hear, of course. But it's almost worse to believe in nothing, y'know?"

Halston nodded. "There's something I'm worried about. Gryff said that he doesn't think there's... anyone left who speaks Wyrdrian. That the memory could've been there for years. Do you think that Tsashin was there that long?"

Jae exhaled. Gods, she hoped not. "Well... I used to hear rumors about men who still spoke it. Besides, if Sterling knows the guy who put her there... her family has to be alive, right? Maybe a fella passed the lorthans, then got away in time to plant the memory there."

Jae wished it wasn't so hopeless. There wasn't much anyone could do for Tsashin but try and keep her out of Sterling's grimy hands. "After we get the silver and go north... I hope she remembers her folks. And I hope she can go home with an armful of stories for them."

They sat in silence for a while. Jae wanted to keep talking, to keep her mind from straying to dark, wild places. So she asked, "What about you? Do you have a favorite story?"

Without a second thought, Halston said, "The Chronicles of Keshav."

"What's that about?"

"*Everything*," Halston said, and Jae realized she'd never heard such brightness in his voice before. "A hero who battles monsters and saves entire nations and falls in love with a goddess. It's an old tale from Surya. My mother's ancestors hailed from there."

To her surprise, Halston then asked, "What's yours?"

Jae chuckled. "I, uh... didn't read many books growing up. Pa taught me most of what I know." He'd tried sending her to school-house once, and she'd thrown mud at a boy for making fun of her clothes—all tailored hand-me-downs from Pa. The teacher had asked her to never come back. Pa had not been happy about it, but he taught her from then on. "He told me most of his stories on his own. But my favorite was 'Edessa of Suncliff.'"

"What's it about?"

"The daughter of a king. The king got sick, so he asked his three kids to bring something to the kingdom to see who he'd give it to. His sons brought him things like gold and jewels, but Edessa trav- eled to a cliff at the edge of the world. She climbed it until she reached the stars and took one and brought it back. It lit up the world, and they named it the sun. At last, things could grow. So her father picked her."

Halston said, "Sounds like a good one."

"It was," said Jae, and she forgot to be quiet. "Pa and I didn't have many books in the cabin, growing up. We couldn't bring them on the road, either. Too heavy. But he told me all the stories he'd learned on his travels, and…"

Her voice trailed off. She remembered the cabin in Banderra, and Pa's voice over the crackling fireplace.

Halston tilted his head. "A cabin?"

Jae swallowed. "Yeah. Sold it a long time ago. Before… well, he's gone now."

It wasn't true. That cabin was still there, for all she knew. And she could have gone back to it after Pa was taken. Slept in a bed and lived off the forest. Would've been an easier life than what she had now, but it felt irresponsible. That cabin wasn't hers; it was both of theirs. Without Pa, she doubted she'd be able to sleep there. The ghosts would keep her up all night. She'd go mad.

"I'm sorry," Halston said softly. And Jae had no doubt that he really was.

"Thank you."

They sat a while longer, until Halston stood up and stretched his arms. "I'm going to sleep now. Lorelin's going to take my place. Wake Gryff up when you get tired."

"Alright."

Halston thanked her and traipsed back to the camp. When he woke Lorelin, she stood and hurried to the rock fast, like she hadn't just been sleeping.

When she sat down, she freed one shoulder from her pack, reached inside and pulled out a hip flask and a deck of cards. "Want to play rummy? I've got wine," she said, waving the flask.

Jae raised an eyebrow. "Where did you get that?"

"A merchant in Calora. I keep it hidden from the boys. They think it's whiskey for wounds." She popped off the lid. "It's a good thing I like you so much. Usually I'm too selfish to share."

Jae shrugged and took a swig. It was tart, but the sip finished with surprising sweetness. She helped herself to two more swallows.

Lorelin dealt her a hand of cards, though Jae had not agreed to play. "What were you and Halston talking about last night?" Lorelin asked, the question spiked with a fiendish tone.

"Sterling. Travel plans."

"Ah," Lorelin said, sounding disappointed. "And what were you talking about tonight?"

"Uh… the Yunah nation and Wyrdrian and stories."

"Hmm." Lorelin grinned. Her hands lingered on the cards, her pretty fingers tracing their corners. Before Jae could ask why, Lorelin began explaining the rules of the card game. Jae was usually good at games, but she could barely listen now, and she figured she'd lose this one.

Lorelin went first, then Jae. She paired up two cards with diamonds. "You look worried."

Jae rubbed her forehead. "My head hurts, I guess."

Lorelin smirked. "Sure it does."

Jae frowned. "What's that supposed to mean?"

"Nothing."

"No. What?"

Lorelin finished a set: a three of spades, a six, and a queen, who had the same pink, plump lips as Lorelin. "Forget about it. It's been a grim week. We could all use a little peace of mind. I'm just trying to teach you how to have fun."

"Fun? I have… plenty of fun."

"Hush, hush." At last, Lorelin emptied her hand of all cards,

286 : Sophia Minetos

and a triumphant grin spread across her face. "Shall we play another game?"

"Sure."

Lorelin shuffled the deck, the stiff cards cracking on top of one another. "Jae?"

"Yeah."

"One more thing." Lorelin began to deal the cards. "I know talking to Halston can be like talking to a fencepost. But I promise you this; he's nothing to be afraid of."

Jae snorted and picked up her cards, perhaps a little too quickly. She wasn't sure what she was feeling. Embarrassment? Wounded pride? She hoped it was neither. No, she *decided* it was neither.

Jae liked Lorelin, but she wouldn't give Lorelin's comment a reply. It'd be like tossing scraps to a hungry bear.

———

Morning came, the day passed by, and the afternoon settled into dusk. Halston and Lorelin ventured to the river to gather roots. Lorelin hummed as they moved downhill, bobbing with each step.

They reached the banks and started harvesting, bending down to pluck the plants. Halston picked a bundle, then dipped them into the water so the current could wash the mud from the stiff white roots.

Lorelin said, "I talked to Jae last night."

"And?"

"I think you should talk to her."

"I already talk to her."

"Not about the right things." Lorelin held the roots, letting water droplets run down their stalks and into the river. "You can tell me anything, Halston. Do you like her?"

"Sure."

"How much?"

Halston supposed he shouldn't have been surprised. Once, he'd struck up a conversation with a merchant's daughter in town, and Lorelin had pestered him about it for a week, asking when they could return so he could talk to the girl again. Now, Halston didn't even remember her name. "I enjoy her company. But she's a gale. I've seen enough storms."

"That's not true."

"It is."

"No, it's not. Otherwise, you wouldn't be turning red."

Halston yanked up another bundle of roots and turned, not bothering to rinse them. "Sterling could be on our trail, Lorelin. We have more important things to worry about."

"I'd say love is pretty damn important."

"Don't you think we have more pressing issues at hand?" asked Halston. "We haven't seen any signs of Sterling. I call that a blessing, but that doesn't mean it won't happen."

Lorelin rolled her eyes. "For heaven's sake, Halston. You act like it's a sin to let yourself feel joy."

Chapter 31

That morning, Jae had a nightmare that Sterling found them and filled her chest with bullets. She woke in her bedroll, clawing at the ground.

Sweat coated her forehead. She sat there, breathing and patting her chest long after she'd accepted that it was a dream.

If that dream were to come true and she wound up dead on the roadside, there'd be no one to blame but herself.

Morning air, cool and moist, nipped at her cheeks. The wildflowers' heads were tipped with dew, and wispy clouds streaked the sky. Everybody stood near the budding fire, save for Hodge, who was missing. Gryff was skinning a carcass while Halston, Tsashin, and Lorelin sat peeling roots.

"Morning, Jae," said Lorelin. "The fire's having some trouble. Think you could find us some more wood?"

"Also, can you find Hodge?" asked Gryff. "He said he was goin' for a walk twenty minutes ago."

"Sure." Jae stood, bunched up her bedroll, and set out downhill.

She walked, gathering wood as she moved along, fingering it to gauge its dryness.

After a while, she came to the river and spied a lanky figure standing by the water. Hodge was perched on the banks, tossing stones into the water.

Jae paced down the river bank, her boots leaving deep imprints in the soft mud. "Hey."

Hodge turned. "Mornin'."

Jae pulled her jacket snugly over her chest. "Wanna head back? You can help me get some more firewood."

"Yeah, in a minute." Hodge tossed a stone in the air, caught it, and tossed it again. "I keep thinking I should thank you."

"Nothin' to thank me for," she said, and she meant it.

"Really." The stone dropped into the river's foam. "Not just for helping us out of that pinch, but… I've seen Halston around you. And there's somethin' different about him. He moves like he's just gotten outta jail. I mean, I guess he *did* kinda just did get out of jail, but it's a good thing to see him glad again."

Not this. "Let's get some firewood."

"You like him, don't you?"

First Lorelin, now Hodge? If Gryff started teasing her, she was going to jump off the nearest bluff. Jae avoided his eyes, but answered the question anyway. "I like all of you."

"Do you like him more than the rest of us?"

"No."

Hodge shoved his hands into his pockets. "I thought there was somethin' funny about you, at first. Seemed like you didn't wanna be here."

Jae considered stepping back, but she held her ground.

"I get it," said Hodge. "Being quiet and all. I just think you ought to say what you mean."

"Alright," said Jae. "Here's what I mean. I mean to get some wood for a fire and for you to help me."

"Fine, fine." They walked up the slope until they found wood that wasn't mossy and waterlogged. Looking over his armload of wood, Hodge said, "Jae?"

"Yeah?"

"Don't play games with him," said Hodge. "I like you and all. But that's somethin' I gotta say."

———

At midmorning, they passed Sienna. Halston led them up a trail winding away from the main road, riding across a tall crest overlooking the town. The rooftops were barely visible past the tree line, and the Briarford peaks towered in the distance.

The sloping trail was strewn about with rocks and branches. The soil was the color of rust. Snorting, the horses trotted skittishly over the pathway. Halston had said that they were bound for Jade Valley, where they kept the silver in a cave.

Jae hadn't talked to Halston for hours. She felt like, at the same time, they'd spoken too much and too little.

At least there were other matters at hand. "I don't think I've been to this valley before."

"It's a small valley," Halston replied. "Maybe twenty square miles. It's almost completely hidden by cliffs. As far as we know, there's only one way in."

"You have to take the Stonespine," Lorelin added.

Jae raised an eyebrow. "Stonespine?"

Halston made a sweeping motion with his arm. "It's a hill that leads into a ridge. Narrow one. If we ride across it, it'll take us straight into the valley."

Unease swam into Jae's chest. "Is it wide enough for horses?"

"Just wide enough," Halston answered. "And it's worth the ride across. I promise."

In the shadow of the pines, the trail grew so narrow Jae didn't trust it was a trail anymore. Wordlessly, Halston led them uphill.

"Alright, everybody off your horses here," Gryff said when they came to a surly thicket of junipers. "Lead 'em by the reins. We've got some duckin' for the next half hour or so."

They stooped under the junipers, live ones and dead ones, rimming the crooked path. The horses grunted as twigs nipped at their faces. Desert plants sprouted in between the trees— yuccas with leaves like daggers, yellow desert blooms, and spiny cacti. Jae couldn't see much beyond the plants, but as they made their way up the path, she felt the air turning thinner as she breathed it in. They were ascending.

The trail stretched upward. Soon, Jae struggled to move forth without stumbling. The incline was getting dangerously steep. Still, they moved on, Halston at the front, leading his horse by the reins.

They began their climb. At last, the trail flattened into a ridge, narrow as Halston had promised. Jae looked to the left, then to the right. The slopes were too steep to call a hill, but not straight enough to be cliffs. She reckoned they stood on the crest of a mesa, or a butte. Pines spanned over the horizon, red rocks jutting through their surface like islands in a vast green sea.

"It's beautiful." Jae could almost taste the clouds. A blue jay swooped over the speckled junipers, and she imagined herself as that bird, weightless and free.

They discussed small things as they traveled—the weather and such—for the next few miles. The ridge widened until they were moving across a long length of flat ground. To the east, the trees stretched on, and to the west, the crest jutted out, the valley cutting through the earth below. The sky turned gold, then violet, then black and pearly. When they reached the flat, wooded ground, they set up camp.

Jae took a look at her map. 'Jade Valley' burned gold on the page.

"I'm positively exhausted," Lorelin yawned. She settled down on her bedroll and placed her hat over her face, her flaxen curls falling over her shoulders. "Don't wake me up, ever."

"Dawn," Halston said firmly.

"Fine."

Tsashin chuckled. "She has a heart of flame, doesn't she?"

"No kidding," said Hodge as he lay down.

"Halston, have you slept at *all* these past two days?" asked Gryff.

"I've slept enough," said Halston.

Gryff waved it away. "I keep thinkin' you're gonna drop dead one of these days. I'm going to go set a few snares, but I'll take the first watch when I'm back."

"Thanks," said Halston.

"Get some sleep," Gryff said, stepping into the woods. "Or I'll make you gut whatever we catch."

Jae smiled as Gryff walked away. "Y'all are an odd bunch."

Though Halston looked close to laughing, he didn't. "Yes, we are. That's not going to change."

"I wouldn't want it to."

"Good."

Shoulder to shoulder, they sat at the edge of the woods. The breeze had died out, but the stars were most alive, pulsing above them. They were close to the sky, here—so close she could almost feel their warmth. Jae wished they could sit there and count them all.

She stretched out her arms. Softly, she said, "I think I'm drunk on the earth."

"No, not now," Halston said with a light laugh, then nudged her. "We need you sober for tomorrow."

"Fine, fine." She settled back, leaning on her palms, and watched the constellations turning in the sky. "Makes me feel small, skies like these. Not that I mind. The world is big so folks like us can try and see every bit of it. I don't ever want to stop roaming."

Halston leaned back as well. He wore a faint, pensive smile. "I wish I could say the same. I think I've had enough roaming for one lifetime."

"Do you think you'll ever settle?" asked Jae.

"I don't know," he said. "I don't think it's something in my control anymore, really."

They stayed quiet for a while, gazing at the face of the night. "Once, my mother told me that the sky is an enormous ocean," said Halston. "And the stars are the sails of sunken ships. I think I'd like to sail up there."

Jae turned to him. "You just told me you might wanna settle down, one day. Now you want to sail up there?"

"Well," he said, shrugging, "I think I'd make an exception for the sky. I wanted to be an astronomer when I was younger."

"What's that?"

"Astronomers are men who study the stars."

Now, she was feeling a little bolder than usual. "You know... you still haven't told me where you're from."

"Well, if you must know, I'm the son of a lord."

She snorted. "A lord?" She wasn't sure what kind of a joke he was trying to get at. He'd told her in the cellar that he was a sea captain's son.

"Yes." He grimaced. "And that makes you a peasant."

She guffawed. "You're unbelievable!"

"You did ask."

"Alright, your majesty, what are *you* the lord of? Smart alecks? Know-it-alls?"

"Yes, both. And it's 'my lord' or 'your highness.' 'Your majesty' is only for kings and queens."

She gave him a gentle shove. "Maybe I'll just call you Halston."

"I'd prefer that, actually."

"You've got yourself a deal."

He cleared his throat. "We lived by the sea. Our home was so close to the edge that you could hear the water spraying the walls. Hodge used to throw rocks off the balconies to see if he could hear them splash."

Jae laughed. "Yeah. That sounds like him."

"It was different," he went on. "From everything here. The waters had so much color in them as the sun went down. The stars lit the sea when they rose over the waves. My brothers and I liked to swim in the bay. We'd see how deep we could dive before coming up for air. Lia always told us we were stupid for doing it."

Jae could have stayed awake all night, listening to him speak of sun-touched waters and sails in the sky. She wanted to ask him more about Lia, about his father, about his mother who'd told him the story of the sky.

But that glint of pain in his eye when he said Lia's name stopped her.

Just then, Gryff came out of the woods, brandishing a coil of rope. Halston took one last look at the moon and stars. "Goodnight, Jae."

"Goodnight, Halston."

They put a comfortable distance between themselves, but they slept side by side that night.

Chapter 32

The next morning, they set out for the stash. Jae surveyed the world around her, savoring the feeling of being so close to the clouds. Junipers with low-hanging branches sprouted here and there, but most of what they saw was curved white rock. A few hours passed, and the morning's soft chill turned into noon's heat. Before long, Halston ordered them to stop. They tied their three horses to a tree, then set out after Halston.

These rocks were different from the red, sandstone mesas and Mescan granite. This stone was pale, peppered with holes and covered in thin coatings of yellowish lichen. Every few yards there was a crater wide enough to store a horde of silver. Or a family of rattlesnakes.

Pa had had a word for this type of rock. Pumice, he called it. Said that once, the earth had been covered in liquid fire, and when Petreos cooled it, it turned to mountains and stone.

That was the first time Jae remembered learning about the gods. She'd listened wide-eyed, considering that if Petreos could do something as wondrous as sculpting mountains, then he could bring back Ma as well so Jae could finally meet her. Pa said no.

Jae reached for a branch and hoisted herself onto a boulder, the slant of the surface hindering her balance. She wheezed, then slid down the other side and landed next to Halston.

They were on the valley's west ridge now, winding through the mountain's stone heaps. There was no trail here, but Halston led them down his own path. Jae reckoned he had it memorized.

Jae kicked the dust from her boots, then helped Lorelin and the Harney boys over a boulder in the path. Tsashin and Gryff didn't need any assistance. Tsashin darted across it, light on her feet, and for Gryff, a single step was enough to climb across.

Halston ducked around a small pile of rocks, swerving with them in an unchoreographed waltz, then pointed to another boulder about ten yards ahead. Atop it was a cairn of flat stones, stacked like a pyramid. "We're close to the caves."

They descended. Tension pulled at Jae's calves, and a slight burn found its way into her muscles. Once or twice, she had to catch herself with a tree trunk and push herself back to slow her steps.

And it only got steeper from there. An hour passed, and with it, their legs grew sore. They passed through gaps, over smooth stone slabs where Jae could hardly get a foothold, through rocky paths where there was only a handbreadth of space between the ground and the gorge.

They came to a large face of rock, slanted like the surface of a pointed roof. At the end of it, jagged pumice spires extended in an uneven row.

"We're almost there. The caves are at the bottom of this rock." Halston took her hand and took the first step down the slope. He whispered just loud enough for her to hear, "I've got you."

The rock was smooth underfoot, but they shuffled to the bottom without falling. Their boots met the thin stretch of dry earth before the stone spires. Halston pointed to the left, where a small, gravelly trail led to the black mouth of a cave.

Jae took a few steps toward it, welcoming the sense of wonder it brought her. The mouth was low, and they'd certainly have to stoop to enter it. A dead tree sprouted in front of the entrance, its thin branches outstretched before the mouth. This was exactly the sort of place where Nefilium would dwell, or some ancient mountain queen.

Jae whirled around just in time to see Hodge stumble on the rock, lose his footing, and tumble down the slant. There was a blur of flying pine needles and wavering arms as twin junipers halted his fall. He yelped as he collided with them.

"Hodge!" shouted Halston.

Jae and Halston hurried back to him. They reached Hodge as he placed his palms on the ground and hoisted himself up. Dirt covered his face. He put his hat back on, then looked at his hands. "Shit."

"Are you alright?" asked Halston.

"Yeah," Hodge murmured, straightening his hat before standing and brushing the grit off his clothes.

Tsashin didn't bother with a careful descent. She slid down the rock, spreading her arms for balance. She skidded to a stop, then said, "Show me your hands."

He did. "Just scratches," said Tsashin. "You'll be alright."

"Hey," Hodge said slowly. He turned to the right, strode forward, and plucked something off the ground. He trudged back to the group. "Look." There, in his scraped palm was a shotgun shell, too shiny and clean to be a remnant from the days of old.

It took Jae a moment to pry her gaze from the shell. Tsashin only looked confused, but the fear on the others' faces was cold and firm.

Halston turned and ran toward the cave.

"Halston!" shouted Jae. She wanted to tell him to be careful, but before she could fully register what was happening, he was rushing into the cave's mouth.

Hodge ran after him. Jae followed Hodge, watching Halston's figure slip into the cave. Hodge slid past him.

Jae shoved her legs into the mouth. The stone was cool under her thighs. She pushed the branches of the dead tree aside, the rough twigs brushing her face and neck. A drop of about five feet led to a tunnel, high but narrow, the walls arched and smooth.

Jae hopped down and ran into the tunnel, following Hodge's swift form. Light streamed in through thin cracks in the ceiling, gaps in the mountain's foundation. The air was cool inside the cave, smelling of rainwater and muck. The inclining tunnel was slightly damp, but Jae didn't let that slow her down. In silence, they ran, covering at least an eighth of a mile.

At last, the tunnel widened into a chamber. The floor was flat and wide enough for about seven people to stand without noticing each other. The ceiling rose above, about as high as the roof of a barn and crowded with thin, craggy steeples of rock. In the upper right, a crevice slashed through the rock, and a thin stream of rainwater trickled down the wall and puddled on the side of the floor.

Halston stood at the end of the flat space, staring ahead and holding still as death. "Hodge."

Hodge stood a few paces in front of Jae. He was looking the stoniest she'd ever seen him. Hodge said, "The silver."

Halston turned, looking like he'd just seen a ghost. He stretched out his arm. In his hand was a crumpled piece of paper.

Hodge snatched it from his brother's hand, then pored over it. Seconds later, he dropped it and dug his hands into his hair.

Jae watched the letter flutter to the ground. She reached for it with quivering fingers, the skin of her forearms prickling into goosebumps. She pinched the paper, and the touch of it made her skin crawl even more.

Hot fear closed around her stomach when she read the words— pitch-black ink in strangely beautiful handwriting.

We have the silver with us at the Lawrence Mine. Bring the girl to us if you want it back. She will not be harmed.

    -S

Chapter 33

*H*odge's hands scrambled across the cave's floor, as if he could pull the silver from thin air. Halston stayed rooted to his spot, the fear flooding through him like wildfire across dry wood.

Halston listened to the footsteps clattering on the tunnel's floor behind him: Gryff's heavy steps and Tsashin's delicate ones, with Lorelin's in the middle. Lorelin gasped, and Halston brought himself to turn at last. Lorelin stood with her hands over her mouth. Jae's arm was outstretched, holding the letter before them.

Halston took the paper from Jae and crumpled it in his fist.

"I…" Tsashin started, her face dimming with confusion. "I can't read your language. I can only speak it. What does it say?"

Halston didn't respond. He didn't want to terrify her. That would only thicken this mess.

A few moments passed, each one more uncomfortable than the last. At last, Tsashin said, "Tell me. Whatever it is, I can handle it."

Breathing in, Lorelin placed a hand on the small of Tsashin's back. "It's from Sterling. He took our silver. And he wants you. He says that you won't be harmed."

Halston watched Tsashin, waiting for her face to change, but it didn't. Her brow stayed creased, her mouth unmoving. "I don't understand. As far as I know... I'm not unlike anyone else. I don't understand the lengths this man has gone to find me."

Neither do we.

"This makes no sense," Hodge muttered, one hand grasping a stalagmite. "If he knew about this place, why ain't he here? Why not line his men up outside for when we came?"

Jae raised a hand to touch the back of her neck. "I reckon he doesn't want another shootout. He wants a clean negotiation. When Tsashin and I were running from his men, one of them shot at us. Sterling threatened to chop his fingers off because the bullet could've hit her."

"He *what?*" Tsashin cried, horrified.

Jae nodded grimly. "He... he didn't do it, though. He stopped."

Tsashin sank back against the wall, tucking her arms to her chest.

Halston inhaled, and the air started to taste stale. He raised a hand. "We have to get out of the cave. We have a lot to talk about, and our heads will be clearer if we do it with some space."

Halston led them out of the cave, anger stirring in his fingertips. He longed to do something with his hands, to strike the wall or toss a stone off a ledge. He feared the heat would only grow if he held onto it, but there was nothing he could do. No amount of cursing would get them their silver back, nor would it guarantee anyone's safety.

They climbed out of the cave, and Halston didn't turn back. He didn't care to see this place ever again.

"We've lost it all," Hodge muttered as he walked behind Halston.

"Hodge."

"The banks and the trains and the shootouts. Every bullet we've dodged. All the bastards we've fled from. Pierce. Sterling. All of it.

For nothing."

Halston didn't respond. He refused to. Because that couldn't be the truth.

There must've been a sickness upon Sterling. To treat them all like pawns, and to treat Tsashin as he would a stack of bonds or a fistful of gold. Years ago, Halston had told Sterling where he drew the line, but he was a fool for thinking Sterling would ever listen. Sterling didn't give a damn about where the line was drawn.

Hatred burned inside Halston. Years ago, his mother had told him he mustn't ever say the word 'hate' out loud. *It is a powerful word. If you speak it, you could leave scars on yourself.*

And he wouldn't say it out loud. But he'd let it simmer in his mind.

Without speaking, they climbed up the trail, trudged back to the horses, and rode until they found a clearing where half the trees were dead. Halston strayed around the edge of the woods, pacing, trying to breathe some ideas to life.

Gryff stood with his back against a tree, eyes fixed on the ground and glazed over. Tsashin sat with her knees up to her chest. Jae and Lorelin lingered near her. Hodge waited close to Halston, hands in his pockets, looking as tired as Halston had ever seen him.

At last, Halston murmured, "Lawrence Mine. It's about a day's ride from here. Picked his location well."

"We've only done business there once or twice," Hodge replied. "Gods, do you even remember what it looked like?"

"Sure." He remembered it well. *Wait.* Halston lifted his head. "That's it. Everyone! Circle up."

Halston opened his pack and pulled out a pencil and his journal. The thing was half as old as he was—thick and wide as a holy book, the spine cracked, the leather cover worn with age. He flipped through all his entries, his sketches of landmarks and calculations from old jobs, until he found a blank page.

He closed his eyes, doing his best to picture the Lawrence Mine. "The mine is in a small gulley," he said, pressing his pencil to the paper. He drew a rectangle, marking the short sides with E and W and the long with N and S. "It's probably a mile away from the Taracoma River. To reach it, you have to walk west uphill. The slope feeds into it." He marked the path on the paper.

"What's on the other side?" asked Jae.

Halston pointed to the long rims. "The ridges don't rise high off the ground. Ten or twelve feet at the most, I'd say. Someone could easily lower themselves down."

He turned his head, looking at each member of his company.

Hodge said, "I have an idea. Jae... do you think you could switch clothes with Tsashin?"

Jae and Tsashin both said, "What?"

Hodge shrugged. "From a distance, Sterling might not be able to tell the difference."

"It can't be from a distance," Halston said. "He'll have to give us the silver. I doubt he'll want to throw the sacks at us."

Hodge muttered something about putting rocks in the bags and flinging them back at Sterling.

Halston pressed his pencil to his brow. "We can't take it by force. We'll be outnumbered. We need some sort of barter. Sterling won't comply without one. But we're not letting him anywhere near Tsashin."

He believed that Sterling didn't want her harmed. He wouldn't have threatened to cut off a man's fingers if that wasn't the case. Regardless, Halston didn't *have* to know what Sterling's intentions were for Tsashin. Whatever they were, Halston doubted it involved returning her safely to her people.

"Hang on," said Hodge. "Sterling took our silver from us. What if we got something of his? That way, we could... y'know, make our own trade."

"Money ain't an option," said Gryff. "But... there's Evia. Or one of his brothers. I doubt he holds any of his other men in high enough regard to trade for 'em."

"That's it," Hodge said. "We'll catch one of them. Then we'll bring them to Sterling, and he'll have to give us our silver back."

"But how?" asked Lorelin. "For a meeting like this, I'm sure they'll all stick together. Doubt any of them will stray too far."

Hodge said, "I'll do it. I'll be bait."

Halston went tense at the mention of 'bait.' He shook his head. "Hodge, no. You don't have to."

"Look, Hal, this ain't gonna be safe either way," said Hodge. "I'll find myself a hiding place, shoot at the sky, and shout for Pierce to come find me. He's mad about me, y'know, trying to kill him and all. Besides, he ain't one to back down from a fight. I'm sure I can lure him in just fine."

Gryff said, "I'll go with you." He patted the golden lasso on his back. "And I'll use this."

Hodge raised an eyebrow. "You sure it'll work?"

"I've used this thing to rope the winds themselves," said Gryff. "I think I can handle a lone man. Granted, Pierce won't be alone, but he's a big fella. He ain't exactly an agile target."

Halston opened his mouth, but Hodge cut him off. "Halston," Hodge said. "I know you're gonna try and fight me on this. Don't. I'll draw them out. It's gonna be alright."

Swallowing, Halston nodded and tried to put as much faith as he could into the bare bones of their plan.

They set to marking their locations on Halston's makeshift map. Hodge and Gryff would enter the gulley from the south rim, then hide in the recesses of rock. Hodge would fire a shot to signal Halston and Lorelin to enter the valley from the eastern hill. Jae and

Tsashin would wait with the horses.

Lorelin glanced upward at the setting sun. "It's getting late. Should we set out?"

"No," said Halston. "We'll stay the night here." He wanted one more night of sleep before facing Sterling. If they set out at dawn tomorrow, they'd reach Lawrence Mine by dusk.

They built a fire for the first time in days, since they knew where Sterling was now. They sat in silence for a while, sipping water and watching the embers escape into the night, their brightness winking out as they drifted higher and higher. Jae went to bed. So did Gryff and Lorelin. Tsashin moved in circles several paces away, arms swaying as if there was music nearby. Halston remained by the fire with his brother.

Halston said what he was sure they were both thinking. "The dagger."

"I know."

"Should we ask him for it?"

"We'd better," said Hodge.

"What if he doesn't have it?"

Hodge shrugged. "We'll figure that out when the time comes, I guess."

In the distance, coyotes barked to one another. Halston watched the breeze dance with the trees' limbs, waving at the ocean of sky.

He tried not to think of what would come tomorrow—but it was no use. They still didn't have enough silver for what they needed. Without Sterling, they'd have to plan their own jobs. That likely meant slimmer pickings and a greater risk for each one. Besides, there was the dagger. What would they do if they lost that blade?

And no matter what they did, the law would chase them. They'd tested their luck enough. There were men who'd pay dearly to see them full of bullet holes, or with nooses around their necks. Maybe

306 : Sophia Minetos

at the same time.

Hodge said, "You should sleep. I'll keep watch."

"You don't have to."

"Yeah, yeah, don't be a martyr. You've done your part for the day." Hodge gave him a sliver of a smile.

"Thanks, Hodge." Halston walked back to his bedroll and lay down near Jae. She was asleep already. She looked younger while she slept, her freckles bright in the firelight, braids draped over her shoulders.

To his surprise, drowsiness took him more easily than it had the last few nights. For all the bad that had happened today, at least they'd learned they weren't being hunted now.

Of course, they were walking into a snake pit tomorrow, but somehow, that didn't stop him from sleeping.

———

Hodge approached Tsashin, who was still moving across the ground on her tiptoes and looking every which way. He pressed a shoulder to a tree trunk, looking in her direction. "Hey. What's on your mind?"

"The plan reminded me of an old story," she said. "I'm imagining it. It's helping me keep calm."

"What's it about?"

"Two warring tribes," she answered. "A warrior from one tribe stole another's wife. He said that he would return her if her husband stole the pelt of a bear cub and brought it to him. But his intentions were cruel. He knew the mother bear would kill the warrior.

"But he found the mother bear and explained to her that a wicked man held his wife captive. She gave him the pelt of a buck and told him to use it, to claim that it was the coat of a cub, and to lead the wicked man back to her cave.

"He dropped the pelt at the wicked man's feet, and the wicked man knew it wasn't from a cub. In his anger, he chased the warrior for many miles, until the warrior stopped inside the bear's cave. When the wicked man ran inside, the mother bear trapped him in her jaws, and the warrior went back to his wife."

"Were they happy after that?" asked Hodge.

Her smile was as sweet as any music he'd ever heard. "Very." Then, she whispered. "I'm sorry. That your silver was taken."

He shook his head. "It ain't your fault."

"You mentioned that your silver was your way to get home. What did you mean?"

He wanted to tell her. More than anything, really. But he couldn't explain it without sounding crazy. The last thing he wanted was to scare her. "It's… it's complicated."

"How?"

Hodge tapped his fingers against his thigh. "It took us a long time to get it all. And a lotta numbers and writing to figure out how much we needed."

She frowned. "That doesn't answer my question."

"I, well—"

"Hodge," she said softly. "You don't have to tell me everything. But for a boy who talks so much, you seem to have many secrets."

He folded his arms. "I ain't keeping secrets to hurt your feelings. Sometimes I keep secrets 'cause they won't make sense to anyone else."

"How do you know that?"

Hodge said nothing.

A breath left Tsashin's lips. She looked at the ground. "I think I'm angry. I'm angry with you and your brother, and I'm angry with Sterling, and I'm angry with whoever buried me."

"W-what are you mad at *me* for?"

"Because you don't answer my questions. You dance in circles instead of saying what you mean."

Hodge opened his mouth to argue, but he couldn't. What she said was pretty much true. At last, he brought himself to speak. "Alright, then. Here it is. Sterling has a magic knife, and we need it to get home, because... our home is really, really far away. Does that make sense?"

Tsashin blinked. "Magic?"

"You don't believe me, do you?"

"No," she said. "I do. Magic kept me alive while I was buried. How could I not believe in it?"

They faced what was left of the fire. The logs were still smoking a little, gray and ashy. Hodge put his hands in his pockets. His palms were still slightly clammy with sweat, and he was uncomfortable with the silence hanging between them.

Tsashin breathed in and out. "What did those evil men have to gain by stealing my life? My memories? By placing me in a hole to sleep while the ages passed above the ground?" She cradled her head in her hands, breathing heavily. Tears began streaming down her cheeks. "I'm scared. I'm scared my anger will burn me alive. I want it to stop."

Slowly, Hodge reached out and touched her shoulder. "If... if I could erase what they did to you, make it so it never happened... I would."

Tsashin said, "You can't."

Hodge swallowed. "Is there anything I can do? To just... help you out?"

Tsashin gulped, wiping the tears from her cheeks with the back of her hand. Softly, she said, "We can sit here. And rest awhile."

So that was what they did. They sat down and waited, listening to the breeze's song and the coyotes yapping in the valley's folds. Together, they watched the full moon move up its starry path.

Chapter 34

They reached the mine just after dusk. The moon was rising, shining like a big yellow coin in the sky. They made their way up the steady incline of the mountain until the trees all but disappeared, giving way to a mass of steep, rocky ground climbing several hundred yards.

Jae squinted. Ahead, she couldn't see much beyond the swath of rugged terrain, but Halston whispered, "It's there. The land peaks up here, and the mines are on the other side. Which way are we facing, Jae?"

Jae took out her compass. The metal was cool and smooth in her hand. She flicked it open. "West."

"Good," Halston said, pointing to the incline. "The slope leads into the gulley, and the ridges line the north and south rims of the pass. Gryff and Hodge will sneak into the west end of the trench and shoot."

They retreated a few yards back into the tree line, then strung up the horses behind a family of short junipers. They all exchanged nods and whispers of luck. Jae and Tsashin positioned themselves a few paces away from the trees. Jae kept a hand on her gun.

Halston stood close to her, a whisper of space between them. He had his head raised to the moon, and the fire in his eyes was so fierce that Jae doubted even an ocean could douse it. And for a moment, she wasn't afraid of what waited for them in this place.

She didn't know if she'd lost control, but her hand jumped to Halston's. Her fingers slipped through the spaces of his own, and she squeezed.

"We'll be alright," she told him.

And to her surprise, Halston's response was, "I know we will." His smile wasn't joyous, but it was still there.

———

Hodge and Gryff hustled along the ridge, careful not to veer too close to the edge. They'd have to travel just far enough that the gang could still hear the gunshots, and so they could drag their prisoner off without covering too much ground.

Silently, Hodge counted one hundred paces before turning so they could make their way to the rim. They skirted around rocks of all sizes, then stooped behind a sharp, crooked boulder that poked its shaft over the gulley's ridge.

Gryff leaned over Hodge. Together, they studied the area. The gulley lay about eight feet below. Shallow, but fairly wide. A thin trail of sand snaked between more rocks, some flat, some smooth and round, others thin and pointed like knives.

Hodge turned east and narrowed his eyes. Sterling and his men stood roughly a hundred feet away, dawdling by their fire and waiting for the Harney gang to bring them Tsashin. Like hell they would.

Hodge glanced to the sky. The night was impossibly clear, without a single cloud in it. The stars were shining like white gems floating in a deep blue sea. Gryff nudged him on the back. "Quick."

Hodge crouched down, then slung his left leg over the rim and leapt to a patch of bare ground. He landed with a soft thud, and his eyes flicked east to make sure that he hadn't caught the gang's attention. Sterling's men kept their heads turned to the hill, waiting for Halston to rise above its crest.

Hodge wove in and out of the rocks, floating to the shadows like a moth to the light. He traveled close to the middle of the trench, then stopped behind a rock a little taller than he was and about three times as wide. He pressed his shoulder to it. The surface was still warm from a day of basking in the sun.

Keeping his breathing steady, Hodge watched Gryff lower himself into the gulley, then select a rock about eight paces from him. Gryff's clawed hands reached behind his back, then clutched the gold rope and slid it over his shoulder. He checked the knot, tugging at it to test its strength, then gave Hodge a quick nod.

Hodge drew one pistol. The weapon felt light and comfortable in his hand. He aimed it at the sky and shouted, "HEY, PIERCE. I'M OVER HERE IF YOU WANT ME." He fired. The shot's echo was like a crack of lightning booming off the rocks.

Gun smoke plumed from his pistol's muzzle. Hodge didn't try to peer at the camp again, but their voices boomed and tangled together like metal tools crashing on a hardwood floor. The arguments went on for a minute or so, then a heavy, grating voice cut the others off. Pierce.

"Argus, Spec, Flynn, y'all come with me. I'll be damned if I don't see Hodge Harney dead tonight. The rest of you stay here and wait."

Carefully, Hodge turned his head, moving just enough to peer ahead of the rock with one eye. The four men came stalking across the flat ground, guns drawn.

Hodge waited. The men stopped about ten yards away, just before the cluster of boulders began. Pierce grunted, his fingers twitching on his revolver's grip. "Come out of the rocks, you coward. Get out here and face me."

Hodge thrust his arm out and aimed at the men's feet, then sent five bullets flying their way.

Someone let out a pained cry. When the smoke cleared, Hodge saw Argus lying on the ground, hands clutching his bloody knee. Pierce and the others stood by him, eyes wide and hands trembling,

A flash of gold soared past their heads. Gryff's lasso flew above the rocks and looped around Argus's neck. Gryff yanked the knot tight as Argus's hands reached for the rope, grasping at it and screaming as Gryff pulled him away.

"Argus!" cried Pierce.

Gryff dragged Argus for a few yards before stepping out from his hiding spot, pistol aimed Pierce's way. Hodge followed him, trailing toward Argus, but not daring to take his focus off the three men positioned before the rocks.

Gryff jerked on the rope, bringing Argus to sit upright. Argus snarled and scratched at the loop until Gryff tugged on it again. Hodge pressed his pistol against the thin man's scalp and said, "Drop your guns right now, or he dies. Put your hands behind your heads and take us to Sterling."

"You're lying!" cried Pierce. It was the first time Hodge had heard something like pain in his voice.

Hodge thumbed his gun's hammer, the click sharp and clear. "I ain't."

Pierce's companions all looked to him. Pierce drew in a deep breath, lifting his broad shoulders. "You'll burn for this, Hodge Harney," he said, and he let his gun hit the ground.

"Maybe so," said Hodge. "But it don't bother me as long as you ain't there to watch."

———

They ran at the sound of the gunshots.

The old mining camp wasn't much to look at—a smattering of log frames across the gulley's floor. Dried bits of wood covered the area. A fire flickered in the center of the ramshackle structures, its light flashing off the stone ridges.

Lorelin and Halston didn't bother being steady. They hustled downhill, the faces of Sterling and his men becoming more pronounced as they approached. They were staring east, in the direction of Hodge and Gryff. Halston heard someone cry out for Argus.

Halston shouted, "Sterling!"

Sterling turned, his glare glassy and firm. He stood near the fire, a stone's throw away from the mining shaft embedded in the north ridge. A trio of burlap sacks sat near his feet. The dimpled swell of metal bars and nuggets bulged through the fabric. Halston itched to sprint ahead and reach for them.

Halston counted the figures standing behind the fire. Four. That meant six men had chased after Hodge and Gryff. Halston tried to see beyond the fire and the outlaws, but he couldn't get a good look.

Sterling bellowed, "Where's the girl?"

"Give us the silver, and give us your half of the knife."

"I ain't bargaining with you! What's going on?"

"Sterling!" shouted Pierce.

Sterling turned his head. Halston watched as Pierce and two others trudged forward, their hands clasped behind their heads. Flynn was with them, his face twisted into a look sharper than glass. The pale man was there, too, but he didn't look angry or fearful. Halston could only describe his expression as disinterested.

Gryff dragged Argus across the sand. Blood flowed from Argus's leg, staining the earth red. One hand was clumsily trying to cover the wound, the other grasped tight around the rope closed around his neck. He looked almost helpless, bound and bleeding, and not much older than Halston himself.

Hodge kept his pistol aimed at Argus, and Gryff had his pointed Sterling's way.

"I'm sorry, Sterling," Flynn said, coughing. "They were gonna kill him."

"You fools!" Sterling boomed. "They won't kill him. They'll never get their precious silver if they do."

Hodge said, "Watch me."

"I ain't giving it to you," Sterling said. "Not without the girl. If you kill him, then y'all are gonna die tonight."

"Without our silver and the dagger, we're good as dead anyway," said Hodge. "Give it to us, and we'll let Argus go free."

Wait.

Flynn, Spec, Argus, and Pierce made four. Sterling and four others stood close to the fire.

They were missing two.

———

Jae just wanted this night to end.

It was barely past dusk, and the moon was still low in the sky. The sounds were muffled here, and somehow, that made them worse. Jae heard the gunshots first, then the shouting. She longed to hear the words themselves, but up here, all she could do was listen to the sounds of anger.

Tsashin kept one hand on her stomach, the other on the juniper's trunk. Without glancing up at Jae, she whispered, "Will they die?"

"No," said Jae. "If we follow the plan, none of us will die."

Anywhere else, she might've snorted at herself for saying such things. She didn't know the answer. For the first time, she understood how Pa must've felt whenever she asked if they had enough money for the winter. Always, always, it was 'yes.'

The world went quiet for a moment. Jae looked from Tsashin, to the hillside, to the woods. The shouting died down.

"Are they finished?" asked Tsashin.

"Don't know," said Jae. She dared to take a step out from behind the junipers. She looked past the hillside, surveying the world around them. To Jae's right, riding away from the gulley's south rim, came the silhouettes of a man and a woman atop a horse.

They were close enough for Jae to see their mouths curl into twisted grins.

"Look!" one of them shouted.

"Tsashin!" cried Jae as a shot rang out.

The world spun around them. Jae grabbed Tsashin's hand and took off, barreling back to the safety of the trees. Hooves pounded behind them, and the hooves were much faster than their feet.

Tsashin screamed, and Jae felt the girl's small hand slip from her own. Jae whirled around just in time to see Tsashin lifted from the ground, kicking her legs in defense. Evia had her arms locked around Tsashin's middle, and began whispering, "Shhh, don't fight me, darlin'. You'll make things harder for everyone."

Jae reached for her gun, ready to order Evia to drop Tsashin, but something cold and blunt struck Jae on the head first. Jae's knees buckled, her legs gave out, and she spilled to the ground. Her knees hit the earth first, then she tipped to the side and fell on her shoulder.

For a moment, the stars in the sky seemed to multiply, but the fog over her vision wasn't heavy, not at all like when she'd been shot in Duraunt. Still, it cost her precious seconds, and she was too dazed to fight back when the rope slipped over her wrists.

"Get up," the man spat. He grabbed her by the shoulder. Groaning, Jae planted one foot on the ground, then the other. The man jostled her as she rose, then shoved her in the direction of the hill. The figures of Evia, Tsashin, and the horse were black in the moonlight, disappearing over the slope towards Sterling's camp.

The man kept a hand on her shoulder as they walked uphill. Jae turned her head slightly, trying to gauge whether a forceful slam of her skull could break the man's nose. When she looked, she realized that she wasn't likely to hit anywhere higher than his collarbone. It figured.

The pain in her head flared with each step, but each twinge was less severe than the previous one. They hadn't taken her weapons yet. If she could just work her way out of these bindings, she could get a gun back in her hand.

Jae's stomach rose at the sight that lay outside the mine below.

A fire burned bright in the center of the pass. On one side, Halston stood with Lorelin. On the other, Sterling's men stood scattered in front of Hodge and Gryff. Pierce was the closest to Jae. Gryff held his strange gold lasso in one hand, and the length of rope was looped around Sterling's younger, reedy brother. Argus.

Sterling snickered, then, white teeth flashing through his smile. "There she is. The beauty. *My* beauty."

The blonde woman snapped her reins, then lowered Tsashin down from the horse. Her hands didn't leave Tsashin's upper arms. Tsashin kept her eyes closed, facing the ground. As Sterling strode her way, Tsashin lifted her head slowly. Her brown eyes opened, brows slanting upward.

Sterling smiled. "Do you think I'd hurt you? Nonsense. You've been away from your family so long. These curs you were traveling with didn't even bother to try and take you home. I'm a better man than that."

"I know who you are," she said. "What do you need me for? I don't know what you seek."

"I seek adamite," Sterling said to Tsashin. "A large deposit in Yunah territory. Your people tried to keep quiet about it, but word didn't make it past the men who snatched you from your lands. Not to worry. They're dead now, and one of them gave me the map to your whereabouts before he passed. But that's beside the point. Come with me, and you can live out the rest of your days in peace."

Tsashin said, "You must promise not to hurt the others."

"Yes, of course. Anything for you." That crooked grin. It was a liar's smile, sure as the springtime rain.

Argus groaned in pain. "Sterling…"

"I'll go," said Tsashin. As soon as the words left her mouth, Evia dropped her arms and Tsashin approached the outlaw.

Jae struggled against her tethers and yelled, "Tsashin, he's a liar! Don't listen to him!"

"Quiet," Sterling snapped. "Listen, Tsashin. It's an easy ride from here. You lead me to your family, and when they tell me where the vein of adamite is, I'll return you. You will be safe with us."

"Tsashin!" Hodge cried. "Get away from him!"

Sterling ignored Hodge's cries. "Just release my brother, Hodge. Here, I'll even give you your damn silver." He paced back to the sacks, then hiked them up and dropped them all in front of Halston.

Halston didn't look at the silver.

Neither did Hodge. "Tsashin! Run!"

Jae wasn't sure how many of them heard Tsashin's soft reply. She hung her head and said, "I don't want to be the reason this man hunts you."

Jae heard her captor snort, then felt a blade slash through her tethers. The rope dropped to the earth, but Jae felt no relief. She couldn't look away from Tsashin, who stood before Sterling, shaking. Sterling placed his hands on her shoulders, and by the way Tsashin tried to draw back, Jae could tell that he was squeezing her with all his might. He looked at Gryff and said, "Let go of Argus, or I'll have my men gun y'all down. You have five seconds."

Gryff lifted the rope from Argus's neck. He got to his feet and limped toward the fire as Hodge and Gryff cast bitter stares his way. The air turned heavy, like summer's most scorching day. In her periphery, Jae watched Halston and Lorelin pick up the silver bags, the contents scarcely rattling as they heaved them up. Nobody moved. Hell, nobody breathed.

And no one spoke until Sterling did.

"We've got the girl. Kill the rest."

Jae's hand flew to her holster, and the movement came to her like a breath of air. She drew.

Pierce was the first man her eyes jumped to. A feeling like fire washed over her, and somehow, it made everything a thousand times clearer. She could see every bead of sweat and speck of dirt on Pierce's face. He had a hungry glint in his eye, ready to spill blood and smile about it.

She cocked her gun and fired.

The shot sent a wave of shock up her arm, but she barely noticed it. Her gaze did not leave Pierce as the bullet tore between his brows. His head jerked back for a second, then his eyes shut tight and he went down like a falling tree.

Jae leapt to the side as Sterling screamed his brother's name. Gunfire exploded around her. She pivoted in the direction of the hill, then raced up the slope.

Hodge and Lorelin were already halfway up the incline. Halston followed, tossing a sack to Gryff, who caught it in one hand. Tsashin ran beside him. Behind them, Sterling's voice blazed like a roaring fire. "*Y'ALL WON'T LIVE TO SEE THE DAWN!*"

Chapter 35

As they raced back to the horses, Halston caught himself wishing for something ridiculous and impossible, as he often did these days. He wished that Hodge was not here. He wished that Hodge was home, and that Elias was there, too.

Every night they'd spent running, bleeding, shooting… he wanted to take it all away and live it three times over for the lot of them, this night included.

Jae caught up to him. The sack thumping on his back made it difficult to run, but he didn't dare slow down.

The shots kept ringing out, bullets flying their way until they reached the hill's peak and sprinted down the other side. The horses snorted and whinnied at the tree line. Hodge saddled up on the palomino, Lorelin and Tsashin on the brown mare. Lorelin shouted, "River!"

The speckled horse waited for them beneath the junipers. Halston didn't leap on until Jae did, but as soon as she was in place, he shoved his foot into the stirrup and settled on the saddle in front of her. Jae held his waist, and Halston flicked the reins until their mare was racing away at full speed.

The forms of Gryff and the others charged a way's ahead—but not so far that losing them was a risk. The land curved beneath them, and the trees here were short and thin and scattered. Just a few minutes passed before they heard the rush of the river drifting over the area. They were close. So damn close.

A gun cracked, and the bullet tore through a branch to Halston's left, sending fragments of wood flying. Halston looked over his shoulder to see a man gaining on them, just close enough for Halston to recognize him as Thumbscrew.

Halston pulled the reins to the side and cut around a tree. Two more shots rang out, one from Thumbscrew, and one from Jae.

Clutching the reins in one hand, Halston drew his gun and cocked it. Sparing as much focus as he could, he fired twice at Thumbscrew. The first shot flew past him, and the second grazed his horse. The poor creature cried out, bucking into the air and kicking its front legs. Thumbscrew shouted and fumbled for the reins again.

Good. A pinch more borrowed time.

The earth slanted downward, and at the bottom of the slope, the river twisted through the land. Beneath the full moon, its rippling current gleamed like silver. The others entered the river, their horses' hooves splashing in the water.

Halston and Jae reached the bank as the company neared the other side. Their horse crossed over a line of scattered stone and tall grass, and just before her hooves could touch the water, a shot thundered behind them.

The bullet cut through the river's surface. The poor mare screamed and bucked like Thumbscrew's had, sending Halston and Jae falling to the water's edge before she ran to the other shore. Lorelin cried out to them.

The water swept over Halston's legs, his hands sinking into mud and gravel. He whirled around to see Thumbscrew, horseless, making his way downhill. Were his allies close behind them, or had they stayed behind with Pierce's fresh corpse?

Halston got to his knees and fired. But Thumbscrew was descending fast, and the bullet didn't bring him down. He gritted his teeth and shot again. This time, Thumbscrew cried out, flinging his arm to the side. His gun tumbled from his bloody grasp, and he fell to his knees.

He was close, now, near the riverbanks. Despite his bleeding hand, he got to his feet and started in Halston's direction. Halston could see the scowl stiffening on his face. Raising his gun, Halston aimed and pulled the trigger. The revolver only let out a hollow click.

Jae jerked herself up. At the same time, Thumbscrew snatched a stone off the ground and hurled it her way. The rock struck her just above her brow, and she spilled to the shore.

Halston and Thumbscrew both raced toward her. Thumbscrew got there first. He pulled a big, meaty hatchet from his belt and raised it overhead, his eyes full of blind, wicked fury.

A cry tore out of Halston's throat.

He was flying—no, he was falling. Jae was beneath him, his body cloaking hers.

He was a shield, a stone. He shifted slightly, and when the blade struck him, it slid clumsily down his skin. The flesh broke on his shoulder, and the wetness of blood sprouted from the tear, but it didn't pain him.

She was safe.

"Halston!" Jae screamed, writhing beneath him.

A shot cracked, but it was not from a revolver. Halston recognized it as the deep, guttural voice of Gryff's rifle. Thumbscrew's body hit the ground, and warm blood sprayed Halston's face. Halston raised his head to meet the man's lifeless gaze. A red river spurted from Thumbscrew's neck.

Jae shouted, "Hal, we have to go!"

Halston rolled off of her, the touch of the ground sending a new flare of pain up his shoulder. He took Jae's hand, and she helped him to his feet. The slash burned as they ran, and their boots sank into the river.

"Come on!" Gryff shouted. He waited on the banks, crouching behind a rotted log. Tsashin sat on the speckled mare. Halston guessed she'd calmed the horse down after the poor animal fled to the other side.

Cold water poured over their knees, their hips, their waists. Jae's arm looped around his middle and pulled, their legs fighting against the current. The riverbed sucked at their boots, and water splashed on his wound. He felt his strength slipping away, and his eyelids were growing heavy, but he forced himself to keep them open. Waves of pain pulsed in his shoulder, begging him to stanch the flow of blood from his wound, but he kept moving forward.

He looked at Jae.

And she said, "Damn it, Hal, don't you fall asleep on me. We're getting out of this, I swear it!"

Overhill, behind them, Halston heard a cacophony of shouts. Halston squinted in their direction, but saw no one emerging from the other side of the hill. He stepped onto the shore, though Jae was dragging him a little by now. She gave him a push in Tsashin's direction, and though his shoulder protested, he took Tsashin's hand and climbed onto the saddle.

They rode ahead, to Hodge and Lorelin, who were waiting for them in the trees. Tsashin leapt from the saddle and ran to join Lorelin again. Jae climbed back onto the horse. She smelled like the river. Before she snapped the reins again, Halston heard her say,

"Don't fall."

Through the dizzy forest haze, through the last dismal hours of night, they rode on. Halston could not say for sure how much time had passed, but he willed himself to stay alert, even after the river's roar faded.

"How do you feel?" whispered Jae.

"I'm alright," he whispered once to her, then to the moon, as if the beaming orb could make it true. "I'll be alright."

Chapter 36

They were riding like bats out of hell, and Jae couldn't catch her breath.

When she closed her eyes, all she saw was blood. Some of it was Pierce's. But it was mostly Halston's.

As they rode, she'd struggled to free her map from her knapsack without jumbling Halston too much. She whispered "hence" and watched the miles fly by.

They couldn't ride like this all night, certainly, no matter how much Halston insisted he was fine. He'd stripped his jacket off and wadded it up to press to the wound. He said it didn't hurt, but Jae knew better. She could feel every one of his movements, and his pained breathing did not cease.

When they'd ridden for a while, and having evaded the sound of angry men, without another gunshot, they found a ring of ponderosas in the woods. The grass and weeds fluttered in the trees' shadows. Gryff paced around the perimeter, on the lookout for any signs of Sterling's men, should they show up. Hodge and Tsashin assisted him. Hodge kept a pistol ready, and Tsashin tread softly around the circle, scattering their tracks with a dead, knobby branch. Jae and Lorelin sat with Halston, tending to his wound.

"Can you hear me?" asked Lorelin.

"Yes."

"Alright. If you feel like you're going to black out, then you need to tell me."

"I'm fine."

On any other day, Halston's grave, self-denying tone would have bothered Jae. She did not believe him for a second.

Jae pinched the hem of Halston's collar and lowered it. Lorelin removed a patch of cloth from her knapsack and blotted up the blood. She took out a second patch, then wet it with alcohol from a hip flask. "Hold still, Hal. This will hurt."

Lorelin pressed the rag to the wound. Halston squeezed his eyes shut and let out a pained, labored grunt through his gritted teeth.

Jae hated this—seeing him hurt and knowing that it was because of her. She should have stopped him. Shot that bastard when she had the chance. "How do you feel?"

"I've had worse."

Jae doubted it.

"Don't be so modest," Lorelin said, wiping away more blood. "You're a conqueror, Hal. You can say so."

Halston smiled, but Jae couldn't bring herself to laugh. She had killed that night. Pierce Byrd was dead.

She should've been praying, preparing to atone for her own sin. But she'd shot Pierce to protect her company, and she would have done it again if she'd needed.

Lorelin passed Jae a dry rag. "Jae, press this to his wound and hold it there. Don't move until I tell you to."

Jae took the rag and pressed it deep into Halston's cut. She whispered, "Do we need to... y'know, sear it shut?" If they did, not only would they have to risk a fire, but they'd have to wait for the metal to heat till it was red hot.

Lorelin shook her head. "It's not that deep. We're gonna get out of here as soon as I get the tourniquet on him." She looked inside her pack. "Shoot. I used up all my bandages after the bank. We need fabric. A long piece."

Without a second thought, Jae took out her knife, drew her arm inside her shirt, and hacked off her sleeve.

"Jae!" Halston gasped.

"What?"

"What are you doing?"

"Making a bandage." The fibers ripped away, the white cotton splitting where she sliced.

"Don't ruin your—"

"Do you think I *care* about my shirt right now?" She passed Lorelin the sleeve.

Lorelin took the sleeve, then reached to the side and fetched a thick stick from the forest floor. "Alright. Take your hand off."

Jae did. Lorelin looped the fabric under Halston's arm, then back around. She wound it thrice around his shoulder, then tied a knot. She placed the stick in between the two ends of the makeshift bandage and knotted it again before twisting the stick. The fabric hitched tighter each time she turned the wood. "Jae, cut a piece of twine. Tie me a circle about as thick as your thumb."

Jae sliced off a small length of twine. Carefully, she looped it around her thumb to form a small loop. She tied it off in a square knot, then passed it back to Lorelin. Lorelin slipped it over the end of the stick and fastened it to Halston's leg with a longer piece of twine.

"How's that feel?" asked Lorelin.

"Snug," said Halston. "Thank you."

Jae helped Halston back onto the saddle. She wanted him to speak, but he just stared forth. Jae didn't think she'd ever seen him looking so worn, so tired, not even in those days in the cellar after Sterling threatened to throw him into the Median.

When they took off again, Jae couldn't stop it. A spark of relief breathed itself to life inside her. It was faint. It was tiny. And considering everything, she shouldn't have been relieved. If it was possible for Sterling's heart to turn even blacker, she'd succeeded in bringing that about. Pierce was gone. To them, Jae was no longer a strange bounty hunter who'd slipped from their grasp. She was prey, and they'd hunt her down.

She should have been scared. And she was.

But that flame of hope, of having lived to see the dawn, was what let her face the dark night and charge into it.

———

Several miles later, they decided they would rest for an hour, and no more. Sterling didn't have a tracker anymore, but that wouldn't stop him from trying. Dawn was approaching, and they couldn't be crippled with fatigue if Sterling caught up to them anytime soon. Nobody spoke when they stopped. As much as she wanted to talk about what was to come, Jae couldn't blame anyone for being silent. The others left her the watch and fell asleep fast. No one bothered to unload their saddlebags or set out their bedrolls, and everyone slept with their hands on their weapons' grips.

Moonlight filtered through the branches. Here, the ground was supple, and fresh grass sprouted in between the blanket of pine needles and outgrown roots. They'd made it out of the rocky area in which the Lawrence Mine spanned. Still in the Briarford Mountains, but a gentler part of it.

Already, it felt like days had passed. Months, even.

As he settled down, Halston whispered to her at last. "Thank you, Jae."

She smiled. "You as well. For saving my life."

"You're a part of the gang," he said. "We look out for each other. Besides, you saved me after Sterling captured us."

Oh, right. She'd hardly thought about that, lately.

Jae hoped Halston would shed his stubbornness long enough to get some sleep and recover. He rubbed his temple, then lay down on his back. He kept one arm over his chest to keep from shifting his tourniquet. "I think I need to stay awake," he said. "To keep my mind moving. Will you talk to me?"

"'Course I will." She slid her hand beneath his, but did not hold it, did not interlock her fingers with his. "What should we talk about?"

Halston shrugged with his good shoulder.

Jae started. "Tell me… tell me about something beautiful. Tell me about the most beautiful place you've ever seen."

Halston said, "Home."

"Where is it?"

He spoke the word like music. "Elsewhere."

She thought he would stop there, but he continued. "There was music in the world around us… in the stars, in the waters, in the sunrise." Halston closed his eyes, and Jae wasn't sure *he* even knew what he was talking about. "The hills rose above the sea, and every day, I passed the faces carved into the stone."

He went on. "It was ancient, and it was new. Like this world. But painted. When I close my eyes, it whirls past me."

"*This* world?"

Halston made no reply.

This didn't feel real. Jae suspected that she might wake up, then, but this felt too strange to even be a dream.

She still wasn't sure who Halston was. But he wasn't a dirty-faced criminal on a poster, a scoundrel with blood on his hands that no amount of rain could wash away.

Runaway. Convict. Thief.

"Halston?"

"Yes?" his voice was small. Muffled.

I don't know how to stop thinking about you. "You should get some sleep. You're hurt. I—I don't think you're thinking straight."

It killed her to see him lie down and brace himself to sleep, to know there'd be a long stretch of time before they spoke again. Had their situation permitted it, she'd have talked to him all night.

She worried she was getting stupider by the day.

Gods, she was selfish. They'd barely escaped with their lives. Here he was, bleeding and dazed, and she was wishing she could talk to him more.

She lay down in silence, her eyes on the stars. She was a small, dark speck in a sea of trees. The sky couldn't hear her, and if it could, it probably wouldn't care for her problems. But she asked anyway.

I'm afraid I've gone crazy. Please tell me what to do.

Just like that, she was a child again, asking the stars for guidance. Or maybe she'd always been one.

Chapter 37

*J*ae recalled the first time she'd tasted dandelion greens. One swallow later, she'd begged Pa not to make her eat more. He told her that the more she ate, the better she'd like them. It worked, at least well enough for her to clean her plate.

Those first few weeks of being alone after Fort Sheridan, she'd lain on the earth for a few minutes each morning, hoping to hear Pa's voice. That spring, she'd had to find her own food, since she'd already sold everything she was willing to part with. She ate plenty of roots and the occasional fish, but mostly, she ate dandelion greens.

Bland, bitter, dandelion greens. She got used to them after a while. Maybe, she thought, she could learn to like them.

The sheriffs often told her to find a husband, or at least a friend, rather than continue bounty hunting. She'd live longer that way. But to do that would be to surrender. It would slow her down, and she'd never see Pa again. Folks had their goals, and she had hers. Loneliness was a small price to pay for seeing Pa again.

Now, she wondered if her solitude was like eating greens. She'd chosen it out of necessity, and in doing so, convinced herself that it was what she wanted.

The morning after they'd fled from Sterling, Jae wasn't sure she'd slept at all. They'd spent the night riding and stopping, riding some more and stopping again, never more than an hour at a time. There were some blurry visions she recalled, but she wasn't sure if they were thoughts or dreams. She'd shifted close to Halston that night. He slept stiffly as ever, arms at his sides. Jae smiled to herself, took his hand and squeezed it. Halston mumbled something in his sleep and rolled to his side, closer to her.

You're running with thieves.

The voice inside her was quiet, but it sure didn't want to shut up. *Thieves, thieves, thieves.*

For years, she'd told herself she was brave. Without courage, she'd be a worthless bounty hunter. But she wasn't brave. Not now. She was scared. Scared of jail cells and nooses and the barrel of Sterling Byrd's gun.

Jae stood up, brushing the pine needles off her pants. Gryff sat with his back to a tree, polishing his rifle. "Ah, good. You're awake."

She cast a glance at Halston's sleeping form.

"I think he'll be fine, Jae," said Gryff. "Boy's made of stone. I reckon it'll take a lot more than a swipe from a blade to knock him down. Let's wake the others up."

"Alright," Jae murmured. She stretched out her neck and studied the full white clouds passing over the branches. The trees seemed to stare at her. Argun's servants, knowing that they'd spilled blood in his woods.

She had killed before, and she doubted she would ever forget it. When she'd started her profession, she'd vowed not to do the gods' work of taking life, if it could be helped. Once, she'd killed a man she'd been chasing, who was wanted for the murder of his sister and her husband. She found him. He lunged for her. She shot. When it happened, she only did what the law would have done in taking his life. Evil flowed through his cold veins. But he'd been heavy—so heavy, when she hauled him onto her horse's back and rode into town.

There, they'd praised her. The undertaker propped him up like a mannequin in his coffin. The reporters asked Jae if she would like her image immortalized with his. She told them to put the damn cameras away, collected her bounty, and rode off.

There had been no one to avenge him. No one had wanted to. Not like Pierce.

She was guilty for killing him, but not for cutting his life short. The good-for-nothing bastard. She would do it again, if she had to, if it would help them escape. Maybe it made her rotten, but right now, she didn't care. What she *did* regret was fueling Sterling's anger. If he found them now, she doubted their deaths would be quick.

Gryff and Jae roused the others. Hodge, Tsashin, and Lorelin all got up quickly and hurried for the horses right away.

Halston stirred a little when Jae nudged him, then lowered his head. "Halston, come on," Jae said, giving him a gentle push.

The night had been cool, but Halston's shirt was warm, like he'd been basking in the sun for a few hours. Something was wrong.

He finally sat up, scratching his forehead.

Tsashin's small voice broke in. "Halston? Are you alright?"

"I'm fine." Halston sounded much older when he spoke, like his throat had dried up overnight. He hobbled over to a crooked old stump, the wood all termite-eaten and parched. "I'm just… gotta take a moment." He ran his thumbs across his knee, like he was trying to sculpt two grooves in his leg.

Jae hurried up to him. "You sure?"

He nodded. Still, she didn't believe him.

She offered him a hand. It took him a long time to take it, and even longer for him to stand.

Jae tried leading him to the horses, but Halston was stomping like someone had replaced his legs with a pair of thick, bulky logs. His hand was damp in her own and hot as June-warmed tin. And when he fell, she cursed herself for not catching him on time.

"Hal!"

He grunted, then tried to push himself back up on his hands. He collapsed again, this time without making a sound.

Lorelin shoved past the horses and knelt down, on it before anyone else got past the shock. "We have to look at the wound. Undo the dressing. Quick."

Biting down on her cheeks, Jae picked the knot loose, then slid the bandage down. She almost emptied her stomach at the sight of it.

The wound itself was fine—not quite scabbed over, and pink and clean. But the skin around it was gray as slate, about the size of a playing card, and Halston's veins were swelling like vessels full of tar. His skin burned hot, slick with sweat.

"Shit," whispered Lorelin, tears forming in her sea-green eyes. "The blade must've been poisoned."

"*Poison?*" cried Hodge. "With what?"

"I've seen this before," Lorelin said. "It's cragmar root."

Halston lifted his head, eyelids barely open. "I've... re... I've read..."

"Slow acting," said Lorelin. "If we're lucky, the river washed some of it out. Willow bark could slow it down, but..."

"But what?" Jae snapped, in no mood to listen to Lorelin ramble.

"Manasia," Lorelin said at last. "Maidheart flower. That'll stop it."

Jae and Gryff hauled Halston to the horses. "How long do we have?" she asked, trying not to let her lip quiver.

Lorelin swallowed. "We have until nightfall, I would guess," she said softly, her voice cracking with pain.

"Nightfall?!" Jae yelled.

"Jae," Lorelin said, her eyes hardening. "Calm down."

"I ain't calming down till he's fixed!"

"Jae," Lorelin said again. "Flailing around isn't going to do him a bit of good. Take out your map. I know where we can get help."

Jae felt a prickle of anger at the remark, but Lorelin was right. Jae whipped her map out and unrolled it. "Hence," she whispered.

Lorelin studied their surroundings. "We're a little north of Jade Valley. That means we're close to the heart of the Briarfords." She nudged Jae. "Do you see a place called Luna?"

"No," said Jae. "Show me the road to Luna," she told the map.

The map wiped itself blank. It stayed empty for a second, then the ink reappeared and depicted a trail following the river and winding to a point between two northern peaks. Jae was shaking so much that it took her a moment to get a good look at it. Luna rested near the mouth of the Taracoma River, at the upper end of the mountain chain with a forest thick around it.

"How far?" asked Lorelin.

"Eighty miles, I reckon," said Jae.

"It's too far," Hodge said, though Jae knew by the pain in his voice that he had to force himself to say it.

"No," Lorelin said. "We aren't trotting. I know the way. If we gallop, we can make it."

"How?" Hodge blurted.

"We'll take the main road," said Lorelin. "Up here, it follows the river. It crooks east near Luna. Jae, you have the map. Ride behind us. Everyone get ready."

Hodge blurted, "With all the slopes? Uphill? It'll be—"

Lorelin cut him off, snapping her fingers shut as if snatching the words away from him. "We're wasting time. Saddle up. I'll lead."

Gryff and Jae helped Halston onto Lorelin's saddle. He shuddered, but his eyes stayed closed. "Come on," Hodge whispered, placing a hand on his brother's head. "You better not black out on me, Hal. Damn it, I'll... Hold on. Just hold on."

Yes, thought Jae, trembling as she let him go. *Hold on.*

She felt heavy as lead, then. She couldn't decide if she wanted to sink into the ground or let the wind carry her off.

Tsashin's hand touched Jae's shoulder. "Be strong for him. It's all we can do, now."

Jae climbed onto the stolen speckled mare. Tsashin followed her, her small body pressed against Jae's back. Gryff waited at the end of their lineup.

Jae had no energy to pray, or to even think. All she could do was watch Hodge hoist himself onto his golden stallion. Lorelin headed the party, sitting steadfast as a colonel on her dark, lean horse. She gave a "Hiyup!" that echoed off the trees and plunged forth. Then they bolted over the earth, leaving a cloud of dust in their wake.

———

They rode like wildfire. They rode like hell.

Cutting through the air like a knife, the horses galloped along the winding banks of the river. Lorelin imagined they were racing against the sun itself, and that its rays had a noose around Halston's neck. As soon as it set, it was taking him with it.

Like hell she'd let that happen.

The day she'd joined these boys, they'd all made a vow: to protect one another. With each mile they'd trekked, it became more than that. It was the nature of things now.

The river dipped into a curve. Gravity tugged at Lorelin's body as they veered around the sweep. She fought against it, clutching her reins, and heaved herself back into a steady position on her saddle.

Lorelin didn't dare let herself breathe easier. These fading seconds were worth more than gold.

They rode through noon, when the sun was a bright, ugly tack in the center of the sky, its heat beating down on them like hailstones. Mocking them.

Lorelin dug her heels into the horse's sides. *Come on, come on.*

She looked over her shoulder at Hodge, who nodded at her to let her know that he was fine. She clutched the reins, her arms keeping Halston from sliding off the saddle, his back to her chest. Even through his shirt and jacket, he was burning like hot iron.

They rode uphill, Lorelin's blood roaring in her veins. She'd ridden like this before, from banks, from lawmen, from Adwell Fisk's home after she'd strung him up like dried meat. Never once had she felt so weightless, so sweltering hot—like she was a plume of smoke, and that she'd drift into the air any moment.

They leapt over small pools and muddy notches in the riverbanks. They plunged through drooping water plants, wove around boulders, dipped beneath junipers and over brambles.

Night would not wait for them.

———

Someone was screaming.

Halston and his brothers ran through the halls and down the tunnel linking the fortress towers together, where pillars divided the open windows. Like always, the floor was slick with seawater, and drops rolled off the ceiling and struck the tiles with sweet, rhythmic chimes.

The sea was black.

Smoke floated above the waters, more than Halston had ever seen before. The cloud was twice the size of a fortress—a storm, bound for their walls.

He followed the screams.

He flew down the steps, circling down, down, down to the ground. He found his father waiting for him there. He was clutching his musket, and his gray eyes were like thunderclouds.

"Boys," he said. "Your mother and sister are bound north. Get the horses. Head for the portal."

Hodge began to protest. "But—"

"Go! Run!"

They ran down the corridors and outside, where the poplars grew thick and tall. They climbed onto their horses, and somehow, Halston could feel the cold shade of the smoke. He kicked his horse's sides and led his brothers north, plunging into the trees. He turned around.

The smoke seeped into the windows and swallowed the rooftops and barracks. Somehow, Halston knew that it did not want to kill his father. He'd seen this kind of smoke before, seen a warlock use it to bind a thief who'd tried to run. It was not here to kill them—it was here to catch them.

Then, he saw his father's figure, clad in his blue uniform and perched on the edge of a window.

The smoke came closer, and his father fell.

Whether his body struck the climbing waves or the jagged rocks beneath the window, Halston did not know. All he knew was that his father was not coming with them.

They rode. They found Lia. They found their mother.

They made it to the portal.

It glowed like a big, bright pool in a circle of willows. The grass was impossibly green and soft, like spun emeralds, and the portal's surface shone like the purest water. It was calm here.

Elias had already stepped through the portal. So had Hodge.

Lia hardly ever cried, but now, her voice strained and broke with each word. "I'm afraid. I'm afraid to go down." But their mother whispered to her, urging her to be strong, to step inside.

Lia clung to their mother's shirt. Halston remembered his mother's face in that moment—her brown skin caked with tears and soil, without a trace of fear in her eyes. There was only her will, stronger than the hardest steel. "I cannot go with you, Lia. Only one person may step in at a time. Watch how Halston does it."

He placed a hand on Lia's small shoulder. "It's going to be alright."

Two things happened at once.

Halston stepped into the portal, and the black smoke burst from the trees.

Lia screamed. His mother did not. She threw her arms around his sister, shielding her, but the black mist shrouded them, engulfed them like stones in the tides. Halston shouted for them, but he was already falling, and his cry followed him down.

Down, down, down.

———

Lorelin's horse began to cry.

Lorelin jerked the reins, bringing the poor mare to a halt. They stood on a thin part of the trail, where the trees grew around them in abundance. The pines were much taller this far north. Light still shone through the green cover of branches, but barely. The sky was turning pink.

Hodge stopped his own horse, skidding just a hair away from Lorelin's. "Why are we stopping?!"

"My horse needs to rest. She can't gallop much further."

Jae silently brought her mare to a halt. Tsashin lifted her head to peer over Jae's shoulder, and though her eyes were wide with worry, she did not speak. Gryff stopped too, then took a moment to lean over and clutch his side, breathing heavily.

Hodge glared. "Alright, let's stop and make a fire, then. We can spend our whole night resting," he snapped.

"Stop it," Lorelin said. "I'm doing the best I can, Hodge!"

Hodge's eyes darkened, and his glare disappeared. "Gods, I… I'm sorry Lorelin."

340 : Sophia Minetos

"I know." Lorelin hopped down from her horse, keeping one hand on Halston to hold him steady. "I know how you feel. But the horses can't go on like this. They need water. Halston needs water, too."

Hodge and Lorelin helped him down from the saddle to the side of the trail. They picked a rock that was flat enough, with soft moss coating its face, and lay Halston down. Lorelin pressed her palm to his forehead. Still hot as hell, but it was damp—a good sign that he hadn't sweat himself dry. Lorelin poked his mouth open with the neck of the waterskin and poured a little into his mouth. His throat bobbed as he swallowed.

"Ten minutes," Lorelin said. "Just ten minutes of rest. Even a trot is better than nothing. I've been here before, too. I'd wager we're ten miles away."

There was no comfort on their faces. No hope. She wanted to give it to them, but she was powerless.

Lorelin dug her fingers into her hair, shutting her eyes tight and trying not to let her breathing turn swift and shallow. Ten miles. It was better than eighty, but it was still a lot. She wanted to scream. She wanted to curse at the sun for moving. But she didn't. If she broke down, so would Hodge, and then their heads would fog up and they wouldn't reach Luna on time.

When Lorelin opened her eyes, she glimpsed a hint of motion in the woods. First, she made out a long, wavering tail, then a lithe body, moving forth on four surefooted paws. Lastly, she glimpsed the yellow-green eyes, slit, staring at them from the greenery that lined the path.

Tsashin screamed.

The cougar pounced, claws-bared, hungry eyes bolted to Lorelin's mare. It plunged down, braced to strike the horse's flank. At the same time, the horse shrieked and took off down the path, and the sound of Hodge and Gryff's guns blasted off the trees.

The cougar yowled, falling to its back. Lorelin leapt a few yards away, but Hodge was still close. Blood streamed from the animal's front legs. Hodge aimed his pistol at its head. The cougar's teeth glittered like white knives in its jaws, and before anyone could shoot, its paw lashed out at Hodge's legs. He screamed, the sound of ripping fabric merging with his strained cry.

Swiftly, Lorelin drew her own gun before the creature could swipe again, and fired two shots at its head. One bullet slammed into the beast's eye, the other its nose. A shudder passed over its body, its muscles twitching. Then it fell still.

Lorelin tried not to look at it—the blood matting its fur, the jaws locked open in death. Hodge cried out again, sitting down now, and his trembling fingers touched his calf. Three gashes pooled through the tears in his pants, sitting just below his left knee.

"Hodge!" Tsashin cried. She hurried forward and offered him a hand. Her voice was heavy, wavering with each word. "Stand. Can you walk?"

Hodge nodded, but winced as Tsashin helped him to his feet.

The poor mare was nowhere in sight, but the palomino was still here. "Jae," said Lorelin. "Help us get Hodge onto your horse. Gryff, sling Halston over the stallion."

Tsashin and Lorelin helped Hodge half-walk, half-limp over to Jae's mare. He took her hands and grappled with the stirrup for a moment, then groaned softly as he slung his bad leg over the side of the saddle.

"Press your hand to your leg, if you can," said Lorelin. "Try not to let the blood trail behind you."

"Will he be alright?" Tsashin whispered.

Lorelin wanted to answer, but she couldn't. She just watched Gryff pick Halston up like a bale of hay, then place him onto the stallion's back. Fear buzzed in her mind. Halston wasn't anywhere close to consciousness now. If he was, the shrieking lion, gunshots, and his brother's screams would've roused him.

Hodge's pained cries killed Lorelin, but they had to get going. Damn it. They were down a horse, now.

"Tsashin," said Lorelin. "Do you think you can fit with Hodge and Jae?"

Gryff answered for her. "No. Three on a horse? That'll slow us down." Gryff sighed. He approached Tsashin, then bent his knees and motioned to his back. "Come on, little one."

On any other day, she would have laughed to see Tsashin climb onto Gryff's back, but the second Lorelin was sure that Gryff had a steady hold on her, she was running for the stallion.

Lorelin mounted the golden horse, then touched Halston's neck. Still warm. Still sweaty. Heart still beating. They had to keep it that way.

Again, they rode.

———

When they reached the new world, there wasn't much left to do but take up honest work.

They came to Emberhill Ranch, and a warmth filled Halston's body, one he hadn't known since he was young. A glimmer of hope.

Elias got them jobs. Elias was seventeen, then, and Gus Emberhill said he'd hire him gladly, but he wasn't too keen on hiring boys of twelve and thirteen. Elias promised the rancher that his brothers were hard workers, and that they'd be a pair of worthy employees.

"Alright," Gus said at last. "They'll have to start small, though. Shoveling the stables and cleaning them. They'll have to work their way up to ropin'."

Gus hired them on, and they joined the crew. Halston learned their names. There was Vince, Gus's son, and Delilah, his daughter. The others were Doug,

Hovis, Jace, Miguel, Fermin, and Miles.

Still, when everyone else slept, they whispered. He and Elias discussed what they knew about portals and how they could open one in a world where magic ran thinner. They needed silver, but they also needed a conduit, with the runes of the old language. The only ones Halston knew of were in the fortress halls—a world away.

Two years passed, and the brothers saved every deon they made. Gus used to joke about how cheap they were. He said that they'd let their clothes turn to rags before they even considered buying new ones.

Travelers came to the ranch, too. Some were quiet, but many had interesting stories to tell. There was a man who'd seen the last herd of bison trek across northern Mesca, before the poachers killed them all. There was another man who'd come from a place called Conbern— a nation all the way across the sea—and fought in their war for freedom. And there was a woman who said that she'd been to the vast Dunes of Monvallea and seen a herd of the fabled Sempahi horses running through. Halston wasn't sure he believed that one, but it was fun to hear.

Then there was the stranger.

He'd sat with the men and paid for a plate of food. He spoke little, but the others made up for it. Halston sat with his journal in his lap, scribbling down a few notes. He was trying to calculate the amount of silver one would need to open a portal large enough for one person to step through.

"What's that?" asked the stranger.

Halston swallowed. "It's…"

Vince laughed. "Hal's got quite the imagination. Always writing in his journal. C'mon, Hal. Show us."

Sheepishly, Halston lifted the journal, not looking at the others.

"Shoot, Hal," said Vince. "You're the only person I know who does math for fun."

Most of the others laughed. The stranger didn't. He stared in Halston's direction long after he shut his journal. The stranger said, "Interestin' stuff.

Smart boy like you shouldn't waste his talents as a cowhand."

The other cowboys narrowed their eyes at the stranger. Before any of them could pipe up, the stranger took out a pen and a couple of deons. He scribbled something on the paper, then placed the coins on the table. "Thank you for the meal, gentlemen, but I can't stay the night. My family's waitin' for me."

No one saw him slip the note to Halston.

I have something that may be of interest to you, regarding portals. Meet me outside the bunker in twenty minutes.

-S

That night, a criminal had passed right under their noses.

Sterling was one hell of a lender.

Halston could hardly believe his luck when they first met. He was only fifteen... He'd still trusted too quickly, too blindly. But this stranger had a conduit: a magic dagger. Broken in two, but still useful. It could open a portal, with the right amount of silver.

"It ain't much use to me," the stranger said. "But it's made of the rarest metal on earth. I could snatch up quite the fortune for it. 'Course, I'd be willing to sell it to you, if you have about a thousand crowns to your name."

A thousand crowns! "If I did, I wouldn't work here."

The stranger laughed. "Tell you what. I'll give you one half now. Consider the other half collateral."

He passed Halston the first half. The hilt was indescribably smooth in his hand. Halston couldn't believe it. This broken weapon could be his way home. "How... how would you like me to pay it off? Where can I meet you? And how often?"

The stranger passed him a slip of paper and said, "Keep this to yourself. If you show anyone else... the deal's off the table. And let's just say we'll have to settle it some other way. Understood?"

Halston nodded, then watched the stranger ride off.

———

To someone else, this might have seemed a dream. To Lorelin, it was too real. Overwhelmingly real.

Hodge's pained grunts had stopped, but Halston hadn't woken. Lorelin felt as though she was being smothered by heat and her own sweat, but they kept on.

The path to Luna was easy to miss. It extended about a mile away from the river, and at first glance, it didn't look like a trail at all. Pale boulders and stones dotted it, and moss sprouted around it in thick clumps. The pass snaked between two enormous plateaus, where the path was barely wide enough for a horse to slip through.

The horses trotted between the rock faces. Lorelin stared straight ahead. The ground climbed up, and the sides of the pass loomed like giants in her periphery, ready to crush them. She reminded herself that this trail would take them to Luna. The gem at the end of this blood-spattered road.

The path thinned so much that the stone walls nearly brushed the horse's sides. Lorelin could not see a thing around her, save for the strip of lilac sky overhead. She cursed. There was a star.

At last, the pathway widened, and the two plateaus gave way to a stretch of flat, solid ground. Lorelin urged her mare on further and further, until the ground's rocky knobs turned to a long stretch of soft, grassy land.

When she spied Luna's rooftops, its bricks shining like a pearl on a collar of green, she scarcely felt like herself. It sat in a wide patch of cleared land, several acres wide, with the forest framing its edges. Sheep grazed in the pasture, and chokecherry trees dotted the grass surrounding the enormous structure.

The poor horse was wailing beneath her, but Lorelin whispered her will in the mare's ears. "Almost there."

The hooves ripped the dust from the road, and grit flew so high it stung Lorelin's eyes. She did not dare blink. Her breath was thin and ragged, the dry air plunging like blades down her throat.

They stole across the crooks in the path, horses swerving. The branches were missing Lorelin's head by inches. She gripped the reins, nails digging deep into her palms.

As the sun sank lower, the sanctuary of Luna grew brighter. Its roof, the shingles polished and red. Its stones, the color of ivory, curled pillars and awnings rippling past Lorelin's vision. Candlelight glowed through the windows.

When they reached the courtyard, Lorelin tugged the reins. Her horse skidded to a stop. Lorelin leapt down. Her hands burned with blisters, and clumps of hair stuck to her sweaty forehead.

Her feet carried her to the carved oak doors, and she pounded on them like a woman possessed.

Long ago, she'd passed this same threshold, fresh from the grasp of Adwell and her mother. For years they'd tried to tame her, wrapping her heart in golden chains and stitching her lips shut with silk thread. At last, she broke free, but she did not *feel* free… until she came here.

And for the first time in ages, she cried a name. "Martina!"

———

Halston never thought Elias would've killed a man. But it happened.

Halston loved Elias. He knew that. But in those days, he wondered if anger was strong enough to bury love.

He'd forgotten most of the time between the day they'd fled and the day they were jailed. Maybe no one was at fault, or maybe everyone was. But Halston looked at Elias, and with a fire that had been foreign to him before, shouted, "Haven't you done enough?"

Halston wanted to forgive him, but the anger was hotter. Fuller. Easier to hold.

The night they'd escaped, the bullets flew thick and fast. Men died, and blood watered Arrowwood's scorched earth. They fled the town limits, fled from the gallows, fled from the law itself.

Then Elias died, and Halston could not ask for forgiveness, nor could he dole it out.

But they kept going. There was no stopping. They'd forgotten how to stop. They stole for Sterling. They began to pay off their debt, one heist at a time. Sometimes, Sterling would let Halston touch the flat of the blade, and he would wonder what it would feel like when he saw its magic thrumming, opening the sky…

Sterling whipped them. He praised them. He scorned them. He thanked them. He threatened to spill their blood if they crossed him. Other times, he let it pass, tacking numbers back onto their loan.

Sterling didn't always let Halston take Hodge's place, or Gryff's, or Lorelin's, when at last she joined them. But he did when he could, despite their protests.

He'd met Sterling on that night outside the ranch. Halston was the reason Sterling crossed over from his world of theft and ruin and into their lives. Halston had leapt into this debt without looking. Hodge had not had a say in it, nor had the others. It was Halston's weight to carry.

Haven't you done enough, Elias? Haven't you done enough…

Haven't I done enough?

Chapter 38

The others stayed on the horses while Lorelin pounded on the door. She waited. She hardly breathed.

Everything around them—the rich moss, the pines, and the dark earth seemed to gaze at them. Many moons ago, Lorelin had turned her back on this place. Luna was the heart of the land, a temple of healing and prayer. She'd sworn to herself that she'd never return, and that it was for the best, but nothing could break a promise faster than desperation.

Two women, wide-eyed and slim, answered the door.

One was around forty. Her black hair fell past her collarbone, an embroidered stole dangling from her shoulders. The other was young, twenty, if Lorelin remembered correctly. A beauty straight from a painting. Or a theater's stage. Her skin was brown, and her lips were red as silk dyed with ripe berries. She wore her raven hair in a knot, a few stray curls framing her delicate face.

Martina, and Jimena, the Prioress.

Martina's voice was like warm honey. "Lorelin?"

"Gracious, dear," said the Prioress. "Where have you been? What's happened?"

Lorelin managed to speak, though she felt like the tears were braced to shatter her throat. "Please. My friend, he—Poison. Cragmar. And Hodge got scratched by a cougar."

Just like that, Martina's eyes softened, and she spoke as though she'd been waiting for them. "Come. Quickly."

Jae and Tsashin helped Hodge inside. Jae had tied a frayed scrap of cloth around Hodge's leg for a makeshift bandage. Bloody patches were seeping through the cloth.

Martina and Jimena helped Halston down from the horse. He hung limp as they carried him, but his throat rippled with a swallow every few moments—a good sign. They moved in a jumbled line as they passed into the sanctuary.

They shouldn't even be here. Halston deserved to be on his feet and talking.

Lorelin heard Jae murmur, "If I'd shot that bastard a second sooner, before he tossed the rock at me, and got him in the *head*..."

They followed Martina and the Prioress down shining halls, their multicolored skirts trailing on the tiled floor. The corridor was sweet-smelling, but sharp as well, like cinnamon. The color in this hall was rampant, each corner lit like the most fruitful days of summer. Paintings and mosaics lined the white walls, and wooden beams stretched across the arched ceiling. They passed by room after room, and Lorelin felt the stunned gazes of the women inside. They all must have looked a fright in a pretty place like this—wounded, covered in dirt and rumpled from a day of riding like hell through the woods.

They ran past a wide, colorful portrait of the gods, past the painted gaze of Argun, with his pine-green eyes, and Cressien and Nerea, the sweet goddesses, and Petreos, with the mountains in his hands. Lorelin asked each of them to let Halston live.

At last, they passed a portrait of a dancing woman, with herbs in her hands a sheaf of wheat slung over her shoulder. Grass sprouted around her ankles, and the land around her was green and vibrant, as though she was sowing life itself into the earth.

Her name was Arilaya, a half-goddess, who had blessed Luna with her touch. There were many of her sanctuaries spread across Hespyria and Quierra, abodes for healers and protectors of the natural world.

Martina and Jimena led them into a room lined with bottles and jars. The air was thick with the smell of herbs. They brought Halston to a bed and laid him down. His head sank into the pillow. Martina wet a rag with liquid from a clay bottle, lowered Halston's bandages, and pressed the cloth to the wound.

She said, "Jimena, will you help the other young man with his leg? Lorelin and I will take care of Halston."

Jimena nodded, then motioned for Hodge to follow her. "Come."

Gently, she took Hodge out of the room. Lorelin felt the weary gazes of Gryff and Tsashin before they followed Hodge and the Prioress into the hall.

Jae didn't go with them. "I'm stayin' here."

"Not now," said Martina. "We need to work alone. Do try to understand."

Jae opened her mouth to protest again, but Lorelin shook her head at her. She saw the stubbornness spark in Jae's eyes for a moment before it disappeared. At last, Jae tipped her head at Lorelin, knowingly, and she returned the gesture as they passed out of the room. When they were gone, she kicked the door shut with her heel.

Martina leaned over Halston. She'd hung his shirt from the headboard. Sweat beaded on his bare chest. The tiled floor bore stains of candle wax, and though the walls were spacious, every inch of them was lined with shelves filled with bottles, jars, and boxes of every color and size.

"I gave him a dose of willow bark," Martina said without looking away. "With a pinch of manasia in it. Have the spasms started yet?"

Lorelin shook her head.

"Good. That means we have time." Martina touched a finger to Halston's wrist. "His spirit is still strong, but his body is fading. It will not hold him much longer. We'll have to work quickly."

Lorelin pushed up her sleeves, ignoring the twinge of pain it brought to her hands. She'd been gipping the reins so hard they'd cut through her callouses. She knelt on the floor next to the bed, where Martina had laid out three vials, a bowl, a strip of muslin, a cruet of water, a knife, and her mortar and pestle.

Martina pinched the bandages on Halston's shoulder. "Do you remember how to do this?"

"I think so."

"I'm here to help you," Martina said as she untied the knot, then let the dressing fall away from Halston's arm.

Lorelin rinsed her hands, then emptied the vials into the mortar—ripe-smelling melot root, brittle stalks of amorayah, and the large, pear-shaped manisia petals. She filled a third of the basin with water, watching the herbs swirl and dance across the surface, then ground them into a pulp. The paste turned the same color as the manisia—a deep purple rich as the robes of long-dead queens.

"Put pressure on his wound," Martina said, taking the mortar from Lorelin. "I'll handle the next part."

Lorelin bit down on her cheeks, then pressed a hand to Halston's wound. She tensed at the feel of his hot skin beneath her hand, and her heart splintered at the sight of his closed eyes and parted lips, but she forced herself to keep her arm steady.

Martina worked swiftly as always, each movement light and

graceful. Lorelin watched Martina spread the tincture evenly over the knife's blade, exhaled, and steadied the tool in her hand.

Martina passed Lorelin a damp cloth. "Wipe it down, please."

Lorelin released her hand, then wiped down the wound. The patch of graying skin was about the size of a footprint now.

When Martina had taught Lorelin about healing, she'd said that one had to pour all their thoughts and prayers and hopes into the act itself. So that was what Lorelin did.

For you, Halston.

Martina nudged Lorelin's hands to either side of the graying skin. Martina said, "Squeeze when I tell you."

Martina ran the tip of her knife across his skin, parallel to the scabbing hatchet wound. She let the tincture run off the blade into the original cut. Halston's black and red blood seeped like tar from the slit. A low, stiff sound came out of his mouth, but he did not stir any more than that.

Martina collected the thick, sticky blood in the bowl, let it sit for a minute, then ordered Lorelin to squeeze. They sat there as the night rolled by, draining Halston's poisoned blood bit by bit. They worked together, as they once had. Lorelin only wished the circumstances had been different.

Lorelin's hands ached, her muscles straining… but at last, when she looked at Halston's skin, the gray veins had softened and dulled, and his feverish heat had cooled.

Lorelin raised her tired, burning eyes to the windowpane. Outside, the sky was turning pale with daylight.

"That should do it," Martina said, lowering the bowl. "Will you find me fresh bandages?"

Nodding, Lorelin hurried to the shelf, one of many that she'd memorized moons ago. She snatched up the bandages and hurried back to Martina's side. Martina lifted Halston's arm. Blotting up the last of his blood, which now bloomed a bright, healthy red, she dressed the wound and tied off the bandages.

"Will he be alright?" Lorelin whispered.

"He should be fine," Martina said at last. "He may be numb for a few days, but I'd say we caught this in the nick of time."

Lorelin wanted to say something. Exhaustion muddled her mind, and she felt words budding on her lips, but they were drowned out by the raw tightness in her throat.

She placed her head on Martina's shoulder and wept.

Martina did not tense at Lorelin's touch. She did not hesitate to wrap an arm around Lorelin's waist, and her whisper was as familiar as the sunrise itself. "It's alright, Lorelin," she whispered. "It's alright."

Chapter 39

orelin wasn't sure she'd sleep that night. After Martina
assured her that Halston would live, she hurried to find the
Prioress.

Jimena was standing in the hallway beside an icon of Argun,
facing Lorelin and looking like she'd been waiting there for hours.
Lorelin ignored Jimena's furrowed brow and folded hands. The
expression reminded her too much of her own mother.

"Jimena," she said, breathless, as she reached the Prioress. "I can
explain."

"There is no need for you to explain," said Jimena. "Luna is
always open to those who need healing. Your friend is fine. His
wounds were shallow enough that they only needed to be cleaned.
No stitches. But I am concerned about why you chose to return."

Lorelin swallowed. "We needed help."

"When you came here, you said that you wished to denounce
thievery. Forgive me if I've assumed incorrectly, but by the looks of
things, you've returned to it."

What was Lorelin supposed to say? That she'd had no choice? That wasn't true. She could have stayed in Luna.

"Yes," said Lorelin, not bothering to try and hide her shame. "I have."

Jimena nodded grimly, then stepped to the side. "I'm not here to berate you, Lorelin. But you should reconsider this life. It will only bring you closer to your grave." She straightened the stole on her shoulders. "Your companions are in the guest quarters. How long will you be here?"

"Just a day or two."

"Very well. Rest now," said Jimena. Then she disappeared down the hall, her shoes thudding softly on the tiled floor.

Lorelin waited until Jimena was out of sight before moving again. She took a deep breath, then hurried down the hallway and up a short flight of stairs. Past more murals, wide windows, and milk-white walls.

She found the rest of her gang outside a string of bedrooms. Hodge and Tsashin sat on a cushioned bench against a window with an elaborate, gilded frame while Gryff and Jae stood in the center of the floor. The moment Jae glimpsed Lorelin, she rushed forward. Hodge joined her, though he immediately grunted when he put some weight on his bad leg.

"Halston is fine," Lorelin said. "He needs rest, though. As do we."

Lorelin watched the relief pass over them. They all dropped their shoulders, exchanging soft glances with one another. She expected them to start chattering, to begin discussing their plan, but then she figured they were all too tired.

"How are your scratches, Hodge?" she asked.

"Said they should be fine, as long as I don't provoke them." He grinned, motioning to his bandages. "If I ever want to tell someone that I tackled the cougar, don't ruin it for me, alright?"

Well… if she'd had any doubts that Hodge wasn't back to himself yet, then his request put those doubts to rest.

Lorelin bid Gryff and Hodge goodbye, letting them know they'd speak again in the morning. Quietly, she led the girls into one of the guest rooms. The chamber was spacious, smelling of pine and soap. White, gauzy curtains dangled above the windows. The tiled floors paired nicely with the ivory walls and linens on the three beds. An oval mirror framed with brass was mounted to the wall.

Tsashin sank into one of the beds almost immediately. She didn't bother to tuck herself under the covers. Within moments, she was asleep.

Lorelin sat on one of the beds. Jae didn't. Instead, she carried herself to the window and pressed her forehead against the pane.

"You should sleep, dear," said Lorelin.

"How did you know about this place?"

Lorelin stroked the bed linens. "I came here after I escaped Adwell. I had to leave, though."

"Why?"

"It's not important," said Lorelin. "I'll tell you later, alright? It's a long story. You need to get some rest."

"I don't know how I can rest," Jae said. "Not after all…" she waved her hands. "*This.*"

Lorelin didn't argue with her. "Very well, then. Sleep if you want, though. That's what *I'm* going to do."

Lorelin lay down and closed her eyes. Eventually, she heard Jae walk to her bed and rustle the covers. Even if sleep hadn't found Jae, her breathing was steady enough to pass for it.

It didn't come for Lorelin, though. She kept her eyes closed and held herself still, but sleep did not pass over her. She tossed and turned, shifting from her side to her back to her stomach until morning light peeked in through the window.

She sighed, rising. If she couldn't get some rest, then she may as well get through the day. There was no dodging what would happen. She'd have to talk to Martina.

Lorelin crept into the washroom. A clean bucket of water waited for her, but she didn't bother heating it. She stripped down, wiped herself clean, then patted her skin dry. Her clothes weren't perfect, but they looked clean enough. She slipped them back on, then headed outside.

When Lorelin had lived here, she'd often find Martina in the gardens, reading amongst the roses or filling a basket with herbs. Sure enough, Lorelin found her there. Martina was sitting on the little porch overlooking her rose bushes. Behind her was a mosaic, the tiles as bright in color as the plumes of birds in warm, faraway places. Her hands were folded in her lap.

"Martina?"

Martina turned around and grinned. "I thought you'd be resting."

"Yeah, well... I figured it wouldn't be easy to get any rest. I've got a lot on my mind."

"I know. So do I. Have a seat."

Lorelin did as she was told. She tried to hold Martina's gaze, but those brown eyes sent a jolt of fear through her, and blood rushed to her cheeks. She stared at the roses instead.

"Thank you," said Lorelin. She swallowed. "And I'm sorry. I know it must have been a lot, with me showing up like that. But we were desperate. Halston... he would've died."

"You don't need to apologize. I was glad to help him." Martina hesitated, and then came the question Lorelin had been dreading. "Why did you leave?"

Lorelin forced herself to look at Martina, then regretted it. The hurt in her eyes cut through Lorelin like a knife. "Do you... really want an answer?"

"Of course, I want an answer. I've wanted one for ages now, Lorelin."

Lorelin bit her lip, trying to ignore the dizziness whirling in her stomach. "I thought you'd have forgotten me."

"Forget you? After all the time we spent together? You meant the world to me, Lorelin. So imagine how I felt when I found that you had gone." Martina's eyes glistened, but the tears failed to fall.

"I know how it must have felt. It wasn't easy for me, either."

"Then why? Why did you have to go?"

Lorelin stared at the jade-studded toes of her boots. "You wouldn't understand."

"Yes, I would. Once, you told me that I understood you better than anyone else ever had. Has that changed?"

There was no fighting it, then. "I left because you deserve better than this life." Lorelin gestured to herself. "I've done a lot of things I'm not proud of. And that was true before, too."

Noise followed Lorelin wherever she went. Gunfire, pounding hooves, sacks full of jangling coins. The chaos that dragged itself behind Lorelin did not belong in Martina's quiet world of healers.

Martina sighed. "Who are they? The travelers who came with you?"

"The Harney boys. I'm sure you've heard of them."

Martina sucked in her cheeks. "Last time, you told me you worked alone."

"I know. That changed." Lorelin shuffled in her spot.

"You were happy here. Luna was your home. I thought our time together meant something to you."

"Of course it did," Lorelin replied. It killed her to see Martina like this. "That hasn't changed. But even if I'd stayed, it wouldn't have protected me from the law, or the Fisks. Adwell would pay dearly to see me hang. I won't be surprised if he's placed a substantial bounty on my dead body, and even if he hadn't, I was a wanted thief. If they'd found me here, you would've been charged, too. You could have lost everything. I wasn't about to be responsible for that."

"Last you were here, you told me about your past. I took that risk. You were worth it. You still are."

"I know." Lorelin didn't know what else to say. "I know."

Silence dangled between them for a moment, then Martina spoke. "I remember when you came to me."

So did Lorelin. It was the first time Lorelin had been certain she was going to die. She'd fled a shootout and escaped with a bullet below her belly. After riding for a few miles, pressing a hand against her wound, she'd fallen from her horse and curled up under a pine tree. Darkness took her.

She hadn't expected to wake up. But she did, and Martina was there.

Martina went on. "You were covered in bruises, getting by on luck and anger alone. I was with you when you changed. Each day, you laughed more. You were happy. *We* were happy."

That was true. If Lorelin's life had been different, if the path that had led her to Martina had been cleaner, perhaps she would have stayed. Lorelin missed the long walks around the estate, laughing with Martina over supper, how she had wanted to bundle up every ounce of joy she'd ever felt and give it to Martina. And Lorelin was tempted to say so, but she didn't want to complicate the matter any more.

Martina stood and faced the garden. "I believed you would stay in Luna with me. It was the perfect place for you. For us."

"Yeah. It's a dream," Lorelin said, watching the rosebuds dance with each other. "A dream I don't deserve."

Martina turned. "*I* believe you deserve it."

"I told you. It's... it's a life I can never have. And I've made peace with that. I'll never settle down. I can't take that away from you."

"I understand. But I need to know, Lorelin—did it hurt when you left?"

"Absolutely." Lorelin stood, reached out, and touched Martina's shoulder. "It was the hardest thing I've ever done."

"This was your home." Martina's eyes met Lorelin's, and suddenly, there was no fear left in her body. "And it can still be your home."

"I want that. I really do. But... we've run into some trouble."

"I figured as much," Martina murmured. "What happened?"

Lorelin told Martina everything, starting with their empty cave and finishing with Thumbscrew's ax hitting Halston's shoulder. Martina didn't speak, but a hundred different feelings passed over her face as Lorelin told her the story.

"We'll leave as soon as Halston recovers," Lorelin finished. "Tomorrow, or the next day, I'd imagine. After that, we're heading north."

"I'm not afraid," said Martina. "Luna is well hidden. It's blessed by Arilaya's grace. Our lands have gone undisturbed for decades. I doubt Sterling will come here. Besides, he would be outnumbered, and I know how to use a gun."

The idea of Martina wielding a gun rather than an herbal compress almost made Lorelin laugh. She raised an eyebrow, grinning a little. "Who on earth would be stupid enough to mess with the daughter of the great Callista Reyes?"

"You'd be surprised."

Lorelin couldn't fight the smile that came. "I've missed you."

"I've missed you, too."

Gods, what had she even hoped for? That Martina would forgive her at once and abandon everything she'd ever known to join the gang? Lorelin was old enough now to know that such boldness only belonged in dreams.

Lorelin's fingers shifted across the porch's wall. She almost touched Martina's hand, but stopped herself at the last moment. *Don't. Don't take her hand if you don't mean it.*

Martina cleared her throat. "You're a friend to me, Lorelin. I have not found peace with why you left, but I understand why you did."

"Don't make any excuses for me." Lorelin snorted. "I'm... I should've done something. Left a note, or—"

"If we spend all day crafting explanations, we'll be here a long time."

"Alright." Lorelin wanted to stay, but she wasn't sure how much longer she could linger before she felt too heavy to speak. There was no apology she could offer, no more to be said.

When all else failed, she liked to end things with a joke. So that was what she did.

"I must look frightful," Lorelin chuckled as she walked away, gesturing to her ragged clothes. "I'm probably the oddest girl that ever was here."

"Not the oddest, no," replied Martina. "But you were always my favorite."

Chapter 40

*H*alston forced himself to open his eyes.

He smacked his lips and found that his breath tasted faintly of herbs. His hands tingled with numbness. He was warm beneath a pile of quilts, but not burning, and he'd stopped shivering. He jiggled his ankle and winced, feeling like ants were swarming beneath his skin.

He remembered swallowing something dry and powdery, a slash of pain on his shoulder, a pair of hands squeezing his arm… Where was he?

Daylight streamed in through the window pane. Its frame bore an intricate design that cast a lacey shadow on the smooth floor. Every inch of the walls was lined with containers of glass and clay. A woman in a white blouse, a flowing blue skirt, and scarlet sash stood in the corner, stacking bottles on the shelves. The glass containers' surfaces chimed and clinked against each other.

Halston opened his mouth to speak, but started coughing instead. The woman turned, then smiled. "Gods be praised. You're awake. How are you feeling?"

Dumbly, he said, "Alive."

"I would hope so. I'm Martina, by the way. I'm a friend of Lorelin's." She walked up to the bedside and knelt. Her motions were graceful, smooth as polished marble. "I'll look at your shoulder."

He lowered his bandages, and she took a look as promised. "You've slept on and off for a few days. The wound looks better, but it may take a few days for the numbness to wear off."

"T-thank you. How *can* I thank you?"

"Consider it a favor," she said, and stood. "In Luna, we help whomever we can. I've never met anyone who did not deserve to be healed."

She opened the door. "I'm going to find Lorelin. Your brother, too. I believe he's doing much better."

"Wait... better? What happened to him?"

"He was slashed by a cougar."

"He... *What?*"

"Shh." Martina walked back to the bed, then pressed a soft hand to his forearm. "Don't fret, he's fine. His scratches weren't very deep. I take it all of you have had... quite the week. Just rest easy, alright? I'll go get the others." She slipped out of the room.

Halston groaned, slapping his hand to his forehead. How much had this delayed them? For the gods' sake, his little brother had been attacked by a cougar, and he'd slept through the whole thing!

Halston heard Lorelin shout from inside the hall: "Hodge, stop running! You'll open your wounds again!"

Hodge came barreling into the room so fast he nearly sent the bottles crashing down. "Hal, you stubborn ass, I knew you'd make it through!"

His laugh came easily. "Good to see you, too, Hodge." He felt lighter, then, like he had not seen Hodge in years. Halston realized how much he'd missed him, how grateful he was that Hodge was here. His brother. The oldest friend he'd ever have.

Tsashin, Gryff, and Lorelin hustled in after him. "Thank goodness you're awake!" cried Lorelin.

"We'll I'll be," Gryff said with a deep, warm laugh. "You made it. How are you feelin'?"

"Well enough." Halston rolled out his wrists, hoping to shake out some of the numbness. "Where are we, Lorelin?"

"Luna," she said. "A sanctuary of Arilaya. Martina is one of the healers. She's a dear friend of mine."

Sometimes, Halston forgot that Lorelin had a history before they'd met in Arrowwood. Martina certainly didn't look like the kind of person who cavorted with outlaws, but he didn't question it. "Is Jae here?"

"Yes," said Tsashin. "She's resting, though I don't know if she's actually slept. I heard her weeping this morning."

"We'll give the two of you a moment," Lorelin said, gesturing to Halston and Hodge. She walked out of the room. The others followed.

Hodge sat at the foot of the bed. Halston flexed his fingers, still trying to get some of the numbness to dissipate. "Well. This has all been... an ordeal."

"No kidding," Hodge snorted. "Retirement sounds awfully swell, right now."

Halston tried to recall the last time he'd spoken to Jae, before the fever took him. The night she'd bandaged him, he scarcely remembered the moments after she tied the dressing off. If he'd said something, it had surely been garbled nonsense, though perhaps he could not trust his memory right now. But he did recall the fierce determination in her eyes when she'd pulled him from the river.

"So," said Hodge. "What now?"

Halston sighed. "The plan is the same, I suppose. We'll head for Monvallea and put as much distance between us and the gang as possible."

They sat there a moment, listening to the rain sliding down the window. Halston cleared his throat. "There's something I need to tell you."

"Yeah?"

"I'm sorry," said Halston. "I was the one who talked to Sterling that night he visited the ranch. I took the knife from him. Before telling you. Or Elias. I'm the reason we're here now."

"Yeah, so?" said Hodge. "I would've done the same thing. He offered you a conduit. And now... well, we've still got half of it. That's... *something*. Maybe we'll find another one. It ain't like we're gonna run out of time by tomorrow."

"I know," said Halston. "But... if we hadn't met Sterling, none—"

"I know what you're gonna say, Hal. That none of this would've happened. But then what? Elias would still be gone. Arrowwood still would've gone to war. We'd still be running. Maybe we'd have fewer scars, but we'd also probably have less silver. Things happen. I don't think it really matters whether we're okay with that. We just have to keep moving." Hodge slouched, staring at the bottles lining the walls. "You came through. You fought it off. Scared me half to death, though. I thought you might die."

"I'm not going to die," said Halston.

"No, I ain't kidding," said Hodge. He raised his fist to his mouth, biting on his knuckles for a second. "Sometimes I think the gods are laughing at us if they're real. They put Elias in the river, and back there, I thought they were gonna do the same thing to you."

"No," Halston said, shaking his head. "No. Don't say that. I made it out."

"Seems like everybody wants to kill us nowadays. Can't say I blame them." Hodge tugged at his sleeve.

They sat in silence for a while. "What are you thinking?" asked Halston.

"When I'm dead, I hope I get a decent send-off."

"Stop. Don't talk like that."

"No, I mean it." Hodge chuckled darkly. "I want to go down shouting. Die like a hero. Then you all run off and live long lives and write songs about me and my glorious death."

"Stop. I mean it."

"I'm just poking fun."

"No, stop it. I don't care if it's a joke for you. I'm not going to lose you too, Hodge. Don't even pretend that you think that's funny."

Hodge quieted down. Then he said, almost inaudibly, "Just trying to make things a little lighter, Hal. I'll let you rest now. I'll see you later tonight."

Halston didn't want to stop talking. He wanted to stay there until dusk, swapping stories of their youth, of how they used to dream of becoming scholars and explorers and seeing the world. He tried to imagine Elias and Lia sitting with them, laughing, as though nothing had changed.

But Hodge had left the chamber, Elias was dead, Lia was a world away, and Halston was alone now.

Chapter 41

There was something magical in these woods.

The grass was too tall, the soil too rich, the leaves too full and green. Once, Pa had told Jae the story of a man across the sea, who sailed to a faraway island in search of gold. It was always summertime there. The trees burst with fruit each day, the pools yielded clear water, and the people who lived there never grew old. That was what Luna made Jae think of.

Jae had learned about the sanctuaries of Arilaya before. She'd even stumbled across one in Banderra, shortly after Pa was taken, and stayed for several days. The women there seemed to have knowledge that most folks had forgotten. They knew about each nerve and vein and bone beneath a person's skin, of all the herbs one could use against ailments and illnesses, and they knew about the souls inside bodies, too.

When she'd had the chance, she'd asked them about ghosts.

The healers told her that ghosts were spirits who'd carried sickness with them into death. Not illnesses like fevers or hacking coughs, but ailments that scraped at their souls. Vengeance. Grief. Anguish. Things that kept them rooted to this world.

Jae had spent years combing through Pa's stories, wondering what he'd done to make those spirits angry enough to turn their backs on death itself and come for him. Pa had never been anything but kind.

Hatred burned inside her for those ghosts. Now, those flames were dancing with new fires she'd lit for Sterling and his men. If she died, she wondered if she'd stick around, walk this earth, and come for them like those spirits had for Pa.

It'd been days since Halston had fallen. That morning, she took a walk by herself, thinking of little but him. She'd woken about half an hour earlier, and when she asked where he was, Martina had said that he was resting. Jae wandered through the gardens now, thinking it best to give him space. The memory of his body shielding her flickered in her mind's eye.

He could have died. It would've at least partially been her fault.

Jae had no place here. She pitied him. Had he gone as crazy as her? Throwing himself in harm's way like that. Would she have done the same for him?

Damn it, she was selfish. If he died on her account, if *any* of them did, then she was no better than a lawless, rotten scoundrel.

Jae walked around the edge of the estate, past willow trees and bushes full of flowers. There was a mural across the wall. Its tiles were no larger than her thumbnails and came in every color she'd ever known, crafting a lively scene.

A woman in loose clothing stood upon the stump of a tree. She hiked a knife above her head, and a circle rippled in the sky from the tip of her blade. Two fiery-eyed men stood at her sides, knives drawn, and behind them were long-legged, shadowy beasts baring their claws. A river, rich and full, flowed far beneath them, while above them, the stars flared in a vast tract of sky.

Jae had never seen anything like it. She'd heard that in the eastern provinces there were museums and galleries full of treasures like these—marble statues and oil paintings and gilded sculptures. What was life like beyond the Beltaire River if the folks there could afford to craft things like this?

"Hello, Jae."

Jae turned and found Martina standing there. She looked like a maiden from a song in her flowing skirts, a basket slung over her arm.

Jae pointed to the mural. "Did you make this?"

Martina's laugh was bright. "I wish. I used to come here often with my mother, before she died. She loved this mural. Said it reminded her of the days before she came to Luna and became a healer."

Jae tilted her head. "What did she do? Before she came here?"

"She was a treasure hunter," Martina explained. "Led quite a few expeditions in her day. She was the youngest of eight. I'm sure her parents had other ideas for her, but... she did make them proud."

She sounded like the sort of woman Jae hoped to be. "What sort of treasures?"

Martina rubbed her chin. "Untapped gem quarries in northern Monvallea. A forsaken mine in eastern Mesca. The fortune of an eccentric baron hidden at the roots of the Cannocs. She left her last adventure with a crippled foot, and pregnant with me. She wound up here and... never left," she said, motioning back to the sprawling white structure.

Jae fought back the urge to blather like a lunkhead. "Have you ever... y'know, gone on an expedition?"

Martina shook her head with an understanding smile. "No. Sometimes I wonder what it would have been like, but... I'm content to let my heart beat at a steady pace. I'm happy here in Luna."

Jae nodded. "Have you known Lorelin long?"

"A few years," said Martina. "We met by chance. I found her wounded in the forest. She stayed with us for a long time before she set out again. I'm glad that she's returned, if even for a time. Most of the other healers adore her. It's difficult not to." She laughed. "She's... she's something else. A dear friend. She always brought out the wilder side of me. My mother would have liked her."

Martina spoke with such grace Jae almost forgot how young she was. Jae envied those starry eyes of hers.

Curiosity rippled through Jae. She pointed to the mural. "Who's this picture of?"

"Oh, that's Hemaera."

"Hemaera!" Jae squinted, hoping to get a closer look. How had she not recognized *Hemaera?*

"It's the story of her... ascent," Martina said. "Though I can't say I remember the whole thing. She fled from beasts and demons in the north, then escaped to another world."

Jae hung onto the phrase like a lifeline. "How?"

She wasn't sure why she'd asked. Martina looked puzzled. "I'm not sure. I can't say I'm an expert on the myth."

Myth. Something about the way Martina said it bothered Jae. "Do you think it's true?"

"I believe Hemaera was real, but... I think some of the stories are exaggerated. Then again, all stories are."

The faded circle above Hemaera's head looked darker now, like someone had outlined it with ink while Jae was not looking. She felt like she was sinking for a moment, treading water in a restless river.

She thought of Sterling tossing Halston into the Median, or Halston bleeding out, and her being unable to stop it.

Matters were not in her hands and likely never had been. Simple as it was, she didn't like the truth of it.

"Jae, are you alright?"

She swallowed, biting down on her cheeks. "Yeah. I'm fine," she said as she stumbled away. "I've... I've got some things to think about."

———

That evening, Halston walked again. The numbness was all gone. His legs felt stiff and tired from lying still, like a wheel turning on a rusted axle. Still, for the first time in ages, he felt almost free. It was all he could do not to run.

He hadn't seen Jae yet, and he longed to, but he figured she was resting. He would talk to her in good time.

Outside, he found Gryff chopping wood at the eaves of the forest. The plants all burst with colors bright as the tones of jewels, and the land here was black and rich. Around every corner was some eye-catching wonder.

This was a perfect place for Lorelin, who held beauty so dear to her heart. Halston couldn't imagine how she ever could have left.

Gryff set down the axe. "Good to see you up again."

Halston smiled. "Good to see you, too. Why are you chopping wood? We can't carry all that with us."

Gryff grunted as he brought the axe down on another log. "I'm thinkin'."

"Do you need to chop wood to think?"

"Yes."

Halston sighed. "Alright. What's the matter?"

Gryff just kept chopping. "I'm thinkin' about Sterling. We ought to leave soon. Lorelin's friend has been good to us. But I don't want Sterling findin' us while we're here. Martina and the healers have no business in this."

"I know," said Halston. "Let's go tomorrow."

"Good," said Gryff. "We should leave as soon as we can. Before things go to shit."

Halston laughed humorlessly. "Haven't they already?"

"Fair point. We ought to get ourselves ready tonight. We'll thank Martina for everythin' and set out. Before anyone finds us."

Halston walked to the edge of the woods. He reached for an aspen, tracing the round knots in the bark. "Gryff?"

"Yeah?"

"I've been thinking." He swallowed. "When we first went to the jail in Arrowwood... I blamed Elias for it. He killed Jackson Poole. I told him the blood was on his hands. And I said... I told him that he'd done enough."

"I know," said Gryff. "I was there."

"Things between us cooled down a bit. Before he died." Halston closed his eyes. "But I never told him I was sorry. And I should've."

Halston remembered racing along the river's edge. At that point, the gunmen who had chased them down were the last of his concerns. He hoped to see his brother's head bob above the waves, arms flailing, so he could reach out and pull him to safety.

They did find him, after an hour or so, in a waterlogged clump of wood submerged in the river. The current was slower, there, and the world seemed to tilt to a halt when Halston saw the black hair, the head poking above the surface, the water parting where his brother's body lay.

He'd cried out, reached in, and pulled Elias from the current. They were too late. The water had poured into him, dammed his breath and flooded his lungs. He was gone.

"You were waitin' until you were ready," said Gryff. "I didn't know him long, but he was a smart kid. I reckon he understood his hand in things. I ain't sayin' killing Poole was a smart move, or anything, but... it wasn't without reason."

"He probably thought I hated him."

"No," said Gryff. "If you hated him, you would've left. And you didn't."

There were too many unsaid things Halston had buried with Elias, and there wasn't enough time or ink in this world to write them all down.

Halston scratched the back of his neck. "Sometimes I feel like I could've done more. I could've stopped it."

Gryff shook his head. "He fell off that log we were runnin' on. He hit his head."

"I know," said Halston. "But maybe—"

"Maybe nothing," Gryff said. "You can't blame yourself for everythin' or you'll be wastin' away your whole life."

Halston's eyes flicked to his shoulder. The wound was still inflamed. "I worry about Hodge," he admitted. "If I had died, then…"

Gryff snorted. "He'll shape up sooner or later. But Halston… you can't get an iron grip on this world. Your hand ain't big enough for it. Some things just… happen by chance."

Halston wasn't sure if he wanted to hear it. Then again, he wasn't sure why he'd started talking in the first place. "You think everything is left to chance?"

"No," said Gryff. "Some things, not everything. If I believed that nothin' was in my control, I reckon I'd go mad. But in this world… you get by. Through any means you can. That's all anybody can do."

Chapter 42

The window pane was cold against Jae's forehead. She stared outside, eyes unfocused, her breath steaming on the glass.

"Jae?"

Jae turned. Tsashin was reclining on her bed, one arm draped over the side, fingertips grazing the floor. "Are you feeling well? You seem distressed."

Pa always used to say that she did a terrible job of hiding her thoughts whenever she peered out the window. Said that the feelings danced on her face. *Guess I haven't shaken the habit.*

She hadn't seen Halston in days. Now, she was bracing herself to visit him. "I'm alright."

"You don't have to lie to me."

"Don't worry about me."

Tsashin paused, raising her eyelids slightly. "You can talk to me about it. If you want. I'll listen."

Jae chuckled mirthlessly. "I feel like a bit of an ass."

Tsashin's eyes widened.

"Oh, sorry for my, uh—language. I just think I've distracted myself, is all."

"How?"

"Well… my…" She wasn't sure how to explain Pa's kidnapping to Tsashin. "I've been looking for my Pa for years now. He went missing when I was about fifteen. Back in Sienna, when I told you I'd be leaving soon… I meant it. I really did. But I don't know anymore. Halston, he… he saved my life." Who would she be if she threw that away?

Tsashin sat up straight. "You're looking for your family, too?"

"Yeah. I guess I am."

"Then maybe we're supposed to be here. Maybe something brought us to the others. It seems like we're all looking for somebody." She stared at the ceiling while she spoke, as if exploring it, searching for her next story in the plaster.

Then Tsashin said, "If you think it best, I'm sure the others would understand. If you left. But I'd miss you. I think we all would."

Jae paced up to the bed. "Well, thanks. I'd miss you too. How are you feelin'?"

Tsashin did not look away from the ceiling. "Like I'm underwater. Like I'm watching the world from beneath a lake."

"Oh gods… I'm sorry, Tsashin."

"It's not your fault. It's kind of you, Jae. To help a stranger."

"Hey, we ain't strangers now, are we?"

A half-spirited smile crossed Tsashin's lips. "No. Not anymore."

Jae turned to leave. "I'm gonna go downstairs." She put on her jacket.

Tsashin propped herself up on her forearm. "That jacket looks nice on you."

"Thank you."

"Halston seems to think so, too," she said with surprising

wickedness.

Jae tried not to react. "I—well…" she laughed softly, then louder, and realized her laughter sounded fake. "I don't dress for Halston."

"I think he'd like anything you wear."

Jae cursed herself for the heat rising to her face.

Tsashin hid her grin behind a hand. Her smile disappeared a few moments later. "Oh, I'm sorry. I didn't mean to embarrass you."

Jae turned so Tsashin would not see the redness. "There's nothing going on with Halston and me." She repeated herself for good measure. "Nothing at all." And she hurried out the door.

When she stepped outside, Jae counted three stars in the dimming sky. She sauntered onto the porch and couldn't help but smile at the sight of Halston standing there. His arms rested on the low stone wall, and he stared at the forest like a sailor perched on the bow of a ship. Bugs hummed in the glade, and the moonlight cast arched shadows on the walkway. Once, a merchant in a marketplace had told Jae about castles, which they used to build out of stone in faraway lands. Jae reckoned they must have looked something like this.

"Halston?"

He turned so fast Jae reckoned he pulled something in his neck. "Jae!"

She hurried to him, and it spilled from her mouth like all the dams inside her had split. "I should've come to see you sooner. It shouldn't have happened, you getting hurt like that. You shouldn't have—"

"Hey." His touch was light on her shoulder, like a whisper. "I made it. It's part of this life. Someone takes a blow, then we all get back up and move forward."

The warmth in his eyes was nothing like she'd ever seen. An understanding she rarely received from men. It left her wondering if she was on the wrong side of things. It left her wondering if she had a side at all.

He took his hand off her shoulder, and she cleared her throat. "What are you doing out here by yourself?" she asked.

"Just thinking."

She rested her forearms on the wall. In Halston's hand was a jar full of red liquid. "What's that?" she asked.

"Chokecherry wine. I guess Martina makes it here herself. Lorelin gave it to me. Told me it was her favorite."

Jae scrunched up her nose. "How is it?"

"A bit much for me, but feel free to try some."

Jae raised the jar to her lips. The smell of the wine was sharp in her nostrils. She took a sip and puckered at the tartness. The liquid warmed her throat as she swallowed it. Bitter as it was, it left a pleasant aftertaste in her mouth. She took a second sip. "I sort of like this."

Halston shrugged and gave it another shot. "Alright. Maybe the second sip is better."

They passed it back and forth, sipping in companionable silence, until all that remained was a shallow pool at the bottom of the jar. The wine stained their mouths and the rim of the glass.

"You wanna know something?" Halston asked as they neared the bottom of the cup.

"Yeah?"

"This stuff is good. Really, really good." He spoke as though he'd just made a profound discovery.

Jae laughed, because everything seemed funnier now. Warmth buzzed inside her head. "Maybe we shouldn't have drunk all that."

"Oh yeah, I think so too. I might say something I regret." Halston laughed, slapping his forehead. "My life is a real mess, you know?"

Jae frowned. "Oh, don't say that."

"The Byrds wanna kill us. I mean, *shit*." He looked thoughtfully at Jae. "We almost died."

"Stop." Jae waved it away. "You're gonna make me sad."

"Oh, I'm sorry. I don't want to make you sad."

Jae tilted her head and rested her chin on her knuckles. "Lorelin keeps making fun of me."

"She does that to everyone."

"She thinks I like you."

"Really? She thinks *I* like *you*."

"Well, do you?"

Halston didn't answer her, though she didn't blame him. If he'd asked her the same thing, she doubted she would've talked.

Jae said, "Maybe we should've talked about this before we drank the wine.

"Yeah, we should have."

Jae nudged him. "Let's go see if Lorelin has more."

Halston chuckled. "That's a terrible idea."

Yes, it probably was. Her head was bleary, but she also felt ready to conquer the world, which was probably not a good sign. "Then let's explore."

He followed her through the corridors. As they strolled along, they delighted in the tiled ceilings and textured walls. The colors seemed even brighter and grander than they had before, lit by the shining sconces. They pointed to the mosaics on the walls and made up titles for them.

They came upon Lorelin and Martina, who stood talking at the edge of the hallway. There was something lovely about the way they looked at each other, filled with warmth and appreciation. Jae imagined Pa must've looked at Ma that way while she was alive. She caught herself longing for someone to look at her that way.

"Lorelin!" shouted Jae, nearly tripping on the flat floor. She stooped forward, then caught herself at the last second.

Lorelin pursed her lips. "Jae, are you drunk? More importantly,

Halston, are you drunk?"

"We're going outside!" Jae announced, pointing. "Into the evening."

"Martina!" exclaimed Halston. "This sanctuary is magnificent, truly. Exquisite. Jae and I are preparing to enjoy each other's company in your gardens, now," he said, his voice dipping down at the end of his announcement.

Martina smiled slyly at Lorelin. "Did you give them the chokecherry wine?"

Lorelin winced. "Unfortunately."

"I see you enjoyed it," Martina said.

"You have such a pretty voice, Martina," Jae mused. She wished her own voice was that pretty.

"Thank you. That's very kind of you to say. Don't get into too much mischief now, alright?"

"We won't," said Halston. "We're just going for a walk."

Lorelin smirked. "I know what 'going for a walk' means, Halston."

Halston's mouth fell open as Jae burst out laughing. "Oh, you don't have to worry about that," Jae replied. "Halston's a bit... stiff for me."

Now Lorelin was the one to succumb to her laughter.

"Shh! Just—*Goodbye*, Lorelin." Halston stood, and Jae joined him. His face was red as rust. If it weren't so funny, Jae might have felt sorry for him.

Alright, alright. She'd be nicer to him. He *was* taking her for a walk, after all.

———

Stiff. She thought he was *stiff.*

What could that mean?

She didn't dislike him. If she did, she wouldn't have agreed to go

380 : Sophia Minetos

on this walk with him. Then again, she might only want to spare his feelings. But if she did want to spare his feelings, why had she called him stiff?

There was something about Jae that night, though… the way she sat with her forearms rested on the garden's railing, her blue eyes bright and alive as a turning tide. She'd stayed by his side all these weeks. In the cellar and after Thumbscrew had slashed his shoulder. Something told Halston that he wouldn't be able to sleep if he didn't talk to her.

He wasn't sure what that meant.

They walked past the sanctuary, marching into the woods. Spring breathed its warmth into the night air, and colorful blossoms danced in the grass. Halston's head still felt foggy, but the laughter seemed to have abruptly leaked out of him.

Jae nudged him, and Halston prayed she could not somehow read his mind. "Hey, come on now. We were only kidding," she said.

He straightened his neck. "What are you talking about? I'm fine."

"No, you ain't. If you were fine, you wouldn't be acting like this."

He changed the subject. "I… I realized that I don't know you as well as I'd like to. And everything has been rather grim lately, and… I just thought we could try and make it better."

She laughed softly. "Well, alright then. I'm glad to get to know you better."

Halston stepped over a log in their pathway, letting out a long breath. *Ask her. What do you think of me? Six words. Six.* He cleared his throat. "Whatdoyouthink."

Jae's brow furrowed. "Huh?"

"Sorry. What—" Panic twisted his tongue. "What's your… favorite flower?" he blurted. *Damn it.* Of all the silly things to ask…

She smirked. "Honeysuckles."

"Really?"

"Yeah. They're pretty. They smell nice. Taste good, too. When I was little, I'd suck them dry and imagine they were flapjacks with maple syrup." She pressed a hand to her stomach. "I could go for some of those right now."

They passed under the branches into another clearing. Moonlight crowned the grass, which grew as tall and green as jade, and the ground was soft and pliant beneath their boots. Halston breathed in the smell of damp moss and tang of the pines.

They kept walking, passing through a cluster of spruce trees, their needles looking even bluer in the starlight. Jae asked, "What are you thinking?"

"I'm thinking about what comes next."

"What do you mean?"

He breathed out. "Alright. The wine might be messing with my head, but... I've met a lot of people in my life. And you're... you're *different* from them all. I'm trying to figure out what that means. See, I... I like planning. It helps me feel like I'm in control. But I *never* seem to have a plan when it comes to you. I have no clue what it means. I mean, I have so many more important things to worry about, but I still can't get you off my mind."

Jae furrowed her brow.

"No! That's not what I meant! See, I *like* having you on my mind, but... it scares me at the same time, because I—"

"Halston, do you *like* working yourself up?"

"Excuse me?"

"Just calm down," she said. "I ain't gonna bite you. This place... it's beautiful. Don't think about anything else. There ain't nothin' to be afraid of right now."

Halston bit his lip as she turned away. Her hat had shifted lower, making it even harder for Halston to read her face.

Jae stretched her arms out to the sky. "It's amazing, ain't it?" Jae said. "Just a few weeks back, we were riding through the dust-dry desert. And here we are now."

They stepped out to the slope overlooking the valley. Below, the river twisted through the earth, a silver ribbon, stretching far into the horizon. The stars cast their glow onto its waters, and its rush echoed off the valley's slopes like a lone chord.

Jae stretched out her arms, her fingers circling as if stirring the wind. "High as birds, we are," she mused. "Maybe we can't climb to the top of the world, but I reckon this is the next best thing."

Somehow, Halston had a thousand replies and none at all. Bravery spiked inside him, like a spark leaping from a flame. "I think you're beautiful, Jae."

"Am I?"

"And smart. And funny." The more he spoke, the easier it felt.

Her face got brighter, and it filled him with joy.

"And... I'm glad to be your friend."

Wait, shit.

She laughed, bright and loud. Jae's smile was a mystery. Halston figured he'd give up trying to read what lay beneath that crooked grin before long.

Before either of them spoke again, a breeze drifted over their heads. With it came a sound, full and metallic, like the clang of a bell. Halston went tense. "Did you hear that?"

It happened again. It was music, certainly. First, there came the chime of bells, a soft whistle, a drumbeat. Moments passed, then it was gone. But a heartbeat later, the sound reappeared.

Halston stepped toward the valley and peered down. "Where is that coming from?"

"The past," said Jae.

Halston swerved, perplexed. "What?"

Jae swayed her shoulders forward and back, like she was trying to run without moving her legs. "Wyrdrian, remember? The language of memory."

"Sure, but—"

"That means someone wanted to preserve this song. Spoke it into the land. So it could live forever."

"That—"

"That what? Makes no sense? Is impossible?"

"Yes, both of those."

Jae swept her arm over the air. "Well, you hear it, don't you?" The rapid drumbeat was louder now.

"Yes."

"Then it doesn't have to make sense." She shuffled in place. "This song must have made someone real happy. Y'know, for them to make it live on for us to hear."

It had to be said: Jae was not a dancer. She moved without care, lost in the barely-there song. Halston had never seen her like this. It was hard to believe that this was the same girl who sat stoically in corners and shadows, watching and listening. Halston thought he heard a singing voice and the word "night" on the air, but maybe he imagined it. Hell, maybe all of this was a dream.

But it certainly felt real when Jae took his hand.

"Dance with me." Her eyes were bright.

"I—"

"What, don't know how?"

"No."

"C'mon, then. Let's learn together."

He wasn't sure how to move to the sound of the river and the swift, distant music. All he knew was that Jae's arms were warm against his waist. There was joy in this song, even if its players were long dead.

Besides, he could almost hear Elias telling him that he'd be a great fool to turn down a dance with a beauty like Jae.

He lost himself for a moment, then realized he was laughing. There was no need to talk. Nothing to do but sway across the earth with her.

They shouldn't be doing this. Against his wishes, he tried to stop it. "We should—"

"Should what? Go back to the camp? We will. Just not right now."

So he danced with her, laughing, losing his breath, wanting to move until he collapsed.

He recalled something Elias had once told him.

Love will make you wild.

Well, that thought was the last straw. He stopped moving, and at the same time, the song faded away.

Jae raised an eyebrow. Her hands, still holding his, were warm. "Something wrong?"

He breathed in. His limbs felt weak. "I... No."

She taunted him with the speed of her breathing, the flame in her eyes, her grin that was so dangerously close to his own mouth. Daring him. Daring him to take her hand and run.

"I need to sit down," he choked out.

"Tired?"

"Yes."

"It's okay."

He lay back in the grass, and to his surprise, she lowered herself with him and rested her head on his good shoulder. Though he felt like his heart would beat right out of his chest, he circled his arm around her and placed his hand on her waist. A strange feeling rose in his stomach, twisting like a pair of hands wringing water from a rag.

Jae said, "You never tell me anything."

He kept his gaze on the stars. The sky seemed to be opening

wider, and somehow, it felt closer, like he could reach out and touch it. "What do you mean? I tell you lots of things."

"Nothing important. I want to know who you are."

"Alright." Halston cleared his throat. "Here it goes. I'm gonna tell you who I am."

Jae listened.

"I'm Halston."

Jae swatted at his arm as he laughed. "You think you're real damn clever, don't you?"

"Well... maybe a little. It's part of our deal, though, isn't it? No questions asked, remember?"

Jae scoffed. "Look at all the questions I've asked you so far. I clearly didn't stick to the agreement. After all we've been through, you still think that's the case?"

"I don't know, is it?"

Silence.

Finally, Jae murmured, "I wish we were far away from here. I wish Sterling was gone. I wish I had my Pa back. Then I could..." Her voice trailed off.

"Then you could what?"

She just lay there, still resting on his shoulder, the two of them huddled against the earth. Finally, she sat up and pushed herself upright on one hand.

Something came over him, begging him to act. He took Jae's left hand in both of his, and there, they faced each other, blinking the moment away. "Listen," he said. "I'm headed home. I know you said you might leave, and sooner rather than later, but... you could come with me. We'll get away from Sterling. Then I'll take you somewhere far from here. I'll... I'll make you happy, Jae. I swear it."

Still, she was quiet.

"Listen. For a long time, I thought I'd been thrown into this life because I deserved no better. I fought, I stole, and I'm gonna try my hardest to put that behind me. I'm going back where I belong.

"I didn't think this world would ever show me kindness, Jae. Until this girl from the Ameda saloon followed me into the desert and smiled down on me, with the full moon shining on her. I'm not a lucky fellow, so... it's a miracle I wound up with you."

Something was burning inside him, and it couldn't have just been the wine.

She murmured, "My Pa."

"What about him?"

"I have to find him." She inhaled sharply. "I didn't tell you what happened to him, because part of me thought you wouldn't believe me. But ghosts kidnapped him. It's a kicker, you know? He taught me all about ghosts, the undead, all the strange things that happen in this world. Things that ain't for the faint of heart. He told me how to protect myself from them, but they still took him."

"Ghosts?"

"Yes. The worst part is I don't even know if he's still alive. I feel he is. Like the gods are guiding me to him, but... I feel like I'm being pulled two different ways now. And it's tearing at me."

"Why?"

"Because..." She pressed her hands to her head. "Because I want to stay with you, too! But you're trying to find your home, and I'm trying to find my Pa. I feel like I'm betraying him. Things keep getting in my way. First it's a bullet to my arm, then it's Sterling taking us away... and then... damn it, I shouldn't have asked you why you liked working yourself up so much when I keep doing the same thing to myself. And I... I don't think I want to leave you."

"So don't."

She let go of his hands, then hugged her arms to her chest. "This... this is too important a thing to be talking about right now.

We've had too much wine, I reckon."

"I…"

"Shh. Don't worry about it." She motioned to the sky. "It's late. Let's… let's talk in the morning."

He walked with her. They didn't say a word as they went up the stairs and slipped into their separate rooms. The warmth in his chest had turned to something closer to pain.

As Halston stepped into the room, he hoped that Gryff and Hodge would be there. Surely they'd have a morsel of advice for him. But they both lay fast asleep.

Halston sighed. A restless movement churned in his stomach, like grease sizzling on hot metal. Feeling as though the room was spinning beneath him, he wavered on his feet. So he blamed the wine, like Jae had, and vowed to never drink again.

Sleep would help. He was sure of it. Tomorrow, they'd set out, and maybe things would feel certain again.

He climbed into bed, wishing for an answer of any kind.

Chapter 43

L orelin disliked being alone. She'd wasted more than a year of her life that way. But sometimes, it had to be done.

Before the sun rose, she made her way up the stairs to the old hideaway—a little terrace of rock overlooking Luna. She and Martina had spent many days here, talking the hours away. When they ran out of things to discuss, they'd sit there and listen to the crickets sing. Sometimes, Martina would bring pouches of herbs and vials of medicine. She'd recite their names and explain their properties and make it all sound like music.

The valley was a deep, vivid green, richer than emeralds. Sparrows whistled, calling across the woods without a care in the world. Lorelin thought of her first days in Luna, when she'd entertained the idea of staying. Of a life untouched by lawlessness.

Peace found her, then, and for the first time in years, she let herself welcome it.

She sat down and overlooked the estate. The sun was a sliver on the horizon.

Today, they'd have to leave. There was no doubting that. They were squandering precious time here.

For a moment, she pretended that there was no Sterling Byrd, no Adwell Fisk, no lawmen calling for her arrest. What would it be like, Lorelin wondered, to stay? To remain in this world of color and birdsong, at the crook of the river, and never have to draw a gun again? To live out her days at Martina's side?

She drove the wish away. She didn't belong here. Not now, at least.

She remembered Halston's promise to her when she'd agreed to join them. *'If you help us out, I'll take you where it's safe. To our home. You won't be a wanted woman anymore.'*

At the time, she'd convinced herself that it was the perfect escape. Perfect if Martina forgave her and somehow abandoned Luna to come along.

"I figured I might find you here."

Lorelin smiled as Martina climbed up the stairs, then sat down next to her. Lorelin hesitated briefly, then rested her head on Martina's shoulder. She felt safer than she had in a long time.

Martina pulled her in closer.

Lorelin was giddy as a squalling bird, then. She dared to ask an impossible question. "We're setting out for Monvallea tomorrow. I know your place is here. But… part of me wishes you could come with us."

"Shh." Martina stroked Lorelin's shoulder. "Even if you must go today, I am glad. I'm glad you came back to me. Even if it was only for a while."

Lorelin frowned. "I wish things were different."

"I know. So do I."

"What now?"

"What now? Well, I have a proposal. We stay here until the sun comes up, then we'll go back to Luna, and I'll send you on your way.

And you'll run. But you must promise me that if you see Sterling again, you'll face him and win."

"That sounds good to me." Lorelin swallowed. "But what about—"

Martina kissed her. And suddenly, there was no fear plaguing Lorelin. There was just Martina, and the valley below, and the morning was not real.

"Martina?"

"Mhmm?"

Lorelin willed truth into her words. "I'm going to come back for you."

"Lorelin." Martina squeezed her hand. "I'll always love you. But you shouldn't make promises you can't keep."

"I won't," Lorelin said.

"Alright."

And they watched the sun rise into the sky.

Chapter 44

A	t dawn, they left Luna, while the air was cool in their throats and the sky was still dim. They found the main road again, then spent the day bound for the north. Lorelin and Gryff walked. Hodge and Tsashin shared the stallion, and Jae and Halston rode on the speckled mare. Jae missed Lorelin's poor mare already. She hoped the creature hadn't fallen to the wounds from the cougar.

That morning, Jae had felt more tired than usual, with an empty feeling in her stomach that wasn't quite hunger. When she'd told Lorelin about it, Lorelin just laughed. "Half a jar of wine will do that to you, dear. Drink plenty of water."

At the end of the day, Jae followed Lorelin into the thick of the trees to gather firewood, thinking of all the ways she would describe Luna to Pa. The murals, the rich, dark land, the gentle healer with a treasure hunter's blood.

Jae used to dream of having stories of her own. *Callista Reyes.* The name flowed so smoothly across Jae's tongue when she whispered it to herself. She certainly sounded like a legend.

The day had passed by slowly, and she hadn't spoken to Halston at all. Jae thought of his drunken offer. To come with him. To take her... *somewhere*. Somewhere far from here.

Far from Mesca. Far from wind that rubbed her skin raw and the sun that burned it. Far from sheriffs and outlaws and meager bounties in her pockets. Far from the ghosts.

Lorelin tucked a load of firewood under her arm. She frowned, flicking a bit of bark out of her hair and muttering something about the wind messing up her curls.

Jae said, "Lorelin?"

"Hmm?"

"How did you meet Martina?"

Lorelin spoke like she'd been waiting for someone to ask her that very question, and the story fell from her lips. She told Jae about how she'd come to Luna with a nearly fatal wound, how Martina had found her in the woods and saved her, and taught her all she knew about healing, and all the days they'd spent together.

"It was like wildfire, talking to her. Moved so fast that by the time you realized what was happening, it was too late." Lorelin's cheeks went pink. "We did everything together."

Jae tried to picture Lorelin as a healer rather than a gunslinger. Jae imagined that healing involved a lot of sitting still, something that Lorelin didn't seem to like very much. "I'm glad you brought us there."

"So am I." Lorelin reached behind a mossy, slanted rock and fetched a sheet of dried bark. "It gave me quite a scare. Halston is sturdy, though." She flashed Jae a grin, raising her eyebrows. "You like sturdy men, don't you Jae?"

"Stop!" Jae cursed herself. Her reply came out sounding high as a tea kettle's wail. She snorted, then, and laughed a little.

"Apologies," Lorelin said with sharp-edged smugness. "I can't help it. I was the youngest in my family. I never had anyone to tease."

Jae rolled her eyes, but the moment felt light between them. Easy. It was like laughing by the fire with Pa when a day's work was done.

She asked, "Why did you leave Luna?"

Lorelin sighed, rubbing her brow with three fingers. "I wanted to keep her safe."

Jae wanted to ask, *You loved her, though, didn't you?* Then again, she didn't need to. Nobody could ramble on like that about someone they didn't love.

"Was it hard?" she asked instead.

The dozy look slipped from Lorelin's face. She frowned. Jae regretted the question instantly. It was strange, seeing Lorelin's brightness dimmed. Sorrow didn't look right on her. Wasn't fitting.

"Oh. Sorry."

Lorelin sighed, shaking her head. "Not your fault. Martina asked me that, too. Of course it was hard. It took every bit of strength I had to walk away. I knew that the longer I delayed it… the harder it would be to leave."

Jae wondered if she'd have that same sort of strength.

It did not matter how much she slowed her pace. A fork waited for her on this road—and she and Halston would part. She'd go to Pa. Halston would go… elsewhere. Wherever the hell that was.

The gang would go to Monvallea. They were starting over. Safe, at least for now. It was time for her to go.

But she'd be selfish a little longer. *One more night,* she thought. *I'll give myself one more night. To bid everyone goodbye. To thank them for all they've done for me.*

She would set out on the road, and wave to them as she moved away. She would find the nearest sheriff and tell him of the Byrd gang's hideouts: the Mouth, the scrappy house in the basin, the Lawrence Mine. Perhaps she would see their name in the newspaper sooner rather than later, and she'd smirk and sleep well, knowing that they would waste away in jail. Wishful thinking, it was, but she allowed herself to hope for it.

Maybe she would not know if Halston found his way home, though she reckoned there would be more comfort in not knowing. She'd think of them. Pray for them. Remember them.

And when she found Pa, she would tell him of these past two months.

Balancing the wood in the crook of her arm, Jae gave Lorelin's shoulder a gentle squeeze. "Lorelin?"

"Hmm?"

"You deserve to be happy. Just thought I'd tell you that."

————

Jae woke late in the night, and Halston was gone.

Jae let the wave of short-lived fear pass through her. If Sterling had come, the gunshots would have woken her. Still, it wasn't like Halston to abandon his watch.

Kicking down her blankets, she left her empty bedroll. Halston had left his own bedroll untouched, the quilt and tarp smooth and wrinkle-free. He always left it that way, and when they packed up, he folded it neatly instead of stuffing it into his knapsack. It never failed to make Jae snort a little.

They'd set up camp between an aspen grove and a curve of storm-gray cliffs carpeted with moss. Boulders rimmed the cliff, scattered like cows across a lumpy pasture. Something shuffled on the stone.

Leading with her toes, Jae crept over the shadows. She came to an aisle formed by three stone slabs and scaled the slanted path. Up ahead, a figure stood. Halston.

He had one foot propped on a small rock, the other braced on the path. Steadying himself, he removed his journal and something small and jagged from his jacket.

Jae squinted. His hand clutched the handle of a knife. That blade that he'd spent so much time getting worked up about. Even from where she stood, Jae could make out the detailed engravings spanning its handle, though she wasn't too sure what they meant. It could not be from Hespyria, at least not in the territories. Folks out here favored practical things over fancy ones.

The knife's tip was missing. The blade ended in a rugged line.

Halston laid the broken knife on the ground.

Jae sank her teeth into her bottom lip and stifled a shout.

Darkness knit into a wide circle high above Halston's head. Starlight did not bounce off of it. It was as if someone had stitched a circle of pitch into the air. Thin wisps of mist rolled off its edges, escaping into the night.

The calmness on Halston's face was almost laughable. He stood there looking like he'd just come across an ordinary pond in the woods instead of… whatever this was.

He sighed and flipped open his journal. "Not here," he murmured, scribbling something down.

When he lifted his head, he glimpsed her.

Jae lost her balance and fell backward.

"Jae!"

She tumbled. After rolling a few yards, she struck her knee on a rock and cursed as a bolt of pain shot up her leg. "Son of a gods-damn bitch!"

Halston came running after her. Glancing behind him, she found that the circle was gone. She heaved herself to her feet, grunting, ready to ask him what business he had opening circles in the sky.

Even then, Jae wasn't sure what she said. Gaping, she stood there, babbling like a fool while Halston said her name about a million times, pleading with her to calm down. She breathed in once. Twice. Again. She asked, "What is it, Halston? Is it one of those portals again, like Sterling opened up? You didn't tell me you were a warlock, too!"

"I'm not a warlock. And it's not a portal."

"Then what is it?"

Halston said, "I'm checking to see how thin the veil is," as if that was somehow close to an answer.

When she just stood and caught her breath, he exhaled, pressing a hand to his brow. "Gods, you'll think I'm crazy...."

Maybe so. "Hal. Just tell me what's happening."

He rolled his shoulders forward and looked down. "We'd better sit, then. This could take a while."

So they sat. A hundred different expressions danced across Halston's face while he tapped his fingers on his knuckles.

Jae made herself speak. "I don't think you're crazy. A little high-strung, but not crazy."

He laughed softly. "Alright. I can live with that. This... this is about my home." Halston rested his forearms on his knees. He turned his head and looked at her like she was very, very far away. "It's not somewhere you could walk to. Or sail to, for that matter. The tribes in the Outlands have a certain... lore surrounding portals. Gateways to other realms. I'm sure you've heard stories of explorers disappearing out there."

"Without a trace," Jae said. "Not even bones to leave behind."

About seventy years back, two explorers called Wil Decker and Elrem Marchant had led an expedition to open the western territories, from the Avourel Gap in the east to the Orliada Valley in the west. After they'd charted the territories, Elrem Marchant had led a second expedition into the Outlands with several hundred settlers, never to be seen again.

"Right. I'm sure plenty of them disappeared under other circumstances. But what if I told you that a lot of those explorers didn't just vanish into nothingness? That they went... somewhere else?"

She gave him a slight smile, despite her racing heart. "I've heard stranger stories."

Halston breathed out. "And they're not the only ones. Centuries ago, before settlers even came to Hespyria... there were other portals. Suryan explorers opened one. Raiders from Alfir found another. One opened up during a ritual in Quierra."

He looked to the stars. "My great-grandfather crossed into our world several decades ago. He was part of the Marchant expedition. The latest league of travelers to cross in to the Second Realm."

Jae ignored the pounding in her chest long enough to say, "That's where you're from."

Halston nodded. "It's not terribly different from this world. Smaller. Brighter. Still largely unexplored. There were new things lurking around every corner."

"Why did you leave?"

Halston swallowed. "My father created a few enemies for himself. We escaped from our own imprisonment through a portal. It was a... one-way portal, if you will."

"What's that?"

"Think of it this way. You walk through a door into another room, then shut it behind you. Immediately, it locks. There's no going back.

"See, in my home world, there was more magic. It was much easier to open portals and keep them active. Here, it's different. Magic is rarer, so to open a portal, you need to draw the energy to it and weaken the veil. That's what the silver is for."

"Like scoring a wall so you can smash it down later?"

Halston laughed a little. "Yes. Exactly like that. Well... maybe not. It's closer to just sawing the wall down outright."

Jae asked, "How many worlds are there?" It was something she never thought she'd ask. Hell, it was something she'd never thought of at all.

"I don't know," said Halston. "Many. They're always moving, drifting toward each other, then back again." He traced a picture in the dirt of circles on a line. "Think of them as beads on a string, bobbing back and forth. The beads are realms. The string is the Median."

Jae remembered her hand on him after Sterling had opened the circle to that strange, blank landscape.

"And here," Halston said, pointing to the Median in his drawing, "portal magic goes through phases. It's active for a century or so, then falls dormant. Sterling told us that the cycle will end within the next decade. We have about five more years to open a portal."

Halston showed her the broken knife, flashing starlight off its blade. "This can't open a portal on its own, but under the moonlight, I can use it to check how thick the veil is. The thicker it is, the more Median there is to cross." He pointed to the sky. "When the veil is thick, I only see darkness. We could open a portal where it's thick, but then we could be crossing over the Median for years… and who knows what we'd find there."

Jae peeked at his journal. "Have you found a thin spot yet?"

Halston shook his head. "Not yet, but Sterling told us that there are plenty of weak spots in the Outlands, so—"

Jae cut him off. "What?"

Halston said, "The Outlands. Once we have enough silver, we're heading there to find a weak spot in the veil." He paused. "Of course… it might be harder, since we'll have to find another conduit. I doubt we'll ever get the other half of the knife back from Sterling."

"*The Outlands.*" Her eyes stung from shooting open so wide.

"Yes. Are you alright?"

She said it again, just to herself. "For crying out loud, Halston! Why didn't you tell me you were going to the Outlands sooner?"

"Because... you... never asked?"

Something flipped inside her, swift as a turning coin. "Hang on. How're you planning on getting there? The Rangers guard Hemaera's Pass."

"The Nefilium passes," Halston said. "There are several old passes and tunnels leading into the Cannoc Mountains from Hespyria. Crossing through them won't be easy. We've all made peace with that. There are... strange things, lurking there."

Jae breathed out. "I... I've heard of the passes, but my Pa said that the Rangers blocked them all off."

Halston shook his head. "Sterling told me about them when he gave us the knife. He's been there before. Says that they're wide open. The Nefilium didn't pay him any mind, given that he's a warlock."

"How are you gonna get past the Nefilium?" she asked. "Sure, there are kind ones. I've met one. But there are also monsters. Not to mention ghosts and... things that are even worse than that."

Halston sighed. "We don't know yet. We figured we would travel north and find someone who knew about them. It's taken us so long to get the silver, to pay off Sterling for the knife. It's still in the open, I guess."

Jae had planned on leaving the next morning. Going back to the life she'd known for two years.

But now...

No more scrounging on outlaws' trails. It would be dangerous— to keep running with this gang, and to take the Nefilium passes.

But it would take her to the Outlands. It would take her to Pa.

She'd never been afraid of danger, or of dying in itself. Not in the way that kept her up at night, at least. What came after death didn't terrify her. What scared her was leaving this world and Pa, with no one to claim the duty she'd left behind.

Maybe she wouldn't make it past the Nefilium passes when she went with the gang.

Or maybe an outlaw would gun her down. Maybe she'd freeze in the winter, or drown in a river, or catch a fever and wither away. If she went back to bounty hunting, she could enter Hemaera's Pass, and the Outlands could claim her. There were a million ways to die out here.

And suddenly, her choice didn't feel hard anymore. In fact, it felt like the easiest one she'd ever made.

"Halston?"

"Mhmm?"

"I'm in. I'm coming to the Outlands with you. That's where the ghosts took my Pa. And I... My Pa taught me a lot about the things that are up there, I can—"

She stopped talking. Halston was giving her a strange look she'd never seen before.

"Hal? Are you al—"

Then, she was lost in his embrace. He held her tightly, like a treasure locked in his arms. Jae hid her face in his good shoulder. "Your wound."

"I'll be okay."

Carefully, her arms found their way around him. Her heart hummed in her chest, lulling her, steadying her. She felt the stars watching them. They guided her to stay rooted to the ground.

A prayer formed on her lips. A plea to let this last. To drown out the noise that threatened to smother her senses.

Even if it would be simpler to leave now... simple things were hardly ever worth chasing.

They could have walked back to camp, but they didn't. They watched the stars tread across the sky until they disappeared into the dawn. Jae's hand rested on the rock, just a pinch of space away from Halston's.

To her surprise, she was not afraid.

Chapter 45

They traveled the next day, slowly but surely. During the day, Jae did not think of Sterling often. Instead, she thought of the Nefilium Passes and the Outlands. She had spent her childhood dreaming of trekking over them, a thousand skies above her, guided by the winds alone.

There, Pa waited for her.

She was going to find him, and she was going to help her company reach the north. It was still a ways' off, but it didn't scare her.

At dusk, they settled to discuss their plans for Monvallea. The night was growing cold. Jae traced their position on her map. They were in Mesca's far north now, getting close to Monvallea's border.

Halston looked over the map with her. They were short one horse now, and the day of travel had not been easy with half the gang on foot. They sat basking in the fire's warmth, discussing how they could put more distance between themselves and Sterling after they crossed the border.

"How much money do we have?" asked Gryff.

"We have ten crowns that Sterling left us in the Mouth," said Halston. "Plus Hodge's deons."

Hodge rubbed his chin. "Looks like there are some villages nearby. Think we could steal a few horses somewhere?"

Halston shook his head. "No, we're not stealing horses."

"I've got it!" said Lorelin. "We'll take the train."

"The train?" asked Hodge.

"Look. Dolorosa is about ten miles away. It has a train station," said Lorelin, gesturing to Jae's map. "The railroad goes all the way to Monvallea. We've lost a bit of time, but we can gain it back if we take the train north. We could even sell the horses in town tomorrow. That'll put a few miles between us and Sterling for sure."

A relieved smile crossed Halston's face. "That's perfect. How much are the train tickets?"

Lorelin shrugged. "Depends on how much ground we cover. But in my experience, no more than a crown apiece if we ride in the back."

Hodge snorted. "Ain't you still used to first class?"

"I'll make an exception for now," Lorelin said with a wink. "I can live without a velvet seat."

Lorelin left the fireside first, followed by Tsashin. The moon rose into the night. As the other girls settled down, Jae sat and watched Gryff and the Harney boys talk. The subject turned to meat or booze or something else she did not care to listen to.

Jae sat, bounced her heel, and listened to the sounds of the night. She was waiting for Gryff and Hodge to leave. She longed to be alone with Halston, like last night.

Never before had she been so eager to speak to someone, without another soul to listen in. She wasn't sure what it meant… but the feeling excited her. It was thrilling in a way she'd never known.

Go to bed, Hodge and Gryff.

404 : Sophia Minetos

Despite her silent request, Hodge and Gryff did not go to bed. *Go to bed so I can talk to Hal.*

No luck.

She sighed. *Guess it'll have to wait at least the night.* She walked back to her bedroll, lay on her side and dozed off as she tried not to think of him.

———

Halston Harney was, as Hodge would say, one lucky son of a bitch.

His wound was still tender, but there wasn't a trace of numbness left in his limbs. He sat with his brother and Gryff in the quiet clearing, listening to the soft sounds in the clear Mescan night. Perhaps Halston did not count his blessings enough. Plenty of men like him did not live to see nights like this. He was grateful that he had.

"Still no sign of Sterling," Gryff said, looking around at the dark woods. "Suppose we should thank our lucky stars."

"So," said Hodge. "Have you told Jae that you... y'know, fancy her?"

Halston sighed. "Not the phrasing I'd use, but... no. I haven't." Suddenly worried she'd overhear, he looked in her direction. "Is she asleep?"

"Let's find out." Hodge stood up. "HEY, JAE. HALSTON LOVES—"

Halston slammed a hand over Hodge's mouth. Tears of mirth swam in Hodge's eyes. Even Gryff burst out laughing.

"I will feed you to the wolves," Halston vowed as fiercely as he could. He released Hodge.

Hodge shrugged and wiped his mouth on his sleeve. "Hey. Now we know she's asleep."

Halston released a breath.

Hodge offered him a remarkably hollow apology, snickering

the whole way through. "Alright, alright. I'm sorry. I shouldn't have done that."

"Yeah, you shouldn't have."

"Hey." Hodge patted Halston's shoulder. "Go get her. I've seen the way she looks at you. You've got nothing to lose."

Halston disliked being mentored by his little brother, but Hodge did have a point. "She told me she'll stay with us. I just can't shake the fear that she'll walk away for some reason."

"Don't worry about that. If she loves you, why would she leave?" Hodge gave Halston a supportive clap on the back. Gryff gave him an even harder clap, and they both retired to bed.

They'd spent days together cooped in Sterling's musky cellar. Jae could have died in Duraunt's bank. Halston could have died from his axe wound. Either of them could have died as they ran from Sterling's gang, brought down by a bullet.

Tomorrow was not promised to them.

Halston tore out a precious blank page in his journal and wrote:

Jae,

I think I might love you. I wish I had more to say about it, but... I know. I've known for some time.

Did that even sound right? For goodness sake, he should have thought this out before writing it in pen. Nonetheless, he continued.

I could list the reasons why, but then I'd run out of ink. I'd rather talk about it in the morning, if you don't mind.

Sighing, he folded the note up and placed it next to his pouch. It was too forward. He'd have to start smaller.

Downhill, Halston spied a honeysuckle bush. He went and

plucked a large handful of the white, sweet-smelling flowers, then bound them into a bundle, tying off the stems with thread from his jacket.

Halston considered leaving the flowers next to Jae, but Lorelin slept only a few feet away. If Lorelin found them, she wouldn't let Halston hear the end of it. Jae's knapsack sat nearby. That would do.

When Halston opened it, he was surprised to find how many supplies it held. Tools, ammunition, flint, and...

...Why was there a folder labeled 'HESPYRIAN LAW'?

Halston took out the folder and leafed through it. It didn't take long for him to wish he'd left it alone.

The folder was filled with written reports for the capture of criminals, marked with the signatures of various sheriffs. The Clarence twins, the Brenner gang, a horse thief named Thaddeus Glory...

With them came receipts for their bounties, paid to a Miss Jae Oldridge.

The folder fell from his hands and landed in the dirt.

Jae was no thief, like the rest of them.

She was a woman of the law.

And now, she was awake and staring right at him.

Her eyes opened wide as the sky. A strangled cry tore from her lips. "What are you doing?!" She sprung to her feet and gathered up the papers and held them to her chest, like that could erase what Halston had just seen.

Halston couldn't bring himself to look at her. "You lied."

"I—"

"No more games. Tell me the truth. What was your plan?"

Her mouth parted, and a small sound came out.

Anger blazed in his chest. "Tell me the truth. Now."

Shivering, she said, "I was a bounty hunter. And... yeah, I lied. I've spent the past few years bringing outlaws to the sheriffs so I could become a Ranger and find my Pa. They don't let you into the Outlands if you ain't a Ranger." She swallowed, raising her hand with the long, puckered scar. "I thought that thieves were all the same. But you ain't. You… you're different. All of you are. I understand that now."

"But you joined us so you could *turn us in?*" He tried not to let his voice break.

"I don't want to turn you in *now.*"

"Is *that* why you *joined* us?"

"I don't want—"

"Answer me."

Silence. Then, "Yeah. Yeah, it was."

Halston took a step back. He glanced at the others, who lay sleeping about ten yards away. He meant nothing to her. Neither did they. They were all just coins for her to fill her pockets.

She kept talking. "Don't tell them about me. Please."

He blew the air from his lips, wondering how she could even have the gall to ask him for a favor right now. "Why not?"

"Because they'll hate me, Hal! Please. I want to stay with you. All of you."

"You wanted to take our freedom, Jae! You've betrayed us all! Do you really think I'm stupid enough to trust you again?"

He wanted to recognize her. He wanted to wipe what he'd read from his mind, to let her fall into his arms and wash it away.

She'd never belonged here, though. She'd had her sights set on him, but his heart had never been hers.

All the conversations they'd had… Sterling's cellar, Luna, those nights where they shared a watch, speaking under the light of a thousand constellations. Had anything she'd said been true? Hell, was anything she said *now* true? Was she waiting until he told her he loved her so he wouldn't think twice about letting his guard down before she turned him in?

"Hal." She moved toward him. "You don't understand. I was wrong. I'm sorry I lied. I… I was thinking all last night, and today. My offer was real. I want to join you. Stay with you."

Was she just spinning a yarn again? Gods.

He should have known. The way she'd duped their adversaries. Her lies, her ruses. He should have realized that he was no different to her.

In spite of himself, he listened to her plea. "Hal. I know I lied before, but you gotta believe me now. You gotta believe me when I say that you mean everything to me. Please."

"Why?" asked Halston.

Nothing came out of her.

He tossed Jae her knapsack, not bothering to be gentle about it. "Just go."

She sank down a bit, backing away a step or so. "Hal, please…"

"Go now. You don't belong here."

Her gaze hardened, and she put the knapsack down. "So that's it? The lot of us went down this road together. Maybe I tried to walk away a time or two. But I came back. All the times I had your back and you had mine? They don't matter now?"

"I need to protect my family. Go."

Her face turned to stone. "Fine." She slung the bag over her shoulder and turned to leave. "Glad to hear that 'family' doesn't include me. Guess I was bold enough to think it did." Her hand rummaged through her knapsack, then she tossed the folder and a wad of bills at Halston's boots.

"What's this?"

"Money from my last bounty," she spat, then turned her back to him. "Use it to buy your train ticket or somethin'. Use it to get away from Sterling. I won't ever forgive myself if he kills you."

He didn't watch her walk away.

He stayed there, looking at the ground, until his eyes burned from staring at Jae's folder sitting in the dirt. He waited for her to come back, to pick it up and cram it in her bag. Something urged him to pick it up and look through it again, but that wouldn't do him a bit of good. Still, he waited there and stared at it until his exhaustion hung over him like a cascade of fog.

Jae didn't come back.

He finally mustered up the willpower to look away from the folder and turn in the direction she'd walked. All that he saw was a line of pine trees swaying in the meager breeze.

One last time, he whispered her name.

Chapter 46

The next morning, Jae and Halston were nowhere to be found. Lorelin rolled over, furrowing her brow. In the place where Jae's bedroll should have been was a bough of wilting honeysuckles and a folded note. Lorelin recognized the grainy, cream-colored paper. It was from Halston's journal. If he was willing to rip out a page, then it must've been for something pretty damn important.

At first, she told herself she shouldn't give in to her sticky fingers... but she read it anyway.

Her heart swelled when she read the word 'love,' but the note was not beyond criticism. "Halston, you idiot," she murmured. She read the next part aloud in his voice. "'I could tell you all the reasons, but then I'd run out of ink?'"

He should've listed the reasons! Women *loved* hearing specifics!

Halston trudged up the hill, carrying an armload of grass for the horses. The circles beneath his eyes were dark as storm clouds.

Lorelin ran for him, then began to gush. "Okay, forgive me. I found the note for Jae. Did she read it?" She could barely contain her excitement.

Eagerly, she waited for the news, but Halston's expression only gutted her. He looked... empty. Like someone had slashed him up and drained him.

"Where's Jae?" she whispered.

Halston's eyes were bleak.

Lorelin bit her lip. "Oh gods, Hal. You're scaring me. Where's Jae?"

Halston hung his head. "She left."

"Left?" A cold, tight feeling welled up in the back of her throat. Shock washed over her. This couldn't be. "How? She... she was fine last night! She and I were talking all about you!"

"You don't understand," he said. "She doesn't want anything to do with us. And she never did."

Lorelin could find nothing else to say.

Halston roused the others. "Everyone up. There's... there's something I have to tell you."

Gryff and Tsashin silently ambled over. Hodge nudged Lorelin, but she said nothing. She held still as Halston ambled to his bedroll, then took something from a fold of blankets. A folder. Streaks of dirt marred its dun-colored cover. Silently, Halston moved back to the circle. "It's full of bounty receipts. She wasn't a thief. She was a bounty hunter."

Lorelin snatched the folder from his hands. She opened it, leafing through the documents.

"Aw, hell," Hodge muttered. "She lied to us."

A thousand feelings jumbled inside Lorelin. How could this be? She flipped through the receipts again, as if they could help her make sense of it. She wished for it to be a joke, some trick of her eyes and ears.

Gryff's voice was steady. Firm. "Maybe it's a blessin', kid, that we found out now."

Lorelin shut the folder. Hodge took it from her, but she hardly noticed. "It doesn't make sense," she said. "She had plenty of chances to turn us in. But she never did. Besides, with everything that's happened these past few weeks, it would've made more sense for her to save her own skin and ditch us. Leave us to Sterling's mercy."

"I don't think she wanted us gone," said Halston. "Not dead, at least. She just wanted money in her pocket. She saw us as..." He didn't finish. Halston usually kept his words even, speaking as fixedly as a river's flow. Now, something else was flooding through him, drowning his voice. Breaking it.

Lorelin loved him. He'd filled the role her own brother had failed to all those years ago. He was a stubborn, pigheaded stick in the mud, and he probably thought he was smarter than the rest of them. Lorelin had lost count of the times she and Hodge would snicker behind Halston's back over what a stickler he was.

And seeing the way Jae loosened him had brought Lorelin more joy than she'd felt in a while.

Tsashin chimed in. "There's something you don't know, Halston."

"What is it?" he murmured.

"She told me that she wished to leave."

"She told me that, too. She tried, in fact. It was just before we found you. She walked away from us before we dug you up." He didn't mention that she'd come back running and saved Hodge's life.

"No. This was... another time. It was after you found me. I told her that she should take more time to think of it. She sounded frustrated. I didn't believe she was thinking very well. And... I wasn't sure if she would leave. There were nights I wondered if she would. She never did."

"It's not important," said Halston. "It doesn't matter whether or not she changed her mind. There's no way to tell the truth. We've just lost another gun. We'll survive without her, and it's done.

What matters now is getting out of here. Let's go. We have to reach Dolorosa before the end of the day."

The rest of the day felt an awful lot like a funeral.

————

His mind wouldn't stop calling for her.

Jae, Jae, Jae.

The road wound on. The miles passed them by. The sun arched overhead. They moved, but Halston's mind could not move as he did.

He kept his tired eyes on the road. The folder was still in his knapsack. Hodge had told him to get rid of it, but Halston ignored it. *For the love of gods, Hal, throw that thing away. I know you're just gonna look at it so you can rile yourself up. Do I need to toss it for you? Hal, are you even listening to me?*

He did his best to listen. Their boots crunched on the dirt, shuffling over dust and gravel. The day was clear, without wind to funnel through the forest's branches. Halston led their line, and Lorelin walked closest to him. She had a grave expression on her round face, moving without a trace of her usual buoyancy.

Close to the evening, and close to Dolorosa, they stopped briefly to rest. The land was growing cooler and greener each mile. Halston turned his back to the others as they settled, resting on fallen, mossy logs in a dark thicket. He excused himself to trek several dozen yards away, then stopped in the shade of a fir tree.

He pressed his back to the trunk and stared into the woods, at the shadows teeming on the forest floor. Behind him, someone's boots rustled the leaves. Halston did not turn around, even as Lorelin's voice touched him, the sound crisp and warm as September's early days. "Hey."

"Hi," he said. "We'll go soon. I just needed to clear my head."

"Is it working?"

He didn't need to answer her. Lorelin could read him as easily as if he were water in a basin of glass.

"I came to talk to you," she said. "Before we go. I know it stings. I won't say I'm not confused. None of it makes sense to me. Traitor or not, she saved us more than once. But there was something *different* about her. When I met Adwell, I think part of me *knew* that he wore a mask. It took him ages to take it off. But I was desperate, and maybe I denied it. Even if he wasn't perfect... I thought he was better than what I had. Then he left me with bruises.

"It was different with Jae. I never had a trace of doubt about her. I thought that she was... a bit tentative. And odd. But I liked that about her. I felt like we understood each other. She was my friend. Maybe it's wishful thinking, but maybe she *did* change her mind."

"Does it matter?" Halston asked.

"Probably not," she said. "But it's eating away at you. I can tell."

Maybe it was. Maybe he'd let it.

"Halston," she said. "I won't tell you that you can't grieve. I saw how you looked at her. But you have to promise me that you won't let this weigh you down. I know you don't think I notice it, but I do. I see how everything stirs inside you. And I'm scared that you're going to drown."

He lifted his stare from the trees and faced her.

Had he been drowning?

Maybe he had. Maybe he still wasn't used to breathing the unfamiliar air of this world he'd stepped into. Maybe he was clawing his way toward its surface with half a dozen stones in his pockets, sinking.

Dolorosa was not far. Neither was Monvallea.

At last, he could glimpse the surface.

He forced a smile. "Thank you, Lorelin. I appreciate it."

"Do you still want to talk?"

"I'll be alright. I'll be back down in a minute, then we'll head out of here. I think we can catch an evening train."

"Good." She gave his shoulder a tight squeeze. "Don't be too long, alright? You and I can take the window seats. It's going to be a beautiful ride."

She sauntered away, and Halston turned to the woods again.

Tonight, they'd board the northbound train. It would carry them out of Mesca, and into Monvallea. They'd find the rest of their silver. They'd find another conduit, even if it took a hundred different trails. They'd cross the Nefilium passes and reach the Outlands. They'd open their portal and step through.

Home.

It was far, far away.

But it wasn't gone.

So Halston gave himself another moment. He lifted those stones from his pockets. His father, crashing down into the sea. Sterling and his men and all the scars on Halston's back. Elias and Arrowwood and the river that took him away. Jae. Whoever she was, and wherever she would go.

It would be alright, Halston figured, to wonder. Life was not long enough to discover every answer. He would learn to live without knowing.

Because he would *live*.

For his gang. For the portal. For his mother, for Lia, for the ghosts of Elias and his father, sailing somewhere in their ocean of stars.

He took all his stones and turned them into seeds.

He let them go and watched them drift.

Chapter 47

The day inched by like the summer solstice. The sun just went on and on, and when it sank, Jae was grateful. Let this day pass. Let it end.

For years, Jae had loved walking on the open road. All she'd needed was the smell of pine, her compass, and a twisting path. She'd felt about as large as the world itself in those days.

There was nothing good about this road.

That evening, Jae found a small brook flowing downhill. She drank as much as she could before filling her canteen to the rim.

Dusk came. She found a clearing and sat down. The wildflowers were blooming in brilliant colors. Cornflower, harebell, wild forget-me-nots. She nestled herself in a beam of fading light, waiting for the stars to poke their heads out.

She'd left her folder of bounty receipts back in the camp. It was probably stupid, but right now, she hardly cared. Nothing really felt worth doing right now. Someone could walk up to her and rob her, and she'd probably just sit there and let them.

She fingered the petals of a cornflower, leaving a bluish stain on her fingertips. *I won't ever see Hal again. Or the others. Serves me right, I guess. I was a liar.*

She rested her chin on her knees. She wouldn't cry, damn it. She wouldn't cry.

Jae stood up. She had to walk, to move and keep her mind from flying off.

She had a magic map in her knapsack. All she had to do was speak a word and know exactly where she was in this world.

But once again, she was lost.

Pa had told her so many stories, tales of heroes and riders and bounty hunters like her. They did what was right. Tamed beasts and saved villages and foiled scoundrels. But at the end of the story, they were almost always alone. They walked into the desert under starry skies, whistling, never to return.

Jae wondered if she was just like them. Maybe lives like hers weren't meant to be shared.

She got up and walked along the brook, following its crooks. The water was shallow, pouring downhill over heaps of stone, algae pooling around their smooth gray heads. Its banks were thin and muddy, but not too slick, and the earth felt almost springy as she stepped across it. Cottonwoods and spruce trees shaded her pathway, and the breeze tossed the hair around her face.

Somewhere, several yards away, something cracked. She stopped and turned.

To her side, there were only thick clusters of vegetation, their reeds and branches wavering in the gentle wind. The greenery looked beautiful sprouting over the brook, but that didn't stop the lump from knotting in her stomach.

Jae looked left and right again, then lowered a hand to the grip of her gun. She scanned the area before her three times before she caught a glimpse of blonde hair shining in the trees several yards away.

Evia.

Jae pulled her gun out and fired. Her bullet cut through a few spruce branches, scattering pine needles in the air like a burst of dust. The blonde head moved forward, and Jae cursed herself for missing, then took off downhill.

Lead her astray, lead her astray. Her speed picked up, and she came dangerously close to falling more than once. Her heels flew over the slope. Her chest burned. A stitch formed in her side, the pain sharp and hot.

At the last second, Jae whirled around. She leapt across the brook, and her boots nearly slipped in the bed of mud and water. She hopped out, muck flying from her boots, and darted back up the hill. Maybe Evia was like a bear, and switching directions would throw her off just long enough.

The hope was short lived. Strong fingers grabbed a handful of Jae's hair. Evia yanked, pulling Jae to the ground. Jae lost hold of her gun. She broke her fall with her hands, but the ground still struck her knees. She kicked, hoping to let Evia's throat know what her heel felt like.

Jae tried to push herself back up, but Evia's knee slammed down on Jae's back, and Jae watched the woman retrieve her fallen gun. Then, Evia took Jae's boot pistol, knapsack, and her knife. Jae squirmed, lashing out with her foot again. She missed Evia's shin, and the bite of a blade touched Jae's neck. "Stop kicking, you little runt! Hold still."

The metal was cold under her throat. Something soft slipped over her head, cloaking her vision. The drawstring of a cloth bag squeezed her neck. Jae's hands flew up to it, then Evia's long fingers latched onto her wrists and gripped tight as a wolf's locked jaws. Thin rope prickled Jae's skin as Evia looped it around her wrists and pulled.

"Get up." Evia jostled Jae, then yanked on one of her braids. Jae winced, then stood.

Evia wrapped one arm around Jae's side, but kept the blade pressed beneath her jaw. They walked uphill, the incline increasing until her knees felt ready to give out. Jae wondered if she could pretend to faint, to fall and roll downhill, then writhe until this blasted bag slipped from her head.

"You're a quiet one, ain't you?" Evia purred.

"You have the ugliest voice I've ever heard."

"Can it!" Evia yanked on Jae's braid again. Her scalp screamed.

They hiked and hiked, and soon, Jae heard the sound of rough voices blending together from uphill. Evia called, "I've got her! That girl who was with the Harneys!"

The storm of voices bored into her ears. Before she could move, a fist slammed into her back. Jae fell, and she felt rough stone grinding into her hip. A boot heel slammed atop her head, then greasy, gritty hands hiked up her shirt, exposing her skin to the air. Someone ripped the bag from her head, taking a chunk of her hair with it. When her vision cleared, she found Argus, Sterling's remaining brother, pointing his gun at her.

They stood on a rocky ledge overlooking the woods. The land around them was clear, the hard-packed dirt free of trees for a circle of around thirty feet. Sterling's men were scattered across the ledge, and a small fire burned in the center of their camp. Boulders littered the plane in abundance. The ledge jutted out into two narrow lengths of rock, shaped like the two back tips of an arrowhead, no more than six yards of empty space between each point. Laid over the two points was a plank, no thicker than three of her fingers stacked together.

A tall, brawny man holding a length of rope stepped forth. He heaved the rope in Jae's direction. Jae almost screamed as a loop slipped over her head and the man yanked, pulling the knot around her neck.

Argus jabbed his gun toward her, forcing her to take a step back in the direction of the gap. "Step onto the plank," he ordered.

She spat, "What do you want from me?"

"I said step back!" wheezed Argus.

Jae stood and put one foot on the plank. Another. Slowly, she made her way onto the plank, wrists still bound. She couldn't help it—she looked down. The drop wasn't too high, no more than twenty feet above the forest floor, but that didn't matter. If a noose was around her neck, and there was no ground for her feet to find, then one small stumble would snap her neck like a twig.

The brawny man kept the rope in his hands, then paced over to a spire of rock poking out of the ground. He looped the other end of the rope around the rock, wrapped it several times around the point, and knotted it off. Jae stood on the plank, trying to keep her legs still, to ignore the feeling of being weightless in the worst possible way.

When Sterling appeared, she wanted to rip those pretty brown eyes right out of his head.

"I feared I'd never see you again." There was a speck of laughter in his voice.

Desperately, she wanted to spit poison at him, but ugly words wouldn't keep her alive. "I'll ask you again, Sterling. What do you want?"

"I thought it'd be obvious," Sterling replied. "I want to know where the Harneys are hiding."

Jae's mouth parted.

"Do you want to live?" he asked.

"As much as you do." If she didn't, she wouldn't be here now, would she? "But I ain't with the Harneys anymore."

"Interesting," said Sterling. "Tell me, sweetheart, did you leave them, or did they leave you? Finally caught on to your little game, did they?"

Damn it, she wouldn't cry in front of him. She wouldn't let him think she was weak. "I left, and it was *days* ago. I swear, I don't know where they are."

She had told so many lies before, and she'd tell this one again and again, even if it put her in cuffs.

"I thought you might be hesitant," Sterling admitted. He snapped his fingers. "Argus."

"I've got it," murmured the younger man. He paced over to the small fire blazing several feet away. He lifted something long and sharp from it—a fire poker, its tip glowing red hot.

A lie. She'd have to think of another lie.

As Argus lifted the weapon from the fire, nothing but fear sprouted in her mind.

"Tell me where they are," Sterling said with a sickening gentleness.

Slowly, Argus aimed the fire poker, its tip creeping dangerously close to Jae's bare belly. Two things happened at once: Jae finished thinking up a lie, and hot iron seared her flesh.

She screamed before the lie came. "STOP, STOP! THEY'RE HEADING SOUTH! THEIR HIDEOUT IS FORTY MILES EAST OF CARTH! THAT'S ALL I KNOW! STOP!

She turned her legs to stone, forcing herself to hold her balance against the burn. At first, she didn't notice when the metal left her skin. The pain hardly ceased. She'd done it, though. She'd spat out a lie. The gang would be safe.

Her gang.

She stood there, eyes closed, breathing the air as she would gulp down water in the desert. It was deliciously cold in her throat. Sweat dribbled into her brows and lashes.

"What is their hideout, exactly?" asked Argus.

"A cabin. In an old mining camp," she said between breaths, casting her gaze to the forest below. "With a painting of a rose on the walls. That's all I know."

"Do you always look down when you lie, honey?" Sterling asked. "Reckon you oughta work on that."

Jae didn't respond. He'd snatch her words up like stones from a river and hurl them right back at her. But… what did he mean? Why was he wasting his time mocking her? If he knew she was lying, why wasn't he trying to coax the truth out of her again?

A pale, haggard man standing close to Argus spoke up. "Stop it! Don't hurt her again!" His voice was strangely thin, as if he were trying to speak after yelling himself hoarse.

Sterling cast a glare the man's way, but that didn't stop the man from turning his gaze to Jae and speaking. "Say nothing more! He knows where they are already!"

"Damn it, Spec!" Sterling bellowed. "I told you to keep your mouth shut!"

"You're torturing her!"

"Shut your trap!" snapped Argus. "Do as he says, or I'll send you off on the wind."

Jae bit her lip. It was all she could do to keep from screaming, from casting words at Sterling that would surely get this board kicked out from beneath her feet. The bastard. The dirty bastard. He knew where they were headed, and he knew that burning her flesh with a poker wouldn't do him a bit of good.

"You really are something else, Jae Oldridge," Sterling said, crossing his arms and shaking his head. "Bounty hunter turned thief. Can't say I've ever met anyone like you. You don't need to cast your pride aside for them, darlin'. They ain't gonna live past tomorrow, anyway. I know where they're headed. We lost your tracks several nights ago, so we started asking locals on the road. A nice couple in a cabin nearby told us they saw a band of travelers with an Azmarian heading this way. Bound for Dolorosa, by the looks of it."

Jae's heart flamed and twisted in her chest. She must've failed to keep her face blank, because it sent Sterling laughing like a washed-up drunk again.

He'd tracked them here. But if that was the case, why wait until she'd left? Why have Evia follow her to the brook, and take her, when the rest of the gang was waiting for him? They still had Tsashin.

She'd ask him. If she was going to die anyway, she might as well spit out a few choice words while she still could. "What do you need me for, then? You know where they are. You can get what you want. You're a sick man, but you seem to use your time wisely enough."

"We came to your campsite this afternoon," Sterling replied. "Two separate sets of tracks. One led back to the main road, one didn't. Glad that you were the one who strayed, so I could see you burn myself."

Jae narrowed her eyes.

"We're heading for Dolorosa now," Sterling said. "Figured we'd make a raid out of it. Get the Harneys to come out from wherever they are so we can watch them bite the dust. I ain't too sure I want to watch them suffer. I just want them *gone*. But you... I'm gonna leave you here. I'll let you think long and hard about what you did to my brother. I can part with a little silver. I can even handle losing an adamite knife. But Pierce is gone, 'cause of you. My brother, dead. Years before his time."

Tears filled his eyes as he spoke. Even this monster, this beast of a man, was capable of feeling.

He wanted her to beg. He wanted her to throw all her dignity to the side and plead. She wanted to spit. She wanted to tell him that she hadn't felt a speck of remorse after she'd killed Pierce, even though she'd wanted to. That she was glad his brother was rotting beneath the earth now.

But she did not speak.

She wanted to let it end there. Let him think of Pierce on his way to Dolorosa and wallow in his grief.

"I gotta say," said Sterling. "I was baffled on the night you saved Halston. I ain't never seen anything like it. A woman of the law, fallen in love with the man she'd gone out and chased." His lips curled into a sneer. "You played him, didn't you?"

"Shut the hell up."

"You lied to them all. I shoulda let them know about it. I would've laughed to see Halston strike you down. Say it. Tell us all how you played them."

"Fine! I lied!" She spat. Sterling was grinning like a man who'd just struck it rich, now, but she didn't care. She just wanted *out* of here.

She wanted to disappear into the wind. She wanted to soar, to feel nothing but the air that carried her.

Sterling said, "I'm done with you, for now. I'm going to give you some time to think of what you did to my brother, if'n you don't decide to jump first." He turned to Argus. "You and Spec stay here. If she tries to get out, shoot her. We'll be back by dawn."

"Dawn?" questioned Argus, somehow managing to sound like a whining child. "We ain't comin' with ya?"

"I told you. You'll stay here with the girl."

The gang strayed away from the slope, back into the woods and toward the trail. They were going to Dolorosa.

What they'd do there... Jae didn't want to think about it.

She should have been running. She should have been chasing after them, stopping them. Halston, her gang... they were going to walk straight into Dolorosa, thinking they were going to board the evening train and get away from Sterling.

"*I'm sorry,*" she whispered, and sent all their names floating on the wind. Tsashin, Lorelin, Gryff, Hodge, Pa. Halston's name lingered on her lips. It would probably be there forever. "*I'm so, so sorry.*"

Chapter 48

Hours passed. Pain still gnawed at Jae's side. Her skin was freezing cold but beaded with sweat. She wanted her mind to go numb. To forget all this.

Pressure ate away at her legs. The board was so thin, she feared she'd doze off and slip. Which was worse: death by hanging here, or Argus shooting her down? She guessed it depended on how it happened. Maybe her neck would break, or maybe she'd strangle. Maybe the bullet would find her head, or maybe it would find her hip, and he'd let her bleed out slowly.

No. I ain't dying here. She had to live. For Pa. For her gang.

Argus sat tending the fire with that damned poker. His eyelids were dark, like he'd smeared them with ash. Spec stared at the flames with a sad, almost naïve expression, like a child seeing fire for the first time.

He caught her staring. His skin was pale, too pale, like he'd never spent a minute of his life in the sun. "Who are you?" he asked.

She snorted, wondering if he'd paid any attention at all to the confrontation earlier. "I'm nobody," she answered, hardly loud enough for him to hear. "I'm a liar and a traitor and a cheat. That's who I am."

"That makes two of us," he said.

"Shut your traps," Argus spat. The circles around his eyes were gray as slate. "I didn't ride a hundred miles north to listen to your wailin', Spec."

"You're weak," said Spec.

"'Scuse me?"

"Sometimes I have second thoughts about wanting to stay on this earth, 'cause of men like you," Spec spat. "You'll die with a black heart in your chest. You walk around like I did, wanting to fill it with somethin'. And you chose pain. You chose greed and fire and harm. You ain't never loved anything in your life, have you?"

"Spec, stoppit," Argus ordered as he stood. "Remember. You do as I say. I promised you that second chance you wanted, and you ain't got a single right to disobey me."

"Why the hell not?" Spec argued. "Day in and day out, you promise me you'll let me go. And you never do. I sit here and watch you let folks hurt and burn."

"Yeah, you do," Argus said, narrowing his eyes. "You owe me. I saved your pathetic soul when no one else would."

"What's it worth, though?" Spec fired back. "This ain't the life I came searchin' for. I'm tired of it."

"Tired of it?" Argus boomed. "Fine, then. How's about I rip your spirit from your body and send you wanderin'?"

"That's fine," Spec said. "I'll find someone else to follow."

And he pushed Argus over the ledge.

Argus shrieked as he tumbled down, the branches tearing at his clothes, slicing his skin. His screams gave out as he slammed against the ground.

Shock seared through Jae's veins. Even from this height, the whitish body of Argus stood out under the branches. Arms raised above his head, lying flat on his stomach. Dead.

"Quick." Spec untied the noose from the rock spire.

Jae didn't move, at first. She had to pry her gaze from Argus's limp, pale form on the earth below. At last, she looked at Spec, and her heart almost stopped. His skin wavered like candlelight. He stared at Jae as his color dripped away, leaving only a bluish, translucent form.

A ragged breath left Jae's lips. "You're a ghost."

Spec blinked. "I died young. I wanted a second chance at life. Argus was a warlock. He promised he would give me a new body if I helped him steal." He shook his head. "I'm so sorry, Jae. I... I should have said something. I shouldn't have let them burn you. I've been standing by like this for years. I'm tired of it. I'm tired of watchin' them hurt folks like you."

Tears formed in her eyes. "Spec, why did you—"

"My name ain't Spec. It's Jem."

Jae stepped across the plank. The first footfall on solid earth was like stepping onto heaven's grounds. "Jem, why did you—"

"Because I'm tired of it," he answered. He smiled at her once more, though the pain on his face was unmistakable. "I wanted to start another life. As a better man. But I can't do that if I ride with them. Come on, now. You've got some people to find."

She wanted to speak, cry, move... *something,* but she could only stare.

"Come with me," she said at last. "You can help me. We'll... we'll take them down together."

Jem smiled sadly. "I've lost my body, Jae. I can't stay here long. I'd explain it, but we're short on time."

She was crying, now, but she wasn't sad, really. There were too many things brewing and breaking inside her. Too many to name.

"Go," he told her, turning himself to face the expanse of forest. "Don't worry. We'll meet again."

"Jem!" she shouted. "Wait!"

He merely waved at her, then took a step right into the sky. He moved above the treetops, pacing with a rhythm in his legs, as if dancing to an old, forgotten song.

"Jem!" she cried as his form vanished in the clear night.

Gone.

"Jem, I…" Tears began to slide down her cheeks, but there was no time for weeping.

Quietly, she thanked him, though she wasn't sure he could hear her. She fetched her weapons from the pile of supplies the gang had left behind, then hurried back into the woods.

Damn it, Evia had really thrown her off course. She opened her pack, took out her map, and asked it to show her Dolorosa. It was about two miles away. If she ran, she could make it in less than half an hour.

She'd find Halston, find the others, and get them to safety. And if she was lucky, she'd help them strike Sterling Byrd down. That would make almost getting killed worth it.

Chapter 49

They reached Dolorosa a couple hours after sundown. The town sat at the end of the sloping trail, and the northernmost edges of the Briarfords rose behind it. Behind those mountains lay Monvallea. Halston tried to let himself feel a glimmer of peace, of hope at the sight of those blue peaks. He was tired, though. Maybe a night's rest would put his mind at ease. Maybe each day from here would feel a little easier.

They stepped onto the wide main street. There were still a few people out and about, but for the most part, the town was quiet. The windows glowed yellow with candlelight, and men slouched tiredly on their horses as they rode off on the darkening road.

They decided to let the horses rest, and tethered them on a railing outside a bar. Tsashin fed them, letting the animals eat grain from her palm while she stroked their necks.

"It looks like we might be too late for the last train," said Lorelin. "Still, it can't hurt to go to the station."

Halston reached into his pack and pulled out their money, plus the crowns Jae had given him the night before. Lorelin lifted her brows. "Where did you get those?"

"Jae gave them to me before she left."

"That makes no sense," said Gryff. "Givin' that she strung us along so she could fill her own pockets."

Halston waved a hand. "It doesn't matter. It's over." And he'd say that until it felt good and true.

Crickets began to sing. Another day come and gone. Halston scratched his neck. He wasn't sure what day it was. He'd lost track a week or so ago. It was sometime in early May, most likely. Had it really only been two months since that brawl in the saloon?

A gunshot shattered his thoughts.

He did not turn around. His instincts cried out to him to lead his gang into the nearest alley.

They darted out of the street, hurrying for a nook between an inn and a mason's shop. Halston's heart pumped like a bellows in his chest. For a moment, they just waited, frozen in the shadows like startled deer. Gryff's hands trailed to his rifle's grip. Lorelin slung her arm across Tsashin's shoulders, like Halston's mother used to do to him. Tsashin clapped a hand over her mouth. Hodge's face sank into a glare.

Anger poured over Halston's body.

He forced himself to peer into the main street.

More gunshots cracked in rapid succession. Bullets shattered glass and wood alike, backed by the sounds of dark, frenzied laughter. People screamed. Doors slammed. The figures emerged on the road, quick as steam bursting from a geyser. They moved too swiftly for Halston to make out their faces… but the tight, sickening lurch in his gut told him exactly who they were. They brandished their guns, and the unmistakable glare of torchlight blazed over their forms.

Halston didn't see Sterling. But he heard him just fine.

"Harney boys." His voice filled the night. "I know you're here. You can come out now, and we'll leave. This is your first warning."

A few moments passed.

Then a figure stepped outside of the lineup. It was Sterling. Halston knew by the way he carried himself, walking like a man without a fear or care in the world. And when he held his torch to the nearest building, Halston felt himself go cold.

As the dry wood caught fire, more people started to scream. Two of them fled from the front doors, hurrying into the street. The gang seized them, snickering, and they beat the pair to the ground. Halston looked away, staring at the ground instead.

And he spoke.

"We have to split up," he said, already breathless. "Tsashin, Lorelin... go in the opposite direction of the gang. Warn the people up ahead. Get them out.

"Hodge, Gryff... we'll have to sneak around the buildings. We'll meet them in the middle. And we'll face them."

Tonight, this would end.

One way or another.

Halston raised his gaze to Lorelin, and the sad smile on her lips nearly made him stumble. But she spoke softly. There was light in her voice, enough to put the moon to shame. "We'll do it. I trust you. I trust all of you, and I'll see you tomorrow for breakfast."

Lorelin and Tsashin hurried out of the alley, then disappeared north, away from Sterling's gang.

Halston, Gryff, and Hodge stayed pressed to the wall. Gryff pointed to a building across the street. "Look."

Halston squinted. He could just barely make out the outline of someone on a rooftop, aiming his rifle at the chaos below. Gryff said, "If he starts shootin', it's gonna get ugly. I'm going after him. You keep an eye out down here."

As he walked away, Halston didn't want to admit to himself that this could be the last time any of them saw each other.

———

Night was falling faster and faster. Dolorosa, a sweet, boxy little town by a hillside, waited at the end of the road. It sat nestled in the trees like a marble in a green-gloved hand. Jae raced toward the clustered, flat-roofed buildings, hoping to the high heavens that she had made it on time. Then came the shouting, the desperate, pleading cries of townsfolk. The shattering glass. The smoke pluming into the air.

She bit her tongue. The folks in Dolorosa weren't the Fisks, or corrupt railroad barons, or lawmen who preyed on poor ranchers. These were innocents. They deserved better than to have their town burned down by lowlifes. She sprinted down the road, toward the town, praying that she wouldn't find her gang's bodies lying in the street.

But what could she do?

All those times she'd tracked down thieves in the desert, she'd gone in with a plan. This was different. She had one gun in her belt, and one in her boot, but what was that against Sterling and his cronies?

She entered the town. A crowd bustled in the main street, gunshots thundering from a disarray of men and galloping horses. Folks were screaming. Bullets were flying. She hustled toward the first building she saw and pinned herself behind it, then peered out from behind a corner. If she ran into this scuffle, she'd be shot, burned up, or worse, but she couldn't leave these poor folks to the Byrds' mercy.

On the other side, a group of folks huddled outside the cobbler's caught Jae's eye. One had a snake's head. With him was a hothead with a smoking pistol, and Halston Harney.

You son of a gun.

They stood waiting for a moment, talking amongst themselves. Jae's instincts were screaming at her to call out to them, but she held her tongue and stayed still. A few moments passed. The Harney boys retreated back into the shadows, vanishing from her sight. Gryff looked both ways, then hurried into the building to his right.

Maybe she was crazy for doing it, but she didn't care. She gauged the distance of the Byrd gang, decided they were far enough away, and raced into the street.

Her feet flew. Even from this distance, she could feel the heat of the fires. She felt a tug at her insides, one pulling her toward the building Gryff had entered. Though her heart begged her to run for Halston, she raced to the building. There was no sign. The building was nameless, with nothing to distinguish its place in the town. Jae darted up its porch, past the awning supported by painted blue pillars, and burst in through the doors.

Before she even looked around, she cried out to him. "Gryff!"

He whirled in her direction

They stood in a large room, the walls and floor built out of close-packed, tan wood. Jae wasn't sure what kind of store this was—shelves lined the walls, and a glass table sat smack in the center of the room. In the back right corner, a narrow stairway rose to somewhere unseen. Two men in fading flannels were huddled in the corner, but only one of them clutched a gun. Gryff stood in the center, staring right back at Jae.

He said, "You here to turn me in?"

Jae shook her head. "No. I'm here to help you."

"What for?"

"The hell do you mean, what for? Sterling's raiding the town, and that's all you have to say to me?"

Gryff snorted. "I'm headin' upstairs. Someone's up on the roof. I'm gonna go take him out."

Before Jae could speak, the window burst behind them. The two men screamed. One of them stood up, his gun shaking like a quaking flag in his hands. Someone broke through the front doors and shouted, "Get down! Hands where I can see 'em!"

Jae threw her hands up, then peered over her shoulder. Standing in the door was one of those gunslingers with the pretty blue eyes… not Lyle, but one of his brothers. *Gods, you'd be hard-pressed to tell any of them apart.*

One of the two men put his hands up. The other didn't. He raised his gun to fire, but the man in the doorway was quicker. The shot exploded, fast as lightning, and Jae didn't even see the blood blooming on the poor soul's head before he fell. His companion looked at him with wide-shot eyes, and a startled cry escaped his lips.

Gryff looked at the new-made body, then shifted his glance to the front door and said, "Put the damn pistol down, Maxim."

Maxim snorted. "Where's the girl, Gryff?"

"Give it a rest, will ya? Why can't y'all find a gold pit to loot instead of houndin' us for poor Tsashin?"

"Why don't you tell me where she is? If'n you do, I'll step outta here."

"Go to hell. I don't know where she is," said Gryff.

Jae took a step to the side. She backed across the room, further and further, until her boot touched the puddle of the dead man's blood. Maxim finally spied her making her way back, and his chafed lips curled into a sneer. "Am I going mad? Or was we gonna string you up? How'd you work your way outta that pinch?"

Jae stopped. She said nothing, but kept her hands high in the air. She was close to the live man and the dead one—close enough to hear the live one sniveling.

Maxim turned back to Gryff. "I don't gotta keep you around, y'know. I reckon your kids are all still running around this town.

Cowards won't come out. We could draw now and settle this like gentlemen." He chuckled. "But you ain't a man. You're a monster. I heard somewhere that they used to hunt your kind for sport. How's about I bring that back?"

Gryff said, "That's alright, Maxim. I agree with you about settlin' this, though."

Gryff's hand crept toward his pistol, inching down his hip. Without moving her head, Jae flicked her gaze to the dead man's pistol, sitting slick with blood on the floor. She dove its way. Her hand flew to the gun, and she grabbed it, aimed, and fired.

The gun was bigger than she was used to. Louder, too. The noise dug deep into her ears, and the recoil sent a deep blow of pain pounding through her wrist. Maxim screamed in answer, his gun falling to the floor.

Jae didn't bother to check where her bullet had hit him. She ran, trying to dart past him, toward the stairway at the left.

Maxim wasn't dead, and he was quick. A hand grabbed her braid and yanked her backward. She fell, and not to the floor. Her body slammed against the glass table, and it fractured like an eggshell under her weight. Her vision clouded for a second, pain cleaving through every part of her. For a few moments, darkness seized her senses.

When she came to, she watched Maxim reaching for another gun in his belt. Blood trickled from his shoulder.

Jae didn't take her time. If she was going to die tonight anyway, then she might as well try and draw quick. And she did.

She didn't know who fired first: her or Gryff. It was hard to say. All she knew was that one of their shots brought Maxim down.

He fell, the broken glass tinkling as he landed on top of it. Groaning, Jae pushed herself up. Bits of glass cut small nicks into her palms, but she urged herself not to think of the pain.

Gryff offered her one green, scaly hand. "Get up, kid. C'mon."

She reached out and took it. Gryff helped her to her feet. Her boots shifted in the smattering of glass and blood. There were three live folks in this room. The poor fella in the corner just sat there, trembling at the sight of Maxim and the dead man.

Jae told him, "Stay here. We're going upstairs."

Jae followed Gryff up the stairwell. It led to a hatch in the roof. Gryff slid the hook from the latch and pushed, driving his arms and his rifle through the opening.

Jae peeked over the hatch's rim. Lyle turned, but not fast enough. Jae wasn't even sure he knew what hit him. There was a bark of gunfire, and he collapsed, blood pooling on his back.

Gryff hurried to the edge of the rooftop. Jae followed him. Their boots clattered on the flat surface. Without looking at her, Gryff cocked his rifle again and tipped its barrel over the roof. He said, "Go downstairs. Hide."

"I ain't gonna hide."

"C'mon, Jae. You've caused us all a great deal of confusion. You'd best sit this one out. Or are you lookin' to collect Sterling's bounty?"

"No! I came back for you! For all of you!"

For a moment, Gryff just kept his eyes on the street below, waiting. "Well... I ain't here to tell you what to do. If you want to help, the boys are on the edge of the street."

She nodded, then turned to leave. She raced back to the roof. Before she slipped down the hatch, she turned. "Gryff?"

"Yeah?"

Jae said, "Best of luck. Shoot well." And she disappeared back into the building.

———

Lorelin and Tsashin sat huddled in the train station, tucked beneath the windows. The interior was small, with a glass-paned ticket office and two rows of benches spanning the floor. They'd gotten a drove of people out of a few buildings near the center of the town, but when they heard the gunshots growing closer, they'd fled into the train station with two women they'd met on the street. Inside, they pushed a pair of benches to barricade the front and back doors, then settled back against the wall.

The ticket officer crouched beneath the counter. Lorelin and Tsashin sat by the back wall, facing the front windows, but Lorelin couldn't get a good look out of them. There was nothing she could see beyond the flat color of the sky.

Apart from the ticket officer, there were only two other people in the room. Women in puffed skirts and waistcoats—a mother and daughter, judging by their shared dark hair and brown eyes framed with thick lashes. They sat near Tsashin, huddling together while the Yunah girl whispered to them. "It's alright. Things will be alright."

Lorelin decided to take a look out the back windows. She rose, keeping her head just high enough to peer out the glass. Ahead, she could see the boarding platform and the awning hanging overhead. It looked strangely still in the sunset's glow, waiting for motion, for something, anything, to happen.

The minutes trudged by. The women in skirts grew more and more frantic, until Tsashin had to ask them, sweetly, to quiet down. She kept doing her best to comfort them, and Lorelin couldn't bring herself to say it.

The Byrd gang was here, and they weren't leaving until Lorelin and her boys lay dead.

But she didn't imagine death finding her. Instead, she imagined the sun rising tomorrow and knowing that Sterling and his men were gone. They'd still be running, just not from him. It wouldn't feel like peace… but it'd be somewhere closer to it.

Footsteps padded down on the platform, making Lorelin twitch. She ducked down further, but kept watching.

A tall, long-legged woman and a coppery-haired man stepped across the station's platform. Evia. Ned. They moved steadily, taking their time as they trekked along the platform's edge. They cast their gazes in the opposite direction of the window, scoping out the rugged landscape running parallel to the rails.

"To hell with this," Lorelin murmured. She stood and darted to the front door, shoving the bench out just enough for her to slip outside.

"Where are you going?" cried Tsashin.

"Settling this! Stay here."

Lorelin slid out the front door and pulled it shut behind her. Lifting one gun from her holster, she slunk around the corner and crept down the side of the building, braced to cock and shoot.

She reached the edge of the building, where the platform met the back wall. Ned and Evia still looked away, their eyes fixed on the rails. Still leaning out from behind the corner, she aimed and fired thrice.

Ned threw his arms out and jolted back. He fell quickly, but not before Lorelin glimpsed the spot of blood right where his heart was. His body went spilling over the side of the platform and landed hard against the rails. Evia's form turned and ran, her blonde braid flying behind her, darting up the platform and down the other side of the building.

Lorelin carried herself after her. She jogged, but kept her pistol ready in case Evia was pressed to the wall and braced to shoot.

When Lorelin reached the other wall and turned her head, Evia was gone. Lorelin stepped slowly around the wall, trying not to let her hands shake. She took a step, then a breath. Again. Over the rooftop, she spied smoke rising in the distance, and her heart shrank. Shouting and pounding hooves thundered from inside the town. Sterling wasn't just here for Lorelin and her gang. He'd made his own little function out of it.

Evia's shrill, crooning voice spoke from behind the corner, around the front of the station. "Don't hide from me, Miss Winter."

"I'm not hiding from you," Lorelin fired back, stopping in place. "For the gods' sake, Evia. If you just wanted us, why are you plundering this place? What have these poor townsfolk done to you?"

It was a stupid question, and Lorelin knew it. Sterling was preparing to kill the gang who'd kept Tsashin from him and killed his brother. Two birds, one stone.

"We came to lure you out," Evia answered. "Though perhaps you could persuade us to stop the raid soon, provided your friends cooperate. Your lives in exchange for the town's."

Her voice was closer now. Lorelin moved toward the corner, and she tried not to let the terror swallow her whole. "You don't have to do this, Evia. Or do you love it the way Sterling does? Causing this much pain?"

"No," Evia admitted. "But I love Sterling. I'd do anything for him. You wouldn't understand what it's like, I'm sure, to have a man love you. Your fiancé didn't love you. Sterling's told me all about it. Said he beat you like vermin. I would have liked to watch that happen."

Anger flared inside her, but it wasn't greater than the stroke of pity that burst inside her mind. "That's not love, Evia. I'm sorry you don't realize that."

"You little shrew. You think you know what love is?"

Lorelin reached the corner. "Better than you."

She whirled around, just in time to see Evia planted no more than a yard away, and fired.

Evia had her gun raised to shoot, but it didn't matter. Lorelin was quicker. The gun wobbled in Evia's hand for a moment, and she looked down at her stomach, where a wide, fresh wound bubbled like a fountain from her stomach. She took two steps back, putting a hand on her gut before falling. The last look she gave Lorelin wasn't an angry one, or even a hateful one. It was just hurt, pure and empty.

Lorelin granted herself a moment to look at Evia's body, at her wide eyes facing the dimming sky. She looked smaller in death, and younger, too. A lump budded in Lorelin's throat, but she forced herself to swallow. "Gods, have mercy on you," she whispered, then opened the front door.

Tsashin, the ticket officer, and the two women shot upright. "They're gone," said Lorelin. "Stay put, though. We've got some more to deal with."

Chapter 50

Halston and Hodge snuck around the back of the buildings, then hurried between the cobbler's and the brewer's. A long stack of barrels rose at the edge of the brewer's, bathing the alley in shadows and leaving just enough room for Halston and Hodge to walk side-by-side. Guns in hand, they crept to the edge and watched.

Up ahead, someone screamed from inside a shop. Smoke billowed into the air. Halston cursed under his breath. They'd lost track of Sterling. Two figures remained in the street, moving slowly, their eyes darting across the road. With the nearby firelight, Halston could make them out. Gallows. Flynn.

"Get out here, fellas!" Gallows called in his thick, gravelly voice. "You can end this, if'n you're ready for it."

Hodge cocked his pistol.

"Wait," said Halston.

"For what?" whispered Hodge. "They'll be out of range. We've got less than a minute to take 'em out."

"They'll shoot back at us."

"Not if we're quick. Hal. Trust me."

There were few things Halston could say with certainty. One was that he could walk through fire, floods, or falling stars, and Hodge would go with him.

Halston held his gun with both hands. The revolver Jae had gifted him. "Ready?"

"Ready."

They dashed to the edge of the alley, aimed for the two men, and each shot three times. There was a shout, and one of the figures hit the earth.

"Get back!" Hodge shouted, yanking Halston behind two stacked barrels. They ducked down.

Gunfire erupted again. Bullets slammed into the wood, and ale flowed from the holes like water from a broken dam. They pressed their backs to the building, still holding their guns ready to shoot.

"Shit," Hodge breathed. "Did you see which one we missed?"

"I—"

The top barrel came crashing down.

Halston shouted, and his free arm reached for Hodge. The barrel knocked them both off their feet. Ale spilled over them, soaking their faces. Halston scrambled to sit upright. Hodge sat before him, his legs pinned beneath the fallen barrel's side, scrambling to retrieve his pistol, now sitting just a yard or two away from him. Before them, Flynn stood, his gun pointed at Hodge's head.

Halston swung his arm out and fired.

The shot hit Flynn's lower stomach. He howled in pain, falling to his knees in the newly formed mud. He keeled over, and Halston didn't wait to see if he was still holding the gun. He fired again. The bullet sent Flynn falling forward, and he went still.

Halston sheathed his pistol and put both his arms beneath Hodge's. Gritting his teeth, he got to his feet and pulled, freeing

Hodge from under the barrel. The air stank of blood, ale, and smoke.

Hodge grabbed his pistol, then shakily stood.

"Your legs. Are they hurt?"

"Hurt, but they ain't broken. C'mon." They hurried to the back of the building, and listened. No gunfire. No shouting.

A few long, painful moments passed. They stood, trying to catch their breath, soaking in ale and covered in dirt.

There was a patter of footsteps to their left. Halston whirled around, ears ringing, gun pointed, but Lorelin threw her hands up in response. "Stop!"

Thank the gods. Halston lowered his gun. "Where's Tsashin?"

"Getting the people at the other end of town to safety. Ned and Evia are dead."

Halston nodded. "I've got an idea. Gryff is up on the roof that-a-way. Sterling wants us to come out and show ourselves. There's no chance in hell we're doing that. I think we need to get *him* to come to *us*."

Everyone was quiet for a moment, then Hodge said, "Here's what we'll do. I'll stay out here. You two go inside. I'll fire a shot and shout to get Sterling to come this way, then wait in the alley for him to pass. If I miss him, or if he comes down from the other side of the street, you two get him when he goes into the building."

The last thing Halston wanted to do was separate, but they'd made it this far. Just a little longer.

They could do it.

Halston and Lorelin stepped into a dim room, the whole floor crowded with barrels and tubs. Paneled batwing doors waited at the front, and they could feel the night air leaking in through the gap. Nobody in sight. At least whoever owned this place had made it out. Halston snuck to the right side of the room, Lorelin the left. Each of them picked a barrel to crouch behind.

They waited.

From outside, there was the muffled noise of a gunshot followed by Hodge's shout. "Sterling! This way! Inside!"

Halston prayed. *Let him live. Just let Hodge live.*

All was quiet.

Halston did not dare move.

A shadow drifted beneath the doors, then went still on the threshold. Another. A pair of legs, looming at the entrance.

They didn't enter. They just stayed there, as if waiting for an order.

Halston's finger rested on the trigger. Outside, far away, he could hear the flames still crackling, the frantic cries of the townsfolk. They'd led Sterling here. Now, it was their job to put an end to it.

Come in, thought Halston.

The doors creaked, and the figure stepped inside.

It wasn't Sterling.

It was Stone.

Halston waited. Stone's eyes shifted over the darkness, his gaze tired and dull. Snorting, he took another step forward and dropped his pistol on the floor. He kicked it to the side. It could not have been an accident. His worn voice cut through the air. "Kill me."

Halston looked to Lorelin. He could not make out her face in the darkness, but he guessed that she was looking back at him.

"Kill me, damn it!" Stone snapped. "I know one of y'all is here. Go ahead. Or do I have to beg for it?"

It was a trick. It had to be. Sterling was probably waiting outside, trying to get Halston and Lorelin to come out.

"Y'all want to be free, don't you?" Stone asked. "So do I. Sterling's had me in his grip for years. I want out. Tonight's my last night. My last run with him. I'm making this all easier on y'all. It's a mercy to me. Just shoot. Make it fast. Then run. Run and get out of here. You're young. You've got time to do better. You've got time to turn around and do some good in this world. It's too late for me."

Halston stood.

Stone met his gaze. Halston kept his gun pointed at the front door, but he did not fire. Halston said, "Run."

Stone just stared his way.

"Run!" Halston said again. "Go! I'm not killing you!"

"Alright, then," said Stone. He crouched down, and picked up his gun. Halston dropped to the floor, cursing himself for his stupidity.

A shot cracked.

Halston waited on the floor, trembling. Where had the bullet gone?

He waited several moments for another shot, hell, another sound. But nothing came of it. Clutching his gun, Halston stood, and then found where the bullet had gone. Dark blood sprayed the floor.

Lorelin's footsteps creaked. Halston barely felt her soft touch on his shoulder. He wanted to look away from Stone's dead eyes, but he couldn't. "Halston, come on," she whispered. "We have to go out. We have to find the others. We don't know what's happened with Hodge."

Stone's warning echoed in his mind, the words cutting through him like jagged stones. Scanning the area, they stepped out the front and into the street, not daring to loosen the grips on their guns. Halston squeezed the handle of his revolver.

The townsfolk had shifted their attention to the fires. They'd started throwing all the water they could at the flames licking the wood. Halston breathed in, trying not to cough from the smoke. Gallows, along with several townsfolk, lay bloody and swollen in the street.

There was no more shouting, no more bargaining, no more bellowing for Halston to come out and show himself. Again, he glimpsed the townsfolk lying dead. *I'm sorry,* he thought, and he could not smother the guilt that hammered down on him. *I brought this to you. I'm so sorry.*

Halston blinked. Had Sterling run? Or was he tucked away inside one of the buildings, holding poor souls at gunpoint and demanding they surrender whatever they had in their pockets and safes?

Halston forced himself to take a step into the street. He breathed in deep, and the smell of smoke was like hard liquor in his lungs. He didn't check to see if Lorelin was walking behind him. After several paces, he settled in the middle of the street. A few steps away was the body of a young man in a blue shirt. The sky looked black.

He wasn't going to shrink away.

Not anymore.

So he tipped his head back and shouted, "Come out, Sterling!"

Nobody answered. The townsfolk didn't even look away from tending the flames.

"Come out, damn it!" Halston shouted. "I know you're here, Sterling! Let it end!"

Behind him, a gun clicked. Halston turned.

Two figures emerged from the alley in which Flynn lay dead and stepped out of the shadows as slowly as the last bit of sun sinking into the west. The anger in Sterling Byrd's eyes could compete with nothing Halston had ever seen, not even the face he'd worn after Jae had shot his brother down.

Some foolish part of Halston hoped he could blink and make the image disappear, that this was all some sort of illusion. But when he opened his eyes again and the sight of Hodge locked in Sterling's arm remained, and when he saw the gun pressed against his brother's head, Halston felt as though he might shatter.

Halston pointed his gun at Sterling. "Drop him. Now. Or I'll shoot."

"And risk your brother's life?" Sterling spat. He took another step. "Your little bounty hunter took mine from me. An eye for an eye, dontcha think?"

Hodge writhed in Sterling's grasp and shouted, "Run!"

"Quiet," Sterling snapped, his fist digging into Hodge's ribs. "I wonder what it'd be like to hear your brother weep for you. Music to my ears, I'll bet."

"What do you want, Sterling?" Halston roared.

"I'd say I wanted the Yunah girl, but even she can't bring back my men. Or Evia. Or my brother." He gritted his teeth. Tears were in his eyes. "And you should know that I killed your little bounty hunter. She's hanging from some bluff out in the woods."

He couldn't stop the words that tore from his throat. "You're lying!"

"I ain't."

A thousand feelings weighed down on him, too many to name. Sterling had lied before. He wanted him to falter, to break. And he wouldn't.

And for a moment, all Halston could do was wonder. What would it be like to be as overcome with greed and rage as Sterling, to strike through entire towns and set them alight? To let blood fall at his feet as easily as men woke in the morning and stepped onto the earth? Rage burned in Halston's head. It was hot... so hot, he felt he might lose control and shoot without thinking.

But he couldn't let it take him over.

He couldn't risk Hodge's life.

He'd lost Elias, and the last thing Elias had heard from him had been an expression of anger. He couldn't let the same thing happen to Hodge. For a moment, he was tempted to beg. *Let me take my brother's place. Let me take it one last time.* He could say it. What was stopping him?

A tear slid down Hodge's cheek. "Hal. Run. It'll be okay."

No.

Halston's finger shifted on the gun. "If this is going to end, let it end now."

"I agree." Sterling smirked, then his own finger shifted to the trigger.

And end it did.

A gunshot rang out, but not from Halston's gun. It was amazing, really, how shocked Sterling looked, even when the life started to leave him.

The outlaw fell into the dust. He stared up at Halston for a second, fury smoldering across his face. Halston had always thought that the flecks in his eyes resembled sparks, ready to catch flame and blaze like an inferno. The anger left his eyes after a moment, and Sterling gawked at Halston, a gurgling noise rising out of his throat. Trying to speak. To claim the last word.

But he didn't manage to. Sterling let out a final sigh, soft and thin. He collapsed, then, eyes closed, without another sound.

Sterling Byrd was dead.

The bullet had lodged itself in the back of his neck. Hodge jumped away, patting himself down. Unhurt.

Halston leapt for his brother. "Gods! Hodge, look at me."

"I'm alright." Hodge pressed a hand to his chest, then burst out laughing like a madman. Tears shone in his eyes, and he placed his hands on Halston's shoulders. "We're alright."

Halston gathered his arms around his brother and pulled him in close. They stood there, allowing themselves a moment to breathe, for that forbidden word to pass them over.

Free.

They were free.

When Hodge drew away from him, Halston peered ahead. He expected to see one of the townsfolk standing in the street, or perhaps someone in a nearby window pointing their gun out from over the sill.

But behind them, gun smoking, blue eyes shining... was Jae Oldridge.

She didn't even take the time to holster her gun. It fell to the ground, and she ran to him. At first, he didn't realize he was moving, but he was running for her, too.

She leapt into his arms, and he held her tighter than any silver bar he'd ever stolen. She pressed her face into his shoulder and he whispered in her ear, "Thank you, thank you, thank you."

Chapter 51

They met the sheriff that morning. He was a short, sturdy man with a gray-streaked, auburn beard and a turquoise-studded belt. He introduced himself as Burgundy Steele.

This might've been the cleanest sheriff's office Jae had ever seen. It was so much brighter than the one in Ameda, too. The windows were wide, letting the sun spread its rays all across the floor. The wood was polished, the lamps gleaming. Neat stacks of paper lay on the sheriff's desk.

"The raid killed four people," Burgundy lamented. "Don't sound like much, but that's a good chunk of our town. But Dolorosa is made up of hearty folks. We'll rebuild. Y'all saved us from the worst of it.

In the corner of her eye, Jae scanned the wall of handbills. Fortunately, the Harney gang was not there.

"How can we thank you?" asked Burgundy.

Halston shook his head. "There's no need for it."

The sheriff smiled. "Good to see some humility in the young ones." He traipsed over to a narrow desk and scribbled something down. Jae recognized it: a bounty receipt. "Now, the bounty for the Byrd gang comes out to five hundred crowns…"

Lorelin caught Hodge from falling over.

Halston stammered out, "Five hundred?"

"Certainly. I don't think there's a gang with a higher bounty on their heads in all of Hespyria."

Jae had never even *seen* that much money at once.

Burgundy asked, "Now, then. You folks want a name on your receipt, or shall I leave it anonymous?"

Halston broke in. "Anonymous, please. We're… we're bounty hunters, but we don't need our names flying around."

Burgundy nodded. "Smart of y'all. Glad you ain't doin' it for the glory. Are you sure, though? This story is going to be all over the papers. I'm sure everyone on this side of the country will want to know who you are."

"Yes," said Halston. "We're sure. Also, we'll take two hundred crowns. You keep the rest."

Burgundy lifted his head. "Sir?"

"Really," Halston went on. "That's all we'll need. Use the rest of it to rebuild your town."

The sheriff's mouth stretched into a kind, bright smile. "Well, thank you very much, son. You sure I can't have your name? Seems I can't thank you properly without one."

"Go on, Marion," said Hodge. "You can tell him."

Halston chuckled. "Well, there you have it."

Burgundy passed Halston a note for two hundred crowns. Halston spoke up, coughing a bit. "T-thank you, sir. Thank you very much. Could you direct us to the nearest bank, please?"

"Well, our own bank ain't open today. Got some rebuilding to do there. But there's one in Vega. Take the north road for four miles. The road is steep, but easy enough to follow. There's a sign at the end of it pointing to Vega. Follow that for another ten miles."

"That close, eh?" asked Halston.

"Yeah." Sheriff Steele paused. Suspicion flickered on his face. "You folks up to anything?"

"Just traveling," said Jae.

"Are you now?"

"Yep."

He exchanged another kind look with them. The spark in his eyes reminded Jae of her Pa. "Alright, then. Don't let us stop you."

———————

Nobody spoke on the way out of the sheriff's office. The day was young, though the fires had all gone out, leaving thick, black scorch marks on the buildings. The air still smelled of smoke.

They stopped just outside Dolorosa, staring back at the little mountain town. Sterling and his gang were gone, swept away somewhere to be buried. Returned to the earth.

No more running. Well, from Sterling, at least.

Jae faced the others and paused for a moment to look at each of them. Gryff, standing firm and silent. Tsashin, the sweet storyteller. Lorelin, the sorrow gone from her eyes. And the Harney boys.

Jae said, "What Halston found... I can explain."

Maybe they'd still turn her away. If they did... she would bid them farewell and go. Part of her would still yearn for her time with them, but she'd move on. She'd live. But before that, she had to speak.

She told them the story of Pa, of the ghosts, of those two thieves who'd slashed her hand and the Nefili man who'd gifted her the map. She told them about Thaddeus Glory, and the sheriff in Ameda, and how she'd followed them into the desert. She told them about Sterling in the hideout, and how she'd bargained with him for her life, and how she'd realized that thieves weren't all the same. They watched. They listened.

"I... I don't think I was ever cut out for bounty hunting. I was good at it. But I told myself it was what I needed to do. And... that ain't true. Not anymore."

For a minute, they swapped glances with one another. Jae tried to read the looks on their faces, but it was tough.

"Well," Hodge said finally. "You ain't gonna turn us in, are ya?"

"Gods, no!"

"Good." Hodge slapped Halston on the back. "See, Halston? Nothin' to worry about. Now let's set out so we can cash this bounty in and set out for the Outlands." He lifted his chin at Jae. "So, you coming with us?"

"You... you mean it?"

"Sure, I do. You took care of Sterling for us. I say you've earned your spot here."

Lorelin smiled, then motioned over her shoulder. "Come on, Oldridge. We need you with us."

Halston glanced at her, then quickly looked away. Something heavy hung between them, like steam in the air.

Perhaps neither of them was blameless.

Suddenly, she didn't know what it felt like to be a bounty hunter anymore. It felt distant as the north in which she was born. All she knew was that she had a wanderer's heart.

And so they set off down the mountain path. The ground was tender, and sunlight dappled the path. On they moved, climbing over boulders and stooping under branches. It was beautiful here. Jae looked at the silver mountain crags, which seemed to call out their welcome to the gang. At last, there was no one to follow them.

They set up camp that night. The Briarford Mountains rose up like knights marching across the dusk-lit sky. They sat basking in the evening's warmth, the twilight rich with spring's sweetness. They ate squirrel that Gryff had snared, its meat light but flavorful, and listened to Tsashin's story.

"When the world was made, there was only darkness. It was cold, and nothing grew. There were many spirits in the world, though, and they banded together to create the first music. As they sang, their voices created light.

"So they took the light and they molded it into the sun, then the moon, and hung them in the sky. When light filled the world, plants grew. Then came the beasts and the birds and the people.

"There was a reckless spirit amongst them, though. When the plants and animals came into the world, the spirit discovered what he could take from them. He took bones and made flutes, and stretched hides across barrels of wood for drums. He gave them to the other spirits, and the new music allowed the light to flow like a river. So they wound them into little balls. Stars, they called them, and they stored the stars in a sheath for themselves.

"But the reckless spirit grew angry, because he believed the stars should belong to them all. So he stole the buckskin from them and threw the stars into the sky and scattered them across the universe, so all could see them."

Silently, Jae bid her thanks to the spirit, and the gods, and all the strange and invisible things in this world for putting the stars in the sky.

At the end of the story, Tsashin said, "I saw something. In a dream I had last night."

Five heads turned her way. "What was it?" asked Lorelin.

"A lake," said Tsashin. "I'm not sure where it was, but I knew I'd seen it before. Seeing it felt like coming home."

Jae wished she could pluck Tsashin's memories like wildflowers from a meadow and give them to her. "We'll get to the bottom of it."

"And we'll get you home," Hodge added.

Tsashin smiled. "Thank you. For freeing me from the ground. For traveling with me, for protecting me, for helping me find my way home. I hope to help the rest of you find your way home as well."

"Jae," Lorelin said. "You didn't tell us what happened after you left the camp last night. How did you find us?"

So Jae told them the story, from Evia seizing her into the woods to Jem fleeing into the night.

"Spec was a ghost?" asked Hodge.

"Guess so." Jae bit her lip, wondering where Jem had wandered off to.

Hodge looked to the sky. "Hey, Elias. Why can't you do somethin' like that? We could use your help down here."

"He probably needs a break from us, Hodge," teased Lorelin.

Hodge shrugged. "Eh. Can't say I blame him."

"I wonder," Jae went on. "He said he'd find me again. He told me he couldn't stay, though."

"Look on the bright side," Hodge told her. "Now instead of one person to find, you've got two. You'll stay busier longer."

She shoved her elbow into his ribs.

"What? You ain't used to me yet?" he said with a smirk.

As they were settling down, Halston asked, "Jae?"

"What?"

He pointed to the trees. "Might you want to… go for a walk?"

"Oooh," said Lorelin, Hodge, and Tsashin.

Halston waved it away, ignoring their wide eyes. "Gryff, can you keep them entertained?"

"No," Gryff said, but he gave Halston and Jae a sly smile.

Before they walked away, Jae paused a moment to turn back. Two months it had been since she'd ridden into Ameda, and these strangers had turned to allies. Friends. Monvallea waited for them, and the north beyond that. Tomorrow, the sunrise would come. Then another. It would carry them over plains and hills and winding roads. And Jae was ready. She was ready to walk with them.

She walked into the woods with Halston. They found a fairly comfortable log to sit upon, and they stayed silent for so long it was almost funny.

Halston asked, "Your burn. How is it?"

Jae lifted her shirt and looked at it. Earlier that day, she'd poured water and alcohol over her damaged skin. It was pink and blistered, but not a deep, charred red. It would heal. Perhaps it would leave a scar, but a scar was far better than death. She would look at it and remember that she'd won. "It stings a bit," she said, pulling her shirt down. "But it'll heal. It's over now."

She didn't look away from him. His golden-brown eyes were softer than usual. She said, "The knife."

"Gryff asked the undertaker about it this morning," said Halston. "He didn't find it on Sterling. Or any of the bodies, for that matter."

"Well," Jae said. "If that knife is made of adamite, I doubt he tossed it away. We can find it."

Halston passed her a hint of a smile. "Alright."

It spilled out, then. "I'm sorry," Jae choked out. "Halston... when I lost my Pa, I didn't know what to do with myself. I didn't want anybody. Didn't need anybody. Except him. I was gonna do whatever it took to get him back. I had no problem lying, if it got me close to getting him back. Something's... changed. I know how I feel. I know what I'd do for the lot of you. I mean it."

Halston hesitated. "I know. As for what I said to you... I wanted to protect the others. I wanted to believe you. I just didn't want to take the chance."

"I don't blame you."

Halston scratched his neck, not quite meeting her gaze. "I've thought of what you said about your Pa. Maybe we ought to spend some time talking about what comes next. No need to sweep dirt over anything anymore."

"Yeah. I… I reckon there's a lot we didn't tell each other. Maybe we can change that."

Halston said, "I'll help you. I'll help you find him. I mean… I know even less about ghosts than you do, but you've helped us get this far."

Fears surfaced in her mind, fluttering past like grim-faced ghosts. Fears of not finding Pa, or losing Halston, or learning that their time was borrowed and it was coming to an end. Perhaps that fork in the road was still there. Then again… there was a chance it wasn't. And she wanted to snatch her chance up like gold glittering in a stretch of hard-packed earth.

There was a new sort of courage inside her, one that came with a sense of freedom, of belonging, and it rose much higher than her fears.

"Well, Mr. Harney," said Jae. "You've cast your charms on me. I'm afraid I'll have to strike a deal with you."

"What deal would that be?"

She said, "You help me find Pa. In return, I'll help to guide you home. I reckon it's a lot better than our previous deal." Without a second thought, she took his hand. "Wherever this road takes us… I'm with you."

Perhaps she should have been frightened, but she was not. A world lay beyond them, waiting.

He brushed back one of her braids. "Jae?"

"Yeah?"

He kissed her in the glow of the setting sun.

When he held her, she had to wonder, was there anything more to be said? She feared for a moment that this wasn't real, that he wasn't real, that she'd be back on a lonesome road and learn that the

Harneys were nothing but a legend. A dream.

His mouth left hers, and she laughed. Not because it was funny—but because her face was burning and his arms were tight around her and she'd just kissed somebody.

They just watched each other for a moment, then lost themselves in their laughter.

She nestled herself comfortably against his chest. He wrapped his arms around her, and they huddled against the earth, the grass soft against their backs. She was warm, and he was *there*, and she was grateful for that. So they basked in the dusk, not bothering to walk back and tuck themselves into their bedrolls, not caring whether the others walked over and saw them.

"Whatcha thinkin'?" Jae asked.

"Our job's not done yet," said Halston. "We'll have to set out tomorrow morning. For the north. To Monvallea."

"That's fine," Jae whispered. "'Cause I'm coming with you."

Acknowledgements

It's been about four years since the day I said I wanted to write a fantasy-Western, and I am beyond blessed to have received so much support from the folks who helped me turn the concept into a book. Many thanks to all of the amazing beta-readers who combed through this book in its earlier stages. Thank you guys for your feedback and all the laughs we shared along the way. It was an absolute joy working with each of you.

Thank you to Franziska Haase, for the stunning cover, and to Lina Amarego for the Chapter headers. I am in awe of your talents, and thank you for helping to bring my visions of the "Graves" atmosphere to life!

To Josiah Davis, my incredible editor: thank you so much for believing in this story and helping me mold it into its final form. It's been such a blessing to work with someone with such a keen eye and a knack for writing advice.

I would also like to thank my wonderful family: Mom, Dad, Christina, and Sia. Thank you for recommending all of your favorite 20th century Western films, for letting me tell you all about my characters at the dinner table, and for being there for me every step of the way. To Taylor and Maria, my wonderful friends and critique partners: thank you for introducing me to your favorite books, for all the days bouncing ideas back and forth at the coffee shop, and for many years of friendship to come. And to Alex: you're the best part-ner in a crime a girl could ever ask for. I am one lucky sunnofagun. Without you, I'd be lost... and I'd also probably still be working on that dang train heist.

Lastly, to my newest readers: thank you for riding alongside Halston and Jae through this first step of their journey. It's been a pleasure to share this story with you.

Cheers to all the adventures to come!
-Sophia

About the Author

Sophia Minetos was born and raised in Albuquerque, New Mexico. She is an alumnus of the University of New Mexico. *Graves for Drifters and Thieves* is her first novel. When she isn't writing, she can be found reading, knitting, or organizing her tea collection.

For more information, please visit www.sophiaminetos.com